TWICE KNIGHTLEY IN MY BED

by

SERENITY WOODS

ISBN: 9798356876288

CONTENTS

Character Relationship in Hartfield House

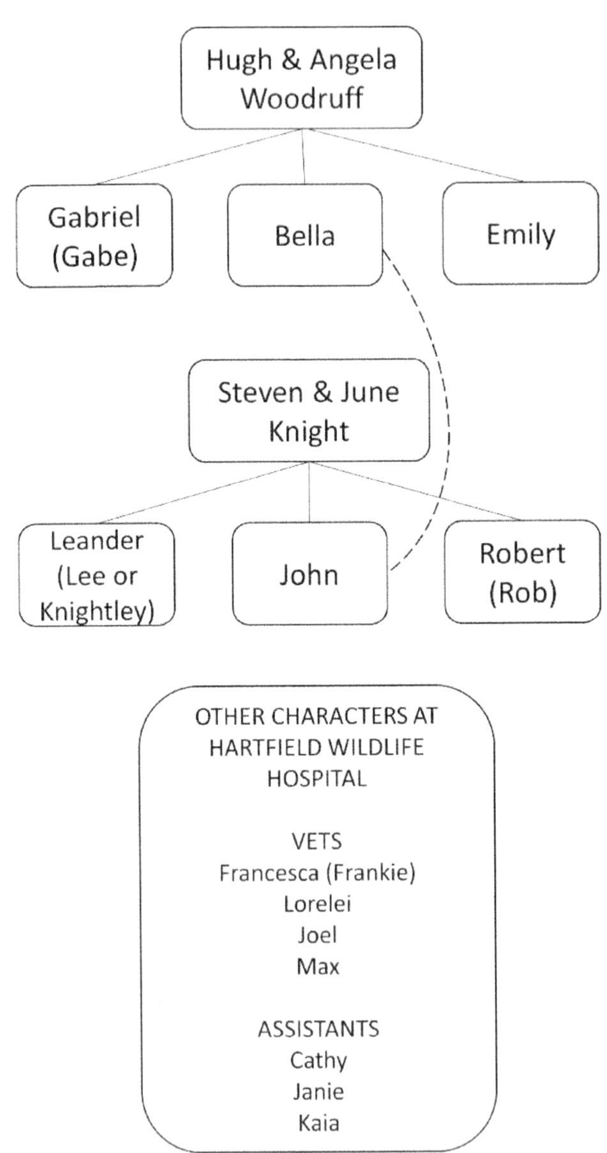

Chapter One

Emily

It's a beautiful January day, the height of summer in New Zealand, and as I cross the car park to the Bay of Islands airport, I'm glad I remembered to smother myself in factor fifty sun lotion this morning. I'm a strawberry blonde (not ginger, even though my friends tease me that I am), and if I'm not careful my freckled skin burns to a crisp in the hot sun. Mind you, this brand of lotion is a tad thick and sticky. I could probably swim across the Tasman Sea to Australia at the moment and not get any chafing.

I go through the automatic doors into the small airport. There's only one arrival gate and one departure gate, joined together by a section of seating and a tiny coffee shop. I glance enviously at it, wishing I had time for a latte, but the passengers are already descending from the plane.

Holding up the hand-written sign I scribbled in the car on a piece of paper, I stand to one side. The first passenger through is an older Maōri woman, and as she enters the arrivals lounge, her family strikes up an impromptu *haka* or ceremonial dance, their voices ringing around the room. It ends with the phrase *Whiti te ra!*—the sun shines! It's so appropriate for the beautiful day. She bursts into tears, and they rush to hug her.

I swallow down a lump in my throat and close my eyes for a moment, sending a kiss up to the fluffy white clouds in the cerulean sky. *Love you, Mum!*

"Emily?"

I open my eyes to see a young woman standing before me with a hopeful smile. I'm twenty-one and she looks a year or two older than me. She's about my height—five foot five—but her hair is as dark as mine is blonde, cut in an attractive long bob. She's wearing a gray pencil skirt, a short-sleeved white blouse, and high-heeled cream sandals. Her carefully applied makeup outlines her big brown eyes and full pink lips. I feel like a country bumpkin next to her, with my faded blue polo shirt, ancient khaki shorts, beaten-up Converses, no makeup, and hair pulled into a scruffy bun. Maybe I should have tidied myself up a bit before I left this morning…

Too late now though, and anyway, I'm a take-me-as-you-find-me kind of girl.

"Naomi!" I hold out my hand, she slides hers into it, and we shake. "Look at you," I say, crumpling my sign into a ball and tossing it into the rubbish, "bringing a welcome touch of city sophistication to the Northland."

She laughs, and we turn and begin walking toward the exit. "I am here for an interview," she says, "so I thought I'd better smarten up."

"Oh, Rob will be pleased. He's always meeting with donors or having fundraising meetings and he usually wears a suit. You don't have a bag to collect?"

"No, just carry-on as I'm flying back this afternoon."

We go out into the bright sunshine and slide on our sunglasses. "Car's over there," I say, gesturing to our left. "The bright-orange ute."

Naomi laughs as we approach the battered pickup truck. "You really are a Northland girl."

"Yeah, sorry about that. Dad told me to take his MG, but I forgot." I click the button to unlock it, then glance at Naomi's elegant skirt and dainty sandals. Eek! I'd better tidy up. I open the passenger door and heave the two bags of goods I've just bought from the hardware shop into the back, then brush the sand off the seat. "I took the dog down to the beach for a run this morning," I explain as I go around to the driver's side. "She likes to sit in the front."

Naomi laughs and gets in. "How far is it to Hartfield?" she asks as we buckle ourselves in, and she glances nervously at the clock on the dashboard.

"Only twenty minutes. We'll be there with plenty of time to spare." Her interview is at eleven, and it's only just gone ten. I start the ute and head it out toward the main road. "Have you been to the Bay of Islands much?"

"I've driven through it once, but I haven't stayed there."

"You're from Auckland?"

"Yes."

"Well, it's very different from the city, but the Northland is an amazing place to live. The weather's fabulous in the summer as you can see. Lots of sunshine. Wet at times, but then so's Auckland."

Her lips twist. "Yeah, tell me about it."

"And the Bay is magnificent. Do you like fishing or boating?"

She chuckles. "I must admit, I'm not much of an outdoor girl, but I'm willing to adapt."

"Oh you'll have to! I'll be dragging you out on the boat to the islands on the weekends. I can teach you to scuba dive if you like? There's nothing better than collecting your own mussels for dinner."

"Wow, it sounds amazing, but I suppose I should wait and see if I get the job first before I get too excited."

I blow a raspberry. "I'll be astounded if you don't get it. Rob hasn't been impressed with the applicants we've had so far. I think you'll walk it, if for no other reason than you're gorgeous." Only after the words have left my lips do I realize how that must sound. "Not that he'd ever act inappropriately with his assistant. His behavior is beyond reproach. He'd never… I mean…"

She grins. "It's okay. I'm not offended."

"Thank God. He's a great guy underneath it all. You have to remember that."

"What do you mean?"

"Well, he can be a tad… grumpy. But there's a reason for it. He had a motorbike accident when he was twenty-one and completely smashed up his knee. He's had three serious operations on it, but it never healed properly, and he has to walk with a cane now. He never mentions it, but he's in a lot of pain most days. Just bear that in mind."

"I will, thank you." She looks out of the window at the feijoa and kiwifruit orchards flashing by, and the stalls by the side of the road selling blueberries, strawberries, and Ladyfinger bananas. "I've done some research on the Wildlife Hospital," she says, looking back at me, "but I'd love it if you could fill me in a bit, give me some background? It's not been around long, has it?"

"No, only six months really." I approach the main roundabout out of Kerikeri and turn south. "Have you heard of Noah's Ark Animal Sanctuary?"

"Yes, it's not far from here, is it?"

"No, it's about ten minutes' drive from Hartfield. It's been hugely successful. It's a veterinary surgery as well as a sanctuary. It does take in unusual animals in an emergency, but it's mainly for domestic animals that have been rescued—cats, dogs, farm animals. My father, Hugh Woodruff, is good friends with Noah and the others who work there. Anyway, just over a year ago, at Christmas, my mum passed away."

She gives me a pitying look. "Oh, I'm so sorry to hear that."

"Thank you." I concentrate on the winding road down the hill. "It was very hard for us all. A few weeks after she died, Dad was out walking the dogs with Noah, and Noah told him they'd had increasing numbers of wild animals come into the sanctuary. They're not really equipped to deal with them, and he said how great it would be if there could be another surgery nearby that could focus on New Zealand's native species, with specialist vets concentrating on treatment, rehabilitation, and releasing them back to their native environment. By the time they came back from the walk, the idea for Hartfield Wildlife Hospital was born. Everyone calls it HWH by the way." I tap the HWH logo on my navy polo top.

"What a great story. So your father runs it?"

"No, he just owns the land. The Hartfield estate is over five hundred hectares, with forest behind it and a generous beachfront. He has his hands full with managing the farmland, orchards, and vineyards. But he donated a peninsula of land to the Trust for the hospital. It took them about six months to build it, and we're still in the process of setting it up, really."

"So you work there?"

"Yes, I'm like an odd-job girl. I do a lot of delivery work, running around, cleaning, gardening, whatever needs doing, really." I smile as her eyebrows rise. "You're wondering why I don't have a more impressive job."

"Not at all! Well, sort of. If your father owns it…"

"I'm not a vet, I don't know much about business, and it's not as if I need the money. So I volunteer wherever they need people. I also work for the local hospice sometimes, delivering and collecting equipment."

"You seem very happy."

"I am. I love the Bay, and the hospital. I'm just grateful to be able to help where I can."

"So who's in the team that runs it?"

"There's a manager of each section. You're interviewing for the assistant to Rob—Robert Knight. He runs the financial side of things and deals with all the fundraising. There's a laboratory where they check the animals for parasites and treat any diseases they might have. My brother, Gabriel Woodruff or Gabe, runs that. And of course, the veterinary services that treat the wildlife, which is the core of the project. There are four vets and six assistants, managed by Knightley—the Manager of Veterinary Services. He's been away in Australia for a month, but apparently he's coming back today, so hopefully you'll be able to meet him."

"Knightley? Is that his first name or his surname?"

I laugh. "Sorry, it's neither. His real name is Lee Knight. When I was four, I overheard my father telling someone that this boy's name was 'Knight, Lee,' and that's what I thought his name was. Everyone's called him that ever since."

She chuckles. "He's an old friend?"

"Well, he acts like he's my big brother, you know, bossing me around."

"Ooh…" Naomi's jaw drops at the sight of the sparkling Pacific Ocean in front of us. "What an amazing view."

"Isn't it? Best in the country, I think." I slow as we approach a roundabout and gesture to our left. "That goes to Waitangi, where the Treaty House is." I signal right and head along the road that follows the shoreline. "This is Paihia, and after that, Opua, which is where Hartfield is."

"I'd love to live here," she says. "It would be so nice after being in the city my whole life." She looks at the boats heading out to sea. "How many islands are there in total in the Bay?"

"One hundred and forty-four."

"Wow."

"Yeah. It'd take a lifetime to explore them all." I drive carefully through the busy center of Paihia, and then take the road toward Opua.

"You were telling me about Knightley," she continues as we go up the hill, the roadside lined with lush palms and ferns. "You said he's like a brother?"

"Mm, yes. Hartfield House, where I grew up, is a large farmhouse. My parents had three kids. I'm the youngest. After I was born, they decided to open the house up for Family Home Care."

"They fostered children?"

"Yeah. Mostly short term until the kids found permanent homes. We must have had twenty or so children pass through during those first few years. I don't remember them much; I was only a baby. But when I was four, three brothers came to the house. Knightley's the oldest—he was thirteen, then there was John, who was eleven. Rob, who you're interviewing with, was the youngest at nine. They were quite…" I hesitate, not sure how to describe the three brothers who were such a handful, without revealing their private history, "…troublesome," I choose, "in the beginning anyway. They had a difficult background, and it wasn't easy for them to adjust to living with us. But my parents were both supportive and strict when needed, and somehow it just worked. Most of the kids who came to the house stayed days, weeks, or months at the most, but the Knight boys lived with us until they left to go to university, and they come back all the time. They're just like family, really. I'm very fond of them all."

"I can't wait to meet them," Naomi says. "You paint a lovely picture of Hartfield."

"I'm very lucky, I know that. Dad and the others have tried to get me to go to university and travel the world, but I'm not interested. I don't see any point in leaving when I love it here so much."

"Fair enough." She smiles. "So Knightley is back today?"

"Yes. He went to another wildlife hospital on the Sunshine Coast in Australia for a month to pick up some tips. Not that we get any poisonous spiders or crocodiles here!"

"Thank goodness."

"Yeah. We're all about penguins, parrots, and seals."

I slow as we approach the sign for Hartfield Wildlife Hospital and turn. The road leads us alongside a strip of bush, thick with wide-trunked kauri and other native trees and lush ferns. After that, it turns toward the coast. To our left are the vineyards, rich with slowly ripening grapes; to our right, mandarin and kiwifruit orchards stand cheek by jowl, backed by rolling fields where sheep graze contentedly in the morning sun.

Ahead of us, Hartfield House sits in a slight dip, sheltered from some of the southerlies by a crest that runs around the side. The back of the house is north-facing, which means that most of the rooms are sunlit and have beautiful views of the ocean.

"Wow," Naomi says. "Is that where you live?"

"Yes, that's home."

"I thought you said it was a farmhouse."

I look at the sprawling house with its many bedrooms, huge decks, rolling lawns, and elegant gardens. She has a point. I pull a face. "It's a working farm, and it's a house, so… When you move up here and have more time, I'll take you around it."

"Stop it," she scolds. "I don't have the job yet and I'm not going to assume anything."

I laugh. "I'm sorry, that's fair enough."

"It's a wonderful place, Emily."

"Please—everyone calls me Em. And yes, it is. When my great-great-great-grandmother came here from England with her parents in the nineteenth-century, a Maōri *rangatira* or chieftain fell in love with her, and they ended up getting married. This was his land, and our family has been here ever since."

"What a lovely story."

"Isn't it?"

The road forks here, the right-hand drive leading up to the front of the house, but I take the left-hand turn and begin the descent toward HWH. It snakes down the hill, flanked by palms and ferns, opening out near the bottom to give us a clear view of the hospital with the sparkling ocean behind it.

Naomi doesn't say anything as I drive, but I know she must be thinking what a beautiful site it is. Signs by the roadside inform us there's a fifteen kilometers-per-hour speed limit, and I cruise through the dense bush. Wooden walkways stretch out on either side, disappearing into the trees. After a few minutes, the bush opens out to a grassy area, and then the Wildlife Hospital appears before us.

I slot the ute into one of the spaces out the front, and we get out. Immediately we're surrounded by Nature in all her glory. Trees, ferns, and palms soar above us, while birdsong mixes with the distant sound of the ocean.

"I'm guessing there are kiwi birds here," Naomi says as we walk toward the buildings.

"Yes, North Island brown kiwi. Knightley took me on a night watch when I was a kid, and we saw two kiwis in the bush—it was amazing."

We approach the front entrance, and I open the door and gesture for her to precede me. We walk into the large, open foyer, and I take her up to Gemma on reception. She's only eighteen, a blonde, ditzy, but friendly chatterbox.

"Gemma," I say, "this is Naomi Smith—she's here for an interview with Rob at eleven."

"Hi!" Gemma beams at her and pushes over the register. "How lovely to meet you! Isn't it a gorgeous day? Wow, I love your blouse, it looks super smart and cool at the same time. And your sunglasses are gorgeous! Can you sign in, please? And if you could put this on…" She passes over a visitor sticker, and Naomi presses it onto her blouse, giving me an amused look.

I check the clock on the wall. It's only ten thirty. "You've got half an hour yet. You're welcome to wait here, or I can show you around the place, if you like?"

"Yes please, that would be great."

"Come on, then."

I lead her through reception, and we turn left toward the sign for 'Veterinary Services.' The four surgeries are separated by glass walls so we can see right through to the labs beyond. At the moment the far rooms are quiet, with only the nearest one occupied.

"Whoa," Naomi says.

I follow her gaze to see a guy bending over, getting something out of a crate. He's wearing a navy-blue polo shirt with the HWH logo, the same as mine—our uniform, such as it is. The dark-green material of his shorts shows off an attractive, tight backside. I'm not surprised she exclaimed.

"Sorry," she adds. "I meant to say something much more professional."

I laugh as he straightens and I realize who it is. "Oh, it's only Knightley."

"Only? You didn't tell me he was gorgeous."

I study him, a little puzzled. Is he? I suppose so. He's tall—a lot taller than me, probably six-one or two. He's trim and muscular—he plays rugby in the winter, cricket and tennis in the summer, and he's always swum every morning. He has thick, dark, springy hair that, if he didn't cut it, would grow into a bouffant style, but when it's short like it is now, it looks as if it's been carefully styled, even though I don't think he ever combs it.

I guess, if I were to really think about it, I'd consider him good looking. But I've never thought about him like that. I mean, he's Knightley. That would just be weird.

He turns toward us, revealing that he's holding a tiny blue penguin. Gently, so as not to frighten the bird, I knock on the glass and wave as he looks over. He grins, revealing the slight gap in his front teeth, then takes the bird over to another crate on the table, places it carefully inside, and closes the door. He says something to Cathy, his veterinary assistant, goes over to the sink and washes his hands, then walks out of the room and through the double doors to us.

"Hey!" I run up to him, jump up, and throw my arms around his neck. "You're back! I missed you."

"Hey, you." He holds me around the waist so my feet remain off the floor and gives me a hug. "Where were you? I've been looking for you everywhere."

I give him a final squeeze. He's been outside—he's all sun-warmed, and he smells of mown grass. I feel a surge of happiness at the thought that he's home.

"You're all sticky," he says, lowering me down. "Did you fall into a vat of olive oil?"

I push him. "It's my new sun lotion. You're always telling me off for getting sunburned, so stop complaining. Look, I was picking up Naomi. She's here for an interview with Rob at eleven."

"Oh yeah, he did mention it." He holds out a hand to her. "I'm Knightley."

"Hello." She shakes it. "Pleased to meet you."

"I was just showing her around," I say. "Want to join us? You know it all much better than me."

"Yeah, right," he scoffs, and then tells Naomi, "Don't believe a word she says. She knows this place inside out." But he gives a good-natured smile. "Come on, then. It's a beautiful day for it."

Chapter Two

Knightley

I lead the way back through the double doors into my surgery. "This little dude has a fractured and swollen flipper," I say quietly, taking them over to the crate with the tiny penguin. "He's dehydrated and underweight."

Naomi bends to look into the crate. "Aw, poor little thing. Can you fix him?"

"I'll operate on him, then we'll keep him here for a few weeks. Hopefully he'll be good as new." I smile as Naomi straightens. She seems nice, and she obviously gets on well with Em, but then so does everyone. Em is the friendliest person on earth. I don't know a single person who doesn't like her.

Although she's not tall by anyone's standards, the incredibly short shorts she favors make her legs look endless—her HWH polo shirt almost hangs past the hem of the shorts. She says her hair is strawberry blonde, but I've always called it ginger to annoy her. She wears it piled on the top of her head in a scruffy bun, and several strands of it inevitably tumble down to hang around her neck. Today they've stuck to her lotion-covered skin.

I think of the way her cheek peeled away from mine when I lowered her down from our hug, and a little erotic shiver runs down my back. I scold myself for it sternly. Jesus. Wasn't this why I went away for a month? I thought I'd conquered my crush. Erotic is not a word I can ever use when connected with Emily Woodruff.

Tearing my gaze away from her, I look back at Naomi to discover that she's been observing me as I study Em. Her lips curve up a very tiny bit. Giving her a wry smile, I turn and lead the way out of the surgery.

"I'm just going to pick up a box of disposable gloves from the store," Em says. "Don't forget to take her back by eleven or Rob's head will explode." She grins at Naomi. "Good luck! I'll come back for you after your interview."

"Thanks."

Em walks off, disappearing around the corner.

"This way," I say to Naomi, leading her along the corridor. I proceed to tell her a bit about the surgery and the animals that have passed through here as we make our way down to the laboratories.

"So," she says as we stop and look in at where Gabe and his assistants are working, surrounded by test tubes, microscopes, and other scientific paraphernalia. "Are you and Em an item?"

"No. Just good friends. We grew up together."

"I see." But her eyes dance, suggesting she suspects there's something more between us.

"She's my best mate's little sis," I say. "And strictly out of bounds."

"Okay." She smiles. "So you're the Manager of Veterinary Services?"

Pleased she's changed the subject, I nod, and we continue along the corridor. I open the door and let her precede me outside. "Mostly I'm based here, but occasionally we get a call from one of the islands to say an injured animal has been found, and I go out and treat it on site."

"It must be a very rewarding job. Where were you before you started up Hartfield?"

A wooden walkway leads us through the trees toward the office block. It gives visitors a pleasant glimpse into the bush, as well as providing access for us to the beach. I won't take Naomi down there as she isn't wearing the shoes for it, but at least she'll get an idea of the layout of the place.

"I've traveled a lot," I reply, pointing out a skink—a tiny lizard—that runs along the wooden barrier to investigate us before diverting onto a fern. "I worked in Nigeria for a while, releasing rescued monkeys back into the forest after years of rehabilitation. That was interesting."

"It sounds amazing. And you've just returned from Aus?"

"Yeah, learning about how they do things over there. I helped look after saltwater crocodiles, amongst other things."

"Eek!"

I chuckle. "It does have… logistical challenges, shall we say. People don't tend to have empathy for them, but they still feel pain and deserve the same opportunity for care."

"I suppose so. I've never thought of it like that."

We emerge from the walkway and stop on the viewing platform we call The Lookout to admire the view of the ocean. In the distance, to our right, the tiny town of Russell nestles in a curve of the coast like a pearl in an oyster shell. To our left, sunlight glints off the cars making their way through the bustling holiday town of Paihia. Straight ahead, I can just make out the flagstaff on top of the hill at the Waitangi Treaty House. And between them all, the Pacific Ocean glitters a deep indigo-blue.

I point out the pool where we put recovering seals and penguins before returning them to the sea.

"It's a beautiful site," Naomi says quietly. "It would be a great place to work."

I glance down at her. She looks wistful. "Where are you working at the moment?" I ask.

She clears her throat and brushes a strand of hair out of her eyes, not looking at me. "I left my last position a month ago." She doesn't elaborate. Personal reasons, I'm guessing.

"Well, I'm sure you'd love it here," I tell her, not wanting to pry. I move away, and she follows, apparently reluctant to leave the beautiful view. "Come on, I'll show you the rest of the place."

I take her on a brief tour of the stores where we stock all the medical equipment, food, and other supplies for the animals, then lead her into the office block. There's no sign of Em, so I don't know where she's gotten to.

"Through here," I say. "Good luck with the interview."

"Thanks." She smooths down her skirt. "I'm a bit nervous."

"His bark is way worse than his bite. I'd say he was grumpy because of his leg, but he's always been like that. He's my brother, by the way."

"Oh of course, Em did say."

"Okay, so this is the office where you'd be working." I take her into the large room, suddenly seeing it through new eyes. Boxes are piled up against one wall, half of them opened, containing stationery, post, kitchen supplies, everything an assistant would need. A printer chunters away on a table, spilling sheets of paper onto the floor, while the phone on the desk rings futilely. The desk is piled high with envelopes, folders, and printed sheets of paper. The phone that sits on it stops ringing, and then a few seconds later it starts again.

"Um, sorry," I apologize, "it's a bit of a tip. We're still in the process of setting things up."

"It's better than it was." A tallish woman with short, spiky, dark hair, lots of eye makeup, and a nose ring appears from behind one of the stacks of boxes. "An hour ago it looked like a bomb had gone off. This is positively pristine."

I grin. "Hey, Frankie. What are you doing here? She's another one of our vets," I explain to Naomi.

"Rob needed some help with putting the mail-out together," Frankie says. She gives Naomi a helpless look. "Please tell me you're here for the job."

"I am," she replies, putting her purse down on the table. "Can I help?"

"Oh, that would be amazing."

"Shall I get the phone?"

"Yes, please."

Naomi picks it up, hesitates, then says, "Hartfield Wildlife Hospital, Naomi speaking, how can I help?"

Something moves behind her, and I turn to see Rob leaning on the door jamb, staring at her. His gaze slides to me, and I hold up a hand. She hasn't seen him yet, and she perches on the edge of the desk, gesturing to Frankie for a pen and paper, then scribbles down a note.

"Yes of course," she says. "I'll ask him to call you back." She hangs up, gives me a bright smile, then glances over and sees Rob. "Oh!" She gets to her feet hurriedly. "Sorry. I was… um… trying to help."

Rob pushes off the door jamb and takes a few steps forward, limping slightly. Interestingly, he's not using his cane. He must want to impress his potential assistant. "Who was it on the phone?"

She glances at her note. "Clint Eastwood." She looks back at him. "Not sure if he's good, bad, or ugly."

I laugh. "He's a potential investor from Auckland."

"I'm Rob Knight." My brother holds out his hand. He doesn't smile, but I know him well enough to guess he's pleased that she knows her old movie stars. He's a big film buff.

She shakes it. "Naomi Smith."

Frankie sends me an amused look. She knows as well as I do that Naomi's going to have to completely screw up the interview to not get the job.

"Oh, you made it," says a voice behind me, and I turn to see Em coming in carrying the box of disposable gloves she'd gone to get. "Just checking that Mr. I-don't-wear-a-watch remembered to bring you over here." She gives me a cheeky grin.

"Are you taking up a life of crime?" I ask her, gesturing at the box as she puts it on the table and pulls out a pair of the bright blue gloves.

"Nope. I thought you might need your prostate checked." She pulls on one and releases the base with a snap. "Bend over."

Rob snorts, and the girls laugh. I meet Em's eyes, and a shiver runs through me at the wicked twinkle in hers.

"Come on," I scold, trying not to think about her playing doctor with my family jewels. "These guys have a job to do and you're distracting them."

"You started it." But she lets me lead her out of the office and into the bright sunlight.

"What a gorgeous day," she says, tilting her face up to the sun.

"Are you working outside today?"

"Yeah. I'm about to clean out the Wing," she replies, naming the place where we keep the animals who are recovering from operations. "Hence the gloves."

"You should really wear a hat."

She pokes her tongue out at me. "Yes, Dad."

"And anyway, Liam can do that," I say, referring to one of the teenage volunteers. "Why don't you help Frankie out in the office?"

"I hate being stuck inside; you know that. I'm an outdoor girl." She stops at the viewing platform and leans on the barrier, looking out across the grass toward the ocean.

"You are," I murmur, leaning next to her. She's like one of the animals I treat. She's not meant to be caged up. She's far more at home in the wild. "Have you given any more thought to the veterinary course we were talking about? I sent you the link."

She shrugs and fiddles with the fingers of the gloves. "I know you mean well, but it's not for me. I'm not smart enough to be a vet."

"Em, come on…"

"No, I'm not being modest. I'm not vet material. And I'm okay with that. I know you think I'm an underachiever…"

"I don't think that," I protest, although I am convinced she could do a lot more if she put her mind to it.

"Not everyone's cut out to go to university. I'm happy doing what I do, helping out where I'm needed. I love my job, and I think I do it well. So don't put me down because of it."

She looks up at me with her big green eyes, and I feel a sweep of shame.

"I didn't mean to put you down. I'm sorry. You're right—you do a great job here, and at the hospice. I won't mention it again."

We look out to sea for a while, not saying anything. Eventually, I bump her shoulder with mine, and she bumps me back. I'm forgiven.

"Naomi's lovely," she says. "She's going to do well here."

"Yeah, she looked like she'd be able to handle Rob okay."

"I was thinking… wouldn't she and Gabe make a great couple?"

"Gabe? I don't think so."

"Why?"

"Because your brother is interested in someone else."

"Who?"

"Frankie."

She bursts out laughing. "Gabe and Frankie? Jeez. They'd murder each other in a week if they started dating."

"If you say so."

"I do, and I'm an expert."

"Oh, sorry, I didn't realize."

"Well, John and Bella wouldn't be getting married if it wasn't for me."

"Em, my brother and your sister grew up together, the same as we did. Their relationship has nothing to do with you."

"She'd never have thought of dating him if I hadn't pushed her into the pool with him that day. She saw him in a different light after he carried her out."

"Well, that's arguable, because I think you pushed her in because she'd had her hair done and she wouldn't stop talking about it. And it certainly doesn't make you a master matchmaker."

"It does. I want that on a T-shirt." She raises an eyebrow. "Who's in charge?"

It's an old argument, something we both say to each other. The youngest of all of us who grew up at Hartfield, she's an independent spirit who's used to getting her own way, and I'm used to attempting to rein her in.

"Em," I chide, "I'm telling you, don't interfere. You can't force two people together who aren't meant to be. It doesn't work like that."

She looks up at me then. "No," she says. Her gaze scans my face. "I'm sorry about you and Tia."

I scuff my boot in the dirt. "Thanks." It's the first time I've seen her since it happened over a month ago. Someone obviously told Em we'd broken up because she texted me a few days after I landed in Aus to say she was sorry to hear the news. She knew me well enough not to press me for details, though.

Two brightly colored rosellas sweep past us into the bush, and she watches them land in one of the trees before continuing.

"Rob said you broke up just before you went to Aus?"

"Yeah. Literally, the day before."

"Did you break up with her, or vice versa?"

I sigh. "It was a mutual decision. Amicable enough."

"You want to talk about it?"

"Not really."

"Okay." She reaches out a blue-gloved hand and pokes one of the coiled-up silver fern leaves.

I clear my throat. "So how are the wedding preparations coming along?"

"Good. Bella's puzzled because John's suit is apparently a bit tight. She makes him a salad for lunch every day—she doesn't know he buys a pie from the corner shop on the way to work."

I chuckle. My brother is five inches shorter than me and finds it much harder to keep the weight off, especially because, as a lawyer, his job means he's far more sedentary than either me or Rob. "How are the bridesmaids' dresses coming along?"

"Mine's done," she says. "It's going to knock your socks off."

"Seeing you in something other than shorts and the HWH shirt will knock everyone's socks off."

"Yeah, but you're the only one that matters." She glances at me then. "Because you're always teasing me about the way I dress, I mean." A light rose color stains her cheeks.

I decide to ignore it. I'm sure she didn't mean to imply my opinion is the only one that matters to her. "What color is it?"

"Pink." She raises her eyebrows. "Why are you laughing?"

"I haven't seen you in pink since you were, like, seven. And don't tell me you're going to wear makeup."

"I am, as a matter of fact. And I'm getting my hair done."

"Wonders will never cease."

"You won't recognize me. I'm even going to wear fashionable sandals. With a heel."

That makes me laugh. "God help us all."

"I might surprise you," she says. "And you should see the girls. They're so adorable in their little fairy dresses."

I smile. Em adores John and Bella's two daughters. She spoils them rotten.

"Dad calls them his little princesses," she says. "He's so proud of them."

I'm sure Hugh Woodruff was a little disappointed that his oldest daughter had had two children out of wedlock. He's very old-school. But he would never say anything, and he certainly adores his two young granddaughters.

"So," I say, "only three and a bit weeks until the big day. Do you have a date for it yet?"

"I'm working on it." She turns her gaze on me. "I'm hoping Finn will ask me."

My eyebrows slowly rise. Finn Weston is a vet at the wildlife hospital on the Sunshine Coast that I've just returned from. Noah King knows the woman who owns the place, and between them they came up with the idea that the two of us swap places for a few weeks to learn about each other's practices. Finn has been working here, covering for me while I did the same for him, but he's decided to stay until after the wedding.

I didn't know he'd also been working on Em at the same time.

"Do you think he will?" I ask, surprised.

She shrugs. "He seems interested, so… we'll see."

I purse my lips and look out at the view.

"All right," she says. "Why the disapproving gaze?"

"I don't disapprove."

"Yes, you do."

"All right, I do." I turn to face her, leaning on the railing. "He'd eat you alive and spit you out."

"One can only hope," she says, somewhat wistfully.

"Em!"

She rolls her eyes. "I want a date! And he's gorgeous and he likes me, so…"

"I wouldn't say he was gorgeous…"

"Yeah, well, I wouldn't expect you to agree."

"His eyes are too far apart."

"No, they're not."

"He looks like Sid from *Ice Age*."

She tries not to laugh. "He does not—don't be mean. You shouldn't say things like that behind someone's back."

"I'd happily say it to his face. I've called him worse." The two of us have had several arguments that have rapidly turned heated, usually because he thinks he's superior and tries to tell me how to run my surgery.

"You two have never got on," she says. "I don't know why."

It's true. The moment I met him, I immediately took a dislike to his arrogant manner.

It had nothing to do with the fact that he teased Em the first time he met her, and obviously liked her.

I blow out a breath. "Seriously, though. Don't go out with him. You can do better than that."

"Not really. I don't get out much. I don't meet many guys, and he's kinda hot."

Her description of him irritates me, because I can see why she likes him—he's young, good looking, and with just the right amount of insouciance to attract the gaze of all the women around him. I might be wrong, but he strikes me as the type of guy who would never be happy tied to just one woman.

"He's a player, Em. And he's going back to Aus soon. He's hardly relationship material."

She gives me an impatient look. "Who said anything about a relationship? You sound like my father. Sometimes it's not about settling down. Sometimes it's just about having a good time."

I push off the barrier, not wanting to think about what her having 'a good time' with Finn Weston would entail. It makes me want to smash the guy's teeth down his throat. "Fair enough. Well, I'd better go back to work."

"Yeah. Me too."

We walk the short distance to the surgery, and we part at the door, Em going through to the Wing, me to my room.

I close the door behind me with a scowl and glare at the blue penguin still sitting in its cage on the table. It looks back at me and lifts its injured wing in a kind of shrug as if to say, Women!

Did I really say, 'He's hardly relationship material'? Em's clearly only looking to have fun. And why shouldn't she? She's young and sexy, and there's nothing wrong with her enjoying herself providing she takes precautions.

I close my eyes. Jeez. I'm this close to watching *Last of the Summer Wine* at night while I munch on a bag of Werther's Originals before I put my teeth in a glass and go to bed. I'm only thirty. So why do I feel so old?

Chapter Three

Emily

"So how was your day?" Dad comes out onto the deck and places the bowl he's carrying on the table. It's a glorious evening. We're sitting under the shade of an umbrella, looking out over the lawn, to the view of the Pacific and the islands in the distance. Minnie, his golden retriever who's still a puppy at eight months, is chasing a butterfly on the lawn. It doesn't get much better than this.

I sniff the dinner, and my stomach rumbles. Mmm—penne pasta with chorizo sausage in a spicy tomato sauce. I help myself to a generous serving as I haven't eaten anything since lunch. "Yeah, it's been a good day. Rob gave Naomi the job."

"Oh, excellent."

"He didn't tell me anything about her interview, but I'm not surprised." I use the salad servers to lift a pile of green salad and squeeze it onto my plate. "If I was a cynic, I'd say there was no way he was going to pass on the curvy brunette with big dark eyes who was also into movies. But I'm not, so I'm putting it down to the fact that she had an excellent CV."

He chuckles and helps himself to the pasta. I'm a terrible cook, so he tends to prepare dinner on the proviso that I clean up afterwards. "When is she moving up?"

I gesture at the bottle of red wine on the table and, when he nods, I pour us both a glass. "This weekend. She's renting a flat in Paihia, but she can't take it over for another week. She said she was going to book herself into a B&B until then, but I was wondering whether she could stay here."

He gives me an amused look and helps himself to a slice of thick, crusty bread. "You don't have to ask me. It's your home too."

"I know. But it's been a bit hectic with all the wedding stuff and I wanted to make sure you were okay with it."

The two of us have been alone for over a year now, since Mum died. The three Knight boys all left home years ago. Gabe, my older brother, and Bella, my sister, both left to go to university when they were eighteen, and both of them live in town now, Gabe on his own, Bella with John and their girls. Although the house is often busy during the day, especially since Bella and John decided they wanted to get married here, in the evenings it's just Dad and me.

Dad took Mum's death hard, and his grief has yet to abate. He sees Mum around every corner, and I know he wanders the house at night when he can't sleep. I don't want to upset him by bringing a stranger in. After saying that, however, for so many years we've had a house full of people, so maybe it would do him good.

He smiles. "You're a good girl. But I'm fine, don't worry about me. Of course you should invite Naomi to stay." He has a mouthful of wine. "And Em… I'm not stupid. I know you're staying here for me, and you really don't need to. You're twenty-one now, and it's time you got a place of your own."

"And start paying rent? I don't think so. I know when I'm well off."

"Em…"

"I'll leave when I'm ready," I tell him. "And I'm not ready yet." It's partly true. I love Hatfield House, and it's only a short drive to HWH. But I also don't want to leave Dad alone, and we both know it.

"You should get out more." He has a mouthful of pasta, then points at me with his fork. "You should be going on dates and getting drunk at parties."

"Euw. No thanks."

He gives a short laugh. "I don't know why you're so different from Gabe and Bella. We brought you all up the same."

I shrug. They were both a little rebellious in their youth, but I've never been even remotely wild. "Don't forget it was as if I had five older siblings. If I'd stepped out of line, I'd have had, like, four different guys putting me over their knee."

"Yeah, but only one would have enjoyed it." Dad chuckles.

"Even so, I think there'd be—" I stop with my fork halfway to my mouth. "Wait, what?"

He's saved by his mobile, which buzzes where it's sitting on the table. "Sorry, it's Noah. I missed him earlier, so I'd better take it." He answers it, propping his feet on the chair opposite, and is soon involved in a discussion about profit margins and investment opportunities that instantly has me zoning out.

As I finish my pasta, I text Naomi. *Hey you! Just wanted to say, why don't you stay at Hatfield with me until your flat's available? We've got loads of spare rooms!*

She comes back almost immediately, *Oh, are you sure? I was just starting to panic as everywhere seems to be booked!*

Of course! It'll be fun.

Cool—I'll be there Friday night.

Look forward to it. Let me know if you need anything.

Will do! X

I put the phone down, pleased she accepted. She's going to be a great addition to the hospital, and I think we're going to get on well. And it might be good for Dad, too, to bring a bit of life into the house.

I look out at the view, feeling a tad wistful. Not far along the deck, near the sliding doors to the main living room, is Mum's favorite outdoor hanging egg-shaped chair. She used to sit there and sketch, and, toward the end, when she could no longer do her artwork, she'd read or just look out at the view. I can't bring myself to sit in the chair now. My throat tightens just thinking about it.

The house holds a lot of good memories for me, too, though. Far to my right is the pool, where all of us spent so many hours as kids, and where I used to watch Gabe and Knightley doing lengths in the morning, cheering them on whenever they decided to have a race. And we had so many parties in the large garden. Mum and Dad always said every holiday should be celebrated: everyone's birthday, Valentine's Day, Yule, Christmas, the Queen's Birthday, Labour Day… Every single one was an excuse to have a party. Over there was where Rob fell in the hostas when he got drunk for the first time. John first kissed Bella under the jacaranda tree, not knowing until we cheered that we were all watching from the living room. I have a vivid memory of Gabe walking on his hands on the lawn and all the change falling out of the pockets of his jeans, right in front of where I'm sitting now. And that's the flower bed I fell into when Knightley told me he'd put a gecko down my neck. (He hadn't—it was a leaf, but it freaked me out just the same.)

The Knight boys have played as big a part in my life as my own siblings. Luckily, I'm able to see most of them on a daily basis now the Wildlife Hospital is up and running. But part of me is aware that I'm trying to cling onto my childhood for as long as I can. At some point I'm going to have to let go and move on with my life.

Not yet, though. I settle back, stretch out my bare legs, and let the evening sun warm my skin.

Yeah, but only one would have enjoyed it. I wonder what Dad meant by that? I'll ask him later, if I remember.

Then I doze off, and forget all about it.

*

Late on Friday, Naomi turns up at Hartfield, tired after the three-hour drive from Auckland, but excited to be starting her new life. I show her into the room I've made up opposite mine. "It used to be Bella's," I say, "but if she and John stop over now, they stay in the room at the end that has a door through to the girls' room."

"It's lovely." Naomi takes in the lavender-colored bedding, the watercolors Mum painted that hang on the walls, and the gorgeous view across the lawn to the ocean. "It's a lot better than my old view of the back of a hotel and a builder's site!"

Dad takes to her immediately, to my relief. Over the weekend, we all chat at mealtimes, and then Dad goes back to overseeing the farm work while I show Naomi around the house and surrounding area.

Monday is her first day at work. We take separate cars as I'm off to Whangarei later this afternoon to pick up some medical supplies, but we leave at the same time and meet up in the car park. When we get to the office block, we discover that Frankie has been in over the weekend clearing up Naomi's room. She's stacked all the boxes neatly to one side, moved the desk over to the window, removed all the rubbish from it, and cleaned it. She's unpacked a new coffee machine that now sits on a table with a box containing a variety of espresso pods and brand-new mugs, and a small fridge sits underneath housing fresh milk and chocolate biscuits.

"We've got two filing cabinets coming this afternoon," Frankie says, "and a stationery cupboard, so you can start getting organized."

"Terrific." Naomi looks genuinely thrilled. "Thank you so much."

"Oh, it was nothing." But Frankie beams. "Glad I could help."

"Where's Rob?" I ask.

"Here." He comes out of his office, carrying a mug in his left hand. He's leaning heavily on his cane with his right, and the fine lines around his eyes seem deeper than usual. I know him well enough to tell that the pain is bad today. "You're late," he says to Naomi.

"No, she's not," I tell him. "it's not even nine yet. Keep your knickers on."

She gives a short laugh, slides off her jacket, and hangs it over the chair. "I'm sorry, usually I'll be earlier than this. It's Hugh's fault for cooking us breakfast."

"You're staying up at Hartfield House?" Rob asks.

She nods. "Just until my flat's available in Paihia." She gestures at the mug in his hand. "Would you like me to make you a coffee?"

He looks at it, then holds it out to her. "Please."

She takes it, goes over to the table, and starts examining the new coffee machine. I think she's going to be good for him. I meet his gaze and smile.

"What?" he growls.

"Nothing. How's the leg?"

"Fine." He turns, limps back to his office, and shuts the door with a bang.

"Try to get him to take his painkillers," I advise Naomi when she gives me an amused look. "He's worried about getting addicted, but his leg is bad today."

"Okay," she says.

"I'll be back later," I tell them both. "Have a good morning."

Frankie waves, and I leave them to it, heading out into the bright sunshine.

As usual, my morning is busy. I check the traps in the surrounding bush for predators like possums, stoats, and rats. Then I help with some maintenance work: I water-blast the walkways free of algae and mold, trim back the ferns that grow so quickly along the side of the paths, remove old leaves from the palms, and pull out the gorse that's popped up behind the storage shed. Even though I'm wearing gloves, my hands are covered with red gashes that are going to sting like hell next time I have a bath.

"Working hard?" The voice comes from behind me, and I turn to see Finn Weston approaching with a smile. His eyebrows rise as he sees the state of my hands. "Ouch. That must sting. And you're bleeding all over your designer outfit." He grins.

I brush a strand of hair out of my eyes, suddenly conscious of how I must look. I'm wearing green coveralls tucked into black gumboots, and I'm hot and sweaty, so I know my face must be scarlet.

Finn wears shorts and tees the same as most people here, but he somehow manages to make it look as if everything he wears carries a designer label. Even his hair looks like a European footballer's, and his short beard is neatly shaped. His stubble never seems to get any longer. How does he keep it the same length all the time?

"Someone has to do all the dirty work," I say. It's hard to keep the defensive tone out of my voice.

"Aw." He comes a bit closer and leans on the railing in front of me. "I like a woman in twill. It's kinda sexy."

I scowl at him. "Now I know you're taking the piss."

"Emily Woodruff. You have no idea how beautiful you look. It's very endearing."

I blush, but I'm so hot he'd never see it. I gesture at the car keys in his hand to cover my flustered demeanor. "Are you going out somewhere?"

"Just taking Kaia and Janie into Kerikeri to pick up a couple of new cages."

They're both veterinary assistants. "Have you told Knightley? I think he was going to call a vets' meeting for midday."

His smile fades. "I don't need his permission."

"I didn't mean—"

"We might get a pie or something for lunch. You want anything brought back?"

"No, it's okay, Dad made me some sandwiches this morning." Jesus. Now I sound like a five-year-old.

He gives me an amused look. "Okay, see ya." He walks away.

I watch him go, cursing under my breath. I wish I knew how to appear smart and sophisticated. Kaia is quite a bit older and has a husky voice and makes a lot of jokes about sex. Janie always wears elegant-sounding clothes like 'slacks' and 'blouses'. She has hoops in her ears and highlights in her hair.

I, however, have blood splashes on my coveralls and sandwiches made by Daddy. What a sex kitten.

Scowling, I put my tools away, take off my coveralls, and stomp over to the office block. Frankie has been in the surgery for most of the morning, but she's back in Naomi's office now, and the two of them are eating takeaway chicken salads from the café on the waterfront.

"Hey!" Frankie gestures to the fridge. "I got you one as well, if you want it."

"Oh, thank you." I decide to eat it and have Dad's sandwiches later. I go over and retrieve the box and a bottle of water, and drink half of it in one go. "Jeez, it's hot out there."

"I hope you're wearing lotion," Frankie says. "You'll get it in the ear from Knightley if you're not."

"Yes, I'm factor-fiftied-up. His lordship will have to pick someone else to moan at."

"Moan being the operative word," Naomi says, digging a piece of chicken out with a fork. Frankie snorts, and Naomi giggles.

I give them an amused look as I perch on the edge of the table and tuck into the salad. "What do you mean?"

Frankie glances at Naomi, then gives me a mischievous look. "I was talking to Tia."

"Oh?" As far as I know, it's the first time anyone's seen Knightley's ex since they split. "How's she doing?"

"All right, I think. We got chatting and she told me a bit about what happened, you know, when they broke up."

"Oh… spill the beans."

"She implied it was to do with his… um… appetite, shall we say?"

Puzzled, I look from one to the other. "He was eating too much?"

"Kinda," Naomi says.

Frankie grins. "I don't mean food. Tia said she got fed up with 'Twice Knightley's insatiable demands.'"

"Twice Knightley…" I repeat, and they both giggle. Then it sinks in. Twice nightly. I'm such an idiot. They're talking about sex. "Oh…" I think about the implications of her statement. "He liked it twice a night? I'm impressed. The man has stamina."

Frankie spears a forkful of lettuce. "She's a nutcase. Imagine being with a guy who wanted you twice a night. I wouldn't be complaining, for sure."

"Mmm." Naomi's gaze drifts off into space.

I blink, having difficulty processing the information. I've never entertained any thoughts about Knightley's activities in the bedroom. It's a road down which I've always refused to travel.

Suddenly, all I can think about is what he's like in bed. The man's a pussycat normally, laidback and gentle, so the thought of him liking it twice nightly is a revelation. If he has a high sex drive, he must be passionate and somewhat… demanding.

And now I think I might faint.

"I don't think it was the main reason they broke up, though," Frankie continues, oblivious. "She called him Mr. Frosty and said he froze her out of the relationship. And she also said she wanted kids, and he didn't. They've been together a while, so I guess she realized she wasn't going to be able to talk him around. An obstacle that big isn't going to be easily surmountable."

"Aw," Naomi says, "I wonder why he doesn't want kids? Do you know, Em?"

"No."

"Shame, isn't it? He's only young. I wonder whether he'll ever change his mind."

While the two of them continue talking about guys and babies, I move the lettuce and chicken around in the box with my fork. I know why he doesn't want children, but it's not something I can discuss with them. I'd hoped he'd have gotten over it by now, but he obviously hasn't. It makes me incredibly sad.

I don't want to be sad, so instead I think about him being called Twice Knightley, but all that does is get me all hot and bothered. I mustn't think about him and sex in the same sentence. But now I can't stop.

He likes sex twice a night. Is that every night? So how's he been coping since he broke up with Tia? Well, come on Em, that's obvious—by indulging in some DIY, no doubt.

Whoa, there's a picture I've conjured up. Knightley. Naked. Taking himself in hand. Lying back and stroking himself until he—

"—and we can pass on the results to the labs at Auckland Zoo…" It's Gabe, coming into the office with Rob. And Knightley. Shit. I blink hurriedly, trying to get rid of the image that refuses to be erased. I think my brain's going to explode.

"It'll be good if we can keep up this exchange of information," Knightley replies as if everything in the world is normal and there hasn't been an atomic explosion destroying every one of my brain cells. "It'll benefit everyone involved."

"Yeah." Gabe comes around the table, reaches over Frankie's shoulder, and pinches a piece of chicken from her box.

"Hey," she says indignantly. "I was saving that."

My brother just grins and goes over to the fridge to get out a Coke Zero.

"So how often do you think we should process the lab tests?" Knightley asks him, nodding as Gabe offers him a bottle of water.

"Twice nightly?" I ask before my brain thinks better of it.

Naomi and Frankie immediately burst out laughing.

The guys all look puzzled. "What?" Knightley asks. He turns his blue gaze on me, and heat rushes through my veins as the image I conjured up reappears.

"I saw your ex," Frankie explains. "She… um… happened to reveal her nickname for you." She presses her lips together, trying not to laugh.

He stares at her, then at Naomi, who's biting her lip hard, and then finally his gaze slides back to me. Slowly, his lips curve up. "I see."

"You've got some stamina," I say, proud that my voice isn't just a squeak. "For an old man."

He gives me a wry look. "I'm not that old."

"Ten years older than me."

"Nine years, nine months, and nine inches taller." It's an old argument.

"Nine inches long?" Frankie suggests, unfurling her fingers by her crotch, palm up.

Rob snorts. "In his dreams."

Oh God, and now I'm thinking about his—

Knightley rolls his eyes and opens his water bottle. "So to get back to the lab results, if we email them through, say, three times a week, and they do the same, we'll have plenty of data to compare to…"

He continues to talk, but I'm not listening. My brain's turning to mush. I have to get out of the room. While they continue, I clean my salad box and put it in the recycling, trying to concentrate on what I have to do before I go to Whangarei. Oh yeah, I want to fill up the bird feeders around the walkway. Jeez, it's so hot today. Can you have hot flashes at twenty-one? I'm wearing my bikini top under my polo shirt, so I peel it up and pull it over my head. Which is fine, except the tag at the back gets caught on my necklace. "Dammit."

"… for comparison," Knightley is saying, "and if we put them side by side, I think we'll f… er… find… several… What *are* you doing?"

"I'm stuck." Exasperated, I turn my back to him, as he's the closest one to me. "Can you unhook me?" There's a little laughter from the others at my comment, and I frown. "My necklace, I mean."

For a moment, he doesn't move.

"Take your time," I snap, afraid of breaking the catch as it's the St. Christopher my mum gave me.

I feel him close the distance between us. "Stand still," he says.

His fingers brush against my shoulder as they move to my neck, and he fumbles at the catch. His skin is warm against mine.

"No hurry," Frankie says. "Wouldn't want to break it."

Again, the others chuckle, and I frown. What's going on?

It only takes him a couple more seconds and then he frees the label, letting me remove the top.

Flushed and flustered, I lower it to discover them all looking most amused. Suddenly worried that I've forgotten to put on my bikini top beneath the top, I look down, but it's okay, I did remember, and my boobs aren't out. I glance up at him. His blue eyes are very bright.

"What?" I ask.

"Nothing." He looks a mixture of exasperated and amused. "You're the bane of my life, Emily Woodruff."

Rob chuckles and even Gabe grins. Irritated because I don't know what's going on, I toss the top onto the chair and say tartly, "If that was true, I'd tell the girls your real name."

Both Naomi's and Frankie's eyes widen. "Oh…" Frankie says. "What's this?"

Knightley gives me a warning look. "Em…"

"What?" I meet his eyes with a taunting look. "*Leander.*" It means Lion Man. That's taken on a whole new meaning for me now.

Frankie's jaw drops. "Your full name is Leander? Seriously? How did I not know that?"

"Because it's not common knowledge. Or at least it wasn't." He glares at me.

"I can see why you'd prefer Twice Knightley as a nickname," I say. "Was Tia really talking about sex? Or was it a reference to how many times you fart?"

Knightley has a wide range of expressions he reserves just for me. Annoyed, irritated, exasperated, indignant, and vexed are just a few. All of those are present today, but also something new, something much… hotter.

The others burst out laughing. I wait for him to give me a witty retort, but instead, he gets up from the table and walks toward me, his gaze fixed on mine.

Alarmed, I back away until my butt meets the table. He walks right up to me, until I have to crane my neck to look up at him. Gosh, he's so tall.

"Careful," he murmurs, and he leans forward. Oh my God, he's going to kiss me. Right there, in front of everyone. My heart hammers, and I can't breathe or move. His lips are just half an inch away from mine, and his breath whispers across my skin as he puts his arm around me.

But he doesn't close the distance. Instead, he tosses his water bottle in the recycling bin behind me. He says, "We're not brother and sister. Remember that." His gaze slips to my mouth for a second. And then he moves away, and walks out of the office.

The breath I was holding leaves me in a whoosh. Rob rolls his eyes and disappears into his office. Gabe just laughs and follows Knightley out.

I stare at Naomi and Frankie, my head whirling. "What… I don't…"

They both giggle.

"What did he mean by that?" I whisper.

Naomi smiles. "He means he likes you."

"I know he likes me. We're best friends. It'd be odd if he didn't."

"No," Frankie says, "she means he *likes* you, likes you."

"I… what?" I can't process that. "No. He's Knightley. He's like a…" I was going to say brother, but my voice trails off. Wasn't that what he was just pointing out? That we're not brother and sister?

My dad's words this morning, when I mentioned the guys putting me over their knee, suddenly ring in my head. *Yeah, but only one would have enjoyed it.* Holy shit. Did he mean Knightley?

"Your dad never adopted the Knight boys though, did he?" Frankie asks.

"No, but—"

"Aren't your sister and his brother getting married soon?" Naomi points out.

"Yeah. But there's only a couple of years between them. He's ten years older than me."

"Nine years, nine months," Naomi says. "As I understand it."

"For God's sake," Frankie scolds, "it's not like he's old enough to be your dad. Anyway, there's something nice about going with an older guy. They know what they're doing. They can show you a few things."

Going with… she means having sex with. *They can show you a few things.* Holy shit. My brain's melting. Can't compute…

"You should've seen his face when you took your top off," Naomi says. "I thought his eyes were going to fall out."

I look down at my boobs, encased in the bikini triangles. They're not huge. I guess they're not bad, though. "Really?"

Frankie gets up to throw her carton in the recycling. "He's known you for a long time, and he's obviously treated you like a kid sister in the past. But you're all grown up now. Boobs 'n' all. You forget, and you still act as if he's your brother, but he's not. He's a guy—one with quite a high sex drive, by the sounds of it. You'd better watch out, Em, or it'll be you who gets the Twice Knightley treatment."

She laughs at that and leaves the room, and Naomi grins and goes back to her desk.

And I just stand there, jaw hanging around my knees, completely bemused by everything that's happened in the last five minutes.

Chapter Four

Knightley

It proves to be a long day. I have to take the boat over to Russell at one point to look at a seal that's been found injured. I manage to treat it there and afterward I let it slip back into the water, but I'm just on my way back when I get a call from Hal, one of the vets at Noah's Ark, and an old friend of mine. It turns out that a stray dog has been hit by a car near the beach in Opua, but they're snowed under at the Ark. He rang Hartfield to see if anyone there might be able to go and see to it, and they told him I was out and about. I tell him that of course I'll go, and so I sail up the coast to the beach, carry the dog onto the boat, and take him back to Hartfield.

We don't usually allow dogs at the hospital because they're a danger to kiwis and other birds, but I'm not about to turn my back on an injured animal, so we'll just have to make sure he stays on a lead. Not that it's an issue at the moment—he's broken his hind leg and he's obviously got internal bleeding. I spend the rest of the afternoon x-raying him, putting him under, repairing the injury, and seeing to his other wounds. The vets take turns doing the night shift, and when I'm done, Lorelei, who's on tonight, takes him off to the recovery room and promises to look after him.

So it's late by the time I leave the building, past seven p.m., and I realize I haven't had anything to eat since breakfast except a muffin late this morning. I totally missed lunch; no wonder I'm ravenous. I'm too tired to cook, though. Maybe I'll get takeout.

I approach my car—a Ford Ranger—my eyebrows rising as I spot Em's orange ute next to it, and then I see her, leaning against the car, watching me.

"Hey." I frown, concerned. "Everything all right?"

She pushes off. She looks tired but gorgeous, strands of her strawberry-blonde hair tumbling around her face. "Yeah, fine. I just finished unloading the stuff I picked up from Whangarei."

"Oh, of course." I'd forgotten she'd gone down there today.

"You look tired," she says. "Busy day?"

"Yeah. I'm knackered. I haven't eaten either, so I'm fading away."

She smiles. "You want to come up to the house for some pizza?"

"Ah… are you cooking it?"

She gives me a wry look. "No, it's one of Dad's." Em somehow manages to burn even the simplest of dishes.

I think about it. It would save me from going into town. Plus Hugh Woodruff makes a damn good pizza. "In that case, yes."

"I'll meet you up there."

"Okay."

We get in our cars, reverse out, and I follow her up the hill.

As we turn onto the long drive and pass the orchards and vineyards, Hartfield looms ahead of me, lit by the evening sun. I will always love this place. When I first arrived here with John and Rob at the age of thirteen, I was a frightened and angry boy, determined to hate the place and the people with whom the authorities had put me. For those first few weeks, all three of us must have been a nightmare to deal with—especially me, I have to say. I was rude and rebellious, and I did everything I could to illustrate my grief for my mother, my fury at my father, and my resentment at having to leave my home.

But gradually Hugh and Angela Woodruff, their three charming children, and the house itself, won me over.

Hugh was—still is—a kind, generous, and no-nonsense guy who was unerringly patient with us. Angela was practical and fun, with a huge heart, and a way of looking at you that made you feel an inch high if you were rude. But when you were polite and well-behaved, she was quick to reward you with food, games, and affection, until eventually it just seemed easier to be good.

And as for their three kids… Gabe Woodruff was the same age as me, an easygoing, fun guy who was happy to share his toys, his bikes, his computer, and his console, and soon became as good a friend to me as my own brothers. Bella was naughty and a bit of a handful, but quickly became devoted to John, and it wasn't a surprise to any of us when the two of them got together in their late teens.

And Emily… at four, she was a delight, the baby sister I'd never had, with the blonde curly hair of an angel and the biggest green eyes I'd ever seen in a kid. Like her siblings, she'd been taught to share and was generous with her toys and, more importantly, her affection.

One of my abiding memories is of me storming out of the house one afternoon after Hugh told me about my dad's verdict and that we wouldn't be going home anytime soon. I walked all the way across the lawn to the seat that overlooked the ocean and sat there bawling my eyes out, a tight knot of misery and fury. When my tears eventually dried up, I noticed with shock that Em was sitting to one side by the fence, watching me.

"Fuck off," I told her fiercely, embarrassed and angry, hoping to shock her with my colorful language. But instead, she got up and came over, and climbed on the bench to sit beside me. Then she put her hand in her pocket and pulled out a KitKat. She opened the wrapper and separated the fingers, passed me two, and proceeded to eat the others while she told me about a honeybee she and Angela had found lying on the deck, and how they'd fed it sugar water until it recovered and flew away.

I ate the chocolate, listening to the little girl doing her best to comfort me the only way she knew how—by talking about animals, because she knew I loved them. It reminded me that Hugh had promised to take me on a boat trip to see the seals at the Hole in the Rock that weekend, because I'd watched the whole series of *Blue Planet* twice. My own father had never made the effort to do anything like that.

And that was the first time I thought maybe everything was going to be all right.

Now, I pull up beside the orange ute in front of the house, and we both get out. This side of the house is in shadow, but as we walk around the west wing to the deck, the sun streams over us, bathing us in warm orange light. It's been a gorgeous January. The Northland summers are to die for.

"Hey." Hugh is in the process of laying out a couple of plates on the patio table. He grins, opens his arms as I walk up, and gives me a bearhug. He always has done, as generous with his affection with me and my brothers as he is to his own children. "You look tired," he says as I move back and bend to greet Minnie, who's bouncing around my feet, looking for attention. "Been a busy day?"

"Just a bit." I gesture at the two plates. "Em invited me up, but I don't want to intrude…"

"Don't be daft. She texted to say you were coming. These plates are for you two. I've had mine. I'll go and get the pizza." He walks off into the house.

Em rolls her eyes and fusses Minnie. "Intrude? This is your house as much as mine."

Her words warm me through, but I say, "I never like to assume."

"Sit down and shut up," she scolds mildly, and I chuckle and take a seat.

Hugh comes out almost immediately and places the pizza between us. Steam coils up into the air, and the smell of bubbling cheese, barbecue sauce, and cooked chicken fills my nostrils and makes my stomach rumble.

"Dig in," he says. "Beer?"

"Go on, then, just the one."

"Em?"

"Please."

He goes back in and reappears with two bottles.

"Are you joining us?" I ask, helping myself to a couple of slices of pizza before piling on some green salad.

"Actually I've got a couple of phone calls to make," he says. "If you're still here, I'll catch up with you later." He gives a wave, calls Minnie to his side, and then vanishes again, pulling the sliding door closed behind him.

Em watches him go, pursing her lips, then glances at me before she helps herself to salad.

"What's going on?" I ask, amused, following it with a long swallow of the beer.

"Nothing. Just Dad being Dad." She tucks into her pizza. "God, I'm so hungry."

"Me, too."

We eat in silence for a couple of minutes, until the first pangs of hunger die down, and then we both sigh, lean back, and stretch out our legs as we work our way through the slices at a more leisurely pace.

She looks over at me once or twice, and there's something in her eyes that makes me frown at her suspiciously. "What's the matter?"

I half-expect her to say 'nothing' again, but this time she studies the crust of her pizza slice for a moment before saying, "You know today, in the office…"

I crunch on a slice of cucumber. "Yeah…"

"What did you mean when you said that we're not brother and sister?"

Oh… I wondered whether she was going to bring that up. She provoked me with her teasing, and the words slipped out. It's probably best if I underplay it.

I have a swig of beer. "Exactly what I said. I was reminding you that we're not related."

"Why did you want to remind me of that?"

"Because you were flirting."

"I was not!"

"Yes you were, even if you didn't realize it. You took off your top—"

"I was hot!"

"And asked me to untangle your necklace, and then you were cheeky."

"Was I?"

"You told them my name's Leander."

She bites her lip. "Oh yeah. I forgot."

"I was just pointing out that if you're going to flirt like that, we're not brother and sister, and it's possible that it might have…" I think of the right word. "Repercussions."

Her eyes widen. "Like what?" She stares at me for a long moment, and I can see her brain whirring behind her eyes, trying to puzzle out what I could possibly mean.

"Do you really have no idea?" I ask softly.

She moistens her lips with the tip of her tongue, a gesture that sends a tingle running through me. "Well, yeah. It's just… I've never thought of you like that." Her gaze drops to my mouth. "Do you… um… think of me like that?"

For a moment, I can't think what to say. Do I tell her the truth? *I didn't used to, Em, because you're my best mate's little sis, and you were just a kid. But lately, something's changed. You've grown up into a gorgeous, sexy young woman. And now, it's all I can do not to think of kissing you.*

No, I can't tell her that. If I was to cross that line, I'd never be able to go back, and I'd destroy our friendship and everything else that comes with it. I'll never be able to show how grateful I am for everything her father and the rest of her family has done for me and my brothers. And I don't want to ruin the relationship we have. Especially when she probably doesn't feel the same way.

Equally, I've never lied to her, and I don't want to start now.

"I don't want to spoil our friendship," I murmur. "It's very precious to me."

"It's precious to me, too," she whispers.

We fall quiet, studying each other for a while. Her eyes hold a touch of wonder and, maybe, longing. She really hasn't thought about me in that way before. It reminds me how young she is. She hasn't been out with many guys. She's not just a girl I can hook up with for fun and then walk away from. She's much more special to me than that. And so I have to be the grown up, and be really careful to make sure our friendship doesn't evolve into anything else.

Eventually, she picks up a piece of pizza crust, dips it in the mayonnaise, and bites into it with a crunch. "Mind you," she says in a tone that tells me she's letting it pass and, as usual, she's going to tease me, "Twice Knightley… it gets a girl thinking."

That makes me chuckle, despite my intention to steer the conversation away from turning intimate. "Does it, now?"

Her expression turns curious. "So… you like sex?"

"Of course I like sex."

"And it's true?"

"What's true?"

"The nickname?"

Oh, for fuck's sake. "You mean do I like to have sex twice in one night? I'll take it as often as I can get it, Em, which isn't very often at the moment." It comes out grudgingly. Breaking up with Tia was hard, and although it was the right decision, I miss being able to relieve the tension of the day in that way.

"I guess you have to use… other methods… to de-stress…"

I meet Em's eyes. They're alight with mischief, and it's impossible not to tease her back.

I glance at the window to make sure Hugh's not listening. "Other methods? You mean like going for a run?"

"I was thinking more like wrist exercises."

We both start laughing.

"Sorry," she says. "I shouldn't tease, you're right, it is sort of flirting. I honestly didn't mean to earlier. I know that's naive of me."

"Eh, no harm done."

"I know nothing would ever happen between us. With you practically drawing your pension, and all."

I give her an exasperated look, and she chuckles. Then she turns her beer bottle in her fingers. "Can I ask you something?"

"If it's which hand do I use, I'll save you the time. It's the right."

Her eyes glaze over for a moment. Then she blinks and says hurriedly, "No! Jeez. Don't put images like that in my head. No, I was going to say that Frankie also said that Tia told her why you broke up. She said it was because she wanted kids and you didn't."

There were several factors involved in our breakup. Me not wanting kids was one. Her insistence that I wouldn't let her fully into my life was another. Both of them were valid accusations. I find it difficult to let women get close to me, and I know I tend to hold back emotionally. Because of this, Tia was hugely envious of my relationship with Em, and she told me if I didn't stop seeing her, we were done. Em is a big part of my life, and I could never be with someone who didn't understand that. So I told Tia it was over and walked away.

But I just say, "Yeah."

"Knightley…"

"What?"

"I thought you'd gotten over that."

"You thought I'd gotten over having a murderer for a father?"

She bites her lip, then says, "No, I thought you'd gotten over the notion of there being bad blood in your veins."

"Nope."

She tips her head to the side. "You're not the same as him."

"I'm his son."

"Yeah, but you could never do what he did."

"You don't know that. I have a temper."

"Ha! I can't remember the last time I saw you lose it."

"Doesn't mean it's not there."

"You were angry when you first came here, but that was understandable after everything you'd been through. You've grown up. You're in control now."

"I'm sure he thought he was in control until he wasn't. I can't risk it, Em. I won't." I work so hard to keep a lid on my resentment and fury and hurt, but it bubbles up inside me. "He was an addict, and he knew it, but he still got drunk and high because he was weak. And because of that, he murdered my mother."

"It was manslaughter," she reminds me. "He didn't mean to do it."

"He pushed her down the stairs, Em, in a drunken rage. It doesn't matter what word you use to describe it. He killed her and the baby inside her. And he scarred me, and John, and Rob, for life. He's always inside me, and I'll never be able to get rid of him. All I can do is make sure he doesn't get the chance to hurt someone I love."

I finish, breathing heavily, my heart banging on my ribs. I glare at her, not because I'm angry with her, but because I need her to understand.

We look into each other's eyes for a long time. Then, eventually, she says, "All right. But you should know, I think you'd make a great father, and I hope one day you'll reconsider."

I lower my gaze, my throat tightening. Then I have a swallow of beer.

"How's Finn?" I ask, when I feel able to speak again.

She crunches on another piece of pizza crust. "Good."

"Has he asked you out yet?"

"No." She studies the crust, then sighs.

"Idiot," I say, and she chuckles.

She looks over her shoulder, presumably checking that her father is still inside. Then she turns back to me and leans on the table. She picks at the label on her beer bottle and says, "Can I ask your opinion on something?"

"Of course." I wonder whether she's going to talk more about Finn and whether he'll ask her out. I'll have to do my best to keep my thoughts to myself, even though I think the guy's a fool for not snapping her up, and it makes me cross that he seems to be toying with her.

Instead, though, she says, "I'm thinking of getting tested."

I stare at her. For a brief moment, I think she means for an STD. Then her lips twist, and I realize what she's referring to. "For Huntington's?"

She nods.

I'm so shocked that for a moment I don't say anything.

Angela Woodruff discovered she had Huntington's disease or HD in her forties, when Em was around ten. She didn't know of anyone who had it in her family, so she had no idea she was at risk. Later, they found out that her grandmother might have had it, although she was never diagnosed. Angela only started developing signs after she'd had her three children, so she had no chance to get tested before making the decision as to whether to have a family. The rare, inherited disease dug its cruel claws into her quickly, and she went downhill fast.

I know that Hugh has discussed getting tested with his children, but all three of them decided against it.

"What's changed your mind?" I ask. "You haven't started getting symptoms?"

She presses her lips together and shakes her head. "It's hard not to wonder when you drop something or walk into a door. But I think I'm just naturally clumsy." She smiles.

I reach out a hand, and she slides hers into it. "You've had no other signs?" I rack my brain to think of the indicators of juvenile Huntington's disease. "No tremors in your hands?"

"No."

"No seizures?"

"No."

"No irritability or fatigue?"

She pauses. "No."

"You're sure?"

"I get tired, but then I work hard."

"What about depression, or thoughts of dying?"

She hesitates again, just a fraction, before she says, "No."

"Em?"

"Everyone gets blue, don't they? I don't know how to tell what's normal and what's not."

"Worse than normal, though?"

"No, not really."

"Anything else?"

"No."

I'm not sure I believe her, but she obviously doesn't want to tell me.

It's the first time we've talked about it like this. When Angela discovered she had Huntington's, I'd just left for veterinary college. I flew home and spent a few days with the family, and to their credit, Angela and Hugh discussed everything in front of not just their own children but us three Knights as well. Since then, I've done my own research, so I know how the disease is hereditary, and of its harsh motor, cognitive, and psychiatric symptoms. I watched Angela's health decline and saw each of those symptoms played out in the flesh when I came home to visit. It's not a kind disease, if there is such a thing. And I feel crushed every time I think that Em—and her siblings—could have inherited it.

I squeeze her fingers. She squeezes back, then withdraws her hand.

"What does Hugh say?" I ask. I'm sure he'd be supportive whatever her decision, but also sad to think the possibility of having it is already affecting her at such a young age.

"I haven't told him. Or Gabe or Bella. It'll make Dad sad, and Gabe and Bella will both be angry. They don't want to know. Anyway, I have to have three sessions of genetic counseling first. I'm not really looking forward to that."

"Can't you take someone with you?"

"I could, but I don't know who. I can't ask Gabe or Bella, and I don't want to ask Dad."

"How about Frankie?" I know the two of them are good friends.

But she shakes her head and scratches at the beer bottle again. "She's a sweetie, and I know she'd try to be all positive and upbeat about it. But there's a one-in-two chance I have it. Those are extremely high odds. I need to be practical. I can't go in there assuming I'm going to be one of the lucky ones."

I want to comfort her, and I can only think of one way to do that. Well, one way that doesn't involve taking her in my arms and kissing her until she forgets, and I can't do that. I dip my head to catch her eye. "Do you want me to go with you?"

Her eyebrows rise. "You?"

"Yeah." She told me about the test, so she must trust me.

"Do you mean that?"

"Of course. I know I'm not a doctor, but I'm a vet, which is kinda the next best thing, so maybe I can help with any medical questions. And all joking aside, we're friends, aren't we?"

Her expression softens. "Of course."

"I'll always be there for you, Em. Of course I'll come with you." I have a swig of beer. "And if Finn doesn't ask you to go to the wedding with him, you can go with me."

That makes her laugh. "You'd be my date?"

"Yeah, why not? I can't think of anyone I'd rather go with." And that's the truth, even if deep inside I feel a flicker of warning.

She smiles, her eyes shining. "Thank you."

"No worries. Now, am I going to have to arm wrestle you for the last bit of pizza, or can I steal it?"

"You can steal it."

I pick it up and eat it, winking at her, glad I could make her feel better, even if only for a short while.

Chapter Five

Emily

The days roll by, and things start to get frantic with the preparations for the wedding. I'm excited for Bella, but I admit I'm beginning to wish she'd chosen to get married somewhere other than Hartfield. I understand why she made that decision, because she loves the house as much as I do, and I'm sure she feels Mum's presence here more. But the place has been in an uproar this week.

I love my sister to bits, but she's been short-tempered and bossy as she tries to get everything organized. She has a wedding organizer, Lulu, but Bella is completely unable to delegate. She's always making anxious calls to the florists, the car-hire company, and the musicians. We've all had numerous visits to the bridal shop to try on the dresses for the umpteenth time. There have been any number of last-minute panics—the florist can't get hold of the particular flower Bella wanted for the bridesmaids' posies; the caterer declared they can't source enough salmon and will need to change the menu; the celebrant, who's a friend of John's, went down with flu and also lost his voice, so they have to find someone else. First-world problems that feel like the end of the world to the already stressed Bella.

I've offered to help with the organization several times, but Bella wants to do it all herself, and I know her well enough to know it's best to leave her to it, and just be there if she needs me.

I miss the peace and quiet I've grown to love, and Dad's the same. When he's not out on the farm or in the orchards, he hides in his study, and only comes out in the evening, when everyone's gone. Then the two of us sit on the sofa and grumble about feeling like strangers in our own home.

It won't be long until it's all over, though, and I can't blame Bella for throwing herself into the festivities. She doesn't talk about it, so I can only wonder whether our mother's illness is a factor in her frenzy. Her attitude has always been that *que sera, sera*, and life is too short to spend it being crippled with worry over something that might not happen.

Gabe's attitude is very similar and has led to him cramming as much as he can into his life, so—I'm sure—he's too busy to think about it. He's traveled a lot, bungee jumped, abseiled, leaped out of airplanes, and slept with a multitude of women, and although he eventually settled down enough to get his degree—and he works damn hard now, along with the rest of the crew at HWH—he still plays just as hard.

I don't understand either of them, although I'd never say as much. Bella has two daughters, but I could never get pregnant knowing I might be passing on an incurable disease to my unborn child, and thus condemning it to a life of misery and pain, the same way that I couldn't enter into a relationship without telling my partner what he might be in for.

But now I've made the decision to have the therapy, and Knightley's coming with me, I feel a lot better, and I find I'm able to put it mostly out of my mind, working hard at HWH and the Hospice in town, delivering, moving, cleaning, and doing any other odd jobs to help out.

A week after my conversation with Knightley over the pizza, I trudge across the wooden walkway to the office after a particularly hard day. I'm exhausted, and for a moment I feel a flicker of fear that it's a symptom rearing its ugly head. Then I decide it's probably because I've spent the day on my hands and knees scrubbing the floors throughout the entire surgery and laboratory.

I'm wearing my overalls, and I'm sweat-stained and covered in grime. But it was a job well done, and the whole place is sparkling. Tomorrow we've got a large group of possible investors coming to look around, and I wanted to make sure it looked its best. Knightley would rather have got a company in to clean, but I didn't want to waste the money when I knew I could do the job myself.

It's nearly six, and if Bella and Lulu were at the house fussing over seating plans, they will have gone by now. I can go home, collapse in front of the TV, and eat a whole tub of chocolate-fudge-brownie ice-cream while I watch Notting Hill for the umpteenth time.

I go into the office block, through to Naomi's office, and stop in the doorway. The whole floor is covered with neat piles of paper. Naomi is on her hands and knees, placing a sheet from a stack she's holding onto each pile.

"You've missed one," Rob says. He's standing behind her.

"No I haven't. Go away." She continues regardless, finishing off the stack, then picking up a packet of brochures.

"They should go underneath," he says.

"No, we decided they'd go on top so the HWH logo is the first thing they see. Please, go and bother someone else and let me do my job."

They're bickering amicably, like an old married couple. Clearly, she knows how to handle him. I chuckle and go in, stepping carefully around the piles. "Leave her alone, Rob. She knows what she's doing."

"If she'd let me help," he says, "we'd have done it in half the time."

She glares at him. "If I'd let you help, you'd have me in a muddle, and it would take us all night. Go away."

He scowls, goes into his office, and shuts his door with a bang. Naomi rolls her eyes, then grins and gets back to dishing out the paper.

"This for tomorrow?" I ask, going over to the box on the wall behind her desk and hanging up my keys.

"Yeah, just a presentation pack for each guest. I'd have gotten them done earlier, but we were waiting for the brochures to arrive, and then the photocopier broke down and the guy didn't get here until four..."

"You need some help?"

Her gaze slides over me, and her lips twitch. "It's okay, I'm good."

"You mean you really don't want my mucky paws all over your nice clean folders?" I hold them up, grimacing at the sight of my dirty nails. "Fair enough. I can clean up, though, and give you a hand?"

"Nah, it's okay, I'm nearly done now. I saw you working away today—you must be shattered. Go home and put your feet up."

"I'm way ahead of you, girl." I take a bottle of water out of her fridge, unscrew the top, and drink a quarter of it. "Ah... that's better. Yeah, I'll head off now. I reckon the coast will be clear at home."

The front door opens, and in comes Gabe. He's taken off his white lab coat, and he's just wearing his HWH shirt and old jeans. "Hey," he says, then stops and stares at the floor. "Wow. It looks like there's been a very neat explosion in a paper factory."

Naomi snorts and carries on dividing up the brochures. "I was just asking Em about the wedding organization," she says. "Is it still a nightmare there?"

I nod. "Let's just say it's totally put me off getting married—not that I was ever big on it. If I were to tie the knot, I think I'd elope."

"Gretna Green is a long way to travel just because you don't like a bit of fuss," Naomi says.

"I'm with you," Gabe tells me. "I can't imagine anything more horrific than having to deal with what John's going through."

"He's marrying the girl of his dreams," Naomi points out.

"Scant consolation," Gabe says. "Bella's hardly anything special."

I laugh. "Not to you."

"It's so much fuss and money for one day. I don't get it."

"It does seem like that." Naomi sits back on her heels. "But you have to look at the bigger picture. They want to stand in front of their family and friends so everyone can witness their promise to love one another until death parts them. So he can place that ring on her finger and show every other guy she meets that she belongs to him. It's primeval and passionate and romantic."

Gabe and I look at each other. "Nah," we both say together, and laugh.

"You two," she scolds, returning to dishing out her brochures. Then she glances at me. "Has Finn asked you out yet?"

I scratch my nose as Gabe's eyebrows rise. "No, still waiting," I admit.

"Really?" Naomi frowns. "He's so flirty with you. I was convinced he'd have done it by now."

"Me too. Yesterday he even mentioned the wedding. He asked what my dress was like, and where the best place was to park. And I thought here we go… And then zilch."

"Men," Gabe says.

I grin. "Yeah. Not a brain between them." I glance at Naomi, who's looking at her brochures, then back at him and gesture at her with my head. He lifts his eyebrows. I gesture at her again. His lips curve up, but he just turns, puts a folder in one of the cubby holes on the wall, and walks carefully through the papers back to the door.

There he hesitates and casts a last glance back at me. "You okay?" he asks.

"Yeah, I'm fine."

He nods. "See you later," he says, and leaves.

I turn back to Naomi. "I think he likes you."

She looks up and glances at the door. "Gabe? Nah. His attention lies elsewhere."

"Are you talking about Frankie? I said to Knightley that she'd kill him in the first week if they started dating."

"They say there's a thin line between love and hate."

"It's hairline where the two of them are concerned. He drives her insane. I thought the two of you would go well together. Want me to ask him out for you?"

She gives me an amused look. "What are we, twelve? No, thank you. I'm not looking to date at the moment."

"Glad to hear it." It's Rob, appearing through his door behind her again. "The last thing we need is something else distracting you from your job."

She pokes her tongue out at him, and I chuckle.

"Don't you think she and Gabe would make a great couple?" I ask.

"This does not sound like a conversation I'm even remotely interested in." He picks up a box of brochures and walks back into his office.

Naomi meets my eyes and we both grin. "Stop it," she scolds, and gets to her feet. "Okay, I'm going to put all this stuff into folders."

"All right. I'll leave you to it. Best of luck. See you tomorrow." I wave and go outside.

It's raining lightly, warm summer rain, and the air smells fresh and earthy. I pause to wash my hands under a tap on the side of the building, then cut across the yard behind the office block, heading for the car park.

I wonder what Dad's cooked for dinner tonight? He mumbled something this morning about a chicken curry—I'm really in the mood for that. With rice and the naans he makes himself, and a big dollop of mango chutney. Oh yeah. My stomach rumbles in anticipation.

I round the corner, still thinking about the curry, and then stop as I see two people ahead. The woman is standing with her back to the building. The guy is leaning one arm on the wall above her, which looks possessive somehow. And he's kissing her, his other hand caressing her waist, just an inch below her breast. Something about the way he's doing it makes it clear that this isn't their first kiss.

Although I didn't mean to, I must have made a sound, because Finn lifts his head and looks right at me. He moves backward, lowering his arms, and Janie looks over then and sees me.

"Em," Finn says.

"I'm sorry." I back away, holding up my hands. "I didn't mean to disturb you."

"No, hey, wait." He murmurs something to Janie, who pushes off the wall, glances at me, then disappears around the corner. He comes over to me. His expression shows guilt and regret. "I'm so sorry."

"For what?" I give him a bright smile. "You haven't done anything wrong."

He runs a hand through his hair. "Maybe not, but…"

Suddenly I'm very conscious of how I must look: filthy dirty, my hair lank and sticking to my head, no makeup, and scratches all over my arms from where I wrangled with the gorse outside the front of the building. I never stood a chance. What a fool I am.

"She's a lovely girl," I tell him as sincerely as I can. "I wish you all the luck in the world."

"Em—"

I turn on my heel and walk off toward my car. He doesn't try to follow me.

It's only when I get to my ute that I stop and lean weakly on the side. I put my head on my arms. I'm so tired. I'm not even sure I have the energy to get in the car and drive home.

"Em?"

My head snaps up, but it's only Knightley, walking across from the veterinary block with concern written all over his face.

"What's up?" he asks. "Are you feeling all right?"

The tone of his voice tells me that his first thought was whether I'm showing symptoms of the disease. "I'm fine," I tell him, frustrated that it's on both our minds. "Honestly. I'm just tired. And I bumped into… well, I didn't actually bump into him, but I saw Finn, and he was…" I stop and, as if the emotion is a tsunami that washes over me, I burst into tears.

"Aw," he says, and immediately puts his arms around me. "Come here."

Sometimes he takes off his HWH polo shirt before he goes home and puts on the tee he wore in that morning, so when I bury my face in it, he smells fresh and clean, unlike me.

"Sorry," I say through sobs. "I smell awful."

"You smell like summer," he says, his lips on the top of my hair.

I bawl, because he's being nice to me, and I can't take it.

"Hey." He rubs my back. "What happened with Finn?"

"Nothing." I lean against him, comforted by his tight hug. "He was kissing Janie."

"Oh… That must have been a shock for you. I'm so sorry."

I take a deep, shuddering breath. Actually, I'm not shocked. I'm not even upset, really. I kind of expected it. I'm not crying over Finn Weston.

I push myself back a little, and he lowers his arms. "I'm all right," I say, and give a little laugh as I wipe my cheeks. "I'm not upset about it, I swear. I'm really not. I'm just exhausted. And it's only because I've been working hard, that's all."

"I told you I'd get a cleaner in," he scolds. "Come on, I'm taking you home."

"But the ute—"

"—will still be here tomorrow. I don't want you coming off the road into the orange trees. Go on, get in the Ford."

I don't have the energy to argue with him, so I get in the passenger side. He waits until I'm in, then closes the door and walks around to the driver's side.

I buckle myself in. It's very much a man's vehicle. An All Blacks rugby sticker decorates the corner of one of the side windows. A bag sits by my feet containing a couple of apples, a banana, an oat bar, and two water bottles, one half empty. On the back seat is a pair of swimming goggles, a Frisbee, a cricket bat and pads, a pair of muddy rugby boots, and a new copy of the biography of the ex-All Blacks' player Richie McCaw. A surfboard is strapped to the rear of the truck. His cars have been like this since he was old enough to drive—the floor covered in a thin layer of sand, the air smelling faintly of his body spray. The familiarity of it comforts me.

He gets in, filling the space with his large frame, buckles himself in, and starts the truck. He glances at me as he looks over his shoulder to reverse out, his bright-blue eyes meeting mine for a second. "You okay?" he asks.

I just nod, not trusting myself to speak. I feel like a ball of emotion, as if I could burst into tears again at any moment.

He scans my face, then puts the car into drive and heads up the hill. "You should watch yourself," he scolds. "You're five-foot-five and there's nothing of you. It's no wonder you're knackered after scrubbing those floors all day."

"It looks good, though."

"Yes, of course it does, because you're very thorough and you'll always make sure it's spotless, but you don't have to do it all yourself. I keep telling you."

"Don't chide me. You'll have to scoop me up into a bucket if you do."

"Aw, Em… I'm just worried about you."

"I'm okay." I pull down the sun visor and look at my reflection. "Jesus. No wonder he was kissing someone else."

Knightley sighs. "I thought there might be something going on between them."

I put the visor back up, looking at him with surprise. "Seriously? Why didn't you say anything?"

"I wasn't sure. And I thought he'd be mad to choose her over you."

"You're kidding me. She's sophisticated with a capital S. And I'm… not."

He glances at me. "Janie might be attractive, but she's shallow and pretentious. You're beautiful inside and out, Em."

A tear runs down my face. I scrub it away, but not before he sees it.

"Is this about your mum and dad's wedding anniversary?" he asks.

I bite my lip and look out of the window. I hadn't thought he'd remembered.

"Did you think I wouldn't know what day it is?" he continues.

"Everyone always says men never remember their own anniversaries, let alone someone else's."

"Well, we all know. John and Rob and I—we asked Gabe whether he thought it was a good idea for us all to come over tonight for solidarity. But he said it was best to leave you and Hugh alone."

"We didn't want to make a fuss."

"Yeah, we get it. But we know, all the same."

I swallow hard. "I thought it would get easier once we got over the first anniversary of her passing. But it hasn't. Every time there's an anniversary or a birthday, it just brings it back that she's not here."

"I don't know why everyone assumes the first anniversary marks the time you should be over your grief. That's not how it works. It's something that happens gradually over many years, with lots of peaks and troughs in between."

Of course, he's been through it himself, with the death of his mother.

He holds out a hand, and I slide mine into it. He squeezes his fingers, and I squeeze back.

"How are you feeling about the wedding?" he asks, releasing my hand and returning his to the steering wheel as he turns onto the drive toward the house.

"What do you mean?"

"I just wondered whether it might feel a bit odd, Bella getting married."

"You mean am I jealous?"

"It did cross my mind."

"God, no. Gabe and I have decided we're going to elope. Not with each other, I mean when we meet someone. Neither of us wants all that fuss."

"Really?" He looks surprised. "I thought every girl wanted the chance to dress like a princess."

"Seriously, do you not know me at all? Can you imagine me being the center of attention like that? I'd die a thousand deaths."

He laughs, pulling up in front of the house and turning off the engine. "Fair enough. I admit I can't imagine you in a big meringue of a dress."

"I'd rip my veil and put the heel of my shoe through the train in seconds. If I get married, it's going to be in shorts and a T-shirt on the beach."

He smiles, turning to face me. "Well, I hope you and Hugh are okay this evening. You can always call me if you need me."

I turn to face him. "Do you want to come in? I think Dad's made curry."

"Not tonight. The two of you should spend some time together."

I lean my temple on the headrest. "I'm sorry about all the tears."

"Jeez, don't worry about that. I'm just sorry Finn disappointed you." He glances out of the window. He thinks I'm upset at losing Finn. How can I explain that's not the issue?

"I misread the signs. It's not the end of the world. I'm jealous, that's all. Not necessarily because he picked her. But the way they were kissing…" I sigh.

His gaze comes back to me, and he frowns. "What do you mean?"

"He kissed her like… he wanted her. And I'd like to be kissed like that. Just once." My face grows warm.

He studies me, clearly bewildered. "You mean… you haven't been kissed like that before?"

I shake my head. "Not even close."

"But… Em…"

Do I tell him? Admit the truth? I can see him putting two and two together. He's already guessed.

"I'm a virgin," I say. "I assumed you knew that."

His face is filled with a mixture of incredulity and wonder. "But you're twenty-one. You must have gone on dates. Jesus. How have you stayed innocent so long?"

"I've lived a sheltered life. I'm like a Jane Austen character without the stays."

"Em…"

The rain on the window casts a mesmerizing pattern over his face. Do I admit what's in my heart? I haven't told anyone about my deepest fears. I can't talk about this to my father or brother. Maybe I'd have discussed it with Bella, but she's not interested in talking about anything to do with Huntington's.

Who else do I trust more in the world than Knightley?

"If I have a relationship with a guy," I say slowly, "I might fall in love. And he might fall for me. How is that fair if it turns out I have the same horrific disease as my mother? I can't go into a relationship without knowing. It would be dishonest. How can I subject someone I love to that kind of future?"

Pity floods his eyes. "You can tell them it's a possibility without knowing for sure."

"What's the point in that? It's always there, always inside me, waiting. If I was entering into a relationship, I'd want to know if there was the chance that he'd develop a devastating disease that could completely change his personality. I know all the symptoms." I'm conscious that my voice is hard. "Movement, psychiatric, and cognitive. Did you know that sexual promiscuity is one?"

"No…"

"Up to seventy-five percent of women with Huntington's experience abnormal sexual behaviors like hypoactive sexual disorder and paraphilia. Do you know what that means?"

"No."

"It used to be called sexual perversion or sexual deviation. It includes things like exhibitionism, voyeurism, sadism, fetishism, and something called frotteurism—which means you touch or rub against a nonconsenting person."

"Jesus, Em, how do you know about this?"

"I told you, I've read all about it. And Mum…" I hesitate. "She didn't sleep around, but occasionally she had moments when…" I look down at my hands. "I don't really want to talk about it."

"Honey, first of all, you don't even know if you've got it yet. And even if you do have it, it doesn't mean you'd develop any of those symptoms."

"I know I'm young to develop it, but juvenile Huntington's is a thing. And…" The words finally spill from me like marbles rolling out of a bag. "I know you're going to laugh at this, but… I'm afraid that once I start having sex, it'll open the door to me sleeping around, and somehow that's going to trigger the onset of the disease. I know that's really stupid. Nothing is going to trigger it. I've either got it or I haven't, and if I have, the symptoms will start when they're going to start, and I can't activate it or provoke it. But… I'm still worried about it."

He doesn't laugh. He just looks full of sympathy and sorrow. "I'm so sorry, I didn't realize."

I take a deep breath and let it out slowly. "It's not the only reason. I didn't go to uni, so I haven't had the college experience. I grew up in the place I was born. And I looked after Mum for the last two years of her life."

Even though Dad would have got someone else in to look after the farm, Mum didn't want him to care for her in that way. I understood, and I was happy to do it. But it did mean I didn't get out much.

"And then helping to set up HWH took so much time… And I've not met anyone who's felt that way about me, so I haven't had to question my decision. It's just not happened for me. Yet."

"It will," he says. "One day."

"I don't know," I mumble. I'm so tired, I swear I could fall asleep right here. "Not looking like this."

"Yes, even looking like that."

"Any guy worth his salt would run a mile if he saw my hair."

"Your hair is just fine." He reaches out a hand and picks up a strand. "Did you know that you smell of strawberries?"

"It's my shampoo." I watch him run the strand through his fingers. He's so gentle and kind.

Then his eyes meet mine.

A strange tingle begins at the nape of my neck. I've never thought of him as a possible partner before. He was with Tia for a while, and before that he was just like a big brother. But now he's single. I trust him more than almost anyone else in the world. And he's gorgeous.

He's also private and closed in many ways, and he doesn't want a family. He's not a possible mate. And he doesn't think of me in that way. Or does he? When I asked him, he said, *I don't want to spoil our friendship… It's very precious to me.* Did that mean that he *does* think of me like that but he's just wary of acting on it?

We're not brother and sister. His words.

I remember what Naomi said about him undoing my necklace when it caught on my top, *I thought his eyes were going to fall out.* And Frankie's comment, *You'd better watch out, Em, or it'll be you who gets the Twice Knightley treatment.*

Ooh.

Imagine having a guy like this in your bed. A man who wants you so much, he can't keep his hands off you.

He continues to play with my hair, and a deep longing fills me.

My gaze slides to his mouth. "Will you kiss me?"

I wait for him to look shocked. To exclaim, "Em!" To scold me the way he usually does.

Instead, though, he merely says, mildly, "If you want."

I know he's only doing it out of sympathy. He feels sorry for me. But my heart bangs on my ribs and my pulse races. I don't move, though. I just give a small nod.

He lifts a hand to cup my face, then brushes my cheek with his thumb. His skin is warm, and the touch sends a tingle all the way through me from the roots of my hair to the tips of my toes.

He looks into my eyes. I never realized before, but deep within his blue irises are flecks of gold.

I wait for him to say he's had second thoughts, he can't, it would be wrong, he shouldn't have agreed.

But he doesn't. He leans forward and presses his lips to mine.

I close my eyes.

His mouth is firm and warm. His bristles brush against my cheek.

We've never crossed this line before. Never done anything as intimate as this. Something shifts inside me. The switch that was flicked briefly in the office when he nearly kissed me stays this time in the 'on' position, and heat rushes through me.

Still, I don't move. He lifts his head half an inch, and his breath whispers over my lips. Maybe to see if I pull back or exclaim in shock. I don't, though. My eyes open a fraction, but I just wait, holding my breath.

So he kisses me again. Short and light. A press of his lips to mine.

The third time, he holds it for longer.

No tongues. No fingers clutching in hair or heavy breathing. No fireworks or bells ringing or waves crashing on the shore. Just the soft rain pattering on the windscreen, the smell of his body spray winding around me like ribbons, and the sense of someone blowing across the embers of my feelings, spreading warmth through me, and making me glow.

He lifts his head, and I wait for him to apologize. To say he shouldn't have, he regrets it, and I should forget what he's done.

"G'night," he says.

"Night." I open the door, get out, shut the door, and run through the rain into the house.

Chapter Six

Knightley

The next day, I'm in the process of examining the damaged wing of a pāteke or brown teal—a species of dabbling duck—when my mobile rings in my back pocket.

Nodding at Cathy to take over for a moment, I extract my phone and look at the screen. It says Unknown Caller.

I'm tempted to end the call and continue with the bird, but something makes me say, "I'll just take this. I won't be long." Cathy nods, and I head out of the surgery.

I go into the office that the vets all share. We occasionally do paperwork here, but most of our time is spent in our surgeries, so there's nobody in here today. I walk over to the window that overlooks the bush and answer the phone. "Hello?"

A man replies. "Mr. Leander Knight?"

"Yes, speaking."

"This is Northland Region Corrections Facility."

Despite the stifling heat in the room, I go completely cold.

"We have an inmate," the man continues, "Mr. Steven Knight, who would like to speak to you. This is on his list of approved numbers. Can you please confirm whether you would like to accept the call?"

I lean forward and open the window to let in some fresh air. A tui is sitting on the fence, the white bobble on its throat bouncing up and down as it sings, *Bo-peep, bo-peep.*

I haven't spoken to my father since the day he pushed my mother down the stairs. On that day, the police came and took him, and the ambulance carried my mother away. I was thirteen. My mother's parents were both dead and she was an only child. My father is from the South Island, and his father was dead. His mother and his two brothers were alive, but I'd never met them, and none of them had any interest in looking after three boys. So the authorities took me, John, and Rob to Hartfield House.

Since then, Dad hasn't tried to contact me once. No phone calls, no emails, no letters. His lack of communication has scarred me deeply, and is the reason why I refuse to call or visit him. I've always thought it was his place to get in touch with his children, and I didn't see why I should be the one to initiate that contact.

Now, after seventeen years, it's finally happened, and I don't know what to say. I'm afraid, because inside me, my heart gives a little leap of hope.

"Sir?" the man asks.

"Yes," I say, my voice little more than a whisper. "I'll accept the call."

There's a click, a moment of silence, and then another voice says, "Hello?"

My heart is beating so loud, I'm amazed he can't hear it. "Hello," I reply.

"Lee?"

"Yes."

"Oh. Yes. Lee, it's your father speaking."

"I gathered that."

"Right. I'm glad you agreed to accept my call. I mean, I know you gave them your number, but I wasn't sure if you would."

I slide my left hand into the pocket of my shorts and lean against the wall. I've always let the prison know my mobile number. Mainly so that it wasn't my fault if my father didn't contact me. But after all these years, I never expected him to ring.

"What do you want?" I ask.

"Just to talk."

"What about?"

"I don't have long. Only five minutes. Lee… are you still in the North Island?"

"Yes," I say, oddly reluctant to reveal anything about my life to him.

"Would you come visit me?"

My jaw drops. "Seriously?"

"I want to talk to you, and I don't want to rush it."

My head is spinning. "What do you want to say that you can't say over the phone?"

"Lee, don't make this more difficult than it already is. I need to see you."

"What about John? And Rob?"

"No. Just you." He sounds impatient. "Well, will you come?"

I grip the phone with a shaking hand. What am I waiting for? A declaration of love? An explanation of why he's never contacted me? An apology? I know none of those is going to be forthcoming. Still, I'm shocked that he doesn't ask how I am, or how John and Rob are.

I'm not even sure he knows he has two granddaughters, because I know John doesn't write to him.

My stomach is a knot of frustration, resentment, and anger. "I don't know."

"It's important to me," he says.

My anger flares. "Why would I care what's important to you?" My voice holds all the hurt I've bottled up over the years.

"Lee…"

"No. I won't come. I don't want to see you. I don't want to hear anything you have to say."

He's silent for a moment. Then he says, "Think about it for a while. I have to send you an application form anyway so you can be an approved visitor. If you change your mind, fill in the form. When they've approved you, you can ring to book a visit."

I don't say anything.

"All right," he says. "I'd better go."

"After all these years," I whisper, "that's it?"

"I said I didn't have long." He sounds defensive, terse.

I give a short laugh. "Yeah. Fuck you." I hang up.

Then I throw the phone at the wall with all my strength.

To my surprise it doesn't break, and it's not enough to vent my anger, so I pick up the landline phone and throw that too, then follow it with the pile of books on the desk, the box of paperclips, the stapler, the hole punch. I push over the filing cabinet, and throw a heap of folders, hard enough to make all the contents come fluttering out so they float down to the floor. Finally I lift up the edge of the table and use all my strength to toss it onto its back, where it falls with a mighty crash.

When I'm done, I sink onto a chair and put my head in my hands.

It only takes ten seconds or so, and then I hear feet at the door. Someone pauses, then comes in. "Knightley?" It's Frankie. "Jesus. Are you okay?"

"Get out!"

She hesitates, then turns and walks out, closing the door behind her.

I sink my hands into my hair and close my eyes.

I'm completely rigid with unspent anger, my hands tightened into fists, my jaw knotted. My chest heaves with deep gasps that I can't control.

I daren't look around at the room. Within minutes, everyone in the building will know that Leander Knight lost his cool and ruined the office. How am I going to explain this away? I curse my temper, my lack of self-control, my fucking father, and his abominable action that ruined my life. I curse Angela Woodruff for dying and Hugh for being everything my own father wasn't. And I curse Emily Woodruff and her big green eyes, and the fact that she's never been with a guy, and the way she said, so shyly, *Will you kiss me?*

Fuck, fuck, fuck. What am I going to do?

I don't know how long passes—two minutes? Five? Ten? But after a while, the door opens and someone walks into the room.

Whoever it is stops, and I presume they're looking around in shock at the mess I've made. Then the footsteps sound again, as the person walks closer to me.

"Lee?" Em stops in front of me and drops to her haunches. "Hey. It's me."

I don't reply, unable to open my eyes and look at her.

"Come on," she says. "Let's get you out of here." Gently, she pulls on one arm until I release my hair, and then she takes my hand.

I don't move, though. "I can't." I'd have to walk past everyone. Jesus. I'm so ashamed of losing control like that.

"It's okay. Forget about everyone else. We'll go out the back way. Come on, sweetheart. It'll be okay. Just you and me, eh?" Talking softly, as if I'm four years old, she gradually bullies me to my feet.

I look around in horror. "I should clear this up."

"Not now. I'll help later. Come on."

Meekly, I follow her out of the room. I don't look down the corridor at the surgeries, knowing people will be watching. I let her take me the other way, past the storerooms and through the back doorway, then across the walkway to the car park.

She stops by her orange ute, opens the passenger door, and pushes me toward it. "In you get."

"Where are we going?" As I get in, I have a sudden visage of her taking me to a mental institution and leaving me behind, while they put me in a straitjacket in a padded cell.

But she says, "To the house for a cup of coffee, that's all. Dad's over at the orchards and Bella's having a dress fitting today, so there won't be anyone there." She closes the door and walks around to the driver's side.

Automatically, I buckle myself in. She gets in and does the same, reverses out, then heads up the hill.

Relieved that I haven't had to talk to anyone, I lean my head on the rest and close my eyes.

Em doesn't say anything. She drives to the house, parks out the front, then comes around to get me. Taking my hand again, she leads me inside and through to the large kitchen. She pulls out one of the chairs at the large pine table in the center and pushes me into it. Then she begins making us a cup of coffee, sliding a capsule into the machine, and pouring milk into a jug.

I lean my arms on the table and rest my head on them, watching her. I can remember doing this when I was seventeen. I came home after school one day, shattered after a game of rugby. Angela made me shower and change, and threw my mud-soaked kit into the washing machine. Then I sat in this exact spot, in this position, and watched as she and Em, who was eight, finished making a batch of chocolate muffins. Em had been beautiful even then, with hair the color of sun on copper, and a personality full of sunshine, always laughing and teasing. Always making me smile.

Now, she moves about collecting mugs and pouring the milk over the espresso, and I think about how much she's grown up, and what an amazing woman she's turned into. She works incredibly hard at HWH, and also at the Hospice. Angela would be so proud of her.

I've only seen Em a couple of times since we kissed yesterday, and not long enough to talk about it. I've thought about it non-stop, though. Scolded myself for not having more self-control.

Seems to be a theme at the moment.

She comes over with the two mugs, puts them down, then goes back and retrieves a packet of chocolate biscuits from the cupboard and brings that over too. She takes one out and holds it up.

"Eat this," she says. "And drink your coffee. Knowing you, you haven't had anything all morning."

It's true, I missed breakfast because I didn't have any milk left in my apartment, and I couldn't be bothered to stop on the way to work. I don't admit it, but I do eat the biscuit, and have a couple of big swallows of the coffee. It grounds me, and afterward I take a deep, shaky breath and let it out slowly.

Em is sitting on the other side of the table, her elbows propped on it, holding the mug with both hands as she sips her coffee. The bright morning sun slants through the windows into the kitchen, falling across the table and us in golden bars. Tiny crystals dangle from her ears, sparkling as they catch the light. Her mum gave her those for her eighteenth birthday.

Her green eyes watch me, gentle and serene. I think of how, when I kissed her, her eyelids fluttered shut as she gave a little sigh. Her pale lips were so soft.

I don't know why I did it. When she told me she was a virgin, and how she was worried about developing the disease, I felt a complex blur of emotions. Sympathy and pity, because no young woman should have that kind of weight on her shoulders at a time when she should be exploring all the delights of sex. Tenderness and compassion for the fact that she had to look after her mum. Affection—even love, because I do love her, as a good friend.

But I also felt a surge of something that surprised me. Possessiveness. I felt like Amundsen must have felt on his way across Antarctica, burning with jealous desire to make sure that his boots and no others marked the untouched snow of the South Pole. At that moment, I wanted to be the first to kiss her, before some other guy could march in and stake his claim.

The trouble is, I want to kiss her again. But I mustn't. If today has proven anything, it's that I've inherited my father's evil temper. If I ever hurt Em… I can't bear to think about it.

"Do you want to talk about it?" she asks quietly.

For a moment, I think she means the kiss, then I realize she's referring to my explosion in the office.

"No," I say.

She sips her coffee. "Okay."

I know she won't press me. I lean back in the chair, look up at the ceiling as I inhale, and let the breath escape in a whoosh. I do need to talk, and she knows it. Why don't I just get on with it?

"My father rang."

She doesn't reply, and eventually I lower my head to look at her. Her jaw has dropped, and her eyes have widened.

"Your father?"

I nod.

"You mean, from prison?"

I nod again. Dad was convicted for manslaughter, not murder, because although he pushed Mum down the stairs, he insisted he had no intention of killing her—he just wanted to stop her yelling at him. However, despite that, after she fell, he didn't immediately dial the emergency services or run outside screaming for help. Instead, he calmly got himself another beer and sat and watched the TV until I arrived home from rugby practice thirty minutes later. He claimed he didn't realize she was badly hurt and assumed she'd get up if he left her alone. Never mind that she was four months' pregnant, and the floor was covered in blood. The coroner stated that she hadn't died immediately, and if she'd been taken to hospital, doctors might well have been able to save her life, and maybe the baby too. The judge called him cold-hearted and cruel, and gave him a life sentence.

The minimum period of ten years was up seven years ago, but the nature of the way he acted after the crime has meant that he's been refused parole, and it wouldn't surprise me if he spends the rest of his life inside.

Em knows I haven't heard from him since it happened. She reaches out a hand to cover mine. "What did he want?"

"He asked if I'd go and visit him."

"What did you say?"

"I said no." I withdraw my hand as my fingers curl into a fist. She notices, but she doesn't comment on it.

"Did he say anything else?"

"No. He just said he needed to see me, and he doesn't want to rush it." Resentment flares inside me again. "If you're going to tell me I should go, you can save your breath. I don't want to see him."

"Hey, I'm on your side. If you don't want to go, you don't have to."

I swallow hard, then give a short nod. "I'm sorry. I didn't mean to snap. And I shouldn't have gotten annoyed."

"It's perfectly understandable. He's not contacted you for seventeen years. You don't talk about it, but I know that hurt you. He abandoned you, and John and Rob. He killed your mother. Jesus, who wouldn't be devastated by that? Of course you're hurt and angry."

I lean on the table, touched by the passion she's showing on my behalf. "It was a shock, that's all. Hearing his voice…"

"Did you recognize him?"

"Yes and no. His inflections were the same. His voice is deeper, though—rougher."

I sip my coffee, letting the peace of the morning soothe me. I wouldn't admit what's going through my head to anyone else, but I know Em will understand.

"When I first heard his voice, I was thrilled. I thought maybe he'd rung to apologize for what he did. For killing Mum, for abandoning us. To say he's missed us. But he didn't say any of that. And I was furious for being naive enough to hope he'd changed."

"How long did the call last?"

"Not long. He said he only had five minutes."

"It is possible, then, that he wanted to say more, but he needed to use those minutes to get you to agree to visit him."

I scratch at a mark on the mug. "I guess."

"It's also likely that someone was listening to the conversation."

I lick my thumb and try to rub the mark off. "I hadn't thought of that."

"I'm not trying to make excuses for him. The man has had seventeen years to contact you, and I think it's disgraceful that he never has. I don't blame you at all for refusing to see him. But if we take a step back and look at it without emotion, it is possible that he finally wants to put things right, and he didn't want to do it over the phone."

I lift my gaze to her. She looks at me earnestly, doing her best—as always—to try to help.

"You think I should go?"

She tips her head from side to side. "I'd be interested to know what he wants. I think the main thing you have to think about is what if it's *not* to put things right. What if it's to ask you to give him money, for example? You'd have to be prepared for that, if you did go."

"I wonder if he's in contact with anyone on the outside."

"Mm. The thing you've got to remember is that you'd be in control of the meeting. If he were to say anything you didn't like, you could just walk away. It wouldn't be like he could get up and follow you."

I study her face. She bears my scrutiny for a while, until eventually her lips curve up.

"What?" she murmurs.

"I was thinking about the kiss."

She presses her lips together as if remembering the moment. Then she sighs. "Are you about to apologize?"

"No, because I'm not sorry."

"But you're going to add a clause."

It's my turn to sigh. "You know we can never be a thing, Em."

"I know you're scared."

"I'm not scared."

"Yes you are. Frankie said that Tia called you Mr. Frosty. She said you froze her out of the relationship."

I don't reply, but I look away as shame fills me.

"You're terrified that you've inherited your father's temper, and of hurting someone you love. So you keep your feelings locked behind steel bars, and you tell yourself you don't need love, or children, or a happy future. That you don't deserve it."

I clench my jaw, watching my hand tighten into a fist on the table.

Em puts her hand over it, and forces me to unfurl my fingers. "But you're not a cold man. You have an incredibly warm heart. No guy who is as gentle with animals as you could be cold. You have a lot to give, as a husband and a father. Getting frustrated when something goes wrong doesn't mean you'd lose control the way your father did. For a start, he was drunk and high. You never take drugs, and you rarely have more than two drinks. You have incredible self-control. When your father rang, did you march out and hit someone? Scream at the lab assistants? Drive a car through the cages and kill all the animals in a rage? Of course you didn't. You threw a box of paper clips."

That makes me give a short laugh. "I did a bit more than that."

"Yeah, I know. But it's a rare person who can deal with a shock like that by saying, 'Oh dear,' and then sitting down for a cup of tea. Be kind to yourself. You've had a huge shock. You're allowed to react."

She brushes her thumb over my knuckles. "And to answer your question, I know you're convinced nothing can happen between us long term. And until recently, I hadn't expected it to. But something's changed. I'm interested in exploring it, and I think that, deep down, you are too. I'm not going to turn my back on it just because you're scared."

"It doesn't matter what you think," I say roughly. "If I say nothing's going to happen, then nothing's going to happen."

She gets up, walks around the table, leans one hand on the back of my chair, and bends until her lips are only six inches away from mine.

I know I should push my chair back and get up, but I discover that I can't move.

"We'll see," she murmurs. Then she closes the gap between us and presses her lips to mine.

She kisses me the same way I kissed her in the car. Once, twice, then a longer third time, holding it long enough that my heart bangs on my ribs and my emotions swirl together, like watercolor paint dropped into a glass of water and stirred with a spoon.

Then she picks up our coffee mugs, takes them over to the sink, and proceeds to wash them, as I sit there with an open mouth, my head in a spin.

Chapter Seven

Emily

"Em!" Bella lobs the word at me as if it's a hand grenade. "Will you please get in the car—we're going to be late!"

"You said we'd leave at 2:30, and it's only 2:25." I lock the door where I've placed the gardening tools and make my way over to her car.

She opens the back door. "I know, but our appointment is at three, and the roads are busy, and I don't need you pushing up my anxiety levels by two hundred notches."

"God forbid," I mumble, getting in the back of her Suzuki. Next to me, Naomi chuckles, while Frankie looks over her shoulder from the front and grins.

"I've only been with her for two seconds and I'm already stressed," I tell them.

"You push her buttons on purpose," Frankie says. "It's your own fault."

I stick my tongue out at her, and she laughs.

Bella slides in the driver's seat, then turns and beams at us all. "Ready for the big moment?"

I smile, because even though she can be annoying when she's like this, her enthusiasm is also infectious. She's so excited at the thought of getting married to her childhood sweetheart, and it warms my heart.

We're off today for the last fitting of the bridesmaid dresses before the big day in ten days' time. Frankie is Bella's oldest friend from high school, and her maid of honor. She's also having her two daughters as bridesmaids. Naomi is a recent addition to HWH, but she's fitted in so well with us all that Bella asked whether she'd like to come along for the afternoon, and Naomi was quick to agree.

"Are the girls meeting us there?" I ask as Bella drives carefully along the road leading out of HWH, and then up the hill.

"Yeah. They're with Rosie's mum," she replies, referring to her daughter Ginny's best friend. "She's bringing them to the bridal shop at three." She rolls her eyes in the rear-view mirror. "They are soooo excited. I know that on the day they're not going to want to take their dresses off. They'll be sleeping in them for a fortnight."

"Better that than refusing to wear them."

She laughs. "Yeah, I guess."

Frankie has been helping Bella to organize the wedding and doing her best to keep her sane. My job is much more fun. I'm in charge of Ginny and Lilibet, and on the day it'll be up to me to keep them safe, well-behaved, and entertained until they finally crash out. It's an impossible task, of course, because even though they're gorgeous little girls, they're going to be as hyper as if they've eaten two cartons of ice cream topped with strawberry sauce and sprinkles. But it's one I'm more than willing to take on, because I love my nieces more than life itself, and I enjoy playing the role of fun Auntie Em.

"How's the prep going for Saturday?" Naomi asks Frankie.

In New Zealand, we call a bachelorette party a hens' night or hens' party. We also often have bridal showers. Despite the fact that she's more comfortable being in the limelight than me, Bella's not the type of person who wants to paint the town red. She's a quiet, country girl at heart, the same as me. She loves her family and has a small group of close friends, and she decided she'd rather spend the money on the wedding, and combine the hens' party and bridal shower into a single party this Saturday.

"Good," Frankie says. "I've booked the stripper and ordered extra handcuffs."

Bella huffs, and Naomi and I giggle. "John might enjoy using those later," I say, earning myself a wry glance in her mirror. I'm teasing; John is the most sedate of the three Knight boys, more serious, and none of us was surprised when he ended up going into law. I can't imagine he's amazingly adventurous in bed. Unlike Knightley, who I'm sure has a few tricks up his sleeves.

Now where did that thought pop up from? I blink, looking out of the window. Yesterday I spent the afternoon scolding myself for kissing him. The poor guy was in enough turmoil after the phone call from his father. The last thing he needed—after insisting that nothing could happen between us—was for me to give him a smacker.

But he'd looked so sad, and I'd just wanted to distract him for a few minutes and brighten his day. I think it worked. Afterward, his face looked as if I'd stripped off and run around the room waving my bra in the air.

Ever since he kissed me in the car, I haven't been able to stop thinking of what it might lead to. The traits that have always been a part of him—his teasing sense of humor, his gentle hands, his tanned skin, and muscular body—have suddenly taken on a whole new meaning. I keep thinking about touching him, and having him touch me… Of having his mouth on mine…

But he's right. Nothing can happen between us. I have to respect that he doesn't want a relationship, and I also need to discover whether I have a future before I decide whether there's a hope of sharing it with someone.

I know he loves me as a friend. But I mustn't encourage that to develop into anything further. It wouldn't be fair on him, if I do turn out to have Huntington's. I know it's going to upset him anyway, the same as it will all my friends and family, but if we were an item? It would destroy him.

"Em?" I blink and turn to Naomi, who's watching me with a smile. "Are you okay?" she asks. "You were miles away."

"Yeah, sorry. Just daydreaming."

"I keep meaning to ask, any news on Finn?"

"Mm, yeah. He's going out with Janie."

All three of them look at me in surprise. "Janie?" Frankie asks. "Shit, really?"

"Yes. I caught them snogging by the storage sheds."

"Oh shit, I'm sorry."

I shrug. "Meh. It's okay."

"Aw, now you don't have a date for the wedding," Bella says.

"None of us does," Frankie replies. "She's in good company. You're the only one who's abandoned the Spinsterhood."

"I hate that word," Naomi grumbles.

"Me too," I say. "Anyway, I do have a date. I'm going with Knightley." The words come out of my mouth without my brain vetting them, and I blink in surprise.

Frankie and Naomi both go, "Ooh."

Bella just laughs. "Knightley?"

"Yeah."

"Like a twelve-year-old going with her uncle."

"He's only nine years older than me," I remind her tartly. "And we're not related, any more than you and John are."

She looks at me in the mirror for a moment. "That's true." She looks back at the road. "Did you know that Mum and Dad never adopted the Knight boys because they suspected this might happen?"

"What do you mean?"

"Dad told John when he did the whole asking for my hand thing. Mum and Dad talked about adopting the three of them after it became clear that they were going to stay with us. But they decided not to because if any of us developed feelings for one another, it would preclude us having a relationship."

If I'd stepped out of line, I'd have had, like, four different guys putting me over their knee.

Yeah, but only one would have enjoyed it.

Dad suspected Knightley and I were going to have feelings for one another? How did the old codger know before we did?

"Aw," Naomi says, "that's so romantic."

"It's not a big thing," I point out hastily, conscious I haven't confirmed it with Knightley yet, even if it was him who suggested it in the first place. "We're not dating or anything. I just meant that we said we'd go together so neither of us has to go alone."

"Yeah, yeah." Frankie chuckles. "We saw the way he looked at you in that bikini."

"His eyes are going to fall out and roll along the floor when he sees you in the bridesmaid's dress," Naomi comments.

"No, it's not… I mean he doesn't…"

"I didn't realize," Bella says. "Why didn't you tell me?"

"Because there's nothing to tell." But it's a lie, of course, because otherwise why would I feel a stab of guilt as I say the words? He kissed me. And then I kissed him. That's two kisses to account for. Brothers and sisters don't kiss. And even friends don't kiss—not like that, and dream about each other naked afterward.

Has he dreamed about me naked?

"You're blushing," Naomi says in delight.

"Jesus." I look out of the window.

Bella chuckles, then says, "Okay, I won't tease you. Anyway, we're here, so I want full concentration for the next hour or so!"

"Yes, Bella," we all say dutifully as she slides the car into a parking space down the road from the Bay of Islands Bridal Shop.

"Yeah, yeah, you can mock me all you like," she says good-naturedly, "but you'll all understand when you're in my position. An exceptional wedding takes great organization."

Rolling her eyes, Frankie opens the door to the bridal shop and lets us all precede her, and we go into the cool interior. The shop is split into two, both parts run by the same family. On the left is where they make and sell wedding paraphernalia. On the right, through an archway in the dividing wall, is a café filled with cakes and pastries, many of which have a bridal theme. Once a week on a Thursday night they have informal bridal shows, where the shop owners and their friends model the dresses while the guests sip wine and munch on treats as they watch the show.

Today, Wednesday, it's quiet in the café with just a couple of the tables occupied and a few young women browsing through the dresses in the shop.

"Bella!" Noelle Goldsmith, in her fifties with silver hair cut in a bob, smiles at us and comes over to greet us. "Hello, everyone, last fitting time, right?"

"Yep!" Bella beams at her. "Only just over a week to go now. The girls will be here soon. I was wondering… while the others try on their dresses, can we go over the arrangements for the day again? I just want to make sure I've got everything ironed out."

It's the hundredth time she's said this, but to her credit Noelle just nods and says, "Of course." I guess she's used to neurotic brides. "Go through," she says to Frankie and me. "Phoebe and Bianca have hung up your dresses in the changing rooms and they're ready to make any last-minute alterations."

Leaving Bella with Noelle, and Naomi to browse through the dresses and shelves of shoes and tiaras, Frankie and I walk through the shop to the changing rooms.

Noelle's twin daughters, Phoebe and Bianca, greet us as we approach and show us into the room with our dresses. Bianca goes with Frankie, and Phoebe comes into the room with me to help me put on the gown.

When Bella first asked the two of us to be bridesmaids, we both said we'd love to, but we begged her not to make us wear flouncy ball gowns, as neither of us are princess-y type of girls. Luckily, Bella was happy to let us look through the bridal shop's catalogs and choose something we felt more comfortable in.

Frankie and I tried a frosted velvet jumpsuit, but we both said it made us feel as if we were going to a nineteen-seventies disco. I quite liked an A-line one-shoulder dress, but Frankie said it made her look like Morticia from the Addams Family. She favored a gray satin gown with a kind of thick, twisted rope down the back but once I said it felt like a noose, it put her off it. Neither of us liked dresses with skirts above our knees, or anything with lots of ruffles, layers, or too much fancy embroidery.

It was Phoebe who came up with the idea of going very simple. She sketched out a gown that looked Grecian-goddess-meets-boho-chic, floor-length, the neckline gathered with a pretty cord that twisted across the back in a more elegant version of the rope that Frankie had liked, and with a simple twisted cord belt to show off our waists. She suggested a 'nude' color—a very light coppery pink—for mine to go with my hair, and an elegant beige for Frankie's. I should wear my hair down, she said, and we should both wear a boho-style headband studded with roses the same color as the dress. We both fell in love with the simplicity of the sketch. Bella was just thrilled we'd agreed on something and gave the go ahead.

"Have you made up your mind about underwear?" Phoebe says as I take off my shorts and tee.

I put them on the bench, suddenly wishing I'd taken a shower before I'd come here today. I haven't been working too hard, so I'm not sweaty or anything, but my skin is sun-kissed and my hair is a mess where it got snagged on the gorse I was clipping, and I feel like a milkmaid who's been dragged up to the manor house and told to serve high tea in the dining room.

"Not really," I say, which covers the fact that I'd completely forgotten she'd asked me to think about it. "Normal knickers, I guess. And I suppose I'll have to wear a strapless bra." I speak grudgingly as I hate them. "I know I'll spend all evening yanking it up, even with tit-tape."

Phoebe laughs. "So you obviously don't want an elaborate fitted bodice or anything?"

"God, no. I'd hate to be restricted like that. None of my bras is underwired."

"No pretty lacy teddies or bodies?"

I hesitate. "I don't mean to sound obstinate. It's just that they're not me, you know?"

"Of course. It's an important day for you, too. And it is possible to feel a million dollars while being comfortable in your own skin. Look, we're going for simplicity, right? We designed the dress to emphasize your natural slim figures. You're young and slender, so why not go braless? You're only a B cup so you're not going to be bouncing about all over the place, and if you feel comfortable, you'll be much happier.

Then you can either go commando, or just add a simple, pretty pair of knickers like these." She holds up an extremely beautiful nude lace pair.

"Okay," I say, "let's try it." I slip off my bra and she helps me on with the dress, carefully lowering it over my head so the twist in the cords at the back falls right in the center of my spine.

"You've lost a little weight," she says as she ties the cord at my back.

"I don't know how. I've been eating like a horse." It's partly true. I have breakfast and a huge meal in the evening with Dad, but quite often during the day I'm too busy for lunch.

"Well, try not to lose any more before the big day. You don't want the dress to hang on you. At the moment you fill it out just right. Can you take down your hair?"

"It's a right mess at the moment."

"Doesn't matter. I just want you to try the headdress."

It's the first time I've seen it. She's made medium-sized roses out of the same fabric as the dress and pinned them to a white headband. As I fan out my hair across my shoulders, she lowers the headdress into place.

"Oh," I say, surprised. "I look, um…"

"Beautiful?" She grins.

I stare at myself in the mirror. "Well, um, yeah. A bit."

"With your makeup done you'll look absolutely stunning."

I purse my lips, studying my reflection as she bends to tighten the waist a fraction. I hardly ever wear makeup, so I'm a bit worried I'm going to end up like a character from *The Rocky Horror Picture Show*. In a strange way, I don't want the guys I know—including Finn, who'll be there with the gorgeous Janie, Gabe, Rob, John, and Knightley—to laugh at me because I look so ridiculous, like a teenager trying on her mother's makeup.

But Bella has insisted that I wear some foundation and lip gloss, if nothing else, and as she's the bride, and my bossy older sister, I'm going to have to do what she says.

"There," Phoebe says, standing back. "All done. Want to step out and show the others?"

I nod, and she opens the door. I go out into the waiting area and meet Frankie coming out of the other cubicle, and we both exclaim at the sight of the other. She looks amazing in her beige gown, and the headdress sits just right on her short dark hair.

"Em," she says in wonder, "that looks so good on you."

"And you. Let's show Bella."

So we go out into the shop and let Bella, Naomi, and Noelle exclaim over us before finally returning to change back into our normal clothes.

By the time I come out, the two girls have arrived, and they run up to me crying, "Auntie Em!" Lilibet jumps right up into my arms, and I fall onto my butt holding her, while Ginny throws her arms around me, and they both cover me with kisses on the floor.

"Very elegant," Bella says. "Come on, you two ragamuffins. You've got to try on your dresses."

"Yay!" They both scramble up and dash into the changing area. I grin at Bella, who's looking a bit harassed at the thought of controlling their excitement while she finishes going through the details with Noelle. "Frankie and I will sort them out," I tell her, and we go back to the changing rooms, where the girls are being ushered in to change.

Six-year-old Ginny is like Bella—confident, bossy, happy to perform in front of people, with a love of glitter and sequins and mermaids and unicorns, and I love her to bits. Four-year-old Lilibet is like me, however. She's quiet and shy, and spends hours playing with the set of farm animals I bought her, as well as coloring pictures of wild animals like giraffes and zebras. She loves Knightley and begs him to tell her stories of when he was in Africa, looking after the monkeys. In fact he calls her his little monkey, which she loves.

As I help her into her flouncy, ballerina-style dress that she adores, I can't help but wonder if I'll ever have a little girl like this. For the first time, I think about discovering I'm pregnant, and the baby growing inside me. Giving birth, and holding it in my arms. I imagine looking up at my husband, standing by my side… And there the vision dissipates. Knightley broke up with Tia because he doesn't want children. He's adamant about it, and even if I could persuade him to have a relationship, I don't think I'd ever convince him to have kids.

"Auntie Em?" Lilibet turns and holds her arms up for a hug. "Don't be sad!"

I give her a squeeze, then spin her around. "Aw, I'm fine, sweetheart. Look at you! You look like a princess in that dress."

She dances in front of the mirror, copying a move I've seen Bella make when she's working out, so I know that Lilibet has watched her and probably joined in. And I feel a pang inside so strong it almost takes my breath away.

I want my future to be like this so much. Weddings and children and love. I don't think Knightley is going to be my Mr. Right, but there are plenty more fish in the sea, aren't there?

So why do I feel so glum?

Chapter Eight

Knightley

"Are you nearly ready?"

I look up from where I'm finishing off stitching up a wound on a kōkako—a large gray forest bird—and nod at my brother. "Two minutes. Take a seat."

Leaning heavily on his cane, Rob limps across the room and lowers himself into the chair in the corner.

I watch him before I return my gaze to the kōkako and finish stitching it up. "Leg troubling you today?"

"Nope."

My lips curve up as I give him a wry smile. "Right."

Since he made the decision that he didn't want any more treatment, he hardly ever talks about his leg or the pain he's obviously in. I wish there was something I could do to help, but as a vet I know that, even with all our modern technology and advanced medical knowledge, sometimes an injury just can't be fixed.

Cathy, my assistant, ties up the rubbish bag and leaves the room to dispose of it. Now we're alone, I decide to broach the subject I've been meaning to mention for a couple of days.

"I've got something to tell you."

Rob stretches out his legs and leans back with a soft sigh. "Oh yeah?"

"I had a call on Tuesday from the Northland Region Corrections Facility."

He stares at me. "From Dad?"

"Yeah."

"Jesus."

"Yeah. That was my reaction, too."

"What the fuck did he want?" His voice is hard.

I cut the suture, run my fingers over the bird, then straighten. "He asked me to visit him in prison."

"What did you say?"

"I said no." I lift the bird and place it carefully on the base of its cage. Cathy will take it out to the Wing where it will spend a few days recovering before we release it. I close the door of the cage, then turn and lean against the table. "I've been having second thoughts, though."

We study each other for a moment. Rob turns his cane in his fingers, clearly mulling over the news. "Did he say what he wants to talk to you about?"

"No. That annoyed me at the time. But he didn't have long, only five minutes, and it's also possible someone was listening in." I stop, not wanting to sound as if I'm defending his actions.

"Does he want me and John to come as well?"

"I did ask," I murmur, "but he said no, just me."

Rob's face doesn't reflect his hurt, but I know he must be feeling it. "Right."

"What do you think? If you don't think I should go, I won't. We don't owe him anything."

He blows out a breath and distractedly rubs the area where the old injury is above his knee. "What do you think he wants?"

"No idea. He didn't sound particularly remorseful. Em said maybe he wants money or something."

"You told Em?"

I run a hand through my hair. "After the call, I kinda lost my temper and smashed up the office. I thought you might have heard about it."

"I think Naomi mentioned it. I just assumed you lost your rag over the rugby or something."

I snort at that. "Em came and rescued me. Took me up to the house."

He gives me an appraising look. "Are you and she…"

"No."

"Naomi said Em blushed when they were talking about you yesterday."

Despite myself, my lips curve up at that, and he grins, too.

"Don't know what that was about," I say.

"Apparently Em said you were going to the wedding together."

Oh, did she now? She hasn't mentioned it to me yet. I decide not to blow her cover, though, and say, "Yeah, well, she was upset the other day because she saw Finn and Janie together—she'd been hoping he'd ask her out."

"He's been leading her on, I think."

"Yeah. She was a bit sad. And I said because neither of us had a date, we should go together. Not *together* together, but… you know, for company." It sounds lame even as the words leave my mouth.

"If you like her," he says, "you should do it properly. Ask her out. Go on a date."

I fold my arms and study my feet.

"Do you like her?" he asks. "In that way?"

I clear my throat. "It's not as easy as that."

"Is this about you or her?"

"Both. It's Em, Rob. She's like a sister to both of us."

"But she's not."

"No, she's not. But the last thing I'd ever want to do is hurt her. We could never have anything… casual. I can't just take the girl to bed because I fancy her and then not call her in the morning."

"No, I know what you mean."

Guys don't tend to talk about their feelings to one another. I certainly don't, anyway. And if I ever was to, it would probably be to Gabe, who's closer to me in age. But I can't talk to Em's brother about this. And despite the fact that Rob is four years younger than me, his injury has given him wisdom beyond his years, and he cares deeply for the Woodruff family.

"The thing is," I admit slowly, "she told me the other day that she's a virgin."

"Oh…" he says. "At twenty-one? Wow. Still, I guess she leads a pretty reclusive life."

"Yeah. But it's also to do with the Huntington's. She told me that seventy-five percent of all women with it develop abnormal sexual behaviors."

His brow furrows. "Fuck."

"I never knew, but I think Angela must have suffered in some way. Em didn't want to talk about it. But she's worried she's got it. And she thinks it'd be unfair to have a relationship before she knows. She's getting tested."

"Seriously?"

"Yeah. She has to have counseling first and she wants me to go with her."

"And if she finds out she has it?"

"I don't think she'll let herself have a relationship."

He sighs. "It's a difficult one."

"Even if we were attracted to each other, everything seems against us. It makes sense to wait until she gets the test results. And even if it's negative, the responsibility of…" I hesitate, not knowing how to put it.

"Being her first? Yeah. I know what you mean."

"I'm nearly ten years older than her."

"You're not old enough to be her father."

"Yeah… But she's just a kid."

He laughs. "You keep telling yourself that."

"What do you mean?"

"I saw you looking at her in the bikini. Your tongue practically rolled out of your mouth onto the floor."

I can't deny it because it's true. "But it's Em." I can't think how to explain it better. "I feel like I need to be the responsible one. The grown up."

"Well, you're both fucked if that's the case."

I glare at him, and he grins.

"Look," he says, "as long as you both go in with your eyes open, it'll be okay. The benefit of knowing each other for so long is that neither of you will be able to hide what you're feeling. You're already aware of each other's strengths and weaknesses. Keep those lines of communication open and you won't go far wrong."

I nod and smile at him. "When did you get to be so wise?"

"It's the cane. I'm also going to dye my hair silver and put my false teeth in a glass at night."

I give a short laugh. "So, about Dad. What do you think he wants?"

"I very much doubt it's to beg our forgiveness. I think Em's probably right, and he wants money or supplies."

"I'm not smuggling in heroin or a file in a cake, if that's what he's hoping."

It's Rob's turn to laugh. "What do you want to do?" he asks.

"Em said it's possible he wants to put things right, but to go prepared that it's not the reason. And to remember that I'd be in control of the meeting and could walk away at any time."

"Wise words."

"I guess I feel I need to give him the opportunity to explain himself, or to apologize. I'm kinda curious to know what he wants, to be honest. To know why he's not contacted us all these years." I look out of the window, at the way the leaves of the silver fern that's growing right outside are unfurling against the glass. "I want to look him in the eyes and see what kind of man he is. I need to know—was it an accident? Does he feel guilty? Or is he just a cold-hearted killer?"

I look back at my brother, whose expression is, as always, inscrutable. "So… do you think I should go?" I ask him.

"I think you should do whatever you want. I won't blame you if you do go. Equally I'll understand if you decide he's not worth the hassle. Just remember, he's a fucking arsehole, and he doesn't deserve a second of your time. If you choose to visit him, Em's right—you'd be in charge. If he puts one foot out of place, says one thing you don't like, tell him to fuck off, leave, and don't look back."

I can count the amount of times Rob, John and I have talked about our father on the fingers of one hand. John has always been the most forgiving, taking the view that the manslaughter charge means it was a terrible accident. He's forgiven him, I think, or at least he's tried to so he can move on with his life. But then he's more placid in general. I think he's more like our mother—what I can remember of her. Rob and I are more like our father. And I know that worries us both.

"Do you ever think about her?" I ask, knowing he'll understand that I'm referring to our mother.

He studies the top of his cane. "No." Which means yes.

I don't know how much he remembers about her. He was only nine when she died. Her name was June. She had light-brown hair she used to wear pulled back into a ponytail, and the same brown eyes as John. She worked at a local supermarket on the checkout. I don't remember her having any friends—I don't think Dad liked her going out. I don't recall her having any hobbies either; she wasn't into sports, or painting, or sewing. She did love movies, which is where Rob got his love of them from. And I remember her singing, mainly seventies disco music. I can't listen to ABBA now without thinking of her.

My memories of her are mixed. It's funny how it's often it's the bad things that loom largest in your mind. I can remember her and my father arguing, him yelling, her screaming, both of them throwing things. She used to sit in the kitchen a lot, her face in her hands, crying. I hugged her a few times, filled with teenage fury that Dad made her cry so much.

Once, close to the end, I stepped in and tried to defend her, only to receive a backhander from him myself. If things had been different and our family life hadn't come to an end, I don't know what I might have done as I'd gotten older. I would have struck back one day when I was big enough, I know that. Sometimes I fantasize about it, imagining how I might have saved my mother, if I'd been big enough and brave enough.

As an adult, I've come to understand that relationships are complicated. I know she provoked him and nagged him and accused him, until he got so frustrated that he lashed out. She wasn't completely innocent. But I've grown up watching Hugh, who taught me that when a man is frustrated with his partner, it's best to walk away and come back when he's cooled down. And that it's always best to solve problems by talking, not with violence. He managed to walk the fine line between respecting his wife and treating her as an equal, and yet also privately believing it's the guy's responsibility to protect and look after his partner.

Rob checks his phone. "We'd better go. I promised John I'd be there by six."

"Yeah. Come on, then."

I wash my hands and collect my keys, ask Cathy to take the kōkako to the Wing, and then Rob and I head out to the car park. He picked me up this morning in his BMW Z3 as we'd planned to go up to Hartfield, so I climb in the passenger side, and he goes around and gets in the driver's.

It's an automatic, and so he has no trouble driving with his uninjured right leg. He backs the car out, then heads up the hill toward the house.

"How's the prep for the stag night coming along?" I tease. Rob is John's best man.

He chuckles. We've known friends who've organized flying or driving experiences on their stag nights, or helicopter flights, or jet-boat rides. John is the least adventurous of the three of us, however, and that would be the last thing he'd want. He'd also freak out if he went within a hundred yards of a strip club.

"It's all organized," Rob says.

John's main passion in life—apart from Bella and his girls—is cooking and food. He's watched every episode of shows like *Chef's Table, The Great British Baking Show, Hell's Kitchen*, and all Anthony Bourdain's shows, and he spends most of his free time in the kitchen trying out different recipes.

Rob's organized for us and some of his closest friends to take a trip to *Aqua Blue*, a five-star restaurant in Doubtless Bay. He's rented a separate room in the restaurant, and the acclaimed Kiwi chef, Fox Wilde, is going to spend an evening teaching us all some dishes while we eat and drink as much as we like.

John has no idea. He's incredibly nervous that we're going to get him drunk, handcuff him naked to a lamppost in the center of town, and leave him there. We tease him that we have terrible things planned, but the truth is that he's going to love what Rob's done.

He slows the car as we approach the house and parks it out the front. There are a few cars out here: including Hugh's Range Rover, Bella's Suzuki, John's Toyota, and Em's ute. A host of butterflies immediately spring to life in my belly.

How ridiculous. I've known Em for seventeen years. She's seen me at my lowest point. She knows all my weaknesses. How can I possibly feel nervous at the thought of seeing her?

We go into the house and through the large hallway, emerging into the light, airy, open plan living, dining, and kitchen area. The east wing contains numerous bedrooms and other living areas where we used to play as kids, but this is the main hub of the house, and it holds many pleasant memories for me.

"Hey." John comes over as he sees us, and the three of us exchange bear hugs.

"How are you doing?" I ask him. "How high are your stress levels?"

"Two hundred percent," he replies cheerfully. "It's manic and vastly over-organized, but Bella's loving every minute."

In the garden, we can see Bella, Em, and Lulu, the wedding organizer, showing Ginny and Lilibet where they're going to have to walk on the big day. My gaze lingers on Em for a moment. I watch her as she spins Lilibet around, laughing. As usual, Em's wearing her incredibly short shorts, these ones a custard-yellow, with a light-blue top. She looks fresh and young, like a daisy.

"Knightley's got something to tell you," Rob says to John. I turn and join him at the fridge, where we help ourselves to a cold drink.

"Yeah." I lean against the worktop, open the bottle of water, and have a few mouthfuls. "I had a phone call a couple of days ago. From Dad."

John's eyes widen. "Shit."

"He wants me to visit him at the prison."

"What did you say?"

"Initially? No. But I'm having second thoughts. I didn't want to do anything without speaking to you two, though."

"Did he say what he wanted?"

"No. There was no time for any in-depth conversation."

"Does he want to see us, too?"

"No," I say softly. Just as with Rob, I see hurt flicker in his eyes for a moment.

He looks at Rob. "What do you think?"

He shrugs. "I said it's up to him. Em said to be prepared that he's not going to ask for forgiveness or apologize, and I think she's right."

"You told Em?" Amusement glimmers in John's eyes as he exchanges a glance with Rob. I note that neither of them were annoyed that I told Em before I told them. They think of her as a beloved sister, the same as me.

Well, maybe not quite the same as me.

"Long story," I say. "She said maybe he wants money or something. I don't know. I'm curious. I thought I'd go and give him the opportunity to talk. If he chooses not to, it won't be my fault."

John nods. "Makes sense. I think you should go. Like you said, I'm curious. After all this time." He looks out of the window, toward his bride-to-be. "Let's not tell Bella. I don't want anything spoiling the next week for her."

"Okay," Rob and I agree.

John's gaze lingers on her, but I know he's thinking about our father. Part of me wonders whether I should have told him—it's his wedding soon, too, after all, and I don't want to spoil his big day. But it didn't seem fair to visit Dad without discussing it with him first. Like Em's decision to have the test, what happens will affect all of us. I think he might have gone to visit Dad if Rob and I had been more amenable to the idea. Because we've been so opposed to it, he's held back, but I can see he's happier to agree to it.

His gaze comes back to me, holding a hint of mischievousness. "Bella said that in the car on the way to the bridal shop, Em said you and she were going to the wedding together."

I make a mental note to have a word with the minx. "Yeah. Just for company, you know. She was upset because Finn didn't ask her out."

His look turns impatient. "She's better off without him."

"Exactly what I said."

"You know you were fated to end up together. Jane Austen foretold it."

That makes me laugh. "I think we need a better reason than that."

"Mr. Knightley was sixteen years Emma's senior," Rob points out. "So you can't use the excuse that you're too old for her."

"We're just friends," I scold, trying not to think about the kiss. Kisses. Plural.

"Well, if you end up with Em, it means Rob's got to get together with Gabe," John says, making us all laugh.

"I love him dearly," Rob says, "but not in that way."

"What are you three all chortling at?" It's Bella, coming through the sliding doors and entering the living room, Em behind her with the two girls. Lulu has vanished, presumably off to her car to make her way home.

"We're talking about Rob and Gabe being an item," John says, and Rob snorts.

"Can't see that happening," Bella replies. "Rob's a ten and Gabe's a five. It'll never work out."

"What's going on?" Gabe asks, coming into the room through the front entrance as we all burst out laughing.

"You really don't want to know," I assure him. He raises an eyebrow, and I grin. I'll tell him about Dad's call later, sometime. I know he'll give his support, no matter what I decide to do.

I look around fondly at this group of men and women I've grown so close to over the years. These are my real family—not the man in prison who killed my mother, then abandoned me. Who has ignored me for the last seventeen years, and then contacted me and expected me to go see him as if nothing has happened. Do I really want to stir up old feelings, and run the risk that he almost certainly isn't contacting me to apologize, which is going to hurt me even more?

My gaze slides to Em, and I'm not surprised to see her watching me. She smiles, but I can see the concern in her eyes. She's always been able to read me, just as I can read her. Is John right—were the two of us always meant to be?

Chapter Nine

Emily

"Come with me," Bella says to John. "I want to show you where we're going to put the altar."

He rolls his eyes, but he takes her hand in his and walks off quite happily, so I know he doesn't mind. I watch them go, a little envious of their obvious happiness, but pleased for them both.

Ginny and Lilibet run up to me, Lilibet throwing her arms around my thighs. "Can we have a drink?" Ginny asks.

"Sure." I open the fridge. "Want some orange in your water?"

"Please!"

I take out one that I picked from the garden earlier, cut it into slices, pop a couple into two cups, and pour cold water over them. "Here." I hand them to the girls, while the guys each take a slice of the orange to finish it off.

"Coming over for the rugby match tomorrow?" Gabe asks Knightley. "It starts at six, so I thought we could all sneak off work early and get takeout or something."

"Actually…" I clear my throat and look at Knightley. "I was wondering whether you were available around three."

My first counseling session is scheduled for tomorrow at four-thirty in Whangarei. I haven't had a chance to tell Knightley about it yet. I should have texted him, but I thought I'd be able to catch him alone.

"A secret assignation?" Gabe grins. "Tell me more."

I hesitate. I'd decided not to tell Gabe or Bella that I'd made the decision to get tested, mainly because I didn't want to upset Bella before her wedding, and it didn't seem fair to tell Gabe and not her. Now, though, with Knightley and Rob there for support, I think that maybe I should let my brother know.

"I'm going for counseling," I say. "Before getting tested. And Knightley offered to go with me."

"What does tested mean?" Ginny asks.

"Nothing." I direct the girls down the steps and over to the TV. "Shall I put *Frozen* on?"

I turn the TV on and choose the movie, sit the girls down with their drinks, then finally return to the kitchen. The guys are all quiet. Gabe stares at me. He leans on the worktop and crosses his arms—a defensive gesture, if I've ever seen one. Rob exchanges a glance with Knightley, who then studies the floorboards. Even though we're not related by blood, Dad has never avoided talking about Mum's disease in front of them, and they know how we all feel about it.

"Why?" Gabe asks.

"Because I need to know."

"And if it's positive? How will you feel then?"

"That's why I'm going to counseling. To talk it over." My throat tightens with emotion, but I hold it in, not wanting to cry in front of all the guys.

"I thought we all agreed not to be tested," Gabe says.

"I changed my mind. Woman's prerogative."

"Em—"

"I need to know." I send him a pleading glance, willing him to understand. "Not getting tested—it's just burying my head in the sand. I need to find out before I make decisions that are going to affect my life, like whether to have a relationship, and children." I don't look at Knightley, although I feel my face flush.

Gabe's expression holds a touch of pity. "You can't let the disease affect how you live your life."

"Yeah," I snap, "because you don't let it affect you at all. Taking risks like there's no tomorrow. Sleeping with everything that moves."

"Em…" Rob says cautiously.

Gabe's brow darkens. "And what if you don't have it, and I do? Or Bella does? How is that going to make you feel? They told us about survivor's guilt. Isn't that going to be just as painful as not knowing?"

My eyes fill with tears, and immediately his expression softens and he unfolds his arms. "Aw. Come here."

I walk into them, and he gives me a hug as I fight not to let the tears fall. "You're going with her?" he asks Knightley over my shoulder. Knightley obviously nods, because Gabe says, "Good, I'm glad." He kisses the top of my head. "It's your decision," he says, rubbing my back. "I just think that in a way, there's no happy ending. Not having it will obviously be amazing for you. But the best outcome would be if we all got tested and none of us had it… and we know the odds of that happening."

I close my eyes. I don't want to think about what happened to Mum also happening to Gabe or Bella.

"Don't tell Bella," Rob says as if reading my thoughts. "Or John. Not until after the wedding, anyway."

"I won't."

Gabe releases me. "Does Dad know?"

"No. I don't want to stir it all up again for him."

He's been through so much. The last year with Mum was very hard on all of us, but especially him. When she died, I know it must have been a relief for him, in some ways. He didn't have to watch her suffer anymore, and he didn't have to deal with the exhausting process of coping with her deteriorating mental and physical self. But he misses her terribly, and he's sad enough, without having to think about the fact that his children might have inherited the disease.

I take a piece of kitchen roll, blow my nose, and then toss the tissue away. "I'm going for a walk around the garden."

"I'll come with you," Knightley says, surprising me.

I nod, then call to the girls on the sofa. "We're going outside."

"Okay," they both say, not stirring. They've spent the last half an hour dancing on the lawn, so it doesn't surprise me they've both conked out.

Leaving Rob and Gabe, who are no doubt going to discuss my decision, Knightley and I walk out to the deck and step down onto the lawn. John and Bella are across the other side, having a sneaky kiss and cuddle on the spot where the altar is going to be, overlooking the sea. I glance at Knightley, who smiles, and then the two of us walk along the stepping stones that lead in the opposite direction, toward the orchards.

"You okay?" he asks after a while.

"Yeah. I don't know why I said anything. I wasn't going to tell Gabe, but it sort of popped out."

"You knew what his reaction would be."

"Yeah. No surprises there."

He sighs. "He does have a point. About survivor's guilt."

"I know. I'm fully expecting the counselor to hit me with that. By the way, I should have texted you earlier about the session tomorrow. If you'd rather stay here for the rugby, I understand."

"Of course not. So it's at, what, four-thirty, in Whangarei?"

"Yes."

"At the hospital?"

"Yeah."

"So we'll leave just before three. That'll be okay. Frankie and Lorelei can cover for me if anything comes up."

"Thank you."

I look up at the cornflower-blue sky. It's a blustery summer day, and the breeze brushes the warm sun across my skin. My mother designed this area of the garden, and the air is filled with the scents she loved—including exotic frangipani and the star jasmine that curls around the shed. As we near the orchard, it mixes with the scent of oranges, which always reminds me of Mum, who loved summer so much.

"I've got a bone to pick with you," Knightley says in a teasing voice.

"Oh?"

"Apparently we're going to the wedding together?"

I pull an eek face. "I might have told the girls that yesterday. Sorry. I should have spoken to you about it."

"I'm not offended, Em. I asked you first, remember? I thought it was funny."

I smile. "So it's okay then?"

"It's a date. Kind of." His lips twist, and I laugh.

We turn and follow the line of the orchard. This was one of Mum's favorite walks. Toward the end, I used to push her in the wheelchair so she could smell the oranges.

I glance over my shoulder. Bella and John are heading back to the house. I can't see anyone else. Seagulls cry overhead as they dip and soar in the warm currents, and the sound of the ocean is a subtle orchestra playing in the distance.

"I've been thinking," I say. "Guess what about?"

"The kiss," he guesses.

"Kisses. Plural. Yes."

He sighs. "They were very nice. But I stand by what I said. It can't lead to anything between us."

"No, of course not. I completely agree."

He chuckles. "But…"

"But I've been thinking about that phrase… you know… friends with benefits…"

He throws me a scolding glance. "Em…"

"No, not like that, but the thing is, I know that if I find out I have HD, that'll be the end of the kissing."

"Em…"

"It will, because I won't let myself get involved with anyone if I have it. I don't care what the counselor says about living your life to the full, blah blah. I just won't. But I really enjoyed kissing you. And so I thought that, until I find out, maybe we should be friends with kissing benefits." I take his hand and pull him into the line of orange trees, then turn him to face me. "What do you think?"

His eyes are full of affection. "It's a nice idea."

I hesitate, looking up at him. "Can I ask you something?"

His eyebrows rise. "Sure."

"Is it definitely over with Tia?"

He continues to look surprised, but says, "Yes, unequivocally."

"And there's nobody else?"

His expression softens. "No, Em. No one except you."

His words fill me with warmth.

"Why do you ask?" he says.

"I just wanted to check."

"You think I'd kiss you if I was interested in someone else?" His look is a tad reproving.

I press my lips together. "No, probably not."

"No, definitely not."

"I stand corrected. Don't tell me off."

That makes him laugh. "I'm not telling you off."

"Yes you are. Actually, you can carry on if you want. I kinda like it."

His lips curve up. "Stop it."

I move closer to him and place both hands on his chest, and automatically his hands rise to rest on my hips. He's wearing a dark-green veterinary T-shirt Bella bought him last Christmas that says 'Live, Love, Heal' with a heart and a paw print, beige shorts, and his feet are bare. His hair is all mussed. I so adore this guy.

"You smell nice. He rests his lips on my hair. "Mint shampoo this time."

I sniff his T-shirt. "And you're all mown grass and sunshine."

"Why are you so irresistible?" he murmurs, sliding his arms further around me.

"Skill," I whisper.

He gives a short laugh, splaying a hand on the base of my spine. His thumb brushes up, just beneath my tee, and finds bare skin. We both inhale as if he's done something much more intimate than touch my back.

I lift my face, letting the sun that's slanting through the orange trees fall across my cheeks.

"You have so many freckles." He touches his lips to one cheek, then brushes them across my nose to the other.

I close my eyes and hold my breath, just enjoying being so close to him, being touched.

He lifts his head, but I don't open my eyes. He gives a little, resigned sigh. Then, finally, he lowers his lips to mine.

We kiss slowly, surrounded by the scent of the oranges and the call of the fantails jumping from branch to branch. Briefly, I wonder whether Mum is watching us and, if she is, whether she's smiling her approval. Then Knightley changes the angle of the kiss, and all other thoughts flee my mind.

I thought he'd do the same as before—give a few subtle, playful, innocent pecks, before announcing we should return to the house.

But he doesn't.

Instead, for the first time, he opens his mouth and brushes his tongue across my bottom lip.

I inhale, my own lips parting, and he lifts his head again. Don't stop, I think as I look at him, although I can't bring myself to say the words. But he obviously reads them in my eyes, because his lips curve up.

He takes my face in his warm hands, brushing my cheeks with his thumbs as he looks into my eyes. Can he hear my heart banging? I'm sure it's loud enough to frighten away the birds.

And then he lowers his mouth and gives me what I can only think of as a *real* kiss.

He sweeps his tongue into my mouth, and my face fills with heat as I blush furiously. He must be able to feel my cheeks warming in his hands, but he doesn't stop. I clutch at his T-shirt as the heat from my face flows through the rest of me, and I'm unable to stop a murmur of pleasure escaping my lips as he continues to kiss me, so thoroughly, so deeply, that I think my head is going to explode.

He slides one hand to the nape of my neck, and suddenly it feels as if he's holding me there, telling me he's refusing to let me go, and he's going to kiss me for as long as he wants, whether I like it or not. That touch of possessiveness, of him taking charge, fills me with delight and wonder. It feels like the first time that he's not kissed me out of pity—he's kissing me because he wants me. This was what I needed. To be desired. To have a man kiss me as if there's no tomorrow, as if he never wants to let me go.

Eventually he slides his arms around me, and I lift mine around his neck, and we kiss like that for a long, long time. I feel as if summer is an orange I've bitten into, and the scent and taste has flowed through me from my toes to the top of my head, filling me with sweetness.

When he finally lifts his head, I stare up at him dreamily, as if I'm half asleep. "Mmm," I murmur.

He cups my face again, brushing his thumbs over my warm cheeks. "You're all flushed. Is that the sun?"

"No. It's all you."

He smiles. "I suppose we should get back."

"Yeah."

We return to the pathway, and start heading toward the house.

We walk slowly, not saying anything, although I can feel him beside me with every cell in my body. I wish we could hold hands, but of course we can't, because even though most of them seem to have guessed something's going on, it's supposed to be secret. I don't even know what this is yet, and neither of us is ready to talk about it. But I'm struck with a fantasy that it's six months or a year in the future, when I've found out that I don't have HD, and Knightley and I are dating, and the two of us are going back to the house where we can hold hands in front of everyone before retiring to a room together for the night. What's the possibility of things panning out like that?

We cross the lawn, and we're still not saying anything. And suddenly I'm worried that he wishes he hadn't kissed me.

"Don't regret it," I whisper. "I couldn't bear it if you did."

"I don't," he says as we reach the house. "That's what's worrying me."

There's no more time to ask what he means, because the doors are open, and as we go inside, everyone is standing in the living room, and they all turn to face us. Ginny is sitting white-faced on the sofa, and she bursts into tears as we approach.

"What's the matter?" I ask, alarmed, as she runs up and throws her arms around me.

"I didn't mean to," she wails.

I look at Bella. "What's going on?"

"You're getting tested," she says. It's a statement, not a question.

My heart shudders to a stop. Fuck.

I look down at Ginny, then bend and take her in my arms. She must have asked Bella what I'd meant when I'd mentioned it. "It's okay." I rub her back, feeling her little body quivering. "It doesn't matter."

"Go and play in the garden, please," Bella says to her daughters.

Ginny buries her face in my T-shirt.

"Ginny," Bella scolds, and the little girl tears herself away and runs into the garden. Lilibet jumps off the sofa and runs after her.

I straighten and look Bella in the eye. "Yes, I'm getting tested. I wasn't going to tell you because I didn't want you to have to think about it before the wedding."

"Does Dad know?"

I shake my head.

She looks at Gabe. "Did she tell you?"

"No."

"I've only told Knightley," I reply. "I didn't want to tell either of you because I know how you feel about it. But I didn't want to go on my own. Don't be angry."

"It's your business," she says, "and of course I'm glad he's going with you. I'm not angry, Em. I'm worried about you. About how you'll feel if you find out you have it. It would have such an impact on your life." She hesitates. "You're like a baby sister to all of us. And I don't think any of us could bear to watch it tear you apart."

I bite my lip. I'd assumed she'd be angry, concerned only with how it affected her and her children. I never considered she might be worried about me.

"I'm different from both of you," I whisper. "I can't just pretend it's not there and get on with my life. I can't have a relationship with a guy—if we were to fall in love, and then later I developed symptoms and discovered I had it, how would he feel? I wouldn't blame him if he hated me for burying my head in the sand." I daren't look at Knightley.

Gabe studies the carpet. John and Rob exchange a worried glance. Bella frowns.

"It's different for you," I tell her. "You were so young when you met John, and you've never looked at anyone else. And he's always known. You made the decisions together. But I can't do that. I have to think about my partner's feelings. I have to think about the bigger picture."

John puts his arm around her and rests his lips on her hair. I look at Rob, who smiles somewhat sadly, and finally at Knightley. He winks at me, and the little, intimate movement sends a flurry of butterflies through me.

Something moves at the edge of my vision, and I glance over to see my father leaning against the door jamb, his hands in his pockets. He's obviously heard everything. His face is creased with pity.

"We'd better go," John says. "We're making pizza tonight. Girls!"

They come running in, quiet and pale, and he takes their hands and leads them out.

Bella comes up to me and gives me a hug.

"I'm sorry about the girls," I whisper. At some point she's going to have to explain it all to them. I don't envy her that conversation.

"Don't worry about it." She kisses my forehead. Then she turns and follows John, stopping to say goodbye to Dad on the way.

"Yeah, we'll head off, too," Rob says, and he, Gabe, and Knightley—who gives me a final glance—say goodbye and leave.

I go up to Dad, he puts his arms around me, and we have a big hug.

"You should have told me you wanted to be tested," he scolds.

"I didn't want to stir up bad memories."

"The memories are always there, love. And none of them are bad. They are what they are."

He's shorter than Knightley, stockier, and he smells different—he's been in the woodsheds, probably chopping up logs, as he always says it calms him down.

"I need to know, Dad," I say, my words muffled by his tee.

"I know." He rubs my back.

"I upset Bella, though."

"She'll be okay. She's stronger than you think."

"She's got to tell the girls one day."

"Yeah." He sighs.

"I don't know how she could choose to have children without knowing."

He kisses the top of my head. "You know that both girls were accidents?"

I move back then and look up at him in surprise. "What?"

"Bella came to see me when she found out she was pregnant with Ginny, just after she graduated. They'd used contraception, but she still fell. We talked for a long time about it. About whether she should get a prenatal diagnosis of the fetus."

"I never knew," I whisper.

"Bella was very upset. She and John decided that no matter the diagnosis, they wouldn't want to terminate the pregnancy, and so in the end made the decision not to get it tested."

I walk beside him as we go into the living room and sit. "And Lilibet?"

"Also an accident."

"Jesus! What method of contraception was she using?"

"Condoms both times."

"I thought they were ninety-eight percent effective."

"Apparently, because of human error, it's nearer eighty-five percent."

"I didn't know that."

He nods. "After Lilibet, John had a vasectomy to make sure it didn't happen again. Even though they're young, they're happy with their two girls and they don't want any more kids."

"I didn't realize that either."

"I don't think it's a big secret, and I'm sure she won't mind you knowing. I just think that when you were younger she wanted to protect you from it all as much as she could."

Which is dumb really, when it was me who looked after Mum most of the time, meaning that I was subjected to the disease on a daily basis. But I suppose being the older sister means it's natural that Bella would feel protective of me.

"So she never made the choice to get pregnant knowingly," I deduce.

"No."

"But she chose not to terminate either pregnancy."

"Yes."

I frown. "I don't know if I'd make the same decision."

"I don't think you can say that until you've been there."

I lean back in the chair and rest my hand on my belly, looking up at the ceiling. If I didn't get tested, and then I got pregnant… What would I do? I think about a little life growing inside me. Could I make the decision to terminate it, if it did have the disease?

"How's Knightley?" Dad says.

I lift my head and raise an eyebrow. He gives me an innocent look.

"Stop stirring," I tell him.

He grins. "I hear you're going to the wedding together."

"Yeah, but not, like, a date or anything. We'll just be walking next to each other. Kinda."

He smiles. "He's a good lad."

"He's all right. Did you hear that he had a phone call from his father?"

His smile fades. "What?"

"A couple of days ago. Steven wants him to visit the prison."

"Did he say why?"

"Apparently not, and he doesn't want to see John or Rob either."

"Is Knightley going to go?"

"He said no at first. I think Steven must have been quite terse. There was no apology or anything. Knightley was very angry. He lost his temper and smashed up the vet office."

Dad blows out a breath. "Poor guy."

"Yeah. But we talked about it, and he felt better after that, I think."

He smiles again. "You've always been able to calm him down."

"Have I? Maybe. Anyway, I don't know whether he should go or not, but I told him that if he does, he's in control, and he can always walk away. He's told Rob and John. They've pretty much said it's up to him. I think they're all curious about what Steven wants."

"Me too. Somehow, I don't think it's to say he's sorry."

"Yeah. Me either."

He puts his hands on his knees and pushes up. "Anyway, time for dinner. Something quick tonight, I think. Stir fry? How about beef teriyaki?"

"Sounds lovely."

He nods and goes off to the kitchen.

I stretch out my legs on the sofa and lie back. I'll lay the table in a while and help him serve up. But I'm just going to take five and think about the kiss, and Knightley's last comment when I said *Don't regret it.*

I don't. That's what's worrying me.

Chapter Ten

Knightley

At two-thirty the next day, I start packing up my surgery, ready for the weekend. I was busy this morning, taking a trip out on the boat to treat an injured seal, and when I got back, most of my time was taken up with treatment for a weka—a brown, flightless bird that had damaged one of its legs. But I've left it in Lorelei's good hands, and now I'm all ready to go with Em to Whangarei for her counseling session.

I head out ten minutes later and meet her coming across the car park. She's changed out of her usual working garb—shorts or sometimes her overalls—and now she's wearing jeans and a white shirt with the sleeves rolled up. She looks a little older, and less like the high school students who sometimes help out here.

"All ready?" I ask.

She nods. Despite the very warm weather, she's pale, her freckles standing out on her skin. We get in my car, and when she buckles in her seat belt, her hands are shaking.

"Hey," I say. "Are you okay? We don't have to go today."

"I want to. I'm just nervous about what she's going to say. I don't know why—I'm sure she's not going to tell me anything I don't know."

When she looked after her mother, she read everything she could find on the disease. But learning all the facts and figures and how the different genes are affected is very different from discussing how it will all affect your life in reality.

She gives me a smile. "Let's go."

"All right." I start the engine, reverse out, and take the road up the hill. "Did you hear about the seal I treated this morning?"

She shakes her head, so I spend a while telling her about how it had been found tangled in a fishing line, and how it had taken ages to remove it before I could treat the small wound the hook had given it. By the end, she's relaxed a little, and she chats away about her morning's work.

"I've reorganized the storage sheds," she announces. "They were in such a muddle. Nobody could find anything. I roped in a couple of the guys to help me move stuff around, and I've also done a fresh inventory, so it should make it a lot easier to find everything."

"Sounds great."

She sighs and looks out of the window. "It took my mind off things for a bit."

"The counseling?"

"That too. But also what happened yesterday."

"With Bella?"

"Yeah. I talked to Dad about it last night. He told me that both Bella's girls were accidents."

I nod slowly. "Yeah. John told me."

"I never knew. I've often wondered how she could make the decision to have children without knowing if she had HD. He also said they talked about having the fetus tested, but she and John decided against it, because they wouldn't have terminated the pregnancy even if the baby had it. Did you know that?"

"Yeah. John told us all—me, Rob, and Gabe—one evening, when we went out for a drink. I'm sorry. Are you upset that Bella didn't tell you?"

"Not really. Dad said she feels very protective toward me. It's just… could you do it? Have a kid if you knew there was something wrong with it?"

I slow the car as we approach a junction, and make the turn toward Whangarei. "I suppose it depends how you view the disease. Maybe Bella and John don't consider a baby with HD as having something 'wrong with it'. I mean, Ginny and Lilibet are beautiful little girls. It's possible that if Bella has it, either or both of them could also have it. But would it have been better for them not to have existed, if that was the case?"

She purses her lips. "I hadn't thought of it like that." She studies her hands, maybe feeling ashamed about insinuating that only perfect people have the right to live.

"Even if they have it," I continue, "they might not develop symptoms until very late in life. *And* even if they do show signs of it earlier, you could argue that the years they have when they're young and free of it more than offset the problems it brings."

She examines her fingernails.

"I'm not blaming you," I tell her gently. "Your view is very different from hers because you had to look after your Mum for the last couple of years. You've seen the worst side of the disease, and the emotional impact it can have on a spouse and a child. At the time that Bella had to make the decision, six years ago, your mum's symptoms were relatively mild."

Angela's health deteriorated quickly over the last three or four years of her life until, one day, Hugh apparently walked into their bedroom and discovered an empty pot of sleeping pills next to the bed. Angela was unconscious, and by the time the ambulance got there, she'd passed away. The coroner's verdict was suicide, and he raised no suspicion about her death, as it was well known that she'd suffered from depression toward the end, and had been heard to say several times that she no longer wanted to be here.

Privately, I wonder whether Hugh left the pot of sleeping pills by her bed on purpose, as he usually kept all medication in a cupboard in the kitchen. I asked Gabe once whether he thought it was a possibility, and Gabe said he'd asked his father, but Hugh had snapped of course not, and that had been that. Whether he was telling the truth… I guess we'll never know.

"You're right, of course," Em says. "My views are very black and white because of my experience. I never thought about it before. And you're right about the girls. It's unthinkable to imagine Bella and John terminating the pregnancies and the girls not being here. I shouldn't be so judgmental."

"Hey, come on. We all see things from our own point of view. All we can do is try to put ourselves in someone else's shoes." I glance at her pale face and feel a pang of pity for her. I want to distract her, and on impulse, I choose the one way I'm sure will work. "So, about the kiss."

Immediately, her lips curve up. "What about it?"

"I want to apologize if I came on a bit strong. I kinda got carried away."

"It was nice," she says shyly. "I liked that you were… enthusiastic. It made me feel… wanted."

"Oh you were definitely wanted."

"What did you mean when you said you didn't regret it, and that was what was worrying you?"

"Just that. I feel like I should have regretted it. I know I shouldn't be kissing you, because of Reasons with a capital R. But I can't help it. You're like my Kryptonite."

She giggles. "So we're going to do it again?"

I give her an amused glance. "You want to?"

"Oh yeah." She says it vehemently enough to make me laugh.

I take her hand and change the subject, talking about Rob's organization for John's stag night, and we chat for the rest of the journey about the wedding and work, keeping things as light as we can.

As we near the hospital, though, she goes quiet and pale again. I take a ticket and find a parking space, and then we get out and make our way up the steep slope to the hospital.

"You're not going to faint on me, are you?" I scold. "You've gone white again."

She swallows hard. "I need a stiff drink."

"We'll have one when we get home, I promise."

We go into the hospital and make our way to the Outpatients department. She tells the receptionist she has an appointment, and we take a seat in the waiting room.

"I thought you might have to go to Auckland for this," I say, as I know Angela had to fly down there multiple times.

"The HD Service is based there," she says, "but they hold this clinic once a month so Northland patients don't have too far to travel for counseling."

I try to engage her in conversation again, but she answers monosyllabically, and in the end I leave her to her thoughts, hoping my presence there is helpful in some way.

As the time ticks by, I look down at where she's gripping the edge of the chair. Her knuckles are white, and her hands are shaking. In fact, the whole of her is trembling.

"Hey." I put my arm around her. She doesn't relax against me, but sits there stiffly. "Come on. This isn't like you."

"I don't think I can do this." She glances at me, and to my alarm I see her eyes glisten. "Not on my own. Will you come in with me?"

"To see the counselor? Em… she'll be discussing some really personal stuff with you. Are you sure you want me there?"

She presses her lips together, fighting for control, and nods.

I hadn't expected this. I thought I'd wait outside, and then she'd tell me about it on the way home.

Part of me is reluctant to go with her, because I don't want to hear the counselor tell us all the terrible things that might happen to Em as she ages. She's so young, so beautiful, how can I bear to think about the disease lying dormant in her, ready to erupt at any moment?

But even as the thought enters my head, I think how selfish it is. If Em needs me, I'll be there for her. So I nod, and can't help but feel a rush of pleasure as relief fills her face.

"Emily Woodruff?" A woman in her forties, dressed in a gray skirt and a cream blouse, calls her name, and smiles as Emily gets to her feet. I follow her, and we walk along the corridor until the counselor stops at the door to a room, and we go inside.

"This is Kn—I mean, Lee Knight," Em says as the counselor closes the door behind us. "Is it okay if he stays?"

"Of course." The counselor gestures for us to sit in two of the four chairs grouped around a coffee table. It's a small room, with a gray-carpeted floor, white walls, and a window overlooking a garden. A desk with a laptop and a heap of manila folders sits in front of the window.

"Are you Emily's partner?" she asks.

"No. Just a good friend."

"Okay. My name is Dr. Susie Cunningham, and I'm a Genetic Counselor at the Auckland Regional Huntington's Disease Service. I understand that your mother had Huntington's, and she passed away just over a year ago, is that right?"

"Yes," Em says.

Susie looks at her notes, then back up at Em. "She took her own life?"

Em swallows and nods.

"Okay," Susie says. "Let's go through some of your personal details."

She checks Em's name, date of birth, and the names of her parents and siblings. Then she establishes that none of them have been tested for HD, but that Em has decided she wants the test.

"When a person decides to have pre-symptomatic testing," she says, "we always offer Genetic Counseling first. This is because a Huntington's diagnosis is complicated, and we want to make sure that you understand the range of results that you might receive, and what the implications of those results could be."

Em nods, her face still pale. "Okay."

"I do want to add that I don't want to influence you either way. And I would also like to say that all your feelings and emotions are valid. People who don't have the disease might question your decision to be or not to be tested, but in the end this is your decision and nobody else's."

Em nods again.

"I'm going to tell you a bit about it now," Susie says. "You may know most of it, but there might be some things you're not aware of."

She proceeds to explain that Huntington's is a rare, inherited disease for which there is no cure, and she says it's her job to go through the risks and rewards of getting tested. She describes the various symptoms, most of which both Em and I know. She explains how these often appear when a person is in their thirties or forties, although it can be earlier or later, especially with juvenile onset, which is what I know Em's worried about.

She then describes the causes of the disease, detailing how it's caused by a faulty gene, which results in parts of the brain gradually becoming damaged over time. The human body has twenty-three pairs of chromosomes, and each of our parents contributes one chromosome to each pair. The gene that causes HD is found on chromosome four, and we all get one copy of the chromosome from our father, and one from our mother.

Susie explains that this means if a parent has the Huntington's disease gene, there's a one in two, or fifty percent, chance of each of their children developing the condition—in which case they are also able to pass the gene on to any children they have—and a one in two, or fifty percent, chance that each of their children never develops the condition, in which case they would not pass the condition on to any children they had. We both knew this. It's not great odds.

Susie goes into some detail about DNA. I remember most of it from my veterinary studies, but after a while Em says, "I'm a bit lost."

"It's okay," Susie says. "It's a lot of information. The important thing to understand is what happens in the testing." She passes us a sheet of A4 paper that bears a diagram and begins to explain it. "Genes are made up of the nucleotide letters A, G, C, and T, and they form a code that is read in groups of three. HD is found in a gene called huntingtin. Everyone has the huntingtin gene, and in most people the CAG letters are repeated less than twenty-six times. Twenty-seven to thirty-five repeats is called an intermediate result, and means that person is not at risk of developing HD, but their children might. Thirty-six to thirty-nine repeats is called reduced penetrance, and the person might or might not develop HD, with a chance that future generations might be at risk. If a person has over forty copies, they are what we call affected, meaning they *will* develop symptoms. Over sixty copies results in juvenile onset HD. Basically, the higher the number of repeats, the younger the person is likely to be when they develop symptoms."

She leans back in her chair. "Does that make sense?"

Em nods slowly.

Susie looks at her files. "Your mother apparently had forty-seven repeats, and began developing symptoms when she was about forty-four years old. When a child inherits HD from the mother, the number of repeats usually remains stable. This means there's a high probability that, if you were to have inherited her HD gene, you would also have forty-seven repeats, and would also develop symptoms around the age of forty-four."

Em lets out a shaky breath. "I didn't realize that."

I didn't either. It means she's unlikely to develop juvenile onset HD, which is a huge relief. But of course it doesn't let her off the hook completely.

Susie continues: "This is the most likely outcome if you do have the faulty gene, but exceptions do occur, and therefore the test might not give you a definite result. It could, for example, reveal that you have thirty-six to thirty-nine repeats—reduced penetrance—which means you might still not know whether you will develop symptoms. Or it might reveal twenty-seven to thirty-five—an intermediate result—in which case you won't develop HD, but your children might, and that will also give you difficult decisions to make." She looks at me. "Did I explain that clearly enough?"

I nod, and Em says, "He'll get it—he's a vet."

"Ah, I see."

"I do understand," Em says. "And I've given it a lot of thought. I'd still like to have the test."

"May I ask why?" Susie asks.

"Because it will affect the decisions I make going forward."

"In what way?"

"About relationships, for example."

"Can you explain further?"

Em looks uncertain, then gives me a helpless look.

"She's worried about what will happen if she chooses not to find out, enters into a relationship, and then develops symptoms," I tell Susie. "She thinks her partner might be angry. Because of this, she's chosen not to have a relationship so far."

It might be more than Em wanted to share, but I think it's important that Susie realizes the impact the disease has had on Em.

Susie's expression softens. "You've never had a partner, because of the disease?"

Em blushes. "Not just because of it. But it's partly the reason. Not just because of how he might react, but…" She shifts uncomfortably.

"Do you want me to go out?" I murmur.

She shakes her head and clears her throat. "I know that seventy-five percent of women with HD develop abnormal sexual behaviors. It happened to my mother."

Susie doesn't reply for a moment. The window behind her is open a crack, and outside a bird calls, its song bright and clear. The summer breeze drifts in, bringing the scent of the lavender from the garden. It's too beautiful a day to be discussing such deep, unsettling things.

"Can you describe what happened to your mum?" Susie asks.

Em's hands tighten into fists in her lap. "She'd… um… talk about her sex life with Dad. Tell me private things people don't normally discuss. And…" Her eyes fill with tears, and she presses her fingers to her mouth. Clearly she can't bring herself to tell us everything.

I reach out and hold her other hand, filled with pity, and wanting to help. Hoping to cover her emotion, I say, "I think she doesn't like the fact that she can't tell the difference between what a symptom is and what isn't. Even small things like being clumsy, tripping up, knocking something over—everything becomes a possible sign. And I don't mean to put words in her mouth, so correct me if I'm wrong, Em, but I think she's worried that if she goes to bed with a guy, she's going to see enjoying anything other than straight vanilla sex as a possible symptom. And she's worries how that will affect her relationship with her partner."

"Is that right?" Susie asks.

Em nods, takes a tissue out of her pocket, and blows her nose.

"All right," Susie says. "Well, first, what we call symptom watching is very common. And for someone of your age, of course sexual issues are going to be one of the most important factors. The results of an HD test will obviously have a huge influence on this. It's natural to hope for a negative test, because it would be like getting the green light to have a relationship, and of course that's going to be very important to you at this age. But my job is to help you consider the impact both a positive and negative test would have on all areas of your life."

"Yeah," Em says, "I know."

"Let's look at the disadvantages of getting tested first," Susie continues. "Practically speaking, a positive test could make it more difficult to purchase life, disability, or long-term care insurance."

Em blows out a breath. "I hadn't thought of that."

"And of course it would have an impact on your siblings, who haven't chosen to be tested yet. Or on your friends, some of whom might pull away from you because they can't deal with it. And of course, a positive result will have a profound impact on you. It might stimulate emotions like fear, anger, or despair. And as you've already suggested, it would probably affect your attitude toward developing a relationship with someone."

Em swallows hard. "Could I have a drink of water please?"

"Oh of course, I should have offered. Here." Susie takes a bottle of water out of the fridge by her side, brings over a couple of paper cups, and pours the water into them. We both have a few mouthfuls. I wonder whether Em's wishing it was whiskey.

"A negative result will also have an impact on your life," Susie continues, sitting down again. "You might feel relief and joy. But your siblings could feel resentful because they still have the decision to make. And if they eventually get a positive result, it's very common for the person who had the negative result to suffer from survivor's guilt."

Em nods. "I'd read about that."

"Now let's look at the advantages of getting tested. If it's positive, at least you know. You can prepare for what you know will happen later in life. You can put plans in place for care, and save money for when the time comes when you can't work. If you want to have a family, you could have IVF, and have pre-implantation genetic testing, which means the embryo could undergo genetic testing in the lab before it's implanted. Incidentally, this can be done whether or not you decide to have your own test done."

Em stares at her. "I could make sure the embryo didn't have HD before it was implanted?"

"Yes, exactly. So even if you had HD yourself, you could make sure your children wouldn't."

Em looks at me, and her smile both warms me through and saddens me. She wants a family, babies of her own. It's wonderful to think that she could have a family if she wanted. But it's not something I can give her. I have to remember that.

Chapter Eleven

Emily

Susie talks for a while longer about the advantages and disadvantages of being tested, and by the end of the session I have a lot to think about. We make an appointment for the following week for my second session, and then we shake hands, and Knightley and I head out of the hospital.

We don't say much as we walk back to his car. My mind is a whirr of facts and figures. I'm excited to hear that even if I do have the disease, I can make sure any children I have won't develop it, although it doesn't change the fact that my kids would have to go through what I went through with my mother, and that fills me with horror.

What sticks with me most, though, is that being tested is not all about me. The testing, and the result, is going to have a profound impact on everyone around me—Dad, Gabe, Bella, the Knight boys, and my friends.

And what about Knightley himself? As we get into his car and he starts the engine, still saying nothing, I think for the first time about the impact this counseling might have had on him. He would never have said no to coming with me if he thought I needed him, so in that sense he didn't really have a choice. He has much more of a scientific brain than I have, so he would already have known a lot about the chromosome and DNA stuff. And because of the way the disease has already affected my family, he knew about most of the symptoms.

But what about the emotional impact? Susie must have raised issues he hadn't considered before. I wonder if it's changed how he feels about me?

I look out of the window as he joins the traffic leading out of the city. I saw the shutters come down when Susie mentioned pre-implantation testing. He must have realized I'd be pleased with that, but no doubt it would also have made him think about his own decision not to have children.

"Are you okay?" he asks.

I look across at him. "Yeah, I'm all right. I was just thinking about you, actually."

"Me?"

"Mm. I want to apologize for asking you to go in with me today."

His eyebrows rise. "It's okay. I'm glad I could help."

"You did help—it was great to have you there. But one thing Susie helped me understand is I mustn't be selfish. I have to think about how my decisions will affect the people I love."

He reaches out a hand and takes mine. His hand is much bigger, and a light warm brown against my pale freckled skin.

"You're the most important thing," he states. "Yes, of course your decisions will have an impact on your friends and family. But I don't personally believe you should let that affect what you decide to do. It's your life, Em. And you only have one chance at it. Of course I don't have HD, and like Susie said, I can't understand how it feels to have it hanging over you like this. But it made me sad when you said you've chosen not to have a relationship because of it. Whether you have it or not—you're denying yourself the chance to love and be loved. And that's a crying shame."

I stare at him in surprise. He clears his throat. "Sorry. But I had to say it."

"Fair enough," I say. "But you understand why I've made that decision."

"I do. I get the symptom watching. And because of what happened with your mum—and I'm really sorry about that, by the way—I can see why you're nervous about sex. But the thing is, it's perfectly normal to be adventurous. To want to try things like having sex outdoors, or watching other people doing it, or tying your partner up, or anal sex. It doesn't mean it's a symptom of anything except a healthy sex life."

I blink, and then my whole face lights up like it's on fire.

He glances at me, then starts laughing. "What?"

I can't speak, too entranced by thoughts of him doing all those things. And not with just anyone, but with me, to me.

It's not that I haven't thought about some of them before. I've watched a bit of porn online, and read some steamy romance novels. Although we joke about it, I haven't really stepped out of a Jane Austen novel.

But sex is something I've tried not to dwell on too much because it makes me feel panicky. I haven't spent hours daydreaming about how it might feel to go to bed with a guy. And I certainly haven't imagined going to bed with Knightley. But now, his words sprinkle a fairy dust on my imagination that sends it into overdrive. And suddenly, it's all I can think about.

He glances at me again, laughs once more, then signals and turns the car off the main road and onto the drive of a small café. He parks, puts the windows down a few inches, switches off the engine, and turns in his seat to face me.

"Sorry," he says, still obviously amused. "I didn't mean to make you blush. We joke about sex all the time at home."

It's true—growing up with four almost-brothers led to a lot of near-the-knuckle jokes and innuendo, and some much more direct conversations about who'd done what with whom.

"Yeah," I reply heatedly, "but that's different from hearing you spell it out and imagining…" Too late, I stop myself talking.

His lips curve up. "Imagining… what? Me?" The smile spreads. "And you? Together?"

"No! Well, a bit. Okay, yes. But only, I mean not in a…" I give in and huff a sigh.

We study each other for a moment. His gaze is gentle, affectionate.

I become conscious of my posture, my shoulders tense, my spine stiff, my hands balled into fists. It's been a difficult afternoon, and there's no need to bring that tension home with me. I force myself to unfurl my hands and relax into the seat. I've known this guy for as long as I can remember. I don't have to second-guess everything when I'm with him. He knows what's going on in my head—mostly—and he understands me.

And suddenly I'm tired of keeping everything secret and hidden away. I want it all out in the open.

"Everything's changed," I whisper, "since you broke up with Tia and went away. And maybe because Bella and John are getting hitched, or perhaps because I'm twenty-one now, I don't know… But I see you differently. And I think you see me differently too. Like you said, we shouldn't act on it because of Reasons with a capital R. But I can't help it. I'm attracted to you. I think I always have been, but you were with Tia, and I was too young I guess, and I was looking after Mum, and I never let myself think about you like that. All I know is that now I think about you in *that* way. And I don't know what to do about it."

He sighs, his gaze as gentle as the summer breeze blowing across my skin, and looks out of the window. He's silent for a moment, as if he's wondering how to reply. Then eventually, his gaze comes back to me.

"Tia and I broke up for a few different reasons. Not wanting a family was one. Having different sex drives was another."

"Twice nightly was too much for her?"

He chuckles. "Yeah. She was happy with once a week, and even then sometimes she had to be talked into it." He rolls his eyes. I feel a flicker of curiosity. Why on earth would you date a guy like him and only want sex once a week? If I had a man like Knightley, you wouldn't be able to drag me off him.

Then he gives me a look that's almost… embarrassed. "There was another reason."

"Oh?"

His eyes are the color the summer sky will be at sunset—a gorgeous deep blue. "She knew I had feelings for someone else."

I go completely cold. "Oh. Right." Fuck.

Then he gives me an impatient look, and I remember what his reply was when I asked him if there was anyone else.

No, Em. No one except you.

"Me?" I ask faintly.

On the main road, a car beeps its horn. A couple of kids out playing in a nearby garden yell at each other. But inside the car, it's warm and quiet, the two of us like binary suns, circling each other in our own universe.

"It's why I went away," he says simply. "I've tried to fight it. To look the other way when you walk past me in your short shorts. Not to picture you at night when I…" His lips twist, and he gives a wry laugh.

He means when he does a little DIY. Ooh.

"Reasons," he says. "Reasons, reasons, reasons. So many of them. But holy fuck, right now I don't care. I just want to kiss you again."

Joy bursts inside me like a firecracker, filling me with light. I don't want to stop to think, to make a list of advantages and disadvantages, to analyze possible outcomes, or to think about how other people might be affected. I just want to kiss him back.

As one, like two incredibly strong magnets, we move toward each other and our lips crush together, as I lift a hand to slide into his hair, and he puts his arms around me.

I thought yesterday's kiss in the orchard was hot, but now I understand that it was a slow burn, a gradual turning up of the dial from one to about seven-point-five. I hadn't realized it wasn't the end of the scale. Today, we go straight to eleven, like one of those fairground strength tester machines where you hit the plate with a hammer and the puck shoots up to hit a bell.

He plunges his tongue into my mouth, and when I moan my approval, he growls deep in his throat, and goose bumps pop out on my skin, while all the hairs rise on the back of my neck and arms. I close my eyes, not because I don't want to see him, but because I want to concentrate on all the other sensations. My senses seem to sharpen as everything around me comes into focus—I can smell coffee and warm muffins from the nearby café, the roses in the garden opposite, and the lemony scent of Knightley's aftershave. He tastes of spearmint—his favorite flavored gum that he had before we saw the counselor.

The short hair on the back of his head feels prickly against my fingertips, but it gets longer as I slide my hand up, where the strands are softer, and curl around my fingers. His lips are warm and firm, and the sexy slide of his tongue against mine sends a shock all the way through me, as if I've stepped into a Tom and Jerry cartoon and stuck my fingers in an electric socket.

Then he slides a hand beneath my shirt, and he skates his fingers across my back and around my ribs. His thumb brushes just beneath my bra, and I shudder, aching for his touch there. My nipples tingle beneath the soft lace, and I wish we were at home, alone, so he could unbutton my shirt, slide it off, and release the catch of my bra. I want to remove his clothes, too, so I can feel what it's like to be naked with a guy, skin on skin, and to have his hands and mouth on me. I want him so much. I've never understood before what yearning means, but now I feel it with every cell in my body. I *yearn* for him. I *long* for him.

"Jesus." He tears his lips away and rests his forehead against mine. "I've got to stop or I'll be throwing you onto the back seat, and I don't think the café proprietor will appreciate that."

I give a short laugh, thrilled at his words, then sigh as he laces his fingers through mine. He has feelings for me. It's partly why he broke up with Tia. Why hadn't I realized that? I'm so late to the party. I was bumbling along, thinking that my feelings for him were the same as my feelings for Rob and John and Gabe, but of course they're not. I don't think they ever have been.

It's funny, I'd forgotten, but suddenly I recall that when I was much younger, maybe nine or ten, I used to dream we'd get married. He was about eighteen then and heading off to veterinary college, and he was all long legs and stubble and Lynx body spray, his body tight and muscular from playing continual sports. He seemed like a man where the others were just boys, and I used to write his name with mine on my schoolbooks with hearts around them, and draw wedding dresses, and write Mrs. Emily Knight over and over again.

Then as I became a teenager, and he was away so much, getting his degree and then traveling, I told myself it had been a childish crush, and I pushed it to the back of my mind. He'd come home with tales of adventure and various girlfriends, and ruffle my hair like I was a kid, and I forgot my dreams the way you forget you pretended you were in Narnia and your dogs could speak to you, and you tell yourself it was part of being a child, and feel a bit foolish whenever you think about it.

But it's always been him I've run to for advice and support. For hugs when I'm feeling down. To make me feel better. I've always told myself that one day I'd find myself a man like him. Why did I not see there was so much more to it than sibling affection or even friendship?

He puts his arms around me, and I bury my face in his T-shirt. "I feel bad," he says, tightening his arms. "You're going through so much, and you're so vulnerable. The last thing I should be doing is complicating matters by seducing you like this."

Like most dads, mine is slightly old-fashioned, and still opens doors for girls and offers them his seat on a bus, even though I tell him that modern women prefer not to be treated as if they're fragile creatures who need men's help. And he's brought the guys up the same. They joke about it, Gabe, Rob, John, and Knightley, and they're more likely to share the bill on a date and wait for a woman to ask them for help rather than offer it in the belief that we need it. But beneath it all, that urge to protect is still there.

I nuzzle his neck. "Ever think that maybe it's me doing the seducing?"

He chuckles. "No."

I kiss his skin, then move back a little so I can look up at him. "You're charming, but you're not so charming that I've completely lost my mind."

My mind whispers: *are you sure about that?*

I ignore it. His eyes are warm, enticing, and I want to kiss him again. But he's right. There are Reasons we need to make sure we keep this light and fun.

"Come on," I say. "Let's go get a coffee."

*

"By the way, I got the referral email from the prison," he says when we're back in the car and on our way home, our coffees sitting in the cup holders while we share a box of sandwiches.

"Oh? And?"

He sighs and has a bite of the chicken sandwich. "I filled it in and sent it off."

I smile. "I'm glad. I think it's better to go and find out what he wants, even if ultimately it's disappointing, than not to go and always wonder."

"I hope so. I've convinced myself he's not going to welcome me with open arms, get down on his knees, and beg for forgiveness, and that he's probably going to ask for money. So hopefully I won't be devastated when it happens."

"That's good. I hope he does want some kind of reconciliation."

"If he did, I'd have thought he'd have asked John and Rob to go with me."

"Maybe he found that too daunting. They would have been much younger the last time he saw them, but you were thirteen, almost a man. In a strange way, I admire him for getting in contact after all this time. It must have taken a lot of courage. He must have guessed you'd probably be resentful and angry."

"Do you think Hugh will mind me going? He's been very good to us." He picks up his coffee and has a sip. "When I was younger, I sometimes wondered why he didn't offer to adopt us. Now, I suppose it's a good thing he didn't."

"Bella told me the other day that Mum and Dad never adopted you because they suspected this might happen."

That earns me a stare. "What do you mean?" he asks.

"Apparently Dad told John when he asked him if he could marry Bella. Mum and Dad debated adoption but obviously thought it likely that some of us might develop feelings for one another."

He slows as we approach a railway crossing. "Wow. I did not know that."

"I'm guessing they had John and Bella in mind, but… Dad said something funny the other day. I said that I'd had five older siblings, and if I'd stepped out of line, I'd have had four different guys putting me over their knee. And Dad said yeah, but only one would have enjoyed it."

He gives a short laugh. "Really?"

"Yeah. Do you think they saw something between us, even back then?"

"Maybe." He doesn't elaborate, though, and he doesn't say anything for a while.

"Did I say something to upset you?" I ask eventually.

"Of course not."

"You've gone quiet, that's all."

"I was just thinking about your dad. I hope…" He hesitates. "I wouldn't ever want to disappoint him."

"You mean by having a… thing with me?"

He doesn't say anything, but I know that's what he means.

And I understand, because I couldn't think what to call it just then. He told me in the orchard that although the kisses were nice, it couldn't lead to anything between us. He won't want to start a long-term relationship with me because he knows that I want a family, and he doesn't.

And also, I have to think about whether we're compatible, too. In bed. He's nine years older than me. He's had a lot of sex. It even earned him a nickname. He's probably tried most things in the bedroom. And I'm so naive I blush when he mentions having sex outdoors. I'm so vanilla I don't even have sprinkles or a chocolate flake. I'm hardly a woman of the world. How long would it be before he got bored with me?

He'd never say so, of course, I know he's too fond of me, and too polite, for that. But I'm twenty-one, and I'm already high maintenance. I'm caught up in fear about sex and relationships, and that fear is not going anywhere anytime soon. Only a negative test will make a difference there, and we already know the odds of that. Chances are it'll either be positive or the horrible 'reduced penetrance' that means I still won't know for sure. So I'll be worried about falling for a guy in case I do develop HD, and I'll still have that terror hanging over me that if I enjoy anything in bed too much, I'm turning into a sexual deviant.

I can't curse him with that. He's got enough on his plate. He deserves someone uncomplicated, who can give him all her heart without holding any of it back.

"You okay?" he asks, obviously picking up on my reticence.

I nod and look out of the window. "It's raining," I murmur, as the first spots hit the glass.

Chapter Twelve

Knightley

"I don't know what I've done, but something's gone awry."

I glance to my right at where Gabe is attempting to use the piping bag to write the words All Blacks on top of his cake in white icing. The cake already looks rather sorry for itself, lopsided and oozing cream and jam from its innards. Now the icing in the bag is too thin, and the letters are all running into one another.

It's John's stag night, and we're all at *Aqua Blue*, the five-star restaurant in Mangonui, in Doubtless Bay. It's a side room with long tables forming three sides of a square, the fourth side with a bench bearing a hot plate, a variety of pans and utensils, and ingredients for demonstration. Fox Wilde, the illustrious chef with spiky black hair, a white coat, and checked chef's trousers, has already spent an hour wincing as he watched us all trying to make sushi. Now he comes over to examine Gabe's offering, and he has to stifle a laugh as he says, "You need to add a bit more icing sugar to that mixture, dude."

"You promised me this would get me laid," Gabe grumbles as he scoops the mixture off the cake and puts it back in the bowl.

"And it would, if you did it properly. Women are a sucker for a guy with decent piping skills."

Next to him, John guffaws, and the rest of us start laughing. His cake is, of course, perfect, with the words "Bella and John 4 Ever" written immaculately in neatly formed letters. His relief when we turned up at the restaurant in a minibus was palpable, and he's having the time of his life, drinking scotch, cooking something new, and spending time with his mates. There are seven of us: John, Rob, Gabe, me, Max and Joel—the other two vets from HWH, and John's old school friend, Fraser, and we're all pretty useless in the kitchen.

"Next round," the waitress says, coming into the room with a tray bearing drinks, and the guys all cheer.

"Don't look," Gabe says as she puts his drink in front of him and smirks at the cake. "Fox, I need a learner sticker I can stick on my forehead or something."

"I thought you were supposed to dedicate the cake to someone important to you," the waitress says, amused, as she passes me my glass.

"The All Blacks are important to me," Gabe insists. "Despite losing recently to the Wallabies. But they've turned out to be the love of my life."

"I think Fox meant a lady friend," she teases, giving Rob his G&T.

"I'm currently between relationships," Gabe says.

"A relationship has to last longer than one night," I point out.

"I don't know. You can do a lot in one night."

"One night?" Rob picks up his drink. "You mean five minutes, and that includes eating the pizza."

"You may mock," Gabe says as we all laugh, "but I always make sure there's extra pepperoni. I know how to show a girl a good time."

The waitress chuckles and throws him a glance before she leaves the room. He grins at me, and I roll my eyes. He always manages to pull no matter where he is.

He looks at my cake, which says, 'Minnie,' the name of Hugh's Labrador. "Thought you were going to write Emily," he says.

"Fuck off," I say mildly, as the others grin. "Minnie has won my heart." Hugh has always had dogs as we've grown up. I'd like to have one myself, but I wouldn't want to leave it on its own all day, and dogs are banned at HWH because of all the kiwi.

"Has Em had the test yet?" Rob asks.

I shake my head. "She has to have two more counseling sessions before that."

"How's Bella about it all?" Rob asks John.

He looks into his glass. "She was very upset that it all came up before the wedding. She doesn't want to tell the girls yet. Her plan was to get tested when Ginny turned thirteen because she said there's no point in telling the girls before that if it turns out she hasn't got it. But if Em's test turns out to be positive… I don't know if we'll be able to keep it from Ginny. She's pretty smart and she spends a lot of time with Em, so she's going to pick something up. I think Bella will have to have the test if that's the case."

I have a big sip of my whiskey. I'm not sure if Em has considered that. I've already told her that she has to concentrate on herself, and I still believe that, but there's no doubt a positive test will affect Bella and her girls deeply.

Should I mention it to her? I wipe up a blob of icing with my finger and suck it off moodily. After our conversation in the car yesterday, Em fell quiet and I couldn't draw her out again. I saw her earlier today, too, because we all met at Hartfield House before the minibus picked us up, but she kept her distance from me, and it was obvious enough to convince me she was having second thoughts about the two of us.

And of course, she's right to. It was a stupid of me to become obsessed with her the way I have. It was never meant to be.

Fox is handing out boxes for us all to put our cakes in to take home if we want to, and then he says he's going to show us how to cook crispy chili beef in a proper wok, which we'll then be able to eat, which makes everyone cheer.

I resolve to put Em out of my mind, and enjoy watching Fox dip strips of beef in egg and cornflour before he fries them in front of us and tosses them in his special chili sauce. He serves the dish up with stir-fried veggies and rice, taking the time to do a separate tofu version for Fraser, who's vegetarian. Then while we eat, he shows us how to make simple but impressive individual apple crumbles, and serves them with a custard he makes from scratch. I'd probably buy the custard in a carton, but I could be tempted to make the crumbles if I wanted to impress someone.

Like Em. She loves apples.

Nope, not going to think about her.

We have another couple of rounds of drinks, by which time the guys are very merry. I've had two whiskeys, which I don't have very often, and I feel mellow and relaxed.

I shouldn't stress so much about Em. She's nothing special.

Except she is. She's gentle, and hardworking, and funny, and gorgeous, and caring. And the thought of her going with Finn Weston, or any other guy, for that matter, makes my blood boil. She's mine.

I glare into my whiskey glass. She's not mine. And she never will be.

"You all right?" It's Rob, lowering himself down onto the seat that Gabe vacated five minutes ago when he went off to get the number of the waitress. "You've been quiet this evening."

"Yeah. Just thinking."

He has a mouthful of his G&T. "Did she say no to a date?"

"Who?"

He gives me a wry look. "I thought you were going to ask her out."

"I never said that."

"Not in so many words." He smiles. "John and I knew the two of you would get together one day. It was just a matter of time until you both realized it."

I sigh, lean on the table, and draw my finger through some condensation from the glass. "It's not going to happen."

"Are you worried about getting involved with her because she might end up like Angela?"

I give him a startled look, a tad hurt that he'd even think it. "No! God, no, that's not it at all. It might be stopping her having a relationship, but not me."

"So it's about Dad?"

I sigh.

"Naomi told me you broke up with Tia because you didn't want kids," he says. "Is that true?"

"Yeah. Partly. My heart wasn't in the relationship, and she knew that."

"Because of Em?"

I shrug.

"Why don't you want kids?" he asks. When I don't reply, he says, "Because of what Dad did?"

"Maybe."

"You know having a temper isn't hereditary, right? We develop behavioral traits when we watch others and copy them. Yes, we saw what Dad did, but we've spent our formative years with Hugh. He's the one who's influenced us, and who we've all grown up like."

I pick up my whiskey, look at the amber liquid, and put it down again. "I'd like to think that's true. But I know I have a temper. It's got to have come from him."

"Dude, you don't have a temper, at least no more than any other guy. We all get frustrated when there's something out of our control. John is Mr. Placid, but you heard him yell at the computer when it crashed and he lost the document he'd been working on. I'm fucking grumpy all the time—I know that. And before you say we all share the same father, I've watched Gabe smash up a tennis racket when he lost a match on the last point, and his dad's like Pooh Bear compared to ours."

I run a hand through my hair. "I know you're probably right, but you're younger than me, and you don't remember what it was like at home. How Mum used to wind him up, and how the two of them would spiral out of control. How she'd chip away at him until he crumbled."

Rob cocks his head at me. "Is that what happened with Tia? Was she getting on your nerves?"

"Jesus, that makes me sound like I'm out of the nineteenth century. But… yeah, kinda. We bickered all the time. She knew how to push my buttons, and I didn't like feeling on edge. I was afraid it might get worse over time."

He nods slowly. "That's fair enough. But surely you can't have the same worry about being with Em?" When I shrug again, he laughs. "Are we talking about the same girl? I don't think I've ever seen the two of you have words in all the years we've known her."

"That's not the point…"

"Tia was fun, but she could be contrary. She had a personality like sandpaper. But Em's not like that. She's like satin. Smooth and shiny. She could never rub you up the wrong way."

"You're right," I say grudgingly. "But I still don't want kids. Come on, Rob, you were there. Losing our parents, leaving our home, having to learn to live with another family. Feeling lost and unloved. I don't want the responsibility of bringing up children and having to make their lives not suck."

Even as I say it, I think how stupid it sounds. And sure enough, Rob's expression hardens. "That's just the dumbest excuse I've ever heard for not having a family. What are you, twelve?" Anger flares in his eyes. "Life's short, and you never know what's around the corner. I can see you, refusing to have more than two drinks, terrified of losing control. Well you can't live your life like that. You can't control or rehearse or prepare for everything. You just have to play the hand you're dealt and get on with it. Are you really going to pass up the chance of the perfect relationship out of cowardice? Are you really going to let that bastard ruin your life like that? I've always looked up to you, but I'm beginning to think I should have looked elsewhere for a role model. One who actually had a fucking pair."

I blink and watch him push away from the table and walk out of the room as Gabe returns.

"Dammit." Gabe sits back down. "She's got a boyfriend. She still wanted to meet up, but I'm not into that." He blows out a breath and glances at me. "What's going on?"

"Nothing." I finish off my whiskey. "I think we're about to order the last round."

I'm actually shaking a little after Rob's surprise outburst. As kids, he, John, and I were very close, clinging together when we were cast adrift, and although we've grown up and live our own lives now, we've continued to keep that strong bond. His emotions must be running extra high for him to speak out like that.

Are you really going to let that bastard ruin your life like that? That's what this is about. The fact that Dad is in contact. We'd all done our best to forget him, but the call upset the applecart, and now we're all on tenterhooks, just the same way Em and Bella and Gabe are with the testing.

"What happened?" Gabe asks, obviously guessing something's wrong from the way that Rob walked out.

"Just a lovers' tiff." I force a smile on my face as the waitress comes up to take our order—a different one this time, and for once Gabe doesn't try to chat her up. "Glenfiddich on the rocks, please," I say. "Make it a double." Fuck it. Rob's right. Trying to stay in control hasn't worked for me so far.

There's no time to talk about it more, because Rob comes back in just as John starts giving a half-drunken speech, thanking us all for being there for him not just now but through the years. I smile fondly, so glad he's with Bella. At least one of us is settling down. Rob's shown no sign of finding Mrs. Right. Gabe seems to find at least one a week, but they don't last for long. And as for me…

I don't want to think about it.

The scotch goes down smoothly, and when John pushes me to have another, I give in, not missing Rob's small smile. By the time we all stumble out to the minibus at eleven, we're at least three sheets to the wind, and I'm more than happy to join in with an All Blacks haka, as our driver takes us home along the dark roads lit by the nearly full moon.

We drop off the three other guys along the way, and then the bus turns off at the sign for Hartfield, drives past the orchards, and ends up at the house. We tumble out—we're all staying at the house tonight—and yell thanks to the driver. He grins and waves, keeping the engine running as the door opens and the girls from the party who aren't staying the night spill out the door. Cheers and kisses are exchanged before they get into the van, and it heads off to deliver its precious load to their homes in town.

We burst into the house, almost falling into the hallway in a heap.

"The guys are here," Frankie says unnecessarily as we all start laughing and make our way inside.

"Fair maiden," Gabe says, presenting her with his cake box, "I made you a delicious confectionary." It takes him three goes to get the two long words out.

She opens the box. "What does All Blocks mean?"

"That's not an O, it's an A."

"So you're giving me a rugby cake?"

"It's a symbol of my undying affection."

"You've got icing down your shirt," she says. "For God's sake, go and sit down before you fall down, and I'll get us all a drink."

I grin, watching the rest of the guys go into the living room and collapse on chairs, beanbags, or the floor next to the girls who are still here. They've obviously had a cool evening. Frankie told me she'd booked a lingerie company called Four Seasons who organized bridal showers with a twist, and that one of their staff was bringing a selection of lingerie for the girls to try, as well as other more… intimate items. Frankie thought it was hilarious. All I could think about was whether Em would be buying something for herself.

50 First Dates, one of Bella's favorite movies, is playing on the TV, although the sound is down, and I don't think they're actually watching it. Bella is sitting in the middle of the settee, feet up on the table, surrounded by wrapping paper, heaps of presents, empty chocolate wrappers, and a half-drunk glass of champagne in her hand that I suspect is not her first. She looks blissfully happy, and tips her head back on the sofa as her husband-to-be leans over her to give her a kiss.

I smile and look around for Em, finding her in the kitchen with Frankie, pouring drinks for everyone. I wait until she's placed the last drink on a tray, and Frankie has left to carry it carefully down to the living room, where everyone helps themselves.

Em stays in the kitchen, watching them all over the top of the breakfast bar and smiling. I walk in there and find her in the process of placing mini chocolate eclairs and bite-size pieces of cheesecake onto a large plate. I guess she must have bought them at the supermarket, because by her own admission, she can't cook for toffee.

She doesn't look up at me, but as I get close to her, she stops and leans her hands on the worktop, looking down at the cakes.

When I'm a couple of inches away, I rest a hip on the worktop, facing her.

We don't say anything. I look down at where her lashes are casting a small shadow on her cheeks, which are filled with a light rose blush. She's sucking on her bottom lip, which sends tingles right through me. As usual, her hair is piled on top of her head in a scruffy bun, but strawberry blonde tendrils curl around her face. The freckles across her cheeks and nose are less obvious now her face has some color.

She's wearing shorts, like she always does, and a coral-colored top with three buttons which are undone, leaving the sides to flop open, exposing her breastbone. From my superior height, I can just see the edge of her bra.

I'm close enough to smell her hair—strawberry again. I want to lean forward and bury my nose in it. And then I want to kiss over her eyelids and down her nose to her lips, pull her into my arms, and kiss her properly.

I don't. But I ache for her. Rob's words haunt me, and I think to myself, he's right. Am I really going to pass up on the chance of happiness because of what Dad did?

She's so young and gorgeous. Like a summer goddess, burgeoning with sexuality and fertility. She makes me think of sweet things: apples and honey and peaches. Of warm endless evenings on the beach as the moon rises over the ocean.

I know I must be imagining it—I'm drunk, and it's all in my mind—but it feels as if something's changing between us, as if our bodies are talking even though no words fall from our mouths. Our pheromones are having a private conversation, seducing one another, making out on the sofa, and we can only watch, helpless to stop it, even if we wanted to.

And I'm not sure I do. I've been fighting it, but right here, right now, I can't think of anything I'd rather do than take her in my arms and make love to her.

The rose blush on her cheeks deepens, and she moistens her lips with the tip of her tongue, a gesture that makes my heart leap. She's not unaffected. She feels the same way I do. She's still not moving, and I discover that I can't either. I'm captured, captivated. I'm going to be standing here like this for weeks if someone doesn't do something.

"Excuse me." Frankie leans between us and picks up the plate of desserts. "A person could starve to death waiting for you two."

I finally force my feet to move and step back, and she grins and withdraws with the plate, taking it down to the others.

I open my mouth to speak to Em, but I'm interrupted as the others give a big cheer, and I turn to see Hugh come into the room, smiling.

"I don't want to interrupt the fun," he says, but it's too late—Bella leaps up from the sofa to go and throw her arms around him, and then she brings him back and pulls him down next to her, so he has no chance to get away.

I look back at Em, but she's slipped past me, and with a sigh I follow her down to the living room. She perches on the arm of Gabe's chair, and I lower myself into a beanbag, an act that is surprisingly difficult and makes everyone laugh as I end up falling back in a heap. I'm drunker than I thought, but I still accept a glass of champagne as Naomi offers one to me. What the hell. Em laughs, her eyes warm as they meet mine, and she blows me a small kiss that makes me glow.

Hugh slides a hand beneath himself and withdraws the box he was sitting on, and stares at it for a moment before Frankie squeals and snatches it out of his hand. "Sorry!" she says, going scarlet and stuffing the vibrator she must have bought from the party organizer beneath the sofa.

Everyone starts laughing, and then Gabe announces a toast to the happy couple, and we all raise our glasses and drink.

I'm not going to get a chance to talk to Em alone tonight, but that's okay. I don't have to decide everything right now. The important thing is that I've realized there are possibilities. I need to think in shades of gray, not black and white extremes.

Tonight is for family and friends, and John and Bella. I look at Rob, who gives me a small smile, and I nod in return. I'll think about what he said. I can't promise to change completely, but I'll take it all on board.

Outside, the moon rises in the sky, the laughter in the room spilling out to be swallowed up in the darkness.

Chapter Thirteen

Emily

I stand in front of the mirror with five rare minutes to myself and look at my reflection.

It's a week later, and it's the day of Bella and John's wedding. And wow, it's been a week. My feet haven't touched the ground. Stressed to the eyeballs, Bella finally caved and asked for my help with last minute organization, particularly of all the guests coming, so I've been dashing about picking people up and dropping them off, making every room at Hartfield perfect for the family members who will be staying there tonight, and organizing hotel rooms in town for everyone else.

Because I know Hartfield better than almost anyone apart from my father, who's already flat out getting the grounds perfect, I've also helped Lulu to move chairs and tables and pots and to carry in plants, and I've climbed ladders to pin up streamers and balloons. But my main job is to try and help Bella when things go wrong, as they inevitably do. Frankie is always by her side, providing support and cups of tea and forcing her to take five-minute meditation sessions to keep her calm, and it becomes my job to be the firefighter putting out all the fires that keep springing up—arranging an electrician when the oven suddenly stops working, rushing out to buy a new matching flower pot for the one that broke when the delivery guy dropped it, and keeping Ginny and Lilibet entertained whenever they're around so that they're not under Bella's feet all the time. They're super-excited, and I know that's going to spill over into nuclear excitement on the day. It's going to be a full-time job looking after them. But I'm glad to do it.

And of course I'm still working—I have two shifts at the Hospice during the week, and then tons of work to do at HWH, as there's a sudden influx of injured animals. People are starting to come up from Auckland for the Waitangi Day celebrations on the sixth of February in just over a week, and there are more boats than ever in the Bay, which leads to injuries to penguins, seals, and other birds. I spend mornings making sure the storage sheds are fully stocked with everything the vets and their assistants need. Also, after a few days of rain followed by constant hot sunshine, the weeds are shooting up everywhere and every plant seems to have grown six feet, so I'm constantly trimming, mowing, clipping, and removing debris. Then I spend the afternoons and some evenings up at the house with Bella before collapsing into bed, so tired I can barely move my limbs. If only I could actually get some sleep, I'd be fine. Unfortunately, it continues to elude me.

I don't manage to grab a single moment alone with Knightley, as he's busy at HWH, and often not even there, out on the boat rescuing animals around the Bay. It's probably for the best. On the night of the party, when he arrived back at the house and came to stand next to me in the kitchen, it took every ounce of willpower I owned not to turn to him, slide my arms around his waist, and lift my face to his for a kiss. I could tell by the way he was looking at me that he felt the same. Even though I'd convinced myself after my counseling session that I needed to keep my distance, something happened between us that night, something chemical, physical, that was completely out of my control. I've never had to fight a feeling so strongly.

So it's good that we've not been able to talk about it. We both need time to sort ourselves out. I went to my second counseling session on my own, and talked for a while to Susie about Knightley and how I felt about relationships and letting myself fall for someone. And even though she was very good at pointing out both sides, and she gently encouraged me to try to live for today and not let myself be defined by the HD, she still hasn't convinced me that I'd be better off not knowing. So I need to have my third session, the test, and wait for the result before I can even start thinking about what I do in the future.

Although I've spent this morning running around like—as my father would say—a blue-arsed fly doing last minute tasks, Bella finally shoved me into my bedroom with one of Lulu's team, who shut the door, put on some relaxing music, and then forced me to sit in a chair for thirty minutes as she did my hair and makeup. She's done an amazing job covering up the dark circles beneath my eyes. You'd have no idea that I've hardly slept a wink all week.

After this, she helped me on with my dress, and now I'm standing here looking at the final result. I don't think I look too bad. I'd say elegant and sophisticated, but I can hear Gabe laughing in my head when I think that, so I opt for 'decent' and decide that will have to do.

"Auntie Em!" The door bursts open, and Ginny and Lilibet burst in, talking at the same time. "Minnie ate one of the cakes off the table and was sick on the carpet, so Knightley took her for a walk, and now she—" They both stop and stare at me. "Oh…"

I smile and look down at my dress. "What do you think?"

"You look like a princess," Ginny whispers, while Lilibet's jaw drops.

"Thank you. We all look like princesses, don't we?" Bella let the two of them put on their dresses an hour ago because otherwise they'd have made her life unbearable. However, she's also cleverly made an apron that goes over the top out of a pretty, sparkly material that the girls love almost as much as the dress, which she'll whip off just before the ceremony. They spent last night with their blonde hair in rags and now it's curled up into tiny, adorable ringlets that are tied back in a neat ponytail to keep their face and neck cool. Their dresses are a few inches above the ground with several petticoats so they can flounce around in them without them being over-cumbersome. Their flowery headdress is pinned on with a gazillion clips so the only way it will come off is if their hair comes with it. They're wearing ballerina shoes tied on so they can't fall off. Bella's done a good job at making them almost indestructible.

Suddenly what they just said sinks in and I say, "Knightley's here?"

"Yes, and Gabe," Ginny replies. "Rob's with Dad at home though. Gabe's helping Gramps with all the guests. Knightley said he's going to put Minnie in her kennel for a while when he's taken her for a walk, and then he's going to come back and help."

I check my phone. It's nearly one, and the wedding is due to start at two. I guess it's time to get organized.

"Come on then, you two." I take their hands and lead them out of the room. "Where's Frankie?"

"In with Mum. She sent us out. She said she had a headache."

"Mum or Frankie?"

"Mum. Frankie gave her two Panadol and told her to chill out before she explodes like a squashed satsuma."

I laugh—that sounds like Frankie. "Let's go and see how they're doing, shall we?"

We walk along the corridor to Bella's old bedroom. I knock gently, open the door, and peer inside. "Can we come in, or do you want me to take the girls away?"

"No, come in." Bella's standing in front of the mirror while another member of Lulu's team titivates with her train and veil. Bella's reflection smiles at us. "Sorry I was a bit snappy," she says to her girls. "I feel better now."

"I gave her two Valium and half a pint of gin," Frankie says. "It seemed to calm her down."

"No, she didn't," Bella scolds. "The Panadol got rid of the headache, and John sent me a text, so that helped." Her cheeks flush. She doesn't reveal what was in it, but I'm guessing it was something intimate. Wow, John! I didn't think he had it in him to make her blush.

"Mummy…" The two girls walk in and then stand there in awe. It's the first time they've seen her in her dress. It's more flamboyant than anything I would have worn, but then Bella's a more flamboyant person than me. It's sleeveless with fine lace above her breasts, a floor-length skirt with layers and layers of tulle, and a layer of lace over the top embroidered with small flowers in white and silver that shimmer in the light. It's elegant and sedate and absolutely beautiful, and she looks like a million dollars.

"Do you like?" She turns and smiles at us. She has a minimalist, elbow-length veil in the same lace as her dress, pinned at the top of the bun which is at the nape of her neck, and a medium-length train that will fan out behind her as she walks along the carpet leading to the altar.

Tears fill my eyes. "Bella, you look amazing."

"Oh God, don't cry!" she says in alarm. "You'll smudge your mascara. And as it's the first time I've ever seen you with it, you can't let it run!"

"It's waterproof," I sniff. "I'm never going to make it through the day without bawling my eyes out."

"Not long now," Frankie says. She also looks fantastic in her gown, with her headband around her short black hair, like a nineteen-twenties flapper. I forgot how beautiful she is when she's dressed in shorts or scrubs most of the day.

"I'll get these two out from under your feet," I tell them. "I'll see you in the hall in a little while."

Bella smiles and waves, and I take the two girls out of the room.

"Let's go and find Knightley," I tell them, and we head toward the garden.

It's impossible to take more than a few steps without meeting someone who wants to say hello. John didn't have any family on his side to invite, but as the Knight boys have been with us so long, they all know our extended family and treat it like their own. Dad has two brothers and two sisters who all have children, so there are first cousins and second cousins once removed and aunts and uncles, and distant relatives from the South Island, and even friends of the family from Australia and Fiji. All of them exclaim when they see me and want to give me a hug, and then of course the two girls have to do a twirl and be admired, and not surprisingly they're more than happy to comply.

It takes us ten minutes to get through the house. As we walk outside, we find Gabe and Dad hovering on the deck. All the Knight and Woodruff guys are wearing the same suit today—a black morning coat with tails over a silvery-gray waistcoat and dark-gray trousers. A dark gray tie completes the look. It's very warm today, and I have no doubt that straight after the wedding they'll shuck the coats and turn up the sleeves of their shirts, but for now they both look dapper and elegant. I smile at them, thinking how handsome they both are. Gabe is very like Dad. I remind myself that I want to try and encourage him to dance with Naomi today. I'm still convinced they'd make a great couple.

"You've scrubbed up well," Gabe says to me.

"I could say the same to you. I didn't realize you knew how to do up a tie."

He fiddles with the knot at his neck. "Naomi did it for me."

I grin—I knew they'd be perfect for one another. "You'll have to ask her to dance later."

He raises an eyebrow. "Whatever. We'd better rescue Dad."

Dad's talking to an elderly woman who holds out her hands as we approach. "Emily! My dear."

"Aunt Daisy!" She's actually a great-aunt, Mum's auntie, and the last one left of her generation, as all my grandparents have passed away. I have fond memories of her as a child, when she and her then husband, Bertie, used to come and stay. "We didn't think you'd be able to come!" I say. She had a hip operation a few months ago, and when she received her invite, she rang Bella and said she was still recovering and wasn't sure if she'd feel well enough to make the journey. Bella put her down as a no. That's going to stress her out.

"I was worried about not feeling well," she admits, "but I decided at the last minute that I wasn't going to let fear get the better of me."

"It's lovely to see you," Gabe says, putting his arm around her. "Now I don't have to worry that I don't have a date for the day."

"Oh, you." She smacks his arm with her hand, then smiles at the two girls, who are dancing together on the deck, doing one of their ballet routines. "Oh look at them, aren't they darlings?"

"There's just one small problem," Dad says. "Because it was a last-minute decision, Daisy wasn't able to find a room in town."

"I didn't expect them to be completely booked," she says. "I also forgot it was Waitangi week. I feel like such a fool. I really didn't mean to cause problems." Her brow creases with concern and worry at having nowhere to stay.

"It's not an issue at all," I tell her. "You can have my room, and I'll kip with someone else."

"Oh, Em, I couldn't throw you out of your room…"

"I fully expected something like this to happen. I booked two extra rooms in town for that very purpose but they've already been taken. It's fine. I can sleep on the living room sofa if I have to!"

"Nope," Gabe says. "Uncle Jim's on there tonight. He arrived this morning."

"Oh." We hadn't thought Jim was coming either. "Oh well! I'll find somewhere. Don't you worry at all."

"Why don't we find you a seat?" Gabe offers her his arm.

"Okay, dear." She takes it, and he leads her along the carpet toward the rows of chairs at the bottom of the lawn.

"Thank you," Dad says, blowing out a breath. "I knew this would happen, but I had visions of having to put her in Minnie's kennel tonight."

I giggle. "It's fine. I'll put a camp bed in Frankie's room or something."

His gaze brushes down me. "You look amazing, sweetheart." His eyes turn wistful. "You're so like your mum. I wish she could be here to see you both."

My smile fades, and I swallow hard. "Me too. I understand why Bella wanted to get married here, but all I can think is that Mum should be here with us."

He puts an arm around my shoulder and kisses my temple. "Yeah."

I clear my throat. "Now, anything I can do? I hear Minnie threw up on the carpet."

"Little minx pinched a cream puff. I'm just glad it wasn't a chocolate eclair. Knightley took her for a walk, bless him, and she's snoozing in her kennel now. Here he is. Doesn't he look fine?" Dad's eyes twinkle.

I turn and see Knightley walking toward us from the direction of the kennel. I knew he'd be in his suit. And I knew he'd be gorgeous, because he looks handsome in his scruffy tees and shorts, and all guys scrub up well in suits. But I'm completely unprepared for just how ravishing he looks.

The morning coat hangs superbly well on his tall frame, while his trousers are the perfect length for his long legs. For once, he's used product on his hair, and it complements his strong, clean-shaven jaw and makes him look like a model. I thought Gabe and Dad looked handsome, but Knightley looks amazing.

Heat rushes through me, and my whole body burns.

Usually, he would have laughed at my blush, but he's too busy staring at me to react.

"Jesus," he says.

I touch my hair self-consciously. "What? Have I got a mark on my face or something?"

He seems to have lost the ability to form words and just blinks at me.

Dad laughs. "Close your mouth, son, before it fills with flies."

He closes it with a snap. Dad grins and walks off to greet someone else who's just arrived, leaving the two of us temporarily alone.

"Are you going to laugh?" I ask suspiciously. When I was younger and attempted to do my hair and put on makeup for a night out, the guys teased me that I looked like Marge Simpson after Homer fired at her with his makeup gun.

"No," he says. "Em… you look sublime."

I suck my bottom lip and look down at myself. "Really?"

"Your hair's down."

"Well, yeah…"

"And you're wearing makeup…"

"Um, yeah…"

"And… are you wearing heels?"

I lift the hem of my dress to reveal my new strappy sandals. "Pretty, aren't they?"

He seems speechless again. His gaze travels down from my face to my feet, then slowly all the way back up, lingering in the places you'd expect.

"Finished ogling?" I ask tartly, although we both know I'm enjoying every second of his admiration

"You look…" He smiles. "Grown up."

"I am grown up. I am a full-grown, sophisticated woman. Or hadn't you noticed?"

"I hadn't," he admits. "I'm such a fool."

Our eyes meet. The heat in his gaze sends a tingle all the way through me.

"You look pulchritudinous," he says.

I raise an eyebrow. "That sounds like a disgusting condition one of your animals suffers from."

"It's the longest word for someone who's breathtakingly, heartbreakingly beautiful."

It takes the wind out of my sails. No man has ever called me anything near as wonderful as that before.

"You look pretty cool too," I whisper. Our bodies are doing that strange thing again, communicating without us, having a private conversation. I feel physically drawn to him, as if he's liberally sprayed himself with a new Lynx deodorant that contains real pheromones. I don't want to feel this way, but I can't seem to help it. I moisten my lips, and they feel oddly sensitive, and my nipples tighten beneath the silky fabric of my dress.

He glances down, then back up. "Cold breeze?"

Time for another blush. "No. Cheeky."

He glances again, then frowns. "Are you wearing a bra?"

I'm saved from replying as someone says, "Lilibet, don't do that," and I glance over to see my niece trying to climb over the wire pen to give Minnie a cuddle.

"No, no, no," I call, running over as fast as I can in the high heels. "You'll tear your beautiful dress."

"She looks sad," Lilibet says, letting me help her back.

"She's all right," Knightley tells her, appearing at our side. "She's a bit overwhelmed by all the people. She'd much rather be in there where she feels safe than out here in the sun."

We both take one of her hands, and we lead her back to where her sister is jumping up and down the steps of the deck, singing to herself. "Not long now," I tell them. I can smell Knightley's aftershave, sexy and mouthwatering, and it's making my head spin. I need to get away. "I have an idea. Why don't we go and get a small drink and a snack, then go to the bathroom, and then it will be time to take off your aprons?"

They agree enthusiastically that's a great idea, and so I give Knightley a shy smile and lead the girls inside.

It's busy all through the house, but all our hard work has been worth it. Silver and light-blue balloons bounce in the air, which is filled with the scent of all the fresh flowers placed strategically throughout. Waiters with glasses of champagne move quietly between the guests who are slowly making their way to the lawn to find their seats.

I take the girls into the kitchen, doing my best to avoid the two women working on the canapés there, and pour the girls a small cup of watered-down juice, not wanting to give them too much in case they want a wee during the ceremony. The caterer gives them each a blini spread with cream cheese and a curl of wafer-thin smoked salmon, which they eat enthusiastically, followed by a couple of the chocolate-dipped strawberries.

After that, I take them to the bathroom near my bedroom. They both go to the toilet and wash their hands, and then I help them take off their aprons, leaving them hanging on the back of the door. We make sure their skirts aren't hooked up and there aren't any chocolate smudges on their faces and their hands are clean, and then we go back outside into the living room.

"Daddy!" The girls rush over as they see John, who's standing in the middle of a small crowd of well-wishers come to congratulate him. He grins and hugs Ginny, then picks Lilibet up and twirls her around. "Look at you! You're like two beautiful flowers!"

He glances over and sees me and smiles. "Em… wow. You look absolutely stunning."

"You, too!" I grin at him and Rob, who limps over. "Nice cane," I tell him. It's new, silver topped. "You look like Gene Kelly in one of his musicals."

"It's difficult to tell us apart," he agrees, "except for the fact that I have two left feet."

"Rubbish," I scoff. "I'm going to expect every single one of you to dance with me today."

"We don't dance at Hartfield," Rob points out. Unfortunately it's mostly true. I've never been able to persuade any of the guys to get up and boogie with me.

"I'll get you drunk," I tell them both. "That might work."

"There's not enough gin in the house," Rob says cheerfully.

I chuckle, then catch the eye of Lulu over by the door to the wing of the house where the bedrooms are. "Oh, looks like we need to start getting everyone outside. Bella's ready."

John blows out a long breath. "She didn't run a mile, then?"

I lean forward and kiss his cheek. "Of course not. She was nervous this morning, but then she saw your text and it was as if all her anxiety disappeared." He grins, and I smile. "I'm so glad the two of you are getting married. You're so perfect for each other."

"It was always going to happen," he says. "You can't fight Fate when she's determined." His eyes meet mine. "But you know all about that, don't you?"

"I… wait, what?"

But he's already moving away, smiling, heading toward the door with Rob.

I watch him go, waiting for the two girls to join me, my heart banging against my ribs. Outside, Knightley is talking to a couple of teenage cousins of mine, and he obviously gives them a compliment, because they blush and giggle. He's in full charm mode right now. There are going to be a lot of girls who'll lose their hearts today.

I can't be one of them. I mustn't give in to my girlish infatuation with him. I need to make sure I keep him at arm's length for the rest of the day, and not get caught up in the wedding magic.

No matter how amazing he looks in the suit.

Chapter Fourteen

Knightley

To everyone's relief, the wedding goes smoothly. Bella prepared for every eventuality, but in the end nothing major goes wrong—it doesn't rain, everyone recalls exactly where they need to be, Rob remembers the rings, and the girls behave beautifully.

Even though, like Em, I'm not a big fan of weddings—and I doubt that if I were to tie the knot, I'd do it like this—I have to admit there's a magic to the day. It's the perfect location, overlooking the Pacific, which sparkles in the warm January sun. It's nice to see people I haven't laid eyes on in years—members of the Woodruff family who were so welcoming to me, John, and Rob when we first came, family friends like Noah King from the Ark just up the road with his wife and son, and others who either work at HWH or are connected to it in some way.

John and Bella stand quietly beside each other as the celebrant welcomes everyone to Hartfield and gives a general speech about the sanctity of marriage. "No ceremony can create a marriage," he explains, "only the two of you can do that, through love and patience; through dedication and perseverance; through talking and listening, helping and supporting and believing in each other."

My gaze drifts across to where Em is standing in the aisle, holding the hands of the two girls. As I watch, Lilibet pulls her dress, and Em bends and whispers to her, finishing with a kiss on her blonde hair before she straightens. She has infinite patience with the girls, and she's so good with them.

I couldn't believe it when I first saw her this morning. I can count on the fingers of one hand the number of times I've seen her wearing something other than shorts or jeans over the years. At her mother's funeral, she wore black, and her grief overshadowed her beauty, because she was so pale and thin. Once or twice when there's been a party she might have worn a mini skirt or a short dress. But this is the first time she's ever worn anything like this.

The gown highlights her gentle curves, and because of the way her breasts move beneath the silky fabric, I'm convinced she's not wearing a bra. Her hair has been curled and it bounces well past her shoulders, the first time I've seen it down in years. Her makeup is immaculate, with black eyeliner drawn out to wings either side of her eyes, smoky gray eyeshadow on her lids, and her lashes lengthened with mascara, which she never wears. She looks like a mature, beautiful woman, sexy and sophisticated. And I realized how foolish I've been in continuing to think of her as the girl I grew up with. She's still that girl inside in many ways. But she's also changed. She's had to look after her mother and help her father with his grief. To deal with her own issues with HD. And she also practically runs HWH, although she'd never admit it. She's amazing. And now I have a serious crush on her.

As I continue to watch her, though, it occurs to me that she looks a little sad. She watches Bella and John with a wistful expression, maybe wondering whether marriage and children are in her future. Bella then begins saying her vows, mentioning their mother and saying she wishes she was there to witness the fact that she's found the man who she wants to commit to for the rest of her life. And it occurs to me that maybe that's why Em is sad—because she misses her mum, and the loss is highlighted on a day like this, where she's surrounded by the rest of her family and friends.

She looks tired, too, I think, but then that's not surprising considering how hard she's been working. I wonder whether she's driving herself hard so she doesn't have time to stop and think about her future.

It's a pleasant ceremony, not too long, with a couple of readings. One of their friends who plays the violin performs a short piece. Then, after they exchange rings, they say their vows. "I love you today, tomorrow, and forever," John says clearly and with feeling. At that, Em looks over her shoulder at me, and my heart skips a beat. I wink at her, and she gives a shy smile and looks away.

The celebrant wraps up with a moving speech about marriage and the commitment they've made to one another, and then John kisses Bella, and it's all done. They turn and smile, and everyone cheers, while their two girls run up to give them a hug.

Once they've signed the papers, Lulu gets the guests to form a line over to the jacaranda tree where they'll be having their photos taken, and everyone throws the biodegradable confetti that Em made with the two girls out of dried lavender, flower petals, and shapes punched out of real leaves, while the girls themselves run beside their parents blowing bubbles that fill the air with rainbow colors.

Then it's time for the photos, which, as always, is a rather boring time for the guests as the photographer directs group after group to join the bride and groom to pose. Em and I are in a lot of the photos, but we're placed at opposite ends of the line, so we don't get to chat.

During and after this, waiters move amongst the crowd with trays filled with champagne glasses and tiny nibbles, while people mingle and catch up, until eventually it's time to move over to the marquee.

Unfortunately I don't get any time with Em then either. She has the two girls on either side of her, and she's fully occupied with keeping them entertained while we have dinner and then the speeches. High on excitement and sugar, they're a handful, and I can see her gradually getting more frazzled, but there's not much I can do about it.

Bella's put me on a table with some of her old aunts—I'm not sure whether she wants to punish me for something or if she's just hoping I can keep them entertained. At least Gabe's on the table with me. We spend a couple of hours listening to them discuss what life was like fifty years ago, making them laugh when we say we've never heard of Gene Vincent, and teasing them that we're going to take them bungee jumping tomorrow.

When the meal is finally over, I help the catering staff move some of the tables, and we make space for the dance floor. Some of John's old school friends are in the band. They start off the music with a popular dance song, and soon the kids and the older couples who are always up first take to the floor.

It's around six now, and although it won't get dark until about eight thirty, the sun is descending toward the horizon, and the sky has turned the color of a bowl of fruit salad—plum, cherry, and mango. Around the marquee, Lulu has placed outdoor sprays to keep away insects, along with hanging citronella candles that make the area glow. Later they'll bring out the outdoor heaters, but at the moment it's still warm enough that I don't need my jacket.

To one side, there's a kind of temporary bar. I ask for a soda—later, I'll have a whiskey, but even though I enjoyed letting my hair down for the stag night, I'm still cautious about losing control. I take it over to where Rob is sitting at a table with Gabe and a couple of others, including Gemma from HWH's reception.

"Good speech," I say to Rob. And it was—he doesn't mind public speaking, and his dry wit lends itself well to speeches, plus ultimately it was very touching. He spoke briefly about the journey that brought us to Hartfield, and how he knew John and Bella would end up together from the moment she fell over in the garden on the first day she met us, and John was the one to pick her up and make sure she was all right.

"Thanks." He props his bad leg on a chair. "Ah… that's better."

"Don't get comfortable." Em comes up with Ginny and Lilibet in each hand. "The next song is going to be a slow one, and Bella's instructed me to get everyone up. As you lot are partner-less, I'm expecting you all to ask the single girls here."

"Not a chance," Rob says.

"Yes, you too, Mr. I'm-pretending-to-be-in-agony-so-I-don't-have-to-dance."

Gabe laughs, then pulls a face as she says, "You too. I want you to ask Naomi."

His eyebrows rise. "Why?"

"Because it's polite to make sure single girls aren't left standing alone." The band finishes the lively song they're playing and switch to a smoochy number. "Go on," she says.

Gabe glares at her, but dutifully rises and goes over to Naomi, who's standing talking to Frankie. We watch him ask Naomi, and she looks just as surprised as he did. But she passes her glass to Frankie, then joins him on the dance floor, where they slowly begin to move to the music.

Frankie watches them, and I don't think I'm the only one who spots the wistful look that appears briefly on her face.

Gabe and Naomi chat a little, staying an awkward six inches apart as they dance, looking a tad uncomfortable. Em purses her lips. Is she finally starting to accept that you can't force an attraction between two people?

I glance at Rob. His face is expressionless, but his gaze lingers on Naomi for a long time before he finally tears it away. He looks at me, sees me watching him, and then stands and goes over to get another drink.

"Auntie Em! We want to dance!" The girls jump around her.

"In a minute," she says tiredly. "I just need five minutes to finish my drink."

"They're so bouncy," Gemma says with a high laugh. "I don't think I've ever had that much energy! Maybe when I was eight or nine. You know, at primary school. Once you go to high school you lose all that oomph, don't you? Or was it just me?"

"Just you," Em says, a little snippily.

"They look good together," Gemma says, completely missing the bite behind her comment as she looks at Naomi and Gabe. "I'm so glad she's settling in well. Wouldn't it be funny if they got together? She's so pretty, and he's so gorgeous. I wouldn't have said no if he'd asked me to dance! That would never happen though. But maybe someone will this evening, if I'm lucky."

"If they do, I hope you'll supply the earplugs," Em replies tartly.

I stare at her. I've never, ever seen the presence of a spiteful bone in her body, and her tone genuinely shocks me.

Her gaze rises to mine, and color appears in her cheeks before she turns away.

I look at Gemma, whose jaw has dropped. "Oh," she says. "Yes, of course, I do chatter a bit. I know I go on. I can't help it, my mouth just keeps moving, even though my brain tells it to stop. It must be very annoying. I'm so sorry." She looks thoroughly embarrassed.

Rob returned just in time to hear Em's comment, and he looks as shocked as I feel. He opens his mouth to speak to Gemma, but I beat him to it.

"Would you like to dance?" I ask, holding out my hand.

Her young face lights up. "Oh, um, are you sure? I'll probably crush your toes…"

"I'm sure you won't," I say, "and anyway I'm a hopeless dancer. I make any partner look like Ginger Rogers." I take her hand, lead her onto the dance floor, put my hand on her hip, and we begin to move to the music.

"It's very nice of you to ask me," she says, a tad breathlessly. "I don't have a boyfriend at the moment—not that I'm saying you could be mine, I mean you're far too old for me, not old, but you know, experienced, you'd never be interested in me, but it's so nice to have someone to dance with, I'm always on my own at these things and I sit on the sidelines like a wallflower, and men never seem to ask, maybe they're worried that you're going to read too much into it, but all I want to do is dance. I so wish I hadn't upset Em, I think she's so wonderful, she's looked after me from day one, she's so pretty don't you think? I wish I could be like her…"

She continues on without a break in her sentences. I smile, glad I could make her day. Em might have had a point about Gemma's endless chatter, but of course that doesn't mean she should have said it to her face.

I look over Gemma's head—she's very short—to where Em is sitting on her own now, as the two girls are dancing with Frankie. Rob is looking at his phone, pointedly ignoring her. As I watch, she gets up and goes over to the bar. The guy pours her a small amount of an amber liquid—whiskey?—and passes it to her. She downs it in one, grimaces, then directs him to pour another, which she also downs in one. Then she goes over to a seat on the edge, looking away from the marquee toward the ocean.

I look back at Gemma, and for the rest of the song I smile and nod and tell her how lovely she looks in her dress, and then when we're done, she tells me she has to leave early because she's got to pick up her little sister from another party and take her home, and she heads off in the direction of the house.

For a moment, I study Em. Then I walk over to her and sit in front of her.

I lean forward, elbows on knees, hands clasped, so I'm in her eyeline, and her gaze drops to mine.

"Want to talk?" I ask.

"Not really," she says.

"Come on, Em. I know something's wrong. You've not been yourself all day, and you really hurt Gemma's feelings."

I expected her to look regretful, but instead she glowers at me and says, "She gets on my nerves."

I frown, hurt that she won't share with me what's bothering her. "I don't care—what do you think you were doing, saying it to her face like that? It's not how we've been brought up, and it was exceptionally rude, not in the least because you did it in front of me and Rob. You were the one who told me about her being badly bullied at school because of her ADHD, and how thrilled she was to get a job at the hospital. She looks up to you. All she talked about while we were dancing was how much she admires you."

Her face flushes. "I don't need you lecturing me on my behavior," she snaps. "You're not my father, or my brother. And you're not my partner either."

Our eyes meet. "You're right," I reply tightly. "So why do I feel so disappointed? It was badly done, Em." And I get up and walk away.

I go over to the bar and order a whiskey, then take it with me and walk out of the marquee.

It's a beautiful evening, although the clouds on the horizon mirror the sadness that's crept into my mood. I wish I hadn't scolded Em like that now. I can't remember the last time we had words. Have we ever argued? We must have, when we were young, but I don't remember. And even though I've always acted like her older brother, I've never had to admonish her on her behavior before, not like that. She's always been kind, supportive, and complimentary to her friends.

I stop by the fence surrounding the bottom of the garden, lean on it, looking out at the Pacific, and have a mouthful of whiskey. I shouldn't have berated her like that. Like she said, I have no right to do so. Something's obviously bothering her, and I should have taken the time to encourage her to talk about it. Not run over her with a steam roller.

"Enjoying the peace and quiet?" Hugh appears and leans on the fence beside me. "Very sneaky, although I think you deserve it after having to entertain the aunts all through dinner."

"I need to have words with Bella about that."

He grins. "She thought you and Gabe would be a good double act and keep the old biddies under control."

I give a short laugh and have another mouthful of whiskey.

"You okay?" he asks. "Em told me that you'd heard from your father."

I look at him in surprise. She hadn't mentioned that she'd told him. "Yeah. I was going to tell you, I swear…"

"I'm not cross. It's your business. I just want you to know that you can always talk to me about it if you want to."

"I know. I really was going to chat to you about it. He called me at work. He wants to see me."

Hugh nods slowly. "Have you decided what you're going to do?"

"I heard from them this morning. I'm going on Tuesday the fifteenth, eleven a.m. Bit of a time to wait, unfortunately." I'd rather have gotten it over with. Two weeks feels like an eternity.

"Good." He smiles. "I'm glad."

"I know he's not going to apologize or explain himself. If he was going to do that, he'd have done it long before now."

"Unfortunately, I think you're right. But you never know."

"I feel like I need to give him the chance. And if he doesn't… well, it won't be my fault."

"Makes sense."

There's a burst of laughter from the marquee, and we both glance over our shoulders and smile at the sight of Gabe dancing with Ginny and Lilibet.

"It's a great day," I say. "You must be pleased."

"Relieved. And yes, pleased for Bella and John. They deserve it." His gaze comes back to me, a bit mischievous. "Can you see yourself here in a few years, doing the same thing?"

"Getting married?" I look back out at the view. "I don't know."

"Lee, I just want to say… It's none of my business… But if you ever wanted to date Em, I wouldn't stand in your way."

I stare at him. "What?"

He shrugs. "I know you're a bit older than her, and I thought you might worry that I'd disapprove. But she's always been crazy about you. And, I might be wrong, but I think you're very fond of her."

I scuff my shoe in the grass. "Yeah."

"So I just wanted you to know that I'd be okay with it. If you were interested."

"Even though you know what my father did to my mother?"

He raises an eyebrow. "Why would that change anything?"

"Rob thinks our characters are formed by us watching those around us. And because we grew up with you, he thinks we're more likely to take after you and Angela than our own parents. But that argument doesn't work for me. Firstly, we know the formative years are between birth and eight, and we were all older than that when we came to you. And anyway, what if he's wrong? What if it's in the genes?"

"You think Steven's actions were caused by a defective chromosome?"

I feel a sweep of guilt. "I didn't mean to imply it was like HD…"

"Son, I'm not offended. After all we've been through, it's not surprising that this family asks a lot of questions about nature versus nurture."

"I suppose," I say, glad he's not upset. It takes a lot to offend Hugh. I envy his ability to think before he speaks, to observe rather than to react. He's always preferred to analyze and talk about an issue rather than just throw accusations around, and he does the same now.

"Everyone is worried they've inherited something bad from one of their parents," he says. "My grandfather was an alcoholic, and my father refused to touch alcohol in case he followed in his father's footsteps."

"I didn't know that," I say, surprised.

"Yeah. Well, you're a science man. You know that with each pair of chromosomes we inherit one from our mother and one from our father."

"Yeah."

"I've known you since you were thirteen. That's seventeen years. Don't you think I'd know by now if you'd inherited Steven's violent chromosome?"

I look into his kind green eyes, so like his daughter's.

"If there is such a thing," he continues, "then all three of you boys have inherited your mother's chromosome, not your father's. There's not a violent bone in any of you."

"Did Em tell you about the vet's office?"

"That you threw a box of paperclips? Yeah."

"I did more than that. What if I do have the gene, and it's like Huntington's, and it's lying dormant, waiting to erupt when I'm older? I couldn't bear it if I hurt anyone, Hugh. If I hurt Em."

I thought he'd frown at that, but instead he just smiles. "In that case, I have to agree with Rob. You've grown up with me. You've learned to solve problems calmly, by communicating and discussing how you feel with the other person. There's a vast ravine between expressing your frustration after some crushing news, and purposefully harming someone after an argument. And Lee, we both know that wasn't the worst thing about what your father did. He lashed out, and your mother lost her footing and fell down the stairs. The blow notwithstanding, it was an accident. If he'd rushed to her side… If he'd phoned for an ambulance… If he'd held her in his arms and sobbed over her body that he was sorry… He could have been forgiven. But he didn't. That's what makes it a crime. That's why he deserves to be in prison for the rest of his life. And that's what separates him from you, John, and Rob."

My eyes are stinging, and I have to fight to stop tears falling for a minute or two. Hugh waits, letting the warm sea breeze and the cries of the seagulls above us calm me.

When I'm finally in control, I clear my throat and say, "I was cross with Em just now."

"Yeah," he says, "I know."

I wonder who told him? Rob, probably.

"She doesn't seem like herself," I say. "Do you think it's the counseling and the test on her mind?"

"Possibly. It's a combination of things, I think. Mainly because she's not sleeping."

I look at him in surprise. "Really?"

"She has insomnia. I think it's because she has nightmares."

"Shit, really?"

"Yeah, about her mum. So her body fights going to sleep. It's not intentional. But insomnia is a symptom of HD."

I sigh. "I didn't know that. I knew she was worried she'd got it…"

"She's not worried. She's absolutely terrified."

I look across at him, shocked.

"The last few months were very hard on her," he says. "I did as much as I could, but I still had to run Hartfield. I wanted to get a nurse in to help, but Em refused. She did everything for Angela—fed her, bathed her, helped her to the bathroom. That in itself was hard enough, but you weren't here most of the time, so you didn't see how Angela… changed." He swallows hard. "Sometimes she was normal, and then suddenly she'd be irritable and moody. She'd yell at Em, swear at her."

My jaw drops—Angela never swore.

"She talked about the most intimate things in front of Em," he continues. "Things about our sex life that Em quite obviously would not want to know. She'd talk to me as if Em wasn't there, asking me to… well, you can imagine. She'd take off her clothes, or touch me, or herself, inappropriately in front of Em."

I ran a hand through my hair. Gabe had told me a little of it, but clearly he didn't know everything. "I didn't realize."

"Honestly, it was awful. And it's traumatized Em. You know she sees a counselor in town?"

"No."

"She's been going once a week since Angela died. But recently she's mentioned that she might stop going. She doesn't feel that it's helping. She said it's like opening an old wound every time she goes in. I think she wants to put it behind her, to forget. I don't know what's best. I want to help. But I think maybe it's not me who can help her the most." He smiles.

He means me. I think of Em—small, slender, strawberry blonde, gentle, with her light laugh and warmth of spirit—and the thought of her not sleeping and being so unhappy makes me feel as if someone is sliding a hand between my ribs, grabbing my heart, and squeezing.

"I'll go and find her," I tell him.

"Yeah," he says. "I thought you might."

I head off across the lawn, back to the marquee, with one thought in my head—to help Em, and make her smile again.

Chapter Fifteen

Emily

So why do I feel so disappointed? It was badly done, Em.

I want to curl up and bawl my eyes out, but that doesn't seem appropriate at my sister's wedding. And besides, I like to think I'm a big enough person that I can admit when I've been an idiot. I was rude, and Knightley was right to bollock me.

But I hate that we had words, and that I disappointed him. And I'm ashamed of what I said to Gemma.

Wanting to put things right, I go looking for her, but someone tells me that she left. I run out onto the drive just in time to see her car pulling away and heading up the hill.

"Fuck." I go through to my bedroom where I left my phone, and quickly text her an apology. I wait for a few minutes, but she doesn't reply. Sadly, I leave the phone on the dressing table, then return to the living room.

I go to scrub my eyes, then remember I'm wearing mascara. I'm so tired, I feel as if I could fall asleep standing up like a horse. But I know if I were to go and lie down, I'd end up staring into space for hours, my brain refusing to switch off.

Slowly, I walk back through the house and pause in the doorway, looking out to the marquee. It's gone seven, and the sun is dipping below the horizon. The sky is the color of a deep bruise—dark-blue, purple, forest-green, and a beautiful orange. It's getting cool because of the sea breeze, and Lulu is instructing some of her helpers to carry out the heaters. I need to rejoin the party. It's Bella's big day, and I don't want to spoil it by acting like the sulky younger sister who's not getting any of the attention. Plus the girls are getting tired, and it's not going to be long before I'll have to put them to bed.

I cross to the marquee, which glows in the semi-darkness like a grotto, filled with light and laughter. The girls are currently running between the dancers, causing havoc despite Frankie's attempts to calm them down, so I go up and catch their hands.

"Let go," Ginny says impatiently, pulling against me.

"I'm doing Swan Lake!" Lilibet informs me, trying to do a spin so her dress flares out.

I drop to my haunches, put an arm around each of their waists, and pull them against me. "Listen, you two. It's getting late, nearly grown-up time, and people don't want two silly girls running around spoiling the party. I can either carry you to bed right now, or you can come and sit down with me, have a drink and a sandwich, and then we'll have a couple of last dances. It's up to you."

Ginny quietens immediately. "We'll be good, Em."

"I want to dance!" Lilibet protests, but Ginny whispers furiously, "Do you want to go to bed now?"

"No!"

"Then stop acting like a baby and come with us and have a drink."

I hide a smile, push up, and lead the two of them over to the table where Gabe's sitting with Frankie, Rob, Naomi, John, and Bella. Their dad pulls them into his arms and nom-nom-noms their necks, and they both squeal and push him away.

"Sit down," I say with a smile. "I'll get you something to eat."

Leaving them with Bella, who tells them how wonderful they've been today, I go over to the buffet table, collect a couple of plates, and begin putting on some tidbits I know they'll enjoy—a sandwich, a tiny quiche, a pig-in-a-blanket, a chicken tender, and a breadstick with a spoon of creamy dip.

"Peckish?" someone asks from behind me.

I glance over my shoulder and see Knightley watching me with a smile. Immediately, my face flushes scarlet. The dressing down he gave me earlier made me feel an inch high, and it took all my self-control not to burst into tears in front of him.

"It's for the girls," I say, turning back to the food. "They're getting tired, but I don't have the heart to take them to bed just yet, so I thought they could have a last snack and then a couple of dances before I whisk them away."

"Good idea. I'll help you." He gets two plastic cups and pours some Sprite Zero into them.

I watch him, tongue-tied. He's not wearing his long morning coat, and he's rolled up the sleeves of his shirt. His dark hair is a bit more ruffled than it was earlier—I think he forgot it had product in it, and he's probably run his hands through it half a dozen times. There's a touch of five-o'clock shadow on his jaw. I can smell his body spray where his body has warmed it through.

I think he's forgiven me. I want to slide my arms around his waist and have him hug me. But I don't.

"Knightley… I just want to say…"

"Don't," he says. "There's no need.

"I'm sorry," I say anyway. "I went to apologize to Gemma, but she'd gone. I've texted her, but she hasn't replied. I… I'm not surprised. It was unforgivable."

"Rubbish," he scoffs. "It was a throwaway sentence. She'll come around. She told me she was going early to pick up her sister."

"Oh, so she didn't leave because of me?"

"I doubt it." His gaze caresses me. "Try not to let it worry you. I shouldn't have scolded you like that."

"No," I whisper, "you were right. I shouldn't have said it. I feel terrible." I swallow hard.

"It's okay. Tomorrow you can chat to her, and everything will be fine." He turns away from the table with the drinks. "Come on. Let's sort out the girls, and then you'll be able to relax for the rest of the evening."

I follow him back to the table with the plates, and I sit quietly for a while, listening to the others chat around me while I keep an eye on the girls. They eat some of their snack and drink the Sprite, and then they're ready to dance again, so Frankie, Naomi, Bella, and I take them a little way out of the marquee where they can't run into anyone, and we hold their hands and dance with them, until it's almost dark, and they finally run out of steam.

"I'll put them to bed," I tell Bella, and she gives me a big hug.

"Are you sure?"

"Of course. You stay here and enjoy yourself."

"You've been amazing today," she tells me. She's removed her veil and train, and she looks just like her girls, dancing around and pretending to be a ballerina in her beautiful dress. "Thank you so much for everything you've done," she continues, her eyes bright. "I know I've been a real dragon, and you've been so patient with me. I couldn't have done it without you."

"All your hard work was worth it," I reply. "It's been a fantastic day."

"It has, hasn't it? I can't wait until we change places, and you're the one standing there with the love of your life."

"Me too." I bite my lip.

She glances at Knightley and smiles, but doesn't say anything.

"I'll go now," I say hastily, and I take the girls' hands and tell them it's time for bed. This time, they're so exhausted that their protests are short-lived, and they come with me quite happily as I take them to kiss their dad before they wave to everyone, and we head off. Bella and John are staying here the night, and then tomorrow all four of them are flying out to Fiji for five days. I offered to have the girls so they could have a proper honeymoon, but they decided to make it a family holiday as they couldn't bear to be away from their daughters.

I walk the girls through the house to their room, which has an interconnecting door to Bella and John's. The beds are all ready for them, the covers pulled back.

"I don't want to take my dress off," Lilibet says tearfully.

"I'm going to hang it up on the wardrobe so it's the first thing you'll see when you wake up," I tell her. "Come on."

I help them undress and put their nighties on, make sure they've cleaned their teeth, then get them into bed. Finally, I reveal the secret I've kept from them all day—a new night light. I switch it on, then turn off the main light, and they gasp. The rotating lampshade throws pictures of dancing ballerinas surrounded by stars onto the walls and ceiling, accompanied by a gentle lullaby.

I give them both a kiss, then sit on the chair in the corner for a while, flicking through one of their picture books, while they chat for a few minutes about the night light and their day. But it's not long before they fall silent, and when I look up, they're both asleep.

Smiling, I turn on the baby monitor and leave the room, pulling the door closed.

I take the receiver back outside to the marquee. It's noisy with the music and laughter, but I leave the receiver on the table, knowing that someone will notice if either of the girls wakes.

A glass of champagne sits by my seat. I give Knightley a suspicious glance, and he just grins. I sit and have a big mouthful, sighing as the cool liquid slides down. "Mmm."

"The girls okay?" he asks.

"They're fine." I look at the dance floor. Bella and John are in the middle, turning slowly as the band plays a ballad. They look incredibly happy. The music changes, and the singer starts crooning to one of my favorite songs.

Knightley gets up and extends a hand to me.

I look up at him, surprised. It used to annoy Tia that he hardly ever danced with her. His asking Gemma to dance was very unusual.

I glance around at the others, but nobody's looking. Gabe and Frankie are arguing about something, as usual. Naomi's talking to Aunt Daisy. Rob's having a chat with one of his and John's old schoolmates. Nobody's interested in what Knightley and I are doing.

"Come on," he murmurs, turning his palm up and flicking his fingers.

I slide my hand into his, let him pull me up, and follow him onto the dance floor.

It's dark now past the lights, and I can no longer see the lawn or the ocean in the distance. It feels as if we're in a floating fantasy land. Quite a few couples are up dancing now, filling the floor.

Knightley stops when he finds a space, not far from Bella and John. He turns to face me, holds my right hand, and slides his other hand around me.

I rest my left on his shoulder, and together we begin to move slowly to the music.

The whiskey I knocked back earlier is beginning to have an effect. I was so tense then, but the alcohol has loosened the nuts in all my joints. I take a deep breath and let it out slowly, my breath whispering across his throat, and he shudders.

"I'm sorry," I say. "For everything."

He doesn't answer, but he tightens his arm around me, bringing me closer to him. His lips brush against my temple.

We dance like that for a long time. The song changes smoothly, the band obviously realizing everyone's enjoying this brief respite in the dancing, and so most of us stay with our partners, some talking, others just enjoying the music.

I see Gabe take the floor with Frankie, of all people, and then, to my shock, even Rob appears with Naomi, his cane left behind by his chair. Naomi and I exchange a wry smile, but then I close my eyes and rest my cheek on Knightley's shoulder, and concentrate on the smell and feel of him.

"Have you decided where you're staying tonight?" he asks in my ear after a while.

"No."

"I'm at the hotel," he says. He only lives fifteen minutes away, but he decided to stay in the hotel just down the road with everyone else and take the minibus rather than either having to drive or book a taxi late at night. "If you want, you can have my bed, and I'll take the sofa. I don't mind."

I turn my head and rest my forehead on his shoulder. His lips brush my ear.

"I promise to behave," he whispers.

"In that case, the answer's no."

He gives a short laugh, and soon we're both chuckling away.

"Seriously, though," he says. "The bed's all yours. If anything were to happen between us, it would be because we both wanted it, and we were both ready for it. I want you to know that."

"Okay."

"So you'll stay?"

"Yeah. I'll stay."

I look up at him. He smiles, but there's something in his eyes that makes a shiver run down my back. He's being a gentleman, but that doesn't mean he's not interested.

I think he wants me.

Oh dear.

There's no time to think about it now, though, because the song is coming to an end. The band strikes up a golden oldie, and everyone cheers and begins dancing. Knightley sighs as I give a twirl, then joins in, and Gabe does the same. Both of them have good rhythm, and it's great fun to see them dance.

Rob's the only one who decides to retire to the sidelines, and Naomi joins him. Maybe I got it wrong, and it's not Gabe who's the ideal guy for her?

Relaxed from the alcohol and the fact that Knightley's forgiven me, and fueled deep down by the excitement of staying with him tonight, I lose myself in the evening, dancing, drinking, and snacking from the buffet, and occasionally stopping to talk to old relatives and friends I haven't seen in years. The minutes and then the hours fly by, and I'm shocked when the band announces it's eleven thirty, and they're going to play a last few songs before they wrap up.

Everyone gets up, and we all dance for the final fast songs, and then people begin to pair up for the last slow song of the evening.

"Would you like to dance?" someone asks me. It's a guy of around my own age, some distant cousin from Oz, with floppy surf-dude hair and an eager smile.

"I'm sorry, she's taken," Knightley says, and before I can say anything he whisks me away into his arms.

"Smooth," I say. "That could have been the love of my life."

"Nah," he says. "That position's already been filled."

My jaw drops, but he turns his head to talk to Gabe, who's back dancing with Frankie next to us, and I don't get a chance to question him about it.

His words flutter around in my head like butterflies, though. What was he saying? That he's the love of my life? It's quite an arrogant thing to say to a girl. Especially when she's only twenty-one, and we're not even dating. He must have been joking.

His hand is warm at the base of my spine, keeping me close against him. He's so familiar to me; I could describe his features, the color of his hair and eyes, the angle of his lopsided smile, without looking. But how I feel about him… the way my pulse picks up its pace when he looks at me… that's all new.

He's singing now, murmuring the words to the song, his breath brushing across my ear, and I close my eyes and just try to enjoy being close to this man who I trust more than anyone except my father. It makes me think of Dad, and I wonder whether he's watching us at the moment. I've seen him several times through the evening, always on the periphery, making sure everyone's glasses are full, and that nobody's left on their own. We had a dance earlier, and I asked him if he was okay, knowing he must miss Mum terribly, but he said he was fine and that he was enjoying seeing everyone.

For the first time, I wonder whether he'll meet someone else. The thought gives me a funny feeling in the pit of my stomach. It's only been a year, and as far as I know there's nobody special in his life. I don't like the idea of anyone replacing Mum. But equally, I don't want him to be alone for the rest of his life. Everyone deserves companionship and love and comfort.

The singer rounds up the song, and everyone stops and claps them, then gradually starts to collect their jackets and bags, and make their way toward the house.

Some of our closer relatives are staying, and I help Dad show everyone their rooms. Bella and John have a final drink, then retire to their room to cheers and waves. All the rest slowly make their way outside, where the several minibuses we booked are waiting to take them to the hotel.

"I'll be off, Dad," I say to him. "Is that okay?" I told him earlier that I'll be staying at the hotel, and I packed a small overnight bag and left it by the front door.

"Of course. We're all set here." He kisses my cheek. "You sure you don't want my bed and I'll sleep on the living-room sofa?"

"Uncle Jim's on there."

"Oh."

"I'll be fine. I'll be back first thing to help clear up."

"No rush," he says. His eyes twinkle. Does he know I'm staying with Knightley?

I clear my throat. "See you tomorrow." And I pick up my bag and head outside.

The moon is a day or two off full, hanging in the sky like a silver coin. Most people are already in the minibuses, but Knightley is standing by one, talking to Gabe, and they smile as I approach.

"Ready?" Knightley says. I nod, and the three of us get in, taking up the last three seats near the front, while the driver puts my bag in the back.

The bus bounces past the orchards and down the hill, then turns toward the town, stopping just a couple of minutes later at the hotel by the sea. I feel nervous as we all tumble out, wondering if the others are going to tease me for staying with Knightley, especially Gabe. But everyone's tired and ready for bed, and he soon disappears off to his own room without waiting to comment on where I'm staying.

I wait until the end, to make sure that all the guests are checked in and everyone has a room. It's close to one a.m. before the guy behind reception tells me that everyone's settled, and Knightley and I finally go into the elevator and emerge on the second floor.

We walk down to the room, carrying our bags. He swipes the key card, opens the door, and gestures for me to precede him.

I go into the room, inhaling with pleasure at the sight of the view out across the dark ocean, the moon reflected on it like a silver path.

"Going to be amazing when the sun comes up," he says, coming over to stand beside me.

"I can't believe the day's over. I feel relieved and disappointed at the same time. All that hard work and stress, and now it's done."

"Yeah, I know what you mean."

We stand there for a moment, side by side. I'm acutely conscious of him again, every cell inside me reacting to his presence. I want to ask him what he meant when he said he was the love of my life. I want to talk about what's going to happen in the future, and about his feelings for me. But I'm dog-tired, and a little tipsy, and I can't think how to phrase anything.

"Come on," he says eventually. "You should go to bed before you fall down. You look so tired."

"Are you really going to be okay on the sofa?"

"I'll be fine." He speaks firmly. It sounds as if he's decided that nothing's going to happen tonight.

My heart sinks a little. It makes sense. I don't know why I thought any different.

I sit on the edge of the bed and flop back onto the pillows. I'm too tired to get undressed or take off my makeup.

"I'll just lie here a while," I murmur, and I close my eyes.

I'll worry about everything else in the morning.

Chapter Sixteen

Knightley

I put Em's case on the stand and mine next to it on the floor, toss my morning coat over the chair, then walk over to the bed to ask her if she'd like a drink.

She's asleep.

I stand there for a moment, drinking in the sight of her sprawled across the bed. She looks like a famous painting, hair fanned out on the duvet, her pale skin like porcelain, the satin dress draped over her curves.

She's so beautiful, it makes me ache. All day, I've watched her walking, talking, dancing, looking so sultry and alluring in her gown, and I've been captivated, unable to think of anything else but having her in my arms.

I wish I could climb onto the bed next to her, strip off her dress, and cover her in kisses until she begs me to take her.

But I promised I'd take the sofa, and I'm not about to take advantage of a sleeping woman.

I also don't want her to wake and discover me standing over her, because that's just creepy. So I retrieve the spare blanket and pillow from the cupboard, and take them over to the sofa.

It's a two-seater, so it's way too short for me. I doubt I'll get much sleep tonight. But that's okay.

I debate whether to get undressed and, in the end, decide against it. Leaving the bedside light on, I take off my tie and undo my shirt, then lie back, legs propped on the wall beyond the arm of the sofa, and look at where the starlight is falling through the open curtains to coat the carpet in silver.

For a while, I think about how it felt to dance with Em, as if we were a couple. My hand fit snugly in the curve of her waist, and later, when she leaned against me and rested her cheek on my shoulder, I felt a strong surge of protectiveness, a need to protect her from the harsh realities of this world.

But of course I can't. All I can do is be there for her when she needs me.

I sigh and close my eyes. In less than a minute, the world fades away.

*

I awake with a start. For a moment, I'm disoriented. The window is on the other side of the room to where it normally is, and clearly I'm not in my own bed. My legs are stiff, and the room is humid and stuffy.

Then, like rebooting a computer, my memory returns. I pick up my phone and check the time—it's not yet two a.m. Only forty-five minutes have passed. What woke me?

A soft moan jerks me into a sitting position. It was Em. I stand and go over to the bed. She's still asleep, but she's muttering, her head twisting from left to right. I think she's having a nightmare.

"Out," she mumbles. She follows with something unintelligible, then says, "Over her head."

"Em…"

"No…" Her face creases with pain. "Get her out…"

"Em—you're dreaming." I put a hand on her shoulder and shake her gently.

"No!" Her eyes open as she gasps, and she stares at me, breathing heavily.

"It's okay." I perch on the bed next to her. "You were having a nightmare, that's all. Everything's all right."

"Lee?" It's unusual for her to use my first name and not my nickname.

"It's all right. What were you dreaming about?"

"My mum." Her bottom lip trembles, and then, to my surprise, she bursts into tears.

Em has hardly ever cried in front of me. Even when she was a kid and fell over, she always put a brave face on it. And although there must have been times when she felt upset growing up, she must have taken herself off, because she never shed tears in front of me. At her mother's funeral, she got emotional, but even then she didn't break down in public. The other day, after she saw Finn kiss Janie, I was convinced she must have been devastated about losing him because she cried. It shocks me now to see her dissolve once again into floods of tears.

"Hey…" I rub her arm. "Come on, it's okay…"

But she covers her face with her hands and sobs her heart out.

"Aw, Em…" I climb onto the bed, then pick her up and bring her with me so I can lean back on the pillows. She sits stiffly for a moment, her spine rigid, but I wrap my arms around her, and after a few seconds she melts against me and buries her face in my shirt.

"It's okay…" I stroke her back and kiss her hair while I wait for the storm to pass. She feels so small and fragile, like a bird in my hands.

It takes a while for her to calm down, but I'm in no hurry. I enjoy the feel of her soft body against me, and hum the song we were dancing to earlier. Gradually she stops shaking, and eventually the tension leaves her.

"There." I lean across to the bedside table, retrieve the box of tissues, and bring them back for her. She takes a couple, blows her nose, and wipes her face, still in the circle of my arms.

"I'm sorry," she whispers.

"It's not a problem, sweetheart. It's been a hell of a day. I'm sure your mum not being there must have been hard for you."

She swallows. "Yeah." She wipes under her eyes. "I forgot that I'm wearing mascara. I must look like a panda."

"A beautiful panda," I say, and smile.

She lifts her gaze to mine. It's true that her makeup is smudged and her eyes are red, but she's still gorgeous.

Her mouth looks so soft and inviting that I can't help it. I lower my lips to hers and kiss her.

She doesn't pull away, but she doesn't respond either. I lift my head to study her.

"Sorry," I say.

She shakes her head. "It's me. I just…" She presses a hand between her eyes. "I just feel so guilty."

It's an odd word to use. "Guilty?"

She rubs her nose. "I'm just going to the bathroom." She scoots to the edge of the bed and gets up.

"Do you want a drink?" I ask. "Something from the minibar? Or a cup of tea or coffee?"

The corner of her lips curve up. "A cup of tea would be nice."

I nod, and she disappears.

I boil the kettle, pop two teabags into mugs, and retrieve some tubs of milk from the fridge. I'm just dunking the teabags when she comes back out. She's still in her gown, but she's removed the headband, and she's taken off her makeup. I liked her smokey-eyed and sultry, but I'm just as fond of fresh-faced Em. Even though she looks younger without her eyeliner and mascara, I'll never see her as a girl again. She'll always be a woman to me now.

I concentrate on removing the teabags and adding the milk. When I finally turn, she's curled up on the sofa. I join her there and pass her a mug.

"Do you want me to put on the air con?" I ask, conscious it's a bit stuffy.

"No, I'll open a window." She puts down the mug and gets up to open one. I watch the silky material of her gown stretch across her breasts as she leans, and I silently blow out a breath and look away.

Outside, it sounds like summer—the woosh of the waves, the occasional late car, and the sound of music far off in the distance from one of the nightclubs that's still going strong. Today has had a surreal feel from the moment it began, a bit like Christmas, as if we're waiting for Santa to pass through the sky.

Em sits back down and curls up again. "My feet are cold," she whispers.

I move them so they're tucked under my thigh. "There."

She smiles and sips her tea.

We sit there like that for a while, not saying anything. I'm partly turned toward her, and I slide down the cushions a bit, stretching out my legs. It feels comfortable and companionable, and I don't find the silence awkward. Like before, our bodies continue to have a conversation of their own, pheromones entwining in the air between us like smoke. I'm hyper aware of her as a woman now, her curves, her mouth, the place behind her ear I want to kiss to see if the skin is as soft as it looks. But I know nothing is going to happen yet.

We've known each other so long, sometimes it feels as if we're almost the same person. But of course we're not. Even the closest of couples will always keep secrets from each other. And I know there's something she's not telling me.

"You said you feel guilty," I say eventually. "What did you mean by that?"

She studies her mug. "I shouldn't have said that."

"Why not? What did you mean?"

She looks up then and gives me a sorrowful look. "I can't tell you."

"Why not?"

"Because I don't want you to think less of me."

"I could never think less of you, Em."

"You don't know that."

"What's this to do with? The wedding?" She doesn't say anything. "With me?" Still nothing. "With your mum?" That's it, she turns her gaze away, unable to look me in the eye.

My brain works furiously, which isn't easy when it's two a.m. and I've had several whiskies. Something to do with her mum, that she feels guilty about…

And then it occurs to me. Oh no…

"Em, did you give her the sleeping pills?" I ask, heart hammering.

A tear tips over her lashes. "No. But I wish I had."

I feel a wave of relief, not necessarily because I disagree with helping a loved one in that way, but because I know how much it would have haunted her if she had. "What do you mean?"

She leans her head on the back of the sofa, and lets out a long sigh. "That last year was hard, so hard. Physically and emotionally. Both Dad and I were exhausted. Mum was on a large cocktail of drugs. Her body was wracked with pain, and her behavioral and mental problems came in waves. Some days she was very bad—irritable, obsessive, and forgetful. At other times when she was lucid, she was horrified at how bad she'd become. She was distraught to see how much it upset us all. And she hated that it was such hard work for me."

I reach out to hold her hand, but I don't think she even notices.

She continues, "She knew it was only going to get worse, not better. She hated being a burden. And she started saying that she wanted it to be over. At first we didn't take any notice. But eventually she told us she couldn't bear it anymore. And one day, she told us she'd spoken to her doctor, and she was being assessed for assisted dying as part of the The End of Life Choice Act."

I know the Act was passed in 2019, and that assisted dying is now legal in New Zealand. "Did she pass?"

"No. The eligibility criteria are very strict. The patient has to be suffering from a terminal illness that is likely to end their life within six months, and the doctor said Mum could have gone on for much longer. They also have to be considered competent to make an informed decision about assisted dying. It doesn't matter that suicide rates for people with HD are highest among people with neurodegenerative disease. Twenty-seven percent of sufferers attempt it at least once and they say completed suicide rates are as high as thirteen percent."

"Jesus."

"Yeah. That didn't seem to matter. She was on medication to treat severe depression, and they concluded it was influencing her decision. We talked about it for weeks after that."

"You and your Dad?"

"And Gabe, sometimes, although he was against it. Mum also mentioned it once to Bella and she completely lost the plot, so we didn't mention it again. But Mum kept saying she wanted it over. We talked about moral and religious issues. I know mum wasn't religious, but Dad kinda is, and I do have faith, of a sort. I said it could be argued that God was testing her, and asked her if she had the right to take her own life. What if, as some people say, it meant she wouldn't go to heaven? But she said it was up to her and nobody else. She begged me to help her finish it."

"Oh, Em."

"I wanted to help her. I know that if I end up in her position, I'll probably feel the same way."

My stomach clenches at the thought that Em has pictured herself like that. She's had to imagine what she will do when it happens to her.

No, *if* it happens. We don't yet know if she has it. Please, God, let the result be negative.

"But you didn't," I clarify.

She shakes her head. "In the end, I couldn't do it. She was so upset. A few weeks went by. I know she asked Dad, too, because they had a huge argument about it. The thing is, it's impossible to remove yourself from the equation. If you agree to help, how do you know that part of the reason you're doing it isn't just to make your life easier?"

"I know what you mean. So what happened in the end?"

"We'd been out for a walk. She was in her wheelchair. It was a bad day for her—her muscle jerks were very pronounced, and she had a bad headache. She was quiet though, not too irritable. We walked around the garden, and then when we came indoors, I stopped off at my room to use the bathroom before I took her back to hers. While I was in the bathroom, she took a pot of sleeping pills from off my bedside table."

She sips her tea. "The thing is, I always kept those pills in my drawer, but that day I'd left them out. And I hardly ever took her into my room. I keep asking myself now, did I do it subconsciously, giving her access to that bottle? I don't think I did… But I don't know…" She stares into her mug.

"I don't think you did," I say. "I think it was a coincidence. An aligning of the planets, if you will. She'd been denied her human right to decide her own fate. She knew it was unfair to ask her loved ones to help her. So she saw an opportunity, and she took it. You can't blame yourself. If you do, in a way it takes away the fact that for once she felt in control. You forget that I grew up with you. I know how much she loved you and your dad, and Gabe and Bella, all of us, in fact. She was so generous with her affection. She had such a big heart. I know how much she would have hated losing control of her body and being a burden on you. So she made a choice. She'd suffered so much. And she wanted to end it on her terms, when she was ready. In that sense, it had nothing to do with you."

She sniffs. "Do you believe in heaven?"

"I'm agnostic. I don't think we can know what lies beyond what we can see. But if there is an afterlife, I can't see why a benevolent god wouldn't recognize suffering and understand why a person would choose to end it. It wouldn't surprise me if there was some kind of counseling service available, where you were talked through your choices to help you be at peace. If there is a heaven, your mum's there, Em. After all the good she did? There's no doubt about it."

She meets my gaze. Then she puts her mug on the table, moves up next to me, and slides her arm around my waist.

I put down my mug and wrap my arms around her.

"Thank you," she whispers. "You always know how to say the right thing."

"I'm smart like that."

She chuckles and wipes her face. Her cheeks are wet, but she's not sobbing like she was earlier.

"There's something I need to say," I tell her, resting my lips on her hair. "I want to apologize for not being there when you were going through it all." Those last few months happened right at the peak of my adventures in Africa, and even though I knew what was happening and I flew home several times to be with my family, I could have done so much more.

"It's okay. She wouldn't have wanted you to see her like that anyway."

"You should have told me, though. Called or emailed or texted. We could have talked about it."

"I… didn't want to step on any toes…"

Her words make me frown. I slide a finger beneath her chin and lift it so I can look into her eyes. "What do you mean? Are you talking about Tia?"

Her lips twist, but she doesn't reply.

"What did she say to you?" I demand.

"It doesn't matter now."

She's not going to tell on Tia, but I can guess what happened. Tia didn't like that I confided in Em, and that we were close. She told me to keep away from her. And I guess she must have demanded that Em kept her distance, too.

"You should have told me," I say, somewhat bitterly.

"It's done now," she murmurs. "We should concentrate on looking forward."

I sigh, then rest my head on the back of the sofa. She's warm in my arms, and soft. I brush her ribs with my thumb, and she shivers.

"Do you want to talk about it?" I ask her. "The future? Us?"

She rests a hand on my chest. My shirt lies open, and she trails a finger through my chest hair. "We should wait and see how things pan out. The test. And your dad."

"Yeah. We should."

After a second or two, she lifts her head and looks at me. "I don't want to, though," she whispers.

My heart skips a beat. "Me neither."

We study each other silently for a moment. There's that feeling again, of time turning, of something changing between us. My pulse has sped up, and I can see hers doing the same in her throat. I want to lean forward and kiss her there, feel her heartbeat thrumming beneath my lips. I want her so badly. But I force myself to wait.

"Tell me what you're thinking," she whispers.

I slide down on the sofa a little, so she's half lying on me, tucked in the crook of my arm. I curl the strand of her hair around my finger. When she saw Finn kissing Janie, she said, *I'd like to be kissed like that. Just once.* She's not just a virgin, I think she's very innocent.

"I don't want to shock you," I say.

She draws a heart on my chest. "Maybe I want you to shock me."

Our eyes meet. "Are you sure?" I murmur.

Her lips curve up. "I'm crazy about you, *Leander*. I want to let the lion king out of his cage."

"Are you sure? He might ravage you."

"God, I hope so."

We both laugh.

"I mean it," she says vehemently. "I'm tired of hearing everyone else joke about sex and not understanding. I don't want to be a girl anymore, innocent little Em, everyone's baby sister. I'm a woman now, and I want to be treated like one."

I stroke down her back. "Fair enough."

She swallows hard. "I know we've kissed, and it was… wonderful. But… do you think there can be more between us? Do you think you can see me as more than a friend?"

Chapter Seventeen

Emily

My heart is racing, and I'm sure he can see my chest rising and falling with my rapid breaths. Part of me expects him to mock me, the way he did when we were kids. But he doesn't.

Instead, he says, "I can't see you as anything but a woman. I haven't for a long time. But especially since we've kissed. You said something's changed between us, and you're right. It's happened at a molecular level. In science it's called an irreversible change. Like wheat ground into flour, or the flour mixed with eggs and baked into a cake." He brushes my back. "Like fruit ripening, or a bud growing into a flower. It can't change back. We'll never return to being just friends, even if we don't sleep together. This," and he moves his hand back and forth from me to him, "what's happening between us, will always be there now."

I wonder whether I should feel sad or frightened by that, but I don't. I just feel excited. Even so, I find myself saying, "If we do sleep together, and it doesn't work out for whatever reason, I don't want to lose your friendship." The thought gives me physical pain.

But he says, "You wouldn't, I swear, and I'm not just saying that. We could never not be friends, could we? We're like binary suns. We're always going to orbit each other."

I rest my cheek on his chest. He strokes my hair, letting the strands slip through his fingers.

I feel as if a huge weight has been lifted after our talk about Mum. I was worried he might think I'd been a coward because I hadn't been able to bring myself to help her, but I should have known he'd always take my side. I should have spoken to him before now. He always knows how to make me feel better.

He smells nice. He has a sprinkling of body hair across his ribs. The sheer masculinity of that stirs something inside me, and I turn my head to where the brown hair curls against his tanned skin, and I bend my head and press my lips to it. He inhales, sharply, telling me that it affected him. He wants me, I know he does. But he's holding back. I think it's partly because I've been so emotional and he doesn't want to take advantage of me, and because he doesn't want to shock me.

He's older than me, and he sees himself as the responsible one. He thinks he's in charge.

I lean on his chest and rest my chin on my hand. "Can I tell you a secret?"

He starts drawing circles on my back, over the satin of the dress. Light and tantalizing, so goose bumps pop out on my skin. "Of course."

I meet his eyes. "I think about you… you know… when I'm on my own. In bed."

His hand stops. He blinks a couple of times. "You mean…"

I moisten my lips again. "Mm. When I'm touching myself. I imagine you're there with me. Kissing me. Stroking me."

I don't think I could have surprised him more. His eyes have widened, and he appears to have lost the power of speech again.

"Sorry," I say mischievously. "Did I overshare?"

"No," he replies hastily. "Not at all. For God's sake, don't apologize. I just didn't expect it."

"You know girls do it, right? It's not just guys."

His lips curve up. "I had heard. I just hadn't thought… I didn't expect…" He runs his fingers up my ribs and gives me a helpless look. "I think my brain's going to explode."

I chuckle. "It turns you on?"

"The thought of you sliding your hand under the covers and touching yourself? Now why on earth would you think that would turn me on?"

My pulse is picking up speed. It's the first time we've ever talked like this. Our relationship has been like a well-worn path, and all of a sudden I've turned off into the wilderness. I don't know where it's going to take me. But I'm filled with a sense of adventure.

My heart is racing, but he seems so in control. I want him to want me as much as I want him.

"Do you think of me?" I ask him, curious. "When you do it?" I fill with heat at the thought of him lying back, taking himself in hand, and stroking himself until he… Oh my.

His eyes are very dark in the soft light. His pupils are huge. "Yes."

I prop myself up on an elbow and lower my hand, so I'm drawing on his belly. A thin line of hair travels down from his navel, disappearing beneath the waistband of his trousers. I love the way guys wear their pants so low on their hips. "What do you think about?" I ask, running a finger along the top of the waistband.

He tips his head to the side, resuming drawing circles on my back. "What you look like naked. The shape of your breasts. What color your nipples are."

I shiver. "What else?"

"I think about kissing you. Touching you. Going down on you." His voice has turned husky. "I wonder what you taste like. And what sounds you make when you come."

I remind myself to breathe before I pass out. "Do you want to find out?"

"Fuck, yeah."

That's it—I've lit the fuse. He slides a hand into my hair, holds me there, and crushes his lips to mine.

Like when we were in the car, heat flares between us. This is no slow burn. And that's fine—I don't want hours of foreplay. I like the idea of spending forever kissing and touching and teasing each other toward the edge, but not tonight. I've waited long enough, and I want him, now.

I tear my lips away and push myself to my feet. Then, before he can move, I lift a leg over him and sink down so I'm astride him.

I don't give him the chance to exclaim. In seconds I'm kissing him again, and this time, on top, I'm able to take charge and give in to my passion, the way I've been dreaming about since the blinkers were removed from my eyes, and I realized what I'd been missing.

I wish I'd done this years ago… only it wouldn't have worked then. We had to wait for the stars to align. But now they have—a rare conjunction that is filling me with starlight.

Oh jeez, I think I'm still drunk. But I don't care. It's giving me Dutch courage. I feel nervous and excited and thrilled and relieved and mischievous all rolled into one. I want him so badly, I'm almost shaking with it. Please God, don't let anything happen to stop this. Don't let him change his mind. Let him want me, too.

Then he puts his hands on my knees, pushes my dress up my thighs so I can widen them, and he pulls me toward him. Now I'm nestled right against him, and for the first time I feel his erection through his trousers, long and hard against my tummy. And I realize everything's going to be all right.

"Mm," I murmur, moving until he's hitting the right spot. Oh yeah, right there. I rock my hips, and we both sigh.

This is heavenly, making out in the semi-darkness, in the warm room, with the sound of the ocean outside. I sink my hands into his hair and concentrate on kissing him, on delving my tongue into his mouth, tasting him, teasing his tongue with mine.

At the same time, he strokes my back, brushes his thumbs up my ribs, and then caresses beneath my breasts.

"I knew you weren't wearing a bra," he says, slightly exasperated.

I hold my breath as he slides his hands up to cup my breasts. He groans as he finds them liberated, and lets them rest in his palms, while he rolls the tips of my nipples with the pads of his thumbs. I catch my bottom lip between my teeth, continuing to slowly rock my hips. Mmm, that feels super-good.

"Em," he whispers as he kisses up to my ear. "You don't know how long I've dreamed about this."

I'd answer, but for a moment the Broca's area of my brain has ceased to work, removing the ability to string two words together. As he takes my nipples between his thumbs and forefingers and tugs, I moan, tipping back my head while he takes gentle bites of my neck and throat.

It's wonderful, but I need more, and I don't want to wait. "Let's do it here," I murmur, sliding my hands down to the button of his trousers. I like the idea of being on top. Of directing the pace.

But he chuckles and moves my hands aside. "Not this time."

"Why?"

"Because I said so." He puts his arms around me, holds me tightly, and moves to the edge of the seat. Then he stands and lowers my feet to the floor.

I pout. "I don't see why we couldn't stay there. Don't I have a say in it?"

"No." He begins to gather up my dress in his hands. "Because a) I want to feel you naked against me, b) I need to get a condom, and c) we need to take our time."

I let him lift the gown up my body and over my head. "You don't need to spend hours seducing me," I inform him. "I'm a sure thing."

He gives a short laugh as he places the dress carefully over the chair, then comes back to stand in front of me. His gaze caresses my bare breasts as he shrugs off his shirt. "It's not about that."

My hands are shaking a little, but I hook my fingers in my underwear, slide them down my legs, and take them off. "You don't have to impress me. I know women tell guys they need hours of foreplay, but I don't care if it doesn't take long."

I'm trying to help, but he gives me one of his impatient, slightly exasperated looks as he begins to undo his trousers. "You know when you're dancing with a guy, you're supposed to let him lead, right?"

"I like taking charge and bossing you around," I tease. "It's what I do. I don't see why that has to change now."

He takes off his trousers, then slides off his boxers. Now we're both completely naked. I glance down. Whoa. He has an erection and it's… my God, very impressive. Leander Knightley has a hard on for me. I think I might faint.

"Get on the bed," he says.

"No." I feel all tingly inside. I want to see how he reacts when I push him.

He cocks his head. "Do I need to tie you down on our first time?"

My heart gives a little bump. "Maybe."

He snorts, then picks me up as if I'm no heavier than a pillow and unceremoniously tosses me onto the mattress. My breath leaves me in a whoosh. He climbs on the bed, and before I can protest, he's straddled me, taken my hands, and pinned them above my head.

"Are you going to put me over your knee?" My pulse is racing now, despite my bravado. He's on top of me, naked, the root of his erection pressing against my mound. I tilt my hips up and exhale at the increased pressure in that sensitive area.

"Okay," he says, "so maybe we should get something clear now. If you've ever won an argument with me, it's because I've let you win. Because it amuses me, and I can't be bothered to argue with you. But in the bedroom, things are going to be different. In bed, I'm in charge."

Ooh, a dictatorial Knightley. Holy moly. I hadn't expected this power play. He's always so laid back and mild.

"We'll see," I say. But I'm melting inside.

He gives me a puzzled look. "We've waited a long time for this. Why do you want to rush it?"

I swallow. "The longer we take, the more likely it is that…"

"That what?"

"That you might change your mind."

He raises his eyebrows. "I'm not going to change my mind, Em."

"I know you have high morals, and you're worried about our age difference, and you don't want to take advantage of me when I've been feeling vulnerable. What if your principles take over at the last minute?"

"I consider myself a gentleman, but I'm not that fucking noble. You're not leaving this hotel room until I've fucked you senseless."

My jaw drops. The corners of his mouth go up. "Too much?" he asks.

"You're so confident," I say, with both admiration and envy. "I'm… nervous? Aren't you?"

"No. But then it's not my first time. You need to trust that I know what I'm doing."

"I do, but…"

He bends and kisses me, cutting off my words, then lifts to look at me again. "We're going to go slowly. You told me you pleasure yourself, so you know what happens when a woman gets aroused."

"Well, um, yeah, but—"

"It's your first time, Em. We want to make sure friction isn't an issue when we get going." He kisses me again. "I don't want to hurt you."

"I thought that was inevitable the first time."

"Not as I understand it. So… trust me, okay?"

I look into his eyes. *You're not leaving this hotel room until I've fucked you senseless.* Oh my God. I give a slow nod.

He smirks. "Good girl."

Ohhh… and now I'm turning molten inside, heated by his possessive stare.

He kisses me then, taking his time, his lips and tongue teasing mine for a while, before he finally releases my hands and starts kissing down my neck. He moves slowly, tasting as he goes, sucking gently, while his hands brush across my skin, as if he wants to touch every inch of me.

I don't move, afraid of breaking the spell, my arms above my head, and shiver as he trails his fingers down from my hands, over the sensitive skin of my underarms, and then down to my breasts. I close my eyes as he kisses a nipple, and catch my breath. My mouth opens, but no words come out.

Ohhh… That feels amazing… He traces the tip of his tongue around the edge, then sucks, gently at first, then a little harder, and I stir beneath him as I clench inside. He kisses across to the other nipple and does the same to that one, then goes back to the first. The curtains billow as the cool sea breeze pushes its way inside, blowing across the wet, sensitive skin, and I shudder.

He doesn't stop, though, continuing to tease me with his teeth, lips, and tongue, until I'm breathing heavily and groaning every time he sucks. Only then does he move down, placing kisses over my ribs, then down my belly. He stops to dip his tongue in my belly button, then, to my shock, continues down. Holy shit, he's going to…

He pushes my knees apart and then lifts and sinks between my legs.

"Relax," he says, brushing his hands on the tender skin of my inner thighs.

Relax? Seriously? All I can think is thank God I waxed and I never thought this would happen and I can't believe he's doing this…

And then all thoughts flee my mind as he slides his tongue down into my folds. Wow… oh my God… I cover my face with my hands, arching my back as he swirls his tongue over my clit and then sucks. Ohhh… I never thought… is he really… how does he know exactly…

It's like sinking slowly, sensually, into a tub of warm caramel. I lift my arms above my head again, wanting to purr like a cat. Mm, I can definitely come like this. Twice Knightley? Jesus. I'm never letting this man out of my bed. He's an expert. He gently teases my entrance with a finger, while he continues to lick and suck… I shiver as, way off in the distance, there's a roll of thunder, and the first signs of an orgasm begin the same way, in the depths of my belly, a gradual tightening of muscles deep inside me, I can feel it coming, and I hold my breath, waiting for it to hit…

And then he stops, lifts up, and moves up the bed to look down at me.

I glare at him, my chest heaving. "Why did you stop?"

He laughs and leans across to get his wallet. "Sorry. But it'll be worth it."

"Lee!" I smack his arm.

He continues to chuckle as he retrieves a condom and remove the wrapper. "I'm not torturing you on purpose. Well, maybe I am." He grins, then rolls the condom on as I watch, eyes wide. When he's done, he leans over me again and looks down. His eyes are dark and sultry.

He pushes up my knees. Reaching down, he guides himself so the tip of his erection presses against my entrance. Then he lowers down and kisses me. Oh, gross, I can smell myself on his lips. Oh, okay, that's actually quite sexy…

He lifts his head to look at me. "Ready?"

"Mm." I close my eyes, worried I'm tensing, and then he'll think I don't want to do this, and he'll stop…

He kisses me again. "Open your eyes."

I look up at him.

"Breathe in," he says.

I blink, then inhale.

He kisses my nose. "Breathe out."

I blow out the breath, long and slow, and as I do, he pushes his hips forward and slides inside me. Ooh. There's a millisecond of, not pain exactly, just tension, of being stretched. And then it's replaced by the sensation of him filling me, all the way up, until his hips meet the back of my thighs.

"Oh…" His brow creases. "Holy fuck, you're tight."

"Sorry."

"It wasn't a complaint." He pulls all the way out, then eases back again. "And you're very wet."

"Wow that's rude… Mmm…"

"Again, it wasn't a complaint." He touches my nose with his. "Okay?"

I look into his eyes and nod. "It didn't hurt at all."

"Good." He kisses me, and starts to move.

There's a storm coming outside—lightning flashes and thunder rumbles a few seconds later, lighting us up for a moment before plunging us into darkness again, while rain begins pattering on the window. But here in bed we're safe and warm, and all there is in the world is his hot mouth and muscular body and tight butt, while he moves inside me.

He takes his time, using long, slow thrusts, sometimes pulling right out before pushing all the way back in. He looks down occasionally, seeming to like watching the way he sinks into my body, before he returns to kissing me.

It's not how I thought it'd be. I thought it'd be hard and fast, and I was prepared for that. Not this gradual seduction. Not this tender, gentle, but sexy teasing of my senses as once again I feel an orgasm waiting in the wings.

And now I think he's finally beginning to lose his grip on the tight control he's had up until now, as he starts moving faster, and his kisses become harder, demanding rather than asking, his tongue plunging into my mouth, while his fingers tug on my nipples, making me groan.

It's so close… just out of my reach, and my teeth tug on my bottom lip as he lifts up onto his hands and looks down at me. He said I wouldn't be leaving until he'd fucked me senseless, and I begin to realize what he meant as he moves with purpose, maybe sure now that he's not going to hurt me.

"Oh God…" The words tumble from my lips again and again with each of his thrusts, and the muscles inside me begin to tighten. "Oh God…" I'm so close…

And then he shifts, moving up an inch, and suddenly with each thrust he's grinding against me, and that's it, that's enough to push me over the edge. I know my face and breasts are flushing red as heat sweeps over me, and then the orgasm slams into me like a train, pulse after pulse, intensified by the sensation of him deep inside me, and it's the best thing in the whole world, and I never want it to stop…

But then I discover something even better, as he shudders, his muscles tensing beneath my fingertips, and he comes inside me. Holy fuck… he's beautiful mid-climax, like a Greek god, and the only thing that's better than watching him is the knowledge that I caused this, I drove him to the edge. It's the best thing in the world.

Chapter Eighteen

Knightley

I finally open my eyes to see Em watching me with a smug smile.

"I did that," she says.

I blow out a long breath and rest my forehead on hers. "And you're very good at it."

"Aw. You once promised you'd never lie to me. I know I'm not going to be amazing on my first try, but I'll get better."

"I wasn't lying."

It's the truth. I know I'm old fashioned, and I believe it's the guy's job to direct the action in bed. I definitely believe that a woman's enjoyment in the sack has a direct correlation to the amount of attention the man pays to her. But even so, it's always nice when the girl is enthusiastic. I didn't leave Tia because she was uninterested in sex, but she was a bit… passive.

That was not a word I'd use to describe Em, though.

Her face and neck bear a sexy flush, her hair is mussed, her lips are blurred from her enthusiastic kisses, and she looks like it's her birthday, Christmas Day, and she's won the lottery all at the same time. The best thing was that she was very vocal, which never fails to turn me on.

I lower my lips to hers and give her a long kiss and then, as gently as I can, withdraw.

"Ooh," she says, drawing her legs up.

I dispose of the condom, then lie back. "Sore?"

She turns to face me. "No. Like you said, no friction is a good thing. I just feel like I've been riding a horse for eight hours."

I laugh and pull her close to me. "So you believe me now? You trust that I know what I'm doing?"

She kisses my chest. "Let's just say that if I was giving marks out of ten, I'd give you eleven."

"Is that all?"

She chuckles and rests her head on my shoulder. "I'm not a virgin anymore."

"That's true. Are you going to wear a black armband?"

"Hardly. I want to declare it from the rooftops. Sex is fantastic. Now I know why everyone's so obsessed with it."

"It is pretty good."

"Pretty good? It's fantastic. It's going to be my new hobby."

"Sex?"

"Yeah. Now I realize why there are so many words for it. Make love, bonk, screw, shag, fornicate, copulate, fuck—"

"Jesus."

"Are they all the same thing? I've always wondered."

"What do you mean?"

"What did we just do? Did we make love? Did we screw? Or did we fuck?" She looks genuinely interested.

I kiss her nose. I adore this girl. "We definitely made love."

"Oh. Maybe later you'll let me fuck you, then."

"Em!"

She laughs, then moves up a bit so she can kiss me. "I want to do it all," she whispers, brushing her lips across mine.

My pulse was slowing down, but now it picks up the pace again. I know I should say no, that this was the last time, but for some reason my mouth won't form the words.

"Every position," she clarifies. "Next time, I'm on top." She nips my bottom lip.

"Ow. What did I say to you about who's in charge?"

"I think we should take it in turns. Next time, I get to direct the action."

Again, she's surprised me, and I realize I'd seen myself as the benevolent older lover inducting his apprentice into the ways of lovemaking. But despite her lack of experience, she's obviously not going to be the shy young girl who relinquishes all responsibility.

"We'll see," I tell her, although I quite like the idea of her being on top.

She leans her chin on my chest. "I didn't think it would be like this."

"Like what?"

"Like it is in the movies."

I chuckle. "I guess that's a compliment."

"Oh definitely. I thought it would be hard and fast."

"Sweetheart, that *was* hard and fast."

"Was it?"

"Pretty much. The whole thing's only taken us… what? Ten minutes?"

"It felt like hours."

"Then you're very easy to please."

"I am," she says. "It never takes me longer than a minute or two."

My head spins. "You have to stop telling me stories about touching yourself. I'm almost a pensioner, remember? My heart can't take it."

She giggles. "Wait till I show you. We'll have to have oxygen on standby."

We both laugh, then exchange a slow kiss.

"Mmm." She licks her lips, then presses them to my shoulder. "Twice Knightley… when can we go again?"

"Jesus, Em. I need a few minutes to recover."

"Have you ever had a threesome?"

"What the fuck?"

"I'm curious. I've never been able to ask you before."

"No, I've never had a threesome."

"I don't know that I'd like one in real life, but I fantasize about it sometimes. Do you?"

I daren't start talking about fantasies or I'll never get to sleep tonight. "Um… sometimes."

"Do you dream about another guy or girl?"

"For God's sake… go to sleep."

She sighs and lets me roll her away so I can spoon her. I yawn and nuzzle behind her ear. "You smell nice," I murmur.

"Thank you. For everything."

"You're welcome." I close my eyes and it's only milliseconds before I fall asleep.

*

When I wake, the room is filled with light.

I also appear to have a massive erection, caused by someone massaging me gently with long, firm strokes.

I open my eyes and look straight into Em's.

"What's the story, morning glory?" she says.

I blink. "Hello. Enjoying yourself?"

"Very. It wasn't my doing. It was like this when I got here. Seemed a shame not to take advantage of it. Want me to stop?"

I yawn and stretch, swelling in her hand. "Not at all. Just be aware it's going to have consequences."

"I'm banking on it."

I chuckle. "You slept?"

"I did, more than I usually do. And now I'm all refreshed and energetic." She moves closer and kisses me, and a wave of contentment rolls over me as she moves her lips across mine. We forgot to draw the curtains last night, and the morning sun is already warm and bright. I can smell the breakfast that's cooking in the restaurant below us and the salty scent of the sea, mixed with the sweet, flowery scent of Em herself. I run my fingers down her back, and she murmurs and stirs beneath my touch. Her skin is like satin, and her hair is soft as silk. She's all womanly textures, round breasts, rose-petal lips, emerald-green eyes. And maybe the best thing about being with her is that I don't have to be someone else. I don't have to try to impress her. She already knows all my faults, all my bad points, and she's here anyway. It gives me a feeling of liberation, like the seagulls must feel as they soar in the currents outside.

"After this, we'll have breakfast," Em says, breaking away to reach over for the packet I left on the bedside table last night. "I hear the Breakfast Boner is the new option at the burger joint." She laughs at her own joke and comes back with a condom, strips off the duvet, then sits astride me. "Will you show me how to put it on?"

"Already? Girl, I know you're eager, but we've got to have some foreplay…"

"I've been having foreplay for five minutes. You're surprisingly difficult to wake up." She leans forward and kisses me. "Honestly, I'm ready. I told you, I don't take long. Trust me. I know what I'm doing. Kinda." She sits back up and waves the packet at me.

Too turned on to argue, I give in, take off the wrapper, show her how to check the condom is the right way up, and then roll it on. I like the way she watches intently, eager to learn.

"Move up a bit," I tell her. I guide myself beneath her, stroking the tip of my erection through her folds and making her purr. Then, when I'm just entering her, I lie back on the pillows. "There you go. You do it. Nice and slow."

She moves her hips and, bottom lip caught between her teeth, pushes down gently. Lifts, then sinks onto me a little more, coating me with her moisture. Then, finally, the third time, she lowers all the way down.

"Mm." She closes her eyes, and I imagine her enjoying this new sensation of letting her body adjust to the strange feeling of having a man deep inside her.

I cup her breasts, brushing her nipples with my thumbs before gently tugging them. She opens her eyes, and a beautiful smile spreads over her face as she starts to rock her hips.

"I can feel you," she whispers. "All the way up. It's amazing."

I curl a hand in her hair and pull her down for a kiss, enjoying the feel of her breasts pressed against my chest, and the way her hair falls around my head like a curtain while she delves her tongue into my mouth.

When she pushes herself up again, her face and chest are lit with the same gorgeous pink flush she had yesterday. "I like this," I murmur, running a finger across her chest, and she gives me a sleepy smile. I move a hand over her tummy, and slide my thumb down into her folds to stroke her clit. She purrs again, arching her back, so I take her hand and put it where mine was. She gives me a shy smile, then begins to arouse herself, tipping her head so her hair falls down her back.

Yesterday, although I made sure to spread any drinks I had throughout the day, and I also had plenty of water, I was definitely very mellow by the end. This morning, now the last vestiges of sleep are disappearing, I feel much more awake and in the moment. The sun falls across Em, coating her with gold. I can't quite believe this is happening.

"I like this position," she murmurs, running her hands over my shoulders and chest. "I like being in charge." She gives me an impish smile.

Filled with delight at her obvious enjoyment, I put an arm around her waist and flip her onto her back.

"Aw," she says, pink-cheeked. "I was enjoying that."

I withdraw carefully and circle a finger in the air. "Turn over."

"Make me."

"Happy to." I catch her arm and pull it across her so she has to roll over, then move between her thighs, and nudge them apart with my knees.

"Wow," she says. "That happened fast."

"I aim to please."

She props herself on her elbows and looks over her shoulder at me. Her green eyes are hot and mischievous. "Are you going to fuck me now?"

I roll my eyes and position myself beneath her. "Whatever the lady wants."

"Yes, I want—-oh!"

With one thrust, I'm inside her. Her fingers clutch at the pillow, and she buries her face in it.

I stop, worried I've hurt her, and bends to kiss her shoulder. "Okay?"

She nods, not lifting her face. "Yes," she squeaks.

I chuckle, then thrust again, burying myself deep into her, and she shudders.

"Get comfortable," I instruct, heat rushing through me. "And mind your head on the headboard."

"Oh my God…"

Smirking, I set up a fast pace, at the same time sliding a hand beneath her so I can stroke between her legs. She moans and spreads them further, and now there's nothing to stop me taking my pleasure from her. I'm conscious she might be a little sore from yesterday, and the last thing I want to do is make it uncomfortable for her, but to be honest she's wet enough again to ensure there's no friction, and she certainly doesn't appear to be in pain. When she eventually lifts her face from the pillow, her cheeks are rosy, her eyes are closed, and she emits an emphatic "Ohhh…" every time I thrust.

As she promised, she doesn't take long to arouse, and it's only a minute or two before she's breathing with deep gasps and pushing back against me. I hold onto the headboard with a hand and ride her through her orgasm as it hits, groaning when her young, strong muscles clamp around me. Jesus, she's tight. If I had any hope of holding on, that rapidly flies out of the window. Half a dozen more thrusts, and my climax hits me, everything tightening and pulsing as I come hard. Whoa. That felt as if I hadn't had sex for six months and it's only been about five hours.

My muscles finally relax, and I sink down onto her and bury my face in her hair where it lies on the pillow. She's breathing heavily too. The warm room has turned our skin damp, and we're now stuck together.

"You're squishing me," she says eventually, trying to move.

"Don't care."

"Ahhh…" She groans and collapses into the pillow. "I'm melting…"

"Serves you right. What did you expect, waking me up like that?"

"I thought we'd have a nice, sedate little session. I didn't know you were in this sort of mood."

I nuzzle her ear. "Then you shouldn't have been so appetizing."

"Have you decided what you're having for breakfast?"

That makes me laugh, then wince. I withdraw, get rid of the condom, then come back and roll her over so she's facing me.

"You," I murmur, kissing her. "You're all the nourishment I need."

She returns it, giving a long, luxurious sigh. "I'd like to say the same, but I'm betting the others are down in the restaurant by now."

"I really don't care. We'll order room service. I don't want to share you with anyone."

She wrinkles her nose at me. "You're not what I expected."

I move back a little so I can look at her. "What do you mean?"

"You're so placid normally. So laid back. I didn't expect you to be so… forceful."

"It's a prehistoric urge. I was close to dragging you up here by your hair."

"Don't mock me. I'm serious."

I rest my head on a hand. "I meant it to sound sexy, but it makes me sound like a Neanderthal. I hope that's not my father coming out."

She smiles, but her eyes are thoughtful. "I'm sure it's not."

"Sorry, I didn't mean to bring the mood down."

"No, it's okay. I was thinking anyway, you know, about the abnormal sexual behaviors that HD can cause, and hoping I haven't set it off. Is that silly?"

I kiss her nose. "I don't think one partner counts as being promiscuous."

"No, I suppose not."

"You're allowed to enjoy sex, Em. It doesn't make you abnormal."

She threads her fingers through mine. "You said in the car the other day that it's okay to want to try things."

"That's right."

"You said about having sex outdoors, or watching other people doing it."

"Yeah."

"I'm guessing you don't mean looking through the keyhole."

"No, Em. But watching a bit of porn is okay. It can give you ideas of new things to try."

She moistens her lips. "You also mentioned tying your partner up."

"Yeah…"

"Do you mean tying me up? Or being tied up?"

"You, definitely."

Her lips curve up at my instant admission. "I see. You don't enjoy being handcuffed to the bed?"

"I'm not keen on giving up control, as you might have noticed. I like directing the action."

"But you didn't mind what I did this morning?"

I smile. "No. That was just fine."

We study each other for a while, quietly, in the warmth and peace of the room.

"We still have a few ghosts to put to rest, don't we," she states.

"Yeah."

"We didn't really take that into account last night."

"No. You were too hot."

She chuckles. "So what do we do now? Go back to normal?"

I don't say anything for a moment. Last night, she told me she was worried about losing my friendship if things didn't work out between us. I should have thought about that more, but I was drunk and tired and I just wanted to get her into bed. But the thing is, I'm not sure I can go back to normal. How do I do that? How do I watch her at work, with our friends, and not picture what's happened between us? How do I watch her date other men and not wish it were me?

"Don't look so worried," she says, kissing two fingers and then placing them on my lips. "I'm not going to freak out on you, whatever happens. I promise."

"You think I'm going to tell you that we shouldn't do this again."

"Well, yeah. Aren't you?"

Outside, a bird calls right by the window, while further down the road a car beeps its horn. But neither of us turns to look. Instead, we lie there in the sun, watching each other.

"I've been an idiot," I say eventually.

"How so?"

"By thinking we could go back to normal. In my defense, I didn't expect to feel like this."

"Like what?"

I hesitate. Then we both smile.

"I've got an idea," she says. "Why don't we postpone any decision making until after you've seen your dad? And I need to wait until I take the test, too."

"It won't change how I feel about you," I say.

Her smile fades. "Maybe. But you have to know, if it's positive, that's it. I will not enter a relationship knowing what's going to happen to me."

I frown. "Em…"

"That's my decision. And I'm not going to change it, no matter how I feel about you."

Her eyes are clear, like beautiful river pools.

No matter how I feel about you. I wonder what she means by that.

"Okay," I say. "We wait."

"I'm having the third counseling session on Wednesday," she says. "And the test soon after that, hopefully."

"You don't think Susie will talk you out of it?"

"Nope. When are you seeing your dad?"

"February the fifteenth."

"I don't know how long the test will take to come through. It could be a couple of weeks." Her gaze drops to my mouth. "Until then…"

I smile. "Yeah?"

"I think we should have sex as often as we can."

That makes me laugh. But I have to add, "Don't you think it will make it harder to end things if we have to?"

"Honestly? No. It's going to hurt like fuck if it comes to an end, no matter how many times we sleep together."

"We probably shouldn't have started," I say, but she shakes her head immediately.

"It's not a good enough reason not to have done it. I refuse to regret it." She bites her lip then. "Please don't regret it."

"I don't. I won't. I swear."

She looks at her phone. "It's nearly nine. We should probably think about checking out. We could get some breakfast in town."

"Yeah, okay." I pull her to me. "In a minute."

I roll onto my back, bringing her with me, and we indulge in a long, sensual kiss that brings me out in goosebumps.

I have to face it: I'm just crazy about this girl. It's already too late for me.

Chapter Nineteen

Emily

"Morning!" Dad meets me in the hallway, carrying a large box.

"Hey." I give him a bright smile. "How's it going?"

"Yeah, good, starting the cleanup. Did you manage to find somewhere to sleep?"

"Um, yes. I kipped on someone's sofa. No problem at all. Had a great night. Lots of sleep. Very relaxing."

He meets my gaze, and slowly starts to smile as my face warms.

"I see," he says. "And how's Knightley? Did he get plenty of sleep too?"

Now my face glows like a furnace. "Oh my God. Just kill me now. Why am I so useless at lying?"

He laughs and leans over to kiss my cheek. "Glad you enjoyed the wedding. Now prepare yourself. Bella will jump on you as soon as you go in the living room and drag you in to help."

"I thought she and John were heading off this morning?"

"They are. You know what she's like. She'll run around directing the action until he forces her out of the house."

I chuckle and let him carry his box outside. I watch him go, surprised at his reaction to discovering that I probably shared a bed with Knightley. I had wondered whether he might tell me I should wait until I get my test results, but if anything he seemed… relieved. For the first time, it occurs to me how worried he must be. He had no idea when he married my mother that she had HD, or that his children had a fifty-fifty chance of developing it. He's seen firsthand what an effect it can have on a marriage. I thought he might have preferred me to remain single, but maybe he doesn't want me to be alone, either.

Musing on that, and conscious that Aunt Daisy might still be in my room, I go through to Dad's bedroom and drop my bag and my bridesmaid's dress off there. I'm back in shorts and tee today, my hair pulled up in its usual scruffy bun. I have had a shower, though. I stop and study my reflection, my lips curving up as I remember the very small shower cubicle that could only just accommodate two people. We had to squash up tightly. I've never had so much fun with a shower puff.

Do I look any different? I study my bright eyes, my pink cheeks. Last night, when we made love, Knightley ran a finger over the blush that consumed the top half of my body and told me, "I like this." I touch my hand there, remembering how it felt when he kissed me.

I should be cross with myself that I gave in and slept with him, because I was convinced it would complicate things. But I don't, because it hasn't. I feel… liberated. And it feels right. Maybe because he doesn't seem to regret it either. *I've been an idiot*, he said, *thinking we could go back to normal. In my defense, I didn't expect to feel like this.*

I don't know what the future holds. But right now, I feel excited and happy, and I'm not going to be cross with myself for that.

I go back to the living room to discover it full of noise and bodies. Most of the family guests who stayed the night are there, having breakfast. Lulu's also there, with half a dozen of her staff. They're carrying plants out, taking balloons down, dismantling tables outside, and stacking chairs. Bella's in the middle of it all with a cloth and a spray can of polish, going around behind them and cleaning up, while Minnie trails behind her as if she's trying to help.

"What are you doing?" I walk up to Bella, take the cloth out of her hand, and put it on the table. "I'll do that later."

"I feel like I should help." She looks around distractedly. "I'm not good at observing."

I chuckle. "Come for a walk with me." I lead her out into the garden, clicking my fingers for Minnie to follow us. It's still busy here, but we walk to the end of the lawn, where the path to the orchard starts and it's a little quieter. It's a beautiful morning, fresh from last night's shower. "Where's John?"

"He's taken the girls out for breakfast. Our flight isn't until four."

"You should have gone with him," I scold.

"We'll have five days together soon. I wanted to make sure the house is back to normal for Dad." Her gaze returns to me. "And you."

My eyebrows rise. "I don't care about the mess."

"I know. But you've got enough on your plate at the moment without tidying up." To my surprise, she puts her arms around me and hugs me.

I return it, smiling. "What's this all about? Are these post-wedding hormones?"

"Kinda. You've been so good to me the last few weeks. I know I've been hard work. I just want to say that I do appreciate it."

"You told me that at the wedding yesterday, don't you remember?"

"Did I? No. I'd had quite a bit of champagne. I think my brain stopped functioning around four-thirty."

"You called yourself a dragon," I say, smiling, moving back as she lowers her arms.

"Oh yes… I do remember now. And I said I couldn't wait until we changed places and you were marrying the love of your life." Her gaze turns mischievous. "How is Knightley?"

"Jeez. Have you spoken to Dad?"

"No, why?"

"Doesn't matter."

She cups my cheek with a hand. "Grab him with both hands, Em."

"He's generously proportioned, but he's not that big."

That makes her laugh. "You know what I mean. You only get one chance at life."

"I guess."

She lowers her hand, studying my face. "When's your third counseling session?"

"Wednesday."

"You're having the test then?"

I nod.

"I hope it's negative," she says fervently.

My throat tightens. "Me too."

"What are you going to do if it's not?"

It's the first time we've ever discussed it. Normally, she refuses to talk about it.

"I don't know," I murmur.

"You won't…" She swallows. "Do anything silly?"

She means like Mum. Sudden tears sting my eyes, and I shake my head.

"If it's positive, we'll find a way to deal with it," she says. "We'll work together."

I take her hand and squeeze it. "We shouldn't be talking about it now. Not the morning after your wedding. You need to go away and spend this time with your family." I smile then. "I wish you'd left the girls with me. You and John could have spent all week in bed then."

"We've been sleeping together since I was nineteen. We're just glad to have a lie in and someone to make dinner for us."

"I'm surprised you waited that long."

She grins, and then her smile fades. "It wasn't long after Mum and Dad told us all about her HD. It was such a shock, and at the time, all I could think was that I wanted to make the most of my life before I found out."

"Didn't you worry at all… about what will happen if you get it, when you develop the symptoms…"

"No. I'm not going to deny myself love and sex because of what might happen," she says vehemently, adding, "and you shouldn't either."

I'd assumed she put it to the back of her mind and didn't think about it, but I realize now how stupid I've been. Of course she's thought about it. "Why haven't you talked to me about this before?" I ask.

"I don't know. I suppose I hoped you weren't thinking about it too much. Which was dumb of me."

"Dad told me both the girls were accidents."

She gives a short laugh. "Yeah. Both times were a shock. That's why John's had the snip."

"But you decided not to get them tested?"

She inhales and blows out a long breath. "That was a really hard decision to make. Both John and I talked to Dad a lot about it. I mean, you know me, I'm not religious, and neither's John particularly. I understand that terminating a pregnancy is necessary sometimes. But we both feel that some things are meant to be. I don't know whether you'll have kids, but when you find out you're pregnant, even when you're only six weeks and the fetus is the size of a tadpole, you suddenly realize it's alive. And it has all this potential—it's going to grow into a thinking, feeling person. Your son or daughter. And the thought of ending that just because it might not be perfect felt wrong."

She's simplifying it tremendously, because it's not only about your child being perfect. It's not about terminating a pregnancy because the child has brown hair instead of blond, or even because it's a girl and not a boy when you already have six girls. It's choosing to give birth to a child that you know is going to struggle in life because it has a disease.

But I think about what Knightley said, *Maybe Bella and John don't consider a baby with HD as having something 'wrong with it'.* I'd felt ashamed at the time, and it's definitely made me think.

Anyway, I'm not going to argue with her now, the day after her wedding. How can I, when her girls are so beautiful? I stop and hug her again, and we stand there like that for a moment in the sunshine before breaking apart, wiping away tears, and laughing.

"Go on," I tell her, "go and find your family. I'll sort out everything here."

"Are you sure?"

"Of course. Lulu's organizing most of it anyway. I'll be fine."

"All right." Her face lights up.

"Have an amazing time."

"Yeah, we will." She turns and runs back across the lawn, then disappears inside.

I look at Minnie, who's stopped sniffing at the lawn and is now looking up at me expectantly. "Come on then," I tell her. "We've got things to do."

I spend a couple of hours clearing up the breakfast things and talking to family members who are gradually getting ready to leave. A few from the South Island or Australia, including Aunt Daisy, are staying for another night, but they're going out for the day to look around Waitangi and the Bay. They've booked themselves a trip on a boat through the Hole in the Rock, and won't be back until after six p.m.

Once they've left, I tidy up the bedrooms, clean the bathrooms, change the beds, and make sure everyone has clean towels. I also transfer Aunt Daisy's things to one of the vacated rooms so I can have my own room back.

Around one p.m., everyone stops to eat some of the leftovers for lunch, and I make tea and coffee and hand out cold drinks while I chat to Lulu and the others.

By this time, the sun is high in the sky, so I cover myself in lotion, don a baseball cap, and spend a while going around the lawn with a pick-up stick and a black bag, collecting all the rubbish.

All this time, I think about Knightley, and what transpired between us last night. And again this morning. It's impossible not to think about it. I might have been a virgin, but I wasn't completely innocent. Nearly every movie and series going today contains sex, so I knew what to expect. But I assumed the sort of passion you see on screen is just fiction. I've read enough Reddit threads to know that many women find sex less than satisfactory.

But it wasn't just satisfactory. It was fucking amazing.

I shouldn't have done it, though. Because now I know what I'm missing. And I want to do it again.

I think about how he took charge, turning me onto my front before thrusting inside me. He told me that he likes to take control. It was fun to fight him, but it might also be fun to play along with that. Hmmm…

I scold myself and grumble as I pick up the litter. When Knightley and I parted, we didn't organize to see each other again. I think he felt as awkward as I did, unsure how far we should take this over the next few weeks. I'll see him at work, of course, but I don't know whether he'll suggest meeting up again. It would be better if we didn't.

To hell with that. I want to go to bed with him again. Desperately. Every cell in my body yearns for it. But I'm going to have to wait at least until tomorrow and I see him again.

Sighing, I take out my frustration by stabbing the litter with the pick-up stick until the lawn is finally clear.

By this point, Lulu's team has finished collecting all the rented furniture, and everything's packed up in their van. Dad, who's back from taking Bella, John, and the girls to the airport, thanks them for everything, and then the van trundles off, leaving the house peaceful for the first time in what feels like weeks.

"I bet you're glad it's all over," I say as we clean up the plates from lunch and begin washing them up.

"It has been stressful at times," he admits, "but it was nice having the place busy again. It's very quiet when it's just the two of us."

I dry a plate and put it in the rack. I know what he means. When I was young, especially when he and Mum started fostering children, Hartfield was a hive of activity. There was always someone yelling or running around, always sport being played in the garden, and the TV was continually on. The fridge door was constantly being opened, and the smell of Mum's baking permanently filled the air. But gradually, his children and the Knight boys have drifted away until I'm the last girl standing.

I should really get my own place, too, but I can't face the thought of leaving him on his own.

"You shouldn't let that stop you moving out, though," he says as if reading my mind.

"Why should I have to pay rent to someone else when Hartfield has so many bedrooms?"

"It didn't stop the others leaving," he points out. "Sometimes it's about having your own space. Your independence."

"Independence is overrated. I like having my dad around to do stuff for me."

He chuckles. "Fair enough. But one day, maybe in the not-too-distant future, you'll want your own space with someone. When that happens, I don't want you to be worried about leaving me."

"Who's going to watch *Game of Thrones* with me if I leave?"

"Your partner?" he asks, raising an eyebrow.

I snort. "I don't need a partner."

"Em, there are things you need that I can't provide."

"Like what?"

He just looks at me. Then his gaze slides behind me, and he smiles.

I look over my shoulder, and a shock goes through me, as sharp as if I've been stung by a bee, or I've picked up static. Knightley is leaning against the wall, hands in his pockets, watching me. He smiles now and pushes off, walking a few steps into the kitchen.

"Hello," he says.

"Hey." Dad tips the dishwater away and wipes his hands. "Have you been down at HWH?"

"Yeah. A boat brought in a seal. Its flipper had been chopped up pretty bad by a propeller, I think." He's talking to Dad, but he's looking at me.

My mind has gone completely blank. I can't think of a single thing to say. He's changed since this morning, and he's now wearing a tight All Blacks' rugby top and faded jeans. He's left his Converses by the front door, and his feet are bare. His hair is ruffled. I could put him on a cracker and crunch him up.

His gaze slides to Dad, then back to me as his amusement grows. Dad clears his throat and says, a little too loudly, "Okay, well I'm taking Minnie out to the vineyard. I'll be back in an hour." He walks past me and gives Knightley a wry look, calls for the Lab, then leaves via the front door.

Knightley looks at me, lips twisted. "You okay?"

I nod.

He walks up to me, takes a strand of hair, and tucks it behind my ear. "You're all sun-kissed," he murmurs. "You're like a snippet of summer."

I study his face, wishing I could explain the longing within me, but I don't know how to put it into words.

He clears his throat. "I just wanted to make sure you were all right. And say thanks for last night. And, you know, I was passing, so I thought I'd call in, make sure everything was good here, and—"

"You want to go to bed?" I ask, finally finding my voice.

Relief washes over his features. "God, yes."

We both start laughing, and I grab his hand and pull him out to the corridor and along to my room. Halfway there, I rip off my T-shirt and toss it away. He does the same, stripping off the All Blacks' top. I tug down my shorts and step out of them, still walking. He grabs me and flips open the catch on my bra, and I toss it away. He cups my breasts and kisses me for the first time, and I return it hungrily, backing into my room.

He closes the door with his foot, then turns me and presses me up against the door as he crushes his lips to mine. Ohhh… it's a heavenly kiss, full of heat and passion, mmm… My blood thunders through my veins and I arch my back as he teases my nipples with his thumbs. All day, I've been dreaming about this… I want him so badly…

"Take these off," he murmurs, tugging at my underwear.

"Yes, sir," I whisper, removing them immediately.

His lips curve up. "You're learning." He drops to his knees before me, trailing his lips down over my tummy as he lifts one of my legs over his shoulder. Then, without missing a beat, he slides his tongue into my folds.

"Aaahhh…" I clutch at his hair, pleasure shooting through me. "Mmm, that feels so good."

He growls his approval, strokes up my inner thigh with his right hand, then slips two fingers beneath me. Gently, he inserts them, and I close my eyes as he moves them inside me. Ooh, I like that… Oh yeah…

He does that for a while, licking, sucking, teasing, and it's not long before I feel the first flickers of tension deep inside. "Stop," I demand, pushing him away. He laughs and gets up, then kisses me on the mouth, hot and hard.

I turn and back to the bed, then climb on. He takes a foil packet out of his wallet, unzips his jeans, pushes his boxers down, and rolls the condom on. Then, without undressing, he gets on the bed and leans over me. Ooh, he's going to do it in his jeans. I don't think I've ever seen anything so hot.

He presses the tip of his erection into me, pushes forward, and in one smooth move he's right inside me.

I gasp, and he takes the opportunity to sweep his tongue into my mouth, which makes me moan.

"Yeah," he mutters, his voice husky. "Tell me what you like."

"You," I whisper, "everything about you. You're so fucking sexy."

He laughs and thrusts hard. "You've got a filthy mouth."

I wrap my legs around his waist. "Maybe you should punish me for it."

He catches my hands and pins them above my head. "Maybe I will."

I give him my best girlish pout. "I've been naughty, Mr. Knightley. I'm so very, very bad…"

He stops and gives me one of his exasperated, you're-driving-me-mad looks, only unlike usual, this one is full of sexy heat.

I blow him a kiss and open my thighs a little, letting him sink deeper into me.

He closes his eyes for a moment, pushing forward, stretching me and making me groan. Then he begins to move again, grinding against me with each thrust.

Still pinned there, all I can do is take it, and I give myself over to the sensations spiraling through me. Oh my God, why did I wait until I was twenty-one to do this?

"Oh fuck… oh fuck…" I can't stop the exclamation, as if he's forcing it out of me.

He grunts and his eyes gleam. I think he likes me talking dirty.

"Yeah…" I say softly, "oh God, yeah, fuck me harder, come on, fill me up, I'm so hot for you, fuck me into next week…"

That's definitely doing it for him. There's nothing like it… To have him right inside me, his mouth on mine… his muscular body taut above me… To know he's going to take me right to the edge and push me over, and there's nothing I can do about it… That thought makes everything clench, and I say his name in a long moan that's muffled by his mouth as he plunges his tongue inside, as if he wants to consume my pleasure, while he rides me through it.

I'm just drifting down to earth when he comes too, tightening, jerking, and then giving a deep groan as he shudders and spills, then finally rests his forehead on my shoulder.

We stay like that for about thirty seconds, catching our breath, before he finally withdraws and then collapses on the bed beside me.

"You're trying to kill me," he says, gasping. "You're actually trying to assassinate me with sex, aren't you? Jesus…"

I look up at the ceiling, and smile.

Chapter Twenty

Knightley

The next morning is the weekly Monday meeting at Hartfield. I arrive at eight as usual, and spend a while checking on my patients in the Wing, reading the reports from the vet assistant who was on during the night, and working out which animals need surgery or other treatment that day. Then, at ten to nine, I wander into the meeting room. Rob's already there, working on his laptop, but the others have yet to arrive.

"Morning," I say, taking a seat.

"Morning." He finishes typing, then leans back. "What's up?"

"Not much. Someone brought in a kiwi found on the roadside. Hit by a car."

"Aw. Will it make it?"

"Dunno yet. I'll do what I can."

He nods. "Enjoy the wedding?"

"It went well didn't it?" I glance over at the door as Naomi comes in with a couple of coffee plungers that she places on the table by the door, next to the mugs, milk, and sugar. "Nice to have it at the house," I add as she pours out three mugs.

"Yeah. If I was ever to get hitched, I think I'd like to have it there," Rob says.

"You?" I snort. "The lucky woman would have to have skin like plate armor."

"What do you mean?"

Naomi laughs and brings the mugs over, placing one before me before taking Rob's over to him. "He means you're a tad grumpy, Rob."

I chuckle. "Understatement of the year."

"Bollocks," Rob says.

"Kinda proving my point," I tell him. "You didn't use to be like this."

"That's because his leg is getting worse," Naomi says.

My eyebrows rise. He hasn't mentioned it. "Is that true?" I ask him.

"No."

She puts a plate of homemade biscuits in front of him. "Don't glare at me. Knightley's your brother and he should know how you're feeling. Look, I made some ANZAC biscuits for you. Coated them in chocolate, too."

When we first arrived at Hartfield, we used to help Angela make them. I can still remember her reading out her list of ingredients, including rolled oats, flour, sugar, butter, golden syrup, and desiccated coconut, and we would all have to search in the cupboards and bring them back to the table. They've been his favorites ever since. Naomi obviously knows this and has made them for him. She must be worried about him.

"Stop fussing," he grumbles, but he takes one anyway.

"Are you seeing anyone about it?" I ask him.

"No point." He dips the biscuit into his coffee. "They'll only offer more painkillers."

"It'd be a start if you took any," Naomi says. "Don't dunk those, they get soggy quickly."

"Stop nagging." He lifts the biscuit, and half of it promptly drops back into his coffee. "For fuck's sake."

She makes an exasperated noise in her throat as I laugh, and passes him a spoon so he can fish it out.

"You're not taking any painkillers?" I ask him. "Why?"

"Because after a while they stop working, and then you need to take more, and I don't want to become dependent on them." He tosses the spoon onto the plate and shifts in his chair. I know him well enough to know how bad the pain must be. But it's his life, and I understand him not wanting to rely on drugs.

"By the way," I say, changing the subject, "I got an email from the prison. I'm going to see Dad on the fifteenth at eleven a.m."

Naomi looks up from her coffee at me, then looks at Rob. Oh… so he hasn't told her about Dad. I'm surprised; I know she's only his assistant, but they seem to get on well, and I thought he might have confided in her.

He doesn't look at her now, and just gives a short nod. "Let me know how it goes."

"I will." I decide not to add anything else as the door opens and people start filing in. I shouldn't have mentioned it in front of Naomi. Rob looks at me, and I mouth, "Sorry." He gives a small smile and a little shrug; he's not annoyed. He's just a very private person, and I guess he doesn't want everyone knowing his business.

Over the next five minutes, the others arrive—Gabe, in his white lab coat, Frankie, Lorelei, Finn Weston, and the other two vets at Hartfield, Joel and Max. The vet assistants and lab assistants won't be joining us, as it's just senior staff, but I'm not surprised when the door opens once more and Em appears, as the others tend to include her in meetings like this because she knows so much about the running of Hartfield.

"Morning," she says, letting the door shut behind her. "Sorry I'm late. I slept through the alarm." She glances along the table, sees me, and our eyes meet briefly before she turns away and pours herself a coffee.

"Unlike you to sleep in," Frankie says, amused. "The organization of the wedding finally catch up with you?"

"Yeah." Em takes the last free chair on the other side of the table from me, one seat down. She's wearing khaki-colored cargo pants that sit low on her hips, and an olive-green vest. Unusually for her, she's braided her hair into one long plait that hangs over her shoulder, and she's applied a little makeup—a touch of eyeliner, and pink gloss on her lips.

"You look nice," Lorelei says. "Something going on today?"

"No," Em says breezily. "Just fancied a change."

I sip my coffee, hiding a smile. She's done it for me. Warmth spreads through me. I'd say it's incredibly sweet, but there's nothing sweet about the raunchy woman who sighed my name as she came yesterday afternoon.

She glances at me. I let my lips curve up. She looks around the table, then drops her gaze to her notepad, pressing her lips together.

"Thanks for coming, everyone," Rob says. "We might as well get started. Did you all get the agenda? Good. Hopefully we won't keep you long today. As you can see, first up is the latest financial report. Then I'd like to cover the Waitangi Open Day. Gabe wants to talk about a new supply schedule. Then we'll cover Any Other Business, okay?"

Everyone nods. I watch Em nibble the end of her pen, and try not to think about kissing her, and the beautiful red flush appearing on her face and chest.

Someone clears their throat, and I look to my right to see Frankie holding out the plate of biscuits to me. She's obviously been doing it for a while, and I guess she's observed me watching Em. She gives me a mischievous grin. I return it with a wry look and take a chocolate ANZAC.

"Naomi's giving out copies of the report," Rob says, as she moves around the table, handing us all a document. "As you can see, it's been a tough month. The new storage shed was more expensive than we thought, and there have also been repairs to the office block after the high winds, the construction of a new walkway to the car park, and increased staffing costs over the summer period to cope with the rise in animal casualties."

"Wow." Gabe studies the figures, then looks up at Rob. "We didn't even break even this month?"

"No. February's going to be tight, too. Waitangi Day brings an influx of tourists as well as Aucklanders on their boats, which always means more injured sea creatures. And also, some sad news—I found out yesterday that Kohanga is closing down."

I stare at him, startled, as everyone around the table exclaims. Kohanga—Maōri for nest—is the biggest bird sanctuary in the North Island, not far from Auckland. I knew it had struggled financially over the last few years, but its closure is a real shock.

"Fuck," Gabe says, summarizing all our thoughts.

"That's incredibly sad," Em says.

"It means more work for Hartfield," Max comments. "Which is good and bad, I guess."

Rob nods. "Obviously, on a purely selfish note, it means increased exposure for us, as Kohanga have already said they'll be directing people up here. But that also means increased workload, and greater pressure on our resources. Do we have the capacity to take on more patients?" He looks at me.

I hesitate. "A few, but we're already busier than we anticipated. The Wing is nearly always full as it is."

"I was thinking about that," Em says. "Since I reorganized the large storage shed, the smaller sheds by the Wing are nearly empty. I think I can find space for the last few boxes in the bigger shed, and convert the two smaller ones into another Wing."

"We'd need more cages," Joel says.

"I'm pretty sure I can get some for a reduced price from the dog kennels if we don't mind second-hand," she replies.

"More animals means either longer hours for existing staff or taking on new vets and assistants," Frankie points out.

"I thought about that as well," Em says. "I wondered what you all thought about approaching the local high school and asking for volunteers."

We all glance around, unsure. "I don't know," I say doubtfully, "having kids around means we'd have to allocate staff for supervision."

"What if one of the animals was to injure them?" Joel asks. "We'd have to think about upping the insurance and getting parental permission. That's a lot of work."

"I'd be happy to take care of that," Em says. "I was talking to the daughter of one of the patients at the hospice. She's a teacher. She was telling me how there's a project called Gateway that gives students workplace learning, to help them transition into the workforce. They have formal unit standards to complete which give them twenty credits toward their NCEA qualification, so there's plenty of incentive for them to work hard—it wouldn't be about them coming here for time off school."

"You've given this a lot of thought," Frankie says with a smile.

Em gives a shy shrug. "I thought it would be a way to get extra help around the place."

"A free workforce?" Finn says, amused.

"You could look at it like that if you're being really cynical," she says. There's no sharpness in her words, but Finn drops his gaze to his mug. She continues speaking to Rob, "We could definitely build in hours helping out with maintenance in both the bush and on the buildings, as well as clearing out the Wing. But it would also be a way to recruit more permanent help, as well as to give something back to the community. Younger staff would be cheaper," she adds, "and we'd be able to train them the way we wanted. We might also be able to offer practical training for university courses, like when vets do placements at surgeries, which would bring in older, more experienced young people. I'd be happy to look into it more."

"It sounds like a great idea," he says. "I'd like facts and figures, though. Can you produce me a report? By the next meeting?"

Her cheeks flush pink. "Yes, of course."

"I'm sure Naomi will help out if you need any help."

"Of course," Naomi says immediately.

"Right," he says, "well I'm open to any other ideas anyone can come up with. Naomi and I are working hard on fundraising options, plus we have a couple of contacts in Wellington with the Ministry, so we'll be keeping in touch with them. Now, about the Open Weekend…" He had the idea a few weeks ago to open HWH to visitors over Waitangi Day, in the hope that it might lead to increased donations. We all agreed it was a great idea, but it's going to mean extra work to keep the place spotless, to organize a route for the visitors to follow, and to make sure there's always someone to show them around.

"I'd like to put myself forward for that, too," Em says. "You lot are going to be so busy anyway, you don't need to take precious time out to ferry visitors, but I can easily put my work off for a few days."

As Rob continues talking about the arrangements, I feel a swell of pride and admiration for her. She's so innovative and full of energy, and the best thing of all is that she's not trying to impress, and it's not all for show—she genuinely wants to help.

She glances up and looks straight at me. I smile, and her lips curve up.

It's only at that point that I become conscious that the room has fallen silent, and I look around to see everyone else looking at me, too.

"Sorry," I say. "What?"

Everyone chuckles, and Gabe says, "Sorry to interrupt your daydreams, but I was talking about the new delivery schedule from Auckland. I wondered how often you'd like the bulk food deliveries?"

"Twice nightly?" Frankie suggests. "What do you think, Em?"

Em coughs into her mug, and everyone bursts out laughing. She delicately wipes her mouth and sends a wry look around the table.

"Once a week will be fine," I say, refusing to be baited. Gabe nods, but his eyes meet mine briefly, puzzled, a little curious. I can feel a conversation coming on about me and his sister. My stomach gives a little flip. He's my best mate, as close to me as my own brothers, and the last thing I'd want is to upset him.

When Gabe's finished, Rob says, "Okay, Any Other Business. Anyone?"

Finn clears his throat. "I've got something. I wanted to let you know that next week will be my last at HWH."

"Aw…" Everyone says. I think most of the sentiment is genuine enough, although for some, including me and Em, it's said more out of politeness.

"Also," he says, "Rob already knows, but Janie's working out her two weeks' notice. She's going to be coming with me to Aus."

Everyone looks surprised, then says things like, "Oh, that's nice," and, "We'll miss you both."

"Congratulations," Em says with a smile.

"Thanks." He doesn't look at her.

That's not the only thing that irritates me. "She hasn't said anything to me," I say.

Rob's eyebrows rise. "Oh, ah, I assumed she'd told you first."

"Nope."

Finn shrugs. "So?"

Frankie and Lorelei look at me. They've seen the two of us lock horns on several occasions. Neither of them like him either.

"Well," I say, "technically I'm her line manager, and I'm also the Manager of Veterinary Services, so she should have spoken to me before Rob."

Finn meets my gaze. "Does it matter now? We'll be out of your hair in two weeks."

Everyone else falls quiet.

"If she wants a reference, it might," I say mildly. I wouldn't deny her one because of this as I suspect it was a genuine mistake, but I'm not going to tell Finn that.

Finn glares at me. "She can ask Rob for one." He looks at him for confirmation.

Rob closes his laptop. "References are always done by the line manager." He glances at me. He knows how I feel about Finn, and there was no way he was going to take Finn's side in this.

"Yeah, you lot stick together, as usual," Finn says heatedly. "You think it was easy coming over here to work with such a close-knit group? You guys don't make it easy to fit in."

"It might have helped if you weren't such an arrogant arsehole," Frankie states.

Gabe bursts out laughing, and the other vets all grin. Rob gives her an exasperated look. I try not to smile, and fail.

Em's obviously amused, but she gathers up her notepad and says to him, "Hey, I need some help carrying a couple of boxes over to the surgery. Would you mind?"

He gets up, his chair scraping on the floor. "Sure."

She leads the way out, and he follows, letting the door bang behind him.

"Wow," Frankie says. "What a wanker."

"What the fuck just happened?" Joel looks puzzled. "That came out of the blue."

"He's never liked me," I say, getting to my feet and taking my mug over to the table by the door. "Don't know why, but the feeling's mutual."

"It's because of Em," Lorelei says. "He told me he was going to ask her out, but every time he started a conversation with her, all she did was talk about you."

I turn back to the room, eyebrows rising. "What?"

Frankie rolls her eyes. "Em was never serious about Finn. We all knew that, even if she didn't."

"There's never been anyone for her but you," Lorelei says.

"I… when… what…?"

The others laugh as they get to their feet. Frankie claps me on the shoulder as she passes me. "Close your mouth, dude. Flies."

I watch them go out, then turn and look at the last people left—Rob, Naomi, and Gabe.

Rob just picks up his laptop, grins, and limps through the doorway toward the other offices. Naomi throws me an amused look and follows him.

Gabe collects the folder he brought and tucks his pen back in the pocket of his white lab coat. Then he perches on the edge of the table and says, "Why am I always the last to know everything?"

"It only happened this weekend," I murmur. "There wasn't much to say before that."

"You and Em… you're an item?"

I hesitate. "Not quite."

He cocks his head. I shove my hands in my pockets and study the floor.

"Is this about her having the test?" he asks eventually.

"Partly." I sigh. "It's not like we've got a written declaration or anything. We just, you know… hooked up." I pull an eek face as he lifts his eyebrows. "Sorry."

"She is my sister, still."

"I know."

He gives a short laugh. "Can't say I'm shocked. Lorelei was right. There's never been anyone for Em but you."

"I didn't know that."

"Then you're less observant than I thought. You know if you break her heart, I'll break your legs, right?"

"Sounds fair."

"Okay. Now I've got that macho shit out of the way…" He smiles. "It'd be nice to have you as a brother-in-law."

I glare at him. "We haven't even been on a proper date yet."

"I'm looking ahead," he says, getting up off the table and walking toward me.

I open the door and let him precede me, then follow him out. "Maybe one day we'll both be old married men."

"Me? Don't think so."

"It'll happen to you eventually," I tell him. "You're thirty next month, aren't you? Cupid's got you in his sights, I'm telling you."

"There isn't a woman born who can handle the mighty Gabe," he advises me.

"Really?" I grin. "I can think of one… dark hair… nose ring…"

He snorts. "In her dreams. We all know who wears the pants in our relationship."

"It's her, right?"

"Oh yeah." He waves and heads off toward the lab.

I chuckle, stopping for a moment and looking around. Then I head over to the storage shed.

Em's not in there. I come back out and listen for a moment—I can hear someone singing.

Smiling, I walk around the back of the shed. There she is, snipping at the ferns trailing over the fence. Her hair looks like a ball of sunshine. Her T-shirt fits snugly to her breasts. I sigh as I remember how they felt in my hands. How soft her mouth is under mine.

She looks around, and her eyes widen as she sees me. She straightens and lowers the clippers, brushing back a strand of hair from her eyes. "Hey."

"Hey." I walk up to her and lean on the fence.

"You okay?" she asks. "That was pretty unpleasant in there."

"I'm a man. I can handle it. And I don't want to waste my time with you talking about Finn Weston." I drop my gaze to her mouth, thinking about kissing her, then return it to her green eyes. "So, you're expanding our workforce?"

She gives a shy shrug. "I wasn't sure whether Rob would be interested, but he seemed keen."

"It was a fantastic idea. I'm proud of you for coming up with it. I don't mean that in a patronizing way. I'd never have thought of it."

"I'm glad you liked it." She looks up at me as I move closer, and this time her gaze drops to my mouth. She wants to kiss me. "Am I going to get a reward?" she whispers.

I chuckle. "A gold star?"

"I was thinking of something a little more… physical…"

I cover her mouth with mine, turn her so her back is against the shed, and give her a long, luxurious kiss.

When I eventually lift my head, she smiles. "This is almost exactly where I caught Finn kissing Janie."

"Oh?"

"I was envious then." She reaches up and brushes her thumb across my bottom lip. "Now, not so much."

"I'm glad you didn't date him."

"Me too." She sucks her bottom lip. "I had a text from Dad. He's gone to Auckland, and he won't be back until tomorrow morning."

"Oh?"

"And all the guests have finally left. Would you… like to come to dinner tonight? Don't worry, I'll get one of Dad's meals out of the freezer."

I smile. "I'd love to."

"You can stay if you want." Her eyes are hopeful.

I feel a swell of tenderness, affection, and eager lust at the thought of having her to myself again for a whole night. "Oh, I'm definitely up for that."

And I kiss her again, because it's summer, and who knows what the future holds? All that matters is right here, right now, and I'm going to let tomorrow take care of itself.

Chapter Twenty-One

Emily

I leave work a little early, wanting to get home before Knightley. Once I'm there, I change into a short summer dress in a pale orange with yellow flowers, let my hair down, and put on a little eyeshadow and lip gloss while Minnie the Lab sits and watches me.

I retrieve a couple of Dad's pasta meals from the freezer and put them in the microwave to defrost, tip a bag of green salad into a bowl and add dressing, then set the table out on the deck with plates, wine glasses, and a bottle of Merlot.

Next I pour myself half a glass and drink it in one go before I sink onto one of the chairs.

Why am I nervous? It's not like it's our first time.

But maybe that's why I'm anxious. This is like a real date. We're not drunk, not yet anyway. We've not been carried away by the heat of passion. This will be our third time together, and that smacks of a burgeoning relationship.

I told him yesterday that we should have sex as often as we can before the test results come through, and I meant it at the time. But I'm beginning to have second thoughts. I told him that it didn't matter how many times we slept together—it's still going to hurt like fuck when it comes to an end. I think that was naive, though. Every time I see him, every time he touches me, I fall that little bit deeper in love with him.

The thought takes me by surprise. Am I in love with him? Then I realize it's a stupid question. Of *course* I'm in love with him. I think I've been in love with him for years.

"Hello."

I get up and spin around at the sound of his voice, relieved I've drunk most of the wine in my glass as the remainder almost slops over the rim. I put it down hastily. "Oh! Hello."

"Sorry, didn't mean to make you jump." He's come straight from work, and he's still wearing his HWH polo shirt and jeans. He lowers down to greet Minnie as she runs up to him, scratching behind her ears and kissing her nose. I love that he loves animals. He's always been like this. He has a huge heart. I don't know how he can think he's anything like his father.

He pushes up, then comes over to me, looking concerned. "Are you okay?"

I feel full of emotion and all mixed up. "Yeah. Just… I don't know."

He studies me for a moment. Then he moves closer and cups my face in his hands.

"You look amazing," he murmurs.

I swallow. "Thank you."

He brushes over my bottom lip with his thumb. Then he lowers his head and kisses me.

I sigh and lift my arms around his neck. It's a beautiful afternoon, and out here on the deck the hot summer breeze blows its breath over us, smelling of lemon and jasmine. I feel a swell of frustration that our lives are so complicated. I want to live in the present, for life to be as simple as me and him, and how it feels when he kisses me, and to forget about everything else.

Sinking my hands into his hair, I open my mouth and touch my tongue to his, and he sighs and wraps his arms around me tightly.

I don't know whether he can sense how I'm feeling, or whether he's just in the mood for sex. Maybe both. But in one smooth move, he lifts me, wrapping my legs around his waist, and he slowly walks back through the house, kissing me all the while.

When we get to my bedroom, he lowers my feet to the floor, then helps me take off my dress. After that, he removes his polo shirt, unbuttons his jeans, and slips them off. Finally we remove our underwear, and now we're naked, warm skin against warm skin.

I wait for him to turn up the heat, maybe toss me on the bed or drop to his knees before me like he did last time. Instead, he just kisses me again, taking his time to kiss across my face, touching his lips to my cheeks, nose, and eyelids, around to my ear, where he sucks the lobe, and then trailing them along my jaw before returning to my mouth.

I put my hands on his chest, brushing my fingers through the curling hairs there, enjoying just feeling loved and admired, happy to let him take his time, while Minnie lies in the doorway and sighs, and outside the rosellas cry as they swoop between the trees.

When he leads me to the bed, lies down, and takes me in his arms, I don't complain at his leisurely caress. This time, on the sunny early evening, alone and with all the time in the world, it seems right to make it last as long as we can.

And that's exactly what he does; he arouses me slowly, so slowly, with gentle brushes of his fingers over my skin and soft kisses that seem to last an eternity. He lifts my arms above my head and strokes down from my hands, along the sensitive skin under my arms, over my shoulders, around my breasts, down over my ribs, over the curve of my hips, and all the way down the outside of my thighs to my knees before returning, taking the same path.

It's a long while before he pushes my knees apart and adds the inside of my thighs to the journey. And it's not until my whole body feels like it's humming that he finally brushes up my core and lowers his mouth to my breasts. Even then, he takes his time, stroking, kissing, teasing until I'm gasping for breath. It feels like a lifetime before he dons a condom, moves on top of me, and slides inside.

There's not an ounce of friction, and he's right up to the hilt in one smooth thrust. Oh wow, I'm never going to get used to this. He rests his forehead on mine for a moment, and I know he's reveling in the feel of being inside me in the same way.

He lifts his head then and looks me in the eyes as he begins to move. He keeps his gaze fixed on mine as he makes love to me, and I find I can't look away. His beautiful blue eyes have hooked me, reeled me in. When I'm close, and my eyelids flutter closed of their own will, he kisses me and murmurs, "Open them." I look up at him again, and this time I try to keep them open, as tiny muscles start tightening deep inside, and then my orgasm sweeps over me.

Only then does he give in to the passion he's kept such tight control on for so long. He crushes his lips to mine, catching my cries with his mouth, and thrusting hard enough to make the headboard bang against the wall. Luckily there's nobody around to hear it, and I sink my nails into his back as he takes his pleasure from me, until the moment he stops and shudders, and finally exhales with a long, long breath.

He withdraws, disposes of the condom, then falls onto the bed beside me. "Whoa."

"Sorry about that," I say. "I should have offered you a drink first."

We both laugh. "It was my fault," he replies. "I didn't give you a chance." He rolls onto his side toward me and props his head on a hand. "I can't keep my hands off you."

"I'm not complaining."

He smiles. Then he leans forward and gives me a long kiss.

When he finally moves back, he says, "Feel better now?"

"Yes," I murmur. "Thank you. How did you know?"

"I've known you long enough to guess when something's wrong. What was bothering you?"

"Nothing really. I was just wishing I could forget about… everything, and live in the present."

He nods slowly. "I thought exactly the same thing earlier today."

I trail a finger along his collarbone. "I wish the next two weeks were all done and dusted. It's going to be a tough time."

"Yeah."

"I know we should have waited until it was all over, but honestly, I think it's the only thing keeping me sane."

He takes my hand in his, and threads his fingers through mine. "Me too."

I kiss his fingers, then lean forward and press my lips to his, and we exchange a long, heartfelt kiss.

Part of me wants to stay there forever, in that warm room, and put off the difficult days I know are coming. But even though we stay there for ages, kissing and touching, we can't stop the sun sinking toward the horizon, and eventually Minnie comes up and puts a paw on the bed, making us laugh.

"I'd better feed her," I say. "And us."

"Yeah, come on."

We get up and dress, then go back into the living room. I take Minnie out and feed her while he heats up our dinner in the microwave, and then he brings out the plates, and we sit and eat the pasta while we talk about our day, looking out at the view.

Like an old married couple, I think… Except that I don't know if old age for me will ever look like this.

The thought makes me sad. I poke at my salad, and he reaches over and squeezes my hand.

There's no need to say anything. He knows what's going through my mind, because I'm sure it's going through his, too.

*

Wednesday

"How did the wedding go?" Susie asks.

"Very well," I reply. "Without a hitch really, which isn't surprising considering the amount of organization Bella did."

Susie smiles. "So you had a nice time?"

"I did." I hesitate and examine my hands. Susie is here to give me genetic counseling specifically related to my decision to be tested. But we've talked a lot about relationships, and last time I was here, I told her a bit about my feelings for Knightley.

"Actually…" I say, a little shyly, "Knightley and I, we… hooked up over the weekend." I don't add that we've met up every day since Saturday and had sex at least twice each time.

"Oh…" She looks delighted. "I'm so pleased for you both. You made such a lovely couple."

I sigh. "I have such mixed feelings about it."

"You mean because of the test? Or because you're not sure about your feelings for him?"

It's only when she asks that I realize I don't even have to think about the answer. "It's because I *am* sure about my feelings for him that I have mixed feelings, I think. That doesn't make sense, I know. But I really like him. I always have, and I think he's always liked me, but we told ourselves that we're like siblings and our feelings are familial."

"Do you love him?" she asks.

"I… don't know." Really, Em? Or is that cowardice talking? "Yes," I admit slowly. "I do. I always have, but now it's new, it's physical, and it's exciting. It feels as if the path ahead is sparkling with promise. And then it ends in this huge brick wall."

"Have you told him that if you take the test, and it's positive, you're not interested in a relationship?"

I nod. I told Susie during my last session.

"How does he feel about that?" she asks.

"I… don't know. I told him before we slept together. We haven't really talked about it since, although I think he knows what's going through my mind."

She turns her pen in her fingers. "Do you think he should have a say about what happens in your relationship?"

I give her a wry look. "I know where you're going with this."

"If he feels the same way about you, don't you think he might want to continue the relationship despite a positive test?"

"I'm sure he'd say that, because he's a nice guy, and he'd hate me to think he was abandoning me for selfish reasons. But I'd always ask myself if he was only staying out of pity. What man would choose to remain in a relationship knowing that something so terrible was going to happen to their partner?" I speak hotly, irritated that she's trying to make me feel guilty for making my own decisions.

But if I'd thought to make her back down, I'm to be disappointed. Instead, she gives me a direct look and says, "There have been several studies carried out on couples in a similar position to yours. In one test, seventy percent of tested persons did not have a change in marital status over the five years of the study."

"Okay, but presumably that means they were married before they found out they might have the disease. That's not the same."

"Fair enough. The study I just mentioned does report some shifts in the balance of the pre-test relationship, where a positive test resulted in the partners of the at-risk people moving toward caretaking roles. Equally, a negative result sometimes caused an increase in self-esteem in the at-risk people, and led to them feeling differently toward their partners afterward. It's very complex, and no two relationships are the same. But what we can say is that relationships can play a significant role in coping with the disease."

"Yeah, I get that. But if I love him, don't I owe it to him to set him free so he can find a less-complicated relationship?"

"Less complicated in what way? His next partner could contract breast cancer, or die in a car accident."

"True. But he wouldn't go into the relationship knowing that. It's a totally different thing to have your partner fall ill when you've been with them a few years, compared to going into a relationship with the knowledge that they have a disease. Marriage vows include 'in sickness and in health' for a reason. We all hope our partners will stand by us if we fall ill. But my situation is different."

"Maybe."

"And what about kids?" I ask. "I'd have to know. I'd have to go down the IVF route with pre-implantation testing. And if I got pregnant by mistake, I'd have to have prenatal testing. I couldn't bear to give birth to a child knowing I'd cursed it like that."

"Em, we've talked about referring to the disease in this way. Plenty of people born with Huntington's go on to lead long, fulfilling lives before they begin to develop symptoms of the disease. I know your experience with your mother has been very hard on you. But it will be a lot easier for you if you can go into this with as much positivity as you can muster."

"You mean leave it to Fate? Tell myself that if my kids have it, it's God's plan, or it's luck, and absolve myself of all responsibility? I can't do that. I couldn't have children without knowing whether I have the disease. And if I had a child and later it discovered it had HD, I'd never forgive myself. Never." I stop, fighting tears.

Susie's expression turns gentle. "I'm not trying to change your mind, Em. The choice is yours, of course. I just want you to make it with your eyes open."

"I am," I say. I take a deep breath. "I'm glad we've had these talks, and you've made me consider lots of things I hadn't thought about before. I do know that it might look as if I'm being selfish, although I'd argue that it's out of love for my friends and family and possible future children that I've come to this conclusion. But I stand by my decision. There's no point us talking about it anymore. I want the test."

This time, she nods. "Okay. I think you're right. We've looked at all sides. And I've explained the range your results could fall into—that it's not necessarily going to give you a negative or positive result."

"Yes. I understand."

"And we've talked about the implications of the results, both positive and negative."

"Yes."

"I'm always here for you to talk to at any stage of the process," she says. "A positive test can take a lot of adjusting to, but equally so can a negative test, which can also bring strong shock and guilt."

"Okay." My heart is racing now we're coming to the end of the process.

"So," she says, "the blood test. Our guidelines recommend a four-week stand down period for the patient to reflect on the pros and cons of having the test."

My heart sinks, and I feel a wave of despondency. "Four weeks?"

"That's the recommended time. However, it's up to the individual discretion of the counselor. You've wanted the test from the beginning. And I believe you've thought carefully about all the pros and cons, and you've never wavered with your decision. Because of this, I'm willing to waive that waiting period. However, if you change your mind at any point before the results are available, you just call and tell me, and we'll file the results away until you're ready. Okay?"

"Okay."

"Now, all this is a very emotional journey, and we do encourage you to have a family member with you along each step of the way. Would you like to return for the test when you have someone with you—Lee, or your father, for example?"

"If I say no, can I have it today?"

"Yes."

"Then I want that. I want it done."

"You're sure?" she asks gently. When I nod, she closes her notepad. "All right, then. Give me a couple of minutes to request the test, then I'll take you down to have it done."

"How long before I get the results?" I ask as she taps into her computer.

"It's usually about two to three weeks. My assistant will call you when they come through and make an appointment to discuss them."

"How long will I have to wait?"

"Oh, we can do it the same day if you can get down here. I won't make you wait, Em. But I must tell you now that it's imperative you bring someone with you. For a start, your mind won't be on the road, which can be dangerous when driving, and you'll need support regardless of what the results are. Do you understand? Do you promise to bring someone with you?"

I nod. "Okay."

"Right. So I need you to sign this consent form to say that you understand what I've told you about the results, and that we've discussed the pros and cons."

I read the sheet, then sign it.

"Come on then," she says. "I'll take you down to Pathology."

My mouth goes dry. I follow her out of her room and through the hospital to the Pathology Department, and all the way my heart bangs so hard on my ribs I'm worried they're going to crack.

Maybe I've been stupid—I should have come back and brought Knightley with me. But part of me is worried he'll try to talk me out of it, and I can't bear to wait any longer. I know I've got a few weeks to wait for the results, but at least I'll be taking action. It'll be done, and I won't need to worry about making the decision anymore.

I follow her into the department. She tells the receptionist who I am, and the receptionist pulls up my details on her screen and nods. Susie then seats me in the waiting area.

"I have another appointment," she tells me, "so I have to go. Are you going to be okay?"

"It's just a blood test," I say, although I have to sit on my hands to stop them shaking.

She smiles. "Just remember that at any point you can change your mind."

"Okay. Thank you, for everything."

"Call me if you want to chat, any time."

"I will."

She walks away, leaving me alone.

I look out of the window. Clouds are closing in, blocking out the bright blue sky. The met office has forecast rain for the foreseeable future. It seems appropriate.

The next couple of weeks will be tough. Whatever the result is, it'll have long-term consequences not just for me but for Knightley, my father, my siblings, and all my friends. It's going to change everything, one way or another. But even so, I feel a sense of relief that I've made the decision.

I don't know how I'm going to get through the days. And I don't know how to rein my hopes in. I'm afraid of hoping for the best because it might make a positive result even more of a shock. I feel as if I need to prepare myself for the worst. But that will mean losing Knightley, and the thought of not being with him, of never having him touch me, hold me again, fills me with a terrible sadness.

The only way I'm going to be able to get through this is to not think about it. I'm going to keep myself so busy, there'll be no time to dwell on it at all.

"Emily Woodruff?"

I nod at the woman who comes out in the white lab coat and get up. "Yes."

"Please, come this way."

I follow her through the door, and it closes behind me.

Chapter Twenty-Two

Knightley

Nine days later

"Wow, you're getting old," Rob says. "It's only seven o'clock, and you're already nodding off."

I jerk awake. It's Friday night, and we're at a bar in town, having a party for Finn and Janie, who are both leaving today. They're currently holding court, explaining their plans for their new life in Australia to everyone. Luckily I managed to secure a seat on the outskirts against the wall, because halfway through my first beer, exhaustion swept over me, and I must have dozed off.

"Sorry," I say, rubbing both hands over my face. "It's been a helluva week."

"It has been busy, true, but I'm thinking your exhaustion probably isn't related to work…" He grins. "Am I right?"

"Um…"

It has been a busy week at work. It began with Waitangi Day on Sunday, which always means more tourists and boats in the Bay, leading to an influx of injured animals the following week. We've been pushed to our limits, and all five of us vets have been working flat out. On top of that, we had the Open Weekend, which was hugely successful. Floods of visitors invaded HWH, eager to look around, and we received lots of small donations and a couple of very generous ones afterward, which made it more than worthwhile, even if it was hard work for everyone. Em, especially, has been run off her feet. She's been working hard keeping HWH running smoothly, and she spent Waitangi weekend shepherding groups of tourists on a pre-arranged route, explaining what we do.

But Rob's right; that's not the only reason I'm knackered. Em and I have met up after work every day, sometimes at Hartfield House, sometimes at my apartment. And the girl has been insatiable. She's taken my nickname literally, and, quite frankly, she's shagged me senseless. It's not a complaint. I'm more than happy to oblige. But I'm so tired I can hardly keep my eyes open.

"Lucky bastard," Rob says.

"You might get some if you ever went out. The perfect girl isn't just going to knock on your door and walk into your office."

I'm being a touch mischievous. I know him well enough to suspect he likes Naomi.

He just gives me a wry look. "I'm too busy for romance."

I smile, although his comment saddens me. He dated lots of girls when he was younger, but after his accident, years of operations and painful physio brought his boyish Casanova days to an abrupt end, and he's never returned to them. I know he's self-conscious of his twisted, misshapen knee because he never wears shorts and no longer plays sports or goes swimming. He did see a girl called Vicky about a year ago, but that ended after a few dates. Although he never discussed it with me, I have a horrible feeling she might have expressed a less than favorable reaction on seeing his injured leg, because since then he hasn't dated anyone, as far as I know. Instead, he's devoted himself to his work and his one other love—movies. He has the biggest DVD and Blu-Ray collection of anyone I've ever known. It keeps him occupied, but it's not going to keep him warm at night.

"How are you and Em getting on?" Rob glances over at where she's sitting listening to Janie talk about how she and Finn are hoping to get married soon. I wonder whether it stings a bit. Em glances at me then, though, and winks. I don't think she's too bothered.

"Good," I say. It's the understatement of the year. We're getting on terrifically. Not that I'd expect anything else. She's the easiest person in the world to be with, and if you add that to the fact that we've always been the best of friends, it's no real surprise that dating her has been so simple.

"Is it likely to be a long-term thing?" Rob asks quietly.

I hesitate. "I don't know. Maybe. We decided to wait until I've seen Dad and she's had her test before we talk about the future."

"When's her test?"

"It was delayed by a couple of weeks because her therapist was fully booked or something. She's having it done next Friday."

"And how long before she gets the results?"

"At least two weeks, I think."

He sighs. "That's going to be hard on her."

"On all of us. I'm not looking forward to it." I can't imagine how horrible it's going to be waiting for that phone call.

"And you're seeing Dad on Tuesday," Rob confirms.

"Yeah. Eleven a.m."

"Are you prepared?"

I shrug. "I've tried not to think about it too much. I'm going to have to play it by ear, anyway."

"Yeah."

We're interrupted by a ripple of loud laughter. Finn's on top form tonight, entertaining the troops. To tell the truth, I'm not in the mood for this. I'm tired, and I feel… uneasy. I'm not sure why.

I feel relieved, therefore, when Em gets up and comes to sit beside me, and whispers, "I think we've done our bit. Shall we make a move?"

"Absolutely," I say with feeling.

The two of us get up and announce we're going. I shake hands with Finn, who—three sheets to the wind—declares I'm a first-rate dude and must stay in touch. Knowing I'll probably never hear from him again, I reply that I definitely will, then I kiss Janie on the cheek and head toward the door.

Em follows me, and we go out into the cool evening air. It's been raining for most of the past week. It's still very warm, so the humidity is high, and sometimes the air can feel like you've got a blanket over your face, but here on the waterfront the sea breeze is brisk and refreshing, scattering misty rain on our skin.

"Shall we go to your apartment?" she asks.

I grin. "Sure." It's only a five-minute walk, and I left the car there tonight, so we set off, holding hands.

"Sad to see Finn go?" I tease.

She smiles. "A bit. Not for any reason other than that it was fun to have someone new at the place. I keep meaning to ask, have you found a replacement for Janie?"

"Yes. Her name's Yvonne, but she's known as Bonnie. She starts in a few weeks, after she's worked her notice at her current surgery. You'll like her, she's young and friendly, and has great references."

"Should I be jealous?"

I chuckle. "Not at all. I have my perfect girl." I put my arm around her and pull her close to me.

She slides her arm around my waist and gives me an impish look. "I hope you weren't dozing off back there in the bar. I need you at your most energetic for what I have planned for tonight."

"Oh?"

"Mm. Let's just say it involves a silk scarf or two…"

I smile, pleased that she's been thinking about what she wants to do in bed, but something in her eyes rings a warning bell in my head. I might be imagining it, but she seems a bit… feverish, panicky even. I can't put my finger on it, though, so I don't say anything as we approach my apartment building and go in.

We take the stairs as it's only one floor up. Even as I'm opening the door, though, she pushes me up against the wall, and pulls my mouth down to hers.

It's not the first time we've been eager for one another, but it's not the same tonight. There's been no build up—no heated looks, no intimate touches, and I'm tired, and sometimes even guys need a little foreplay.

"Steady on." I put my hands on her upper arms and move her back a few inches. "Let me put the lights on and get us a drink."

But she pushes me up against the opposite wall and crushes her lips to mine.

Once again, I feel a prickle of uncertainty, and it's sharp enough to make me lift my head and say, "Em, wait."

She moves back and gives me a hurt look. "What?"

I run a hand through my hair. "I just need five, okay? It's been a really busy day, and I'm shattered."

She flushes then. "I'm sorry. I was excited to be with you, that's all."

"I know, but we've got all evening. Why the rush?"

Her gaze meets mine, then she turns away and walks into the apartment.

I follow her in, flicking on the lamp by the TV. "Is everything all right?"

"Fine."

I watch her walk over to the window, where she stands and looks out at the view of the sea. Her face is wistful, sad.

"What's going on?" I ask.

She folds her arms and shakes her head.

I toss my keys on the coffee table, toe off my shoes, then walk a few steps toward her. Even though the room is dimly lit, I can see the dark circles under her eyes. It's been a tough week for us both, incredibly busy, but there's no doubt that she's worked exceptionally hard, twelve hours most days, often doing physical work out in the surrounding bush. Almost as if she's trying to keep busy… to stop her brain working…

And it's then that I realize what's going on.

"You've had the test," I say, stunned.

She doesn't deny it, so I know I'm right.

"When?" I ask, aghast that she's done it alone, without me.

She studies her feet for a moment, then says, "Nine days ago."

I can't believe she's been worrying about the results for a whole week. "Why didn't you tell me?" I ask incredulously.

She throws me a small smile. "I didn't want you to worry."

"Em…" Pity and hurt swirl inside me. "I thought we cared for one another."

"We do," she says, aghast that I'd question it. "That's why I didn't tell you."

"But when two people are in a relationship, they support each other, don't they?"

She bites her bottom lip. "I wasn't sure if we were."

"If we were what?"

"In a relationship."

My eyebrows rise. "What would you call this?"

"I don't know. An affair? A fuck-fest?"

I glare at her. "I like to think it's a bit more than that."

"Is it?" Her face flushes. "We both said we were going to wait a few weeks before we talked about it. We're not in a 'relationship'." She puts air quotes around it. "We're just having sex."

"Don't be childish. We've known each other for seventeen years. I'd have thought you'd have told me purely because of that, regardless of whether we were sleeping together."

"Don't call me childish," she says hotly.

"Then don't act like a kid," I snap.

We glare at each other. My stomach churns. We've never argued. And I can't believe we're doing it now. She's upset, I remind myself, anxious about her test results, and of what will happen if they're positive. She's trying to cram a lifetime of loving into a couple of weeks in case this is all she gets. This isn't about us at all. I need to be patient with her. She's not making it easy, though.

"Whether or not we've discussed having a 'relationship'," and I copy her air quotes, "I have feelings for you that go far deeper than they would if we were just having a fuck-fest, as you call it so colorfully."

She turns away. "I don't want to hear it."

I catch her arm. "You don't want to hear me say I love you?"

She looks up at me then, jaw dropping, before she gathers herself and tears her arm away. "Don't. I have to go."

"You're not leaving." I move to block her. "Why is that so hard to hear? I know we haven't said it in so many words, but you know how I feel about you. And you feel the same about me."

"I don't." A tear runs down her face, but she dashes it away.

"You do," I insist. "You love me, too."

She shakes her head. "I'm not going to let myself fall in love with you."

"You don't have any control over it, Em, it just happens."

"Maybe. But I can't talk about it now. I won't." She tries to sidestep me.

I move to block her again. "Why? Because if your test is positive, you're going to say it's all over?"

She lifts her head then to look into my eyes. "Yes."

I feel a surge of frustration. "Don't I have a say in it?"

"No."

"That's not fair."

"I don't care."

"So you'll break my heart and take away my chance to be with the love of my life because you're worried about what might happen in twenty years' time?"

She blinks at that. "L—love of your life?"

I reach up a hand and cup her cheek. "Yes. I love you. And I want to be with you. No matter what happens in the future."

A tear runs down her face. "That's so sweet," she whispers. "And you're right. I do love you. But it doesn't change how I feel." She lifts her face out of my hand and takes a step back. "We should have waited before we slept together. And I shouldn't have come around here tonight. I'd like to go now."

Despair washes over me. "At least let's make the most of this week until you get your results." Maybe, if I continue to show her how I feel, I can convince her we have something worth saving.

But she shakes her head. Keeping her eyes down, she says, "Will you let me pass, please?"

I want to tell her no. To refuse to move, and insist she stays here until she agrees with me. But that's not how her father brought me up. That's bullying, and it's unfair. Just because I don't like what she's saying doesn't mean I have the right to force her to stay.

I step to one side. "Please don't go. I'm begging you. Stay. I don't care what we do. Make love all night. Or just sit here and watch TV. I just want to be with you."

She hesitates for a long moment. Her chest heaves, and I can see her fighting with herself.

Then she walks past me, goes out and closes the door behind her.

*

Half an hour later, I send her a text. It takes me about five minutes to compose it so it's lighthearted and yet caring too.

Are you home? Let me know you're okay. You know where I am if you want to talk about anything, even if it's only Game of Thrones! Miss you x

A few minutes later, she comes back.

Yes, I'm home. I'm okay. Thanks. I'm off to bed. Speak to you tomorrow x

I toss my phone onto the table, then lie back on the sofa and look out the window at the night sky. She doesn't want to talk, and I'm going to have to accept that.

Doesn't mean I have to like it, though.

*

The next day's Saturday, but most of us are working to try to catch up on the busy week. When I get there, however, I discover that Em has called in sick.

I'm stunned. She's never had a day off sick since we opened HWH.

"She says she feels like she's coming down with something," Frankie tells me. "Personally, I think it's probably a hangover, but we'll give her the benefit of the doubt."

I send her a text. *Hey! Are you okay? Frankie says you're unwell. x*

She comes back. *Just feeling a bit under the weather. x*

Want me to come up to the house and cheer you up? :-)

Thanks for the offer, but I'm going to rest for a bit. Hope you have a good day.

Okay, I can take the hint. She doesn't want to see me.

Frustrated and cross, I spend the day growling at everyone. Eventually, Frankie comes up to me mid-afternoon and says, "For God's sake, you're like a bear with a thorn in its paw. Go and see her, will you?"

Knowing she's right, I pack up and drive to Hartfield House, park, and get out. It's been raining continuously for the past week, but I barely notice it as I walk across the drive.

The door opens, and Hugh comes out, carrying an umbrella. I can tell immediately by the look on his face what he's going to say.

"She doesn't want to see anyone," he tells me gently, holding the umbrella over both of us. "Don't take it too personally. She's run herself into the ground this week, and she's absolutely exhausted."

"You know she's had the test," I say, half hoping he didn't, and he'll take my side now he knows.

But he nods and says, "Yes. And everything's going to be up in the air until she gets the results. You've just got to give her space, lad. It's not anything to do with her feelings for you."

Hands on my hips, I look toward the house, wondering if she's watching me, then drop my gaze to the gravel drive, full of frustration. "I just want to talk to her," I say looking back up at Hugh.

"I know."

"She says that if the test is positive, she's never going to have a relationship."

"I know."

"Don't I get a say in it?"

"I understand your frustration. All I can say is that you have to give her time. She's terrified of what happened to her mother happening to her. She loves you so much, son, that she can't bear the thought of inflicting that pain on you."

His words take me by surprise, and emotion tightens my throat. "But even if it did," I say hoarsely, "it wouldn't happen for years and years."

"Probably, but it doesn't matter, it's hanging over her like the Sword of Damocles. Most of us don't know how or when the end is going to come, and we all somehow manage to push it to the back of our minds and trust that we'll be in our nineties and die in our sleep of old age tucked up in our beds. Nobody wants to think that they might get cancer or some other disease and die young or in pain. But Em knows what a positive result will mean. She knows what will happen to her.

Can you really say you'd be feeling any different if it was you in that position?"

He's got me there. If the roles were reversed, I wouldn't let Em anywhere near me. I'd break her heart quite happily if it meant she were free to meet someone else and have the chance of a happy, carefree life with another man, even if the thought of it churns up my insides.

"Give her space," Hugh says again, putting a hand on my arm, "and pray, or hope, that we get good news."

I give one more longing glance at the house, then nod. "Call me if you hear anything, whatever the result."

"Of course."

"Do you think she'll be back at work tomorrow?"

"I don't know. Initially she thought staying busy would keep her mind off it, but that was never going to work. I might suggest she takes the week off and the two of us spend some time together. She's not really had any time off since Angela's funeral, so it'll do her good to rest. Sometimes it doesn't do to ignore things. You need to let your brain process it all."

"All right. Well, you know where I am if you need me."

"Thank you," he says with feeling. "For understanding."

"I love her," I tell him honestly. "Very much. And that's not going to change no matter what the result. Make sure you tell her that."

"I will. Take care, son, and good luck with Steven, eh?"

I'd completely forgotten I'm due to meet my father on Tuesday. "Oh, yeah. Thanks."

"Let me know how it goes."

"Will do."

I walk back to my car, get in, and drive away. I'm gutted that she won't see me. But Hugh's right. Maybe she just needs some time to process everything.

I hate that the fate of our relationships rests on the results of the test. I resent that with every bone in my body. It's a fucking horrible disease, but it's not a death sentence, and I can't bear to think that if it's positive, that's it for us, lights out, over and done. Part of me hates that Fate is going to whip away the love of my life just when I've realized who she is.

But there's nothing I can do about it. Now all I can do is wait, and hope.

Chapter Twenty-Three

Emily

Under my father's gentle pressure, I agree to take some time off work. I let him talk to Rob, and I'm not surprised when Rob tells him it's not a problem at all. I think Dad tells him, and maybe Gabe, that I'm waiting for the results, and just to let me be, because normally one of the guys would have called in to check on me, but the house remains quiet, while outside, heavy subtropical rain continues to fall.

Normally Dad's not around much during the day, spending long hours out on the orchards and vineyards, but he spends a while on the phone to the assistant he employed some time ago to help out, and after discussing what needs to be done that week, Dad ends the call and announces he's taking a few days off, too.

I tell him not to fuss, but if I'm honest it's nice to have some company. Truthfully, I don't feel quite right, as if I am coming down with something. Although I don't say anything to Dad, it's impossible not to run through the list of symptoms and see if they match up. Even though Susie told me I'd be likely to follow the same pattern as Mum, there are always exceptions to every rule, and I can't help but think that maybe I've got juvenile onset HD.

If I have… the possibilities go around and around in my head. I don't want to put any of my family or friends through the pain of watching me deteriorate. How can I do that to Knightley? To Dad?

All weekend, and then all Monday, I wander down different mental paths, reach dead ends, backtrack, and continue to new forks in the road. I have a constant headache, and I feel exhausted all the time. But it's impossible to stop my brain churning.

Dad tries to distract me. We cook dinner together each evening, and we watch lots of movies. He gets Rob to drop off some classics we haven't seen for a long time, which I think he hopes will be comforting. But nothing stops me thinking, going over the symptoms one by one, and analyzing what I'm going to do with each potential different diagnosis.

On Tuesday morning, Dad comes into the living room to discover me on the sofa and realizes I've obviously been up all night. "Coffee and cereal?" he asks.

I shake my head. The thought of eating and drinking anything makes me feel ill. "I couldn't."

He studies me for a long moment. Then he turns and walks out to the kitchen.

I curl up and look out at the rain. Is it ever going to stop? I'm sure I'd feel better if I could see the sun. It would be nice to sit outside. But instead there's just this continual downpour. Dad says part of the road down the hill has almost been washed away. I'm sure HWH has suffered damage from localized flooding. I should get back to work. But I just can't face it at the moment.

He comes in with a glass of orange juice and a slice of dry toast. "You need something in your stomach," he says. "Here."

"Nag, nag, nag," I grumble, but I sip the orange and nibble on the toast, and he's right, it does make me feel a bit better.

He perches on the edge of the armchair opposite me, sitting forward, elbows on his knees. "How are you feeling?"

"A bit rough." I swallow the scratchy toast and put the rest down. Maybe it's best I talk about it. "I keep running through all the symptoms. I can't stop myself. I'm having difficulty concentrating. I'm tired all the time. I feel irritable and emotional and achy."

"Those are also all signs of stress."

"I know… But I always feel so well, Dad. And right now… I don't feel right." My eyes water, and I have to bite my bottom lip to stop it trembling.

He purses his lips. "Mind if I ask you something personal?"

I frown. "No, of course not."

"When was your last period?"

I hadn't expected him to say that. "Oh. Um… I'm not sure."

"Will you check for me?"

I stare at him. He lifts his eyebrows.

I pick up my phone with a shaking hand and pull up the calendar. I'm usually relatively regular, and my cycle is twenty-eight or twenty-nine days. I always mark the expected first day of my next cycle. Oh yeah, it sent me a notification on Saturday, but I'd forgotten.

I look up at him. I've gone completely cold.

"How late are you?" Dad asks.

"Two or three days." My voice is a whisper.

"Is that normal?"

"No. But…"

"Work backwards," he says. "Your cycle begins on day one of your last period, right? You're at your most fertile around day fourteen. When was that?"

I look at my calendar. Then I put down the phone. "Bella's wedding."

The first night I slept with Knightley.

"No." I shake my head. "We used a condom."

It's probably a bit TMI, but my father doesn't flinch. "Condoms are only eighty-five percent effective, remember? That means fifteen out of a hundred people get pregnant every year."

"But…"

"Feeling nauseous?" he asks.

I nod.

"Sore breasts? Peeing a lot? More tired than normal?" I nod to each of them. He smiles. "It's not HD sweetheart. You're pregnant."

"Oh no." The enormity of it washes over me with the full force of a tsunami. I put my face in my hands and burst into tears. "No. I can't be. No…"

"Hey, it's okay…" He comes over, sits beside me, and pulls me into his arms. "It's all right. We'll work it out together."

But I'm filled with abject horror. "What if I test positive? Or even if I have an intermediate result? I might not develop it, but it would mean my children could."

"Em…"

"I'd have to have it tested. And if it's positive, I'd have to terminate the pregnancy…"

"Em…"

"And even if it wasn't… If I'm positive, I don't want kids, I don't want them to see me like Mum, I don't want them to have to look after me, I don't—"

"Em!" He speaks sternly enough to make me jump. My brain, which was going at a million miles an hour, screeches to a halt. I stop speaking and sniffle and snuffle.

He leans over to the coffee table, collects the box of tissues on there, and passes me one. "Blow your nose," he says.

I give it a big blow. "I'm sorry."

"It's all right. It's a shock, I get that. But one thing at a time. First of all, there are other reasons why you might be late. It could be stress. It's pointless to debate too much until you know for sure."

I nod.

"I'll go down to the chemist in a minute," he says, "and get you a pregnancy test. Then we'll know."

I wipe my nose. "If I am pregnant, it's only a few days."

"These tests can tell from the first day you miss your period. Em, whatever happens with the HD test, with this test… We'll deal with it. You're surrounded by loving friends and family. I know what's been going through your mind, and I swear, you don't have juvenile onset."

I blink and look up at him in surprise.

"Don't you think I'd know?" he asks. "I saw the symptoms as Mum developed them, and you haven't shown any signs of them. If you do have it, you're years away from developing it."

I lean against him and rest my head on his shoulder. "I know."

"We haven't talked about it much," he says. "About your Mum, and what she did. But the fact is that she waited until the last possible moment, until she couldn't cope anymore. And I don't blame her for that. But we had so many wonderful years together. We had you three amazing kids. And I know the three of you now have to cope with the issues of the disease, and I'm so, so sorry about that, but if I could change things, if I could have had you tested in the womb, would I have done it? Aborted the fetuses that showed positive? I couldn't have done that."

"I know, Dad, but that's because you've seen those fetuses grow up into real people."

"Yeah, fair enough." He sighs and kisses the top of my head.

We sit there quietly for a while, as I gradually calm, and the realization sinks in, like a spoon settling into a pot of honey.

I could be pregnant. With Knightley's baby.

Actually, it's probably about time I started calling him by his first name.

Leander. Lee. I could be pregnant with Lee's baby.

Tears prick my eyes. "He doesn't want children," I whisper.

"I know he's said that. But I have a feeling that might change after he visits his father today. And if the mother of his children was you." Dad smiles.

But I shake my head. "I don't want him to stay with me because I'm pregnant."

He sighs again. "I know that losing control is one of your biggest fears. But maybe you need to think about letting Lee make some of his own decisions. He loves you, Em, and yes, love is the most important ingredient in a relationship, but it's not the only one. There's also duty, responsibility, respect, and trust. If he's gotten you pregnant, do you have the right to deny him the opportunity to do the right thing, if he decides that's what he wants to do?"

I fiddle with the tissue. "I hadn't thought of it like that."

"I know on the surface of it, we make decisions for other people for the right reasons—mostly to try to save them from pain. But sometimes they're not our decisions to make. Did your mother save me pain by choosing to take her own life? Well, she saved me from a few months, or maybe even a year or two, of having to watch her suffer, and from hard work and emotional turmoil. But am I glad she did it? No. I resent her with every fiber of my being for taking away from me the chance to care for her and be there when she passed away."

His voice, usually so calm, holds a touch of bitterness. I look up at him, shocked. I've never heard him speak about her like that.

My bottom lip trembles again, and more tears spill over my lashes.

"I'm sorry." He tightens his arms around me. "I just wanted you to know that I see both sides."

I cry for a while, but inside I'm already calming as I process what he said.

When my tears finally stop falling, he gives me a squeeze and says, "Right, I'm going to go and get a pregnancy test. Will you be okay?"

"I'll be fine. Thanks, Dad."

He kisses the top of my head, grabs his keys, and leaves.

I'm tempted to have a whiskey for the shock, but then I think maybe I shouldn't until I've taken the test. Two tests, two results that will drastically change my life if they're positive.

I might be wrong, but once the shock wears off, I'm pretty sure Dad's right, and Knightley will want to do what he sees as the 'right thing'. I'm not sure what that would entail. Marrying me? My heart gives a little leap. He is very old fashioned, so that would probably be his logical conclusion. I wouldn't want him to commit himself to me for life just because of a stupid slip up. But Dad said, *Maybe you need to think about letting Lee make some of his own decisions*. Is he right?

I watch the rain run down the window. If I am pregnant, should I get the fetus tested? There's no point, unless I'm convinced I want to terminate it if it's positive. But should I make that decision on my own? Or should Knightley, as the father, have a say in it?

I mean Lee. Dammit. I don't think I'll ever get used to not calling him Knightley.

I shouldn't get carried away—I don't even know if I'm pregnant yet, and anyway, even if I am, I won't need to get it tested if my HD test is negative. What a muddle. But it's impossible not to think about all the options. I'm only twenty-one, but one way or another, my life is going to look quite different in a week's time. Maybe even in a day's time. I've convinced myself I won't hear from Susie until next week, but the truth is that the results could come any day.

Curling up on the sofa, I rest my head on the back and think about Mum. For the past year, I've told myself it's a good thing that she was able to make her own decision about when to end her own life. But now, after Dad's confession, I finally feel able to admit to myself that what she did hurt me terribly. I understand, of course I do, and it's entirely possible I'll make the same decision if I end up in her position. But as her child, her baby, even though looking after her was terribly, terribly hard, I do regret that I wasn't there with her at the end.

And then I think about Knightley, and how he said: *So you'll break my heart and take away my chance to be with the love of my life because you're worried about what might happen in twenty years' time?*

The love of his life. We haven't even really started dating yet. Not properly, going out to the cinema, or telling our friends that we're a couple. He can't really think I'm the love of his life. Can he?

But of course, it's not as if we only met two weeks ago. We've known each for other seventeen years. And we've gradually fallen for each other over that time. I'm happy to admit I love him with all my heart and always have done. I trust him more than anyone else bar Dad. Why am I so shocked that we ended up together?

Resting a hand on my belly, I consider the idea that I might be pregnant. Knightley and I might have made a baby. I've not let myself think about children too much, because I've always known I have the hurdle of the HD test to get over first. But for the first time, I let myself go a few feet down that road. My heart gives a strange flip. If you believe in parallel universes, there is definitely one out there where my HD test is negative, and the pregnancy result is positive... Where Knightley is thrilled that I'm pregnant, and where we end up together, young and healthy, married and with children.

What if it's this universe?

I'm shocked at the joy that surges briefly through me. Forget the test. Forget his insistence that he doesn't want kids. Forget everything except having his baby inside me. Oh my God. I hadn't realized how much I wanted it until now.

Tears prick my eyes. I can't think about it. It's going to be far too painful if it doesn't turn out that way.

I close my eyes, exhausted from all the emotion, and even though I wouldn't have thought I could possibly sleep, I doze a little until the front door opens again and Dad comes in.

"Hey," he says, as I push myself up. "You okay?"

I nod, looking at the paper bag in his hand.

He passes it to me. "Are you going to do it now?"

"Yes. Better to know."

"Okay. Make sure you read the instructions."

"Will do."

I take it into the bathroom and read the leaflet that comes in the box. Dad was right—the test claims it's ninety-nine percent accurate from the day of your expected period. I pee on the stick and put the lid back on. I wash my hands, set a timer on my phone for three minutes, and put the box and leaflet in the trash.

Then, too nervous to wait on my own, I go back into the living room.

"Three minutes," I say to Dad as he looks up.

"Okay."

I sit on the edge of the sofa and put the test face down on the coffee table. He sits in the armchair. His hair is damp—he must have left without his umbrella. Outside, the rain continues to run down the windows, although it seems lighter than it has been. Maybe it's clearing up at last. Or perhaps it's just wishful thinking.

He looks at his watch. "Lee will be going into the prison right about now."

My jaw drops. "I'd completely forgotten. Oh, I should have wished him luck." I feel guilty that I didn't remember. I know how nervous he must have been driving up there.

"He'll understand," Dad says. "I asked him to let us know how it goes. I don't know if he'll phone, or if he'll call in tonight."

"I wonder what Steven will say."

"I think Lee's going in with realistic expectations," Dad says. "That's a good thing."

"Do you think Steven is going to apologize?"

"No."

"Me neither."

He gives me a sad smile.

I look at my phone. Twenty seconds to go.

It's amazing how your whole life comes down to one second. As if you're standing in the middle of a seesaw, and it could tip either way.

I watch the seconds tick down until it says zero.

Then I lean forward and turn over the test.

Chapter Twenty-Four

Knightley

I try not to look as if I'm terrified as I walk into the prison.

I don't know why, but my stomach has turned to water, and my hands are shaking. It might be the fear of seeing my father, but I think it's also some kind of primal terror that the bars are going to close behind me, and they'll refuse to let me out. I can hear Gabe laughing at that in my head.

As I follow the signs for Visitors, I try to imagine how Dad must have felt coming in here and knowing he would never be leaving again. I've spent most of my life trying not to think about him or prison, but it's impossible not to now I'm here.

To my knowledge, what my father did to my mother was nothing to do with me, but even though I pretend it isn't, his act and the place he's in now is still a major part of my life.

It would be horrible if the man inside was a distant relative—a third cousin twice removed. It would still feel like a stain on my clothing I can't get out no matter how much I scrub. But he's not a distant relative. He's my fucking father, and I hate him with every ounce of my being.

I go into reception, tell the guard my name, and hand him the visitor approval letter. He looks at my ID carefully, checks my name against the list of visitors expected for the day, gives me a colored wristband, then lets me through. Next I have to take off my jacket and shoes, then I go through a scanner, and my temperature is taken with a thermal camera. A dog handler with a German shepherd also checks me over. I wait nervously, even though I'm carrying nothing that could be called contraband. In fact I haven't brought my father anything. Maybe I should have done, like when you visit someone in hospital. Even if they don't want anything, it seems polite.

As I put my jacket and Converses back on, I'm told that my visit will last a maximum of thirty minutes, and then I'm shown into a large room with tables and chairs, half of which are occupied by men in orange overalls.

I stand in the doorway, my heart racing. I haven't seen my father for seventeen years. I scan the men, unsure whether I'll recognize him.

But I needn't have worried. The guy sitting on the left under the barred window meets my gaze, and I feel a shiver of recognition.

Slowly, I walk over and stand before the table.

He's older, of course, and his hair is flecked with gray. He's also a lot thinner—he was overweight when he was younger, but he must have lost forty pounds or so. He's clean shaven, but his face is heavily lined, and his skin is dull and a yellowy gray.

"Sit down," he says.

So, no affectionate hug, then. Half-relieved, half-bitterly disappointed, I draw out the chair and sit. I lean back, hands in the pockets of my jacket, and we study one another silently. My heart bangs on my ribs, but I try to keep my cool.

"I didn't bring you anything," I say, wanting to hurt him back.

He shrugs. "Didn't expect you to." He blinks slowly. John has light-brown hair and always took more after Mum, but Dad looks a bit like me and Rob—tall with dark hair, blue eyes, and a straight nose, and to my shock, as I didn't remember, he also has the same slight gap in his front teeth that I do.

It hits me then. This is my natural father. The man who murdered my mother. Who left me, and Rob and John. Who abandoned us at the time we needed him most. And who hasn't contacted me since.

"What do you want?" I ask, my voice husky.

"I wanted to see you."

"Why? After all these years?"

"Because I'm dying."

I stare at him. "What?"

"I have pancreatic cancer. I've had treatment but it's come back. I don't have long."

I sit there numbly, feeling like a robot. I need someone to program me and tell me how I should react, how to feel.

"Are you in pain?" I ask.

He shrugs—it seems his default gesture.

"I'm sorry," I mutter. I don't know if it's true, but I say it anyway. After the words have left my lips, I realize they're sincere. I'm not a vindictive man. I'm a vet. I don't want any creature to be in pain.

"Do you need anything?" I ask.

"No." He studies the table. He seems empty, blank.

"I don't understand," I say. "Why call me here? Why not write and tell me? Or just let me find out when… it's all over? Why did you want to see me?"

He finally lifts his gaze to mine, and he looks at me for a long while before eventually saying, "Hugh Woodruff writes to me. Regular as clockwork, every month."

My eyebrows lift and my jaw drops. "Seriously?"

"He tells me how you boys are doing. He put in a photo of you when you got your vet degree. He sent one last week, with pictures of John's wedding."

"I didn't know," I whisper.

"There was one of you with a pretty girl. Young, slim, blonde hair. You had your arm around her."

"That's Em. She's his daughter. I grew up with her."

"Is she your girl?"

I shift in the chair, uncomfortable talking about her. "Why didn't you ask Rob and John to come too?"

A shrug.

Silence falls between us again.

"Are you afraid of dying?" I ask.

For a moment, he looks away, out of the small, barred window to the cloudy sky. Then his gaze comes back to me. "I'm going to hell for what I did. I know that. I deserve it. But I wanted to see you. I needed to see for myself that I did one thing right in my life."

I don't say anything. I'm too shocked to speak.

A fraction of a smile flickers on his lips. "You've turned out well, son. Better than I could have hoped."

It's no good; although I promised I wouldn't ask, I can't stop myself. "Why didn't you contact me before? Why leave it until now, when it's too late?"

"You were better off without me." He speaks plainly, without emotion. He's obviously come to terms with that. "You didn't need me."

"But you're my father."

He shakes his head. "No I'm not. Hugh's your father."

It's then that I realize—when he said *I needed to see for myself that I did one thing right in my life*, he didn't mean by having children, or seeing how I turned out. He wanted to reassure himself that he did the right thing by letting another, better man bring us up.

I'm going to hell for what I did. I know that. I deserve it. He does regret his act. And he hasn't contacted us because he wanted to set us free. To make sure we were tainted as little as possible by what he did.

Emotion wells inside me, tightening my throat and making my eyes sting.

"What's the Bay like today?" he asks.

He hasn't stood on the sand, felt the sea wash over his feet, in seventeen years.

I clear my throat. "Beautiful. I helped set up a veterinary hospital on the coast, just down from Opua. I take the boat out most days to help injured animals found out on the islands."

He nods slowly, his eyes distant. "Do you go fishing?"

"Yeah. Rob and John come with me sometimes. And Gabe—that's Hugh's son. He's my best friend. The four of us used to go over to Urupekapeka with Hugh when we were teens, camp there for the night, and wake up at dawn to fish. The water would be crystal clear and cold, but the sun would come up, and then the shallows would turn warm. Seals would bask on the rocks, and penguins would swim under the jetty. Stingrays and dolphins in the water. White horses out to sea. You could see for miles. We'd have a portable barbecue, and we'd cook the fish we caught and eat it right there on the beach. Gabe and I would dive for mussels and take them back for the girls. I had a wonderful childhood, in many ways."

Dad nods. "I'm glad."

"It's time," the guard calls.

Already? I stare at my father, shocked that I'm disappointed.

"I'm sorry," Dad says.

I don't know if he's sorry because the time went so quick, or because he wasn't there to bring me up, or because of what he did to Mum. Maybe all of it. He stands, and I get to my feet. We hesitate, and then I go up to him and put my arms around him.

He stiffens, then hugs me back.

We stand there like for a long moment.

Then I turn and walk out of the room without looking back.

*

I drive back to Paihia, then park up by the beach, kick off my shoes, walk onto the sand, and sit, just a few feet from the sea.

My face is wet, and my throat is raw. I press the heels of my hands over my eyes, shutting out the bright sunlight. The emotion reaches its peak, and I feel like a rope that's been knotted in the middle and pulled tight. My whole body tenses with the weight of seventeen years of anger and pain.

And then, just as quickly, it washes over me, and it's gone.

I lay back on the sand, my arms over my face. My feet grow wet as a wave creeps up to cover them, but still I don't move.

He couldn't apologize, not in so many words. I know that now. It would be meaningless. How do you say sorry for something like that? It's such a small word, too small for the enormity of what he did, like trying to cure cancer with a multi-vitamin. He destroyed our lives, and he knows it. He can't excuse it. Say he'd had a bad day, or that he'd had one too many. Nothing he could say would have made it all right. If he'd apologized, it would have made me angry, as if he thought he'd wiped the slate clean. He knows it'll never be clean. But he feels that he did the best he could by letting us go, and leaving us to get on with our lives without him.

I move my arms up a fraction and peek out. The rain stopped about an hour ago, and the clouds have parted to reveal the brilliant February sunshine. It's already roasting hot, and the sand is drying quickly.

I should go back to HWH, but I don't feel like it today. Before I left this morning, I made sure we were on top of the work. The influx of animals has calmed after the mania of the past week. All the other vets are there, and they can cover for me.

Taking out my phone, I sit up and check my messages. Nothing from Em, but that doesn't surprise me. I text Frankie, saying I probably won't be in today.

Next, I text Hugh and ask whether I can call in after lunch. He comes back immediately, *Of course. Whenever you want.* He doesn't ask what happened at the prison. He knows I'll tell him when I'm ready.

After that, I phone Rob. He listens quietly as I summarize my visit.

"Are you going to go and see him?" I ask after I've told him that Dad only has a short time left to live.

"Did he ask for me?"

I sigh and throw a stone into the sea. "I'm sure he'd like to see you."

"Then no. Thanks for letting me know." He hangs up.

Should I have lied? I'm not sure Dad would agree to see him, though, even if he wanted to go. I feel bad that I'm the only one he asked for, and the only one who got to see him. Should I have refused to go unless he agreed to see all of us?

Feeling guilty, I call John and tell him what happened. "Rob's upset," I tell him.

"Yeah," he says. "He would never have admitted it, but he's always hoped Dad would eventually contact us. It sounds as if Dad at least accepts what he did was wrong, which is something. He let us go because he knew it was best for us. That's good, too."

"Yeah. That's what I thought."

"Rob'll come around. Maybe it's what he needed to be able to move on, you know?"

"Maybe. Do you think I should have refused to go?"

"Not at all. Look, don't worry about it. It makes sense that Dad asked to see you. You represent all three of us, and you're the one he'd be able to remember the most. We all wanted to know why he chose to call after all this time. There's no need to feel guilty."

I clear my throat. "I'm glad you see it like that. Hey, did you know that Hugh wrote to him once a month?"

"Really? No."

"He sent some photos of your wedding day."

"Oh… I'm quite touched by that."

"Me too."

"Have you told Dad?"

For a second I'm confused, then I realize he's referring to Hugh. "Not yet. I'm going over there soon."

We talk for a few more minutes before we say goodbye.

Apart from Hugh and Em, Gabe is the one other person I want to tell, but I know he's at a meeting until two, so I decide to call him later.

It's nearly twelve thirty. Scrolling back through my messages, I find the one I got yesterday evening from Hal King, one of the vets at Noah's Ark. We trained at veterinary college together, and he's an old friend, although I've only seen him a couple of times since he had his baby. He asked if I could collect an injured kiwi bird that someone brought in. It was late when he texted, so I replied that I'd pick it up today.

I message him and ask if I can call in. He comes back immediately, *I'm just leaving to go home. Can you meet me there? I'll bring the kiwi bird with me.*

Will do, I reply.

Getting up, I brush the sand from my jeans. It's going to take a while to process what's happened this morning, but I don't think it's a coincidence that the world feels brighter, warmer.

I drive the short distance to Hal's house, up on a high hill overlooking Paihia and the Bay. His car is already there when I pull up, and the front door is open. I walk into the house, leaving my shoes by the door. A covered crate sits in the hallway in the shade, and when I peek in, I see the kiwi asleep in the corner.

Rising, I call out, "It's me."

"Come in. We're in the kitchen."

Hal and Izzy bought the house not long after they were married. He's *rich as*, and the house is gorgeous, wide and open plan, filled with light. The kitchen is huge, with a large, square table in the middle. His son, Daniel, is sitting in a highchair, eating his lunch. He must be nearly a year old now. He bangs his spoon on the tray when he sees me and gives me a toothless grin.

"Hey." Hal comes over and gives me a bearhug. He's taller than me, big, affable, and charismatic. Izzy calls him the Dog Whisperer, and I've seen him cast his magic on more than one animal, and watched them immediately quieten and succumb to his charm. "You remember Uncle Knightley," Hal says to Danny.

"Dog," Danny says, and throws his spoon on the floor.

"Not quite," Hal says, "but gold star for trying."

"Babysitting?" I tease, picking up the spoon.

"Yeah. We have a nanny who looks after him in the mornings. In the afternoons me, Izzy, and Mum and Dad take turns. Want a coffee?"

"Please, as long as I'm not disturbing you."

"No, of course not. When Danny boy here's done with lunch, we'll be settling down for an exciting afternoon watching *Storybots* and snoozing."

"Sounds thrilling."

He grins as he begins to make the coffee. "It's my favorite afternoon of the week."

I sit next to Danny as Hal steams the milk, and I pass the baby one of his breadsticks. He bangs it on the table with the spoon.

"I think you've got a budding Zak Starkey here," I tell Hal.

"He's a damn good singer, too. Show him, Danny."

Danny yells, "Nana, nana, nana."

Hal chuckles. "See?" He pours the hot milk onto the coffee, then when he's done, unbuckles his son from the chair.

I smile. "I have to admit, I never thought I'd see you so comfortable with kids."

He lifts Danny up in the air, blows on his belly, then tucks an arm under his butt. "Me neither. They're pretty easy. You hold them like a rugby ball, pull faces when they're crying, and if they don't stop, you give them back to their mother."

"Yuck," Danny says, showing Hal his biscuit-crumbed fingers.

"Yum," he replies and licks one, and Danny squeals.

Hal grins. "Can you bring the coffees?" He grabs a wipe and cleans Danny's other fingers, walking into the living room, and I follow. The two of us sit on the floor on either side of the baby gym in front of the TV. He places Danny underneath the gym, then clips a couple of toys onto the frame arching over him. Soon Danny's swatting away, cooing at himself in the tiny mirrors that swing in the sunlight.

I sip the coffee, studying Hal, surprised by how content he seems. He was nuclear-powered at vet college, managing to balance top grades and partying with ease, never without a pretty girl on his arm. Izzy also studied at our college. The two of them were the best of friends, and I sometimes wondered why they'd never gotten together. I guess it takes time. I think of Em, and smile.

"How's HWH?" Hal asks.

"Busy, especially over Waitangi."

"Yeah, we were the same."

"Did you hear about Kohanga?"

He nods. "It's going to mean more work for you. Do you have the capacity?"

"We can expand a little. We have a few financial issues though. Rob's doing his best to get funding and donations, but things are tight."

"Get him to call Leon," he says, mentioning their financial manager. "He might have a few contacts."

"I will, thanks."

"I sympathize though. It's not easy running places like ours, and that's even with the Kings' money."

"Yeah."

He has a mouthful of coffee. "By the way, I'm sorry to hear about you and Tia."

"Ah, yeah, thanks."

"You broke up before you went to Aus?"

"Yes. It had been coming for a while."

He nods. "Anyone else on the horizon?"

I run a hand through my hair. "I'm kind of seeing Em."

A smile spreads slowly across his face. "Emily Woodruff? Huh. She's a sweetheart."

"She is."

"How long?"

"Oh, only a couple of weeks. It's a bit up in the air at the moment."

"Why so?"

"Well, she's waiting for her test results for her Huntington's."

"Oh shit, yeah. I forgot about that. What are her chances?"

"Fifty-fifty."

Hal blows out a breath. "Hard on you both."

"Yeah."

"If she's positive… what then?"

"She told me that she wouldn't get involved with anyone because she wouldn't want to burden them with it."

Hal's eyes hold pity. "How do you feel about it? Would it change how you feel about her? If it's only been a few weeks, it's a lot to take on in a new relationship. It wouldn't make you a bad person to go along with her decision."

On the surface, it's a harsh question, but I know him well enough to guess he's playing devil's advocate and forcing me to look at both sides.

"This part is new," I say slowly, "but we've known each other for a long time. Whether we were in a relationship or not, I'd want to care for her when she eventually showed symptoms. It'd be tough to watch her go through it either way."

"Yeah."

"I don't want it to be a factor in whether or not we make a go of it," I add with feeling. "Shit happens in life; it's just usually we don't know when it's coming. In her case, she'd know where she was heading, but it shouldn't change the fact that we could have twenty or thirty good years together."

"What about kids? They'd inherit the same chance, right?"

"If she's positive, yes. She could either have IVF and have the embryos tested, or if she got pregnant, have prenatal testing."

"You want kids?" he asks.

I hold out a hand to Danny, who grabs my finger. "I didn't. I was too afraid of turning out like my father."

Hal knows about my parents, and why I came to stay with the Woodruffs. "But you've changed your mind?"

"I went to see him this morning at the prison. He rang me and asked me to go."

"Fuck."

"Yeah."

"What happened?"

"He told me he's dying. Pancreatic cancer."

Hal sighs. "I'm sorry, man."

"I don't know how I feel about it yet. I asked him why he hadn't contacted me before now, and he said I didn't need him. And when I said that I did, because he was my father, he said, 'No I'm not. Hugh's your father.' And it made me realize how right he was."

I lie on my back and look up at the ceiling. Something is settling over me, and I'm not sure what it is yet, but I can feel it happening, like confetti thrown in the air that gradually drifts to the ground.

"I think because Hugh and Angela never adopted us, I've kept Hugh at arm's length," I say slowly. "Rob and John both call Hugh Dad, but he's never asked me to, and I never have. If I'm honest, I've wondered more than once why he didn't adopt us. He's always treated us no differently than his own kids, but I think I've felt that maybe he loved us, but not quite enough for that. Then I found out he told John that he purposely didn't adopt us because it would preclude any of us having a relationship. I guess he saw the possibility of that happening early on, especially with John and Bella, who were close even when they were kids."

"Smart man."

"Yeah. And today, Dad told me that Hugh writes to him once a month."

"Shit, really?"

"Yeah. He tells him what we've been up to, and sends him photos. I don't think Dad writes back, but Hugh does it anyway, regular as clockwork. It's made me feel so humble. He told me that if violence was caused by a defective gene, I obviously haven't inherited it, because he'd have seen evidence of it by now."

"Makes sense."

"Do you think so? Or is it behavioral? I was thirteen when Dad killed Mum. It's an impressionable age."

"And you're a smart guy. You've been able to compare his behavior with Hugh's. You've seen how a real man deals with frustration and anger. It doesn't matter whether it's nature or nurture. You're one of the good guys. You should take as much positivity as you can from today's visit and run with it. And bring up your own boys in Hugh's footsteps."

He looks at his phone then. "It's Izzy. I'll just take this, won't be long." He gets up and puts the phone to his ear as he leaves the room.

I look at Danny, who's watched his father go. The boy blinks, looks at me, and then his bottom lip trembles.

"Shit," I say, "don't cry."

Danny's face screws up, though, and he begins to wail.

"Can you pick him up?" Hal's voice echoes from somewhere in the house.

I sit up, move the baby gym, then hold my hands out to Danny. My stomach does a strange flip as he lifts up his arms to me.

"Come here, little fella." I get to my feet, pick him up, and slide an arm under his butt, the same way I saw Hal do it. "Shh. Daddy'll be back soon. Look! It's a giraffe." I pick up a soft toy whose hooves appear to be teething rings. Danny munches on one as his tiny fingers rustle its crunchy ears.

He's soft in my arms, and he smells of baby powder and milk. His hair is light blonde and silky soft. I kiss it gently, feeling the fontanelle—the soft spot where the bony plates that make up the skull haven't yet closed—beneath my lips. He rests his cheek on my shoulder and gives a shivery sigh.

I've never considered having kids before. I've always been adamant that I don't want them. But for the first time, I think about what it would be like to hold one of my own.

I imagine making love with Em without a condom, knowing that each time there would be a chance we could make a baby. Finding out she's pregnant. Watching her grow. Being with her when she gives birth. Holding our child in my arms. And then seeing it grow up. If it was a boy, like little Danny, bringing it up in Hugh's footsteps.

I glance over my shoulder and see Hal leaning on the door jamb, watching us, a small smile on his face. I'm not convinced there was actually a phone call; I didn't hear it ring or vibrate. Sneaky bastard.

Chapter Twenty-Five

Emily

At just before two, Knightley's Ford pulls up on the drive.

"He's here," I call to Dad, who's in the living room, having a snooze in the armchair.

He gets up, stretches, and meets me in the kitchen. "You okay?" he asks gently. "You definitely want to see him?"

I nod.

"Okay."

We turn as the front door opens, and Knightley comes in.

He's wearing dark jeans and a white shirt, no tie, with the sleeves rolled up to just below his elbow. His hair is even more ruffled than usual; I suspect he's run his hands through it multiple times today. He's left his Converses by the door, and his feet are bare. God, he's so incredibly handsome.

He bends to greet Minnie as she runs up, wagging. He glances at me and smiles, then looks back at Hugh.

"Hey," Hugh says. "How are you doing?"

Knightley just looks at him, then, to my surprise and, I expect, my father's, he comes up and envelops him in a huge bearhug.

"Aw," Dad says, putting his arms around him and hugging him back.

Knightley stands like that for a good thirty seconds, eyes closed. My throat tightens at his obvious emotion, and I press my fingers to my mouth.

Eventually, he opens his eyes and looks at me, then releases Dad and moves back.

"All right, boy?" Dad says, rubbing his arm.

Knightley nods, leaning his butt on the worktop and folding his arms. "He told me you write to him every month."

My eyes widen. Dad slides his hands into his pockets. "You're not angry about that?"

"No." Knightley smiles. "I told John. We both said we were touched by it."

Dad looks relieved. "I'm an eternal optimist, and I hoped he regretted what he did. I wanted him to know that his boys were doing well."

Knightley studies his bare feet. "He has pancreatic cancer. He doesn't have long to live."

Dad's face creases with sadness. "I'm so sorry."

"Me too," I whisper.

"I don't know how I feel about that yet," Knightley says. "I asked why he hadn't contacted me before now. He said because I didn't need him. When I said he was wrong, he was my father, he said no, that you were my father. And he needed to know he'd done one thing right in his life by letting us go." He stops and smiles, his eyes bright.

My eyes sting. It doesn't make what his father did all right. It doesn't take away the fact that he hurt his sons by not contacting them. He could have written them a letter and explained why he was choosing to keep his distance. But finding out now is better than not finding out at all, and I can see that realization in Knightley's eyes.

Dad puts a hand on his arm. "Tell me the rest later," he says. "I need to check on Angus in the orchard. If you're around for dinner, we're having tacos." He smiles and heads out the front door, Minnie on his heels.

Knightley's gaze returns to me. "Hello."

"Hello."

We're about six feet apart. He doesn't move toward me, but the look in his eyes is gentle. "How are you doing?"

I shrug. "Okay. I wanted to say, I'm sorry about not seeing you on Saturday. I was a mess, and I just couldn't deal with it."

"It's all right. I get it. I'm guessing you haven't heard yet?"

I shake my head. "Not yet. But I—"

"I've got something to say," he says, interrupting me. I stop speaking and raise my eyebrows.

"I've been thinking about it a lot," he continues. "I'm going to blurt it all out, and it might not make a lot of sense, but let me go before you say anything, all right? So, seeing my father, and Hal, too—I called in after I left the prison—seeing them both brought it all into focus, you know? And now I get it. The only thing that matters is you. And me, and how we feel about each other."

I stare at him. His eyes are blazing, and passion radiates from him like a thousand-watt bulb.

"Nothing else matters," he continues. "Not any fucking test, not what's happened to either of us in the past, or what will happen in the future. Do you get that? You said to me that it's going to hurt like fuck if it comes to an end, no matter how many times we slept together. I told Hal today that it'd be tough to watch you develop the disease whether I was with you or not. And I realized I don't want it to be a factor in whether or not we make a go of it. I don't think you should let yourself be defined by HD. I think we're strong enough to deal with whatever life throws at us. It's not about avoiding the bad things, because you can't. It's learning to deal with them. I want to share my life with you. Or at least, I want that to be an option. I want to date you, to spend time with you, for us to try each other on and see if we fit, like normal people do. I'm not going to let the disease run my life, and I don't think you should either. I think we should fuck it up the arse and tell it that it has no power over us."

I blink. "Fuck it up the arse?"

"Metaphorically speaking."

I give a short laugh, overwhelmed by his speech and the strength of emotion behind it.

"You don't have to decide anything now," he says. "But I want a future that includes marriage and children."

That makes my jaw drop. "Children?"

"Hal said that it doesn't matter whether violence is something we inherit, or whether it's behavioral, that either way I'm one of the good guys. It's what Hugh said too. And I think I'm finally beginning to agree with it."

I stare at him again. Emotion wells up inside me.

"I was going to confess something," I whisper, "but you beat me to it."

"What?"

"I'm pregnant."

It's his turn to stare at me. "What?"

"I know we used a condom, but… I don't know, I guess it broke or something. I'm sorry, I didn't plan for it to happen, but it did, and I took a test today, and it was positive, and now I'm so mixed up—I'm excited and panicky and upset and relieved and thrilled and—"

He takes my face in his hands and kisses me, ending my ramblings with a press of his lips.

When he finally lifts his head, I have to blink tears away. "You're not mad?"

"No," he murmurs, brushing under my eye with a thumb, "I'm not mad."

"If my HD test is positive, we'll have to talk about whether we get the fetus tested."

He nods. "First things, first."

"Yeah."

He kisses my forehead, then wraps his arms around me. I bury my face in his shirt, and we stand like that for a long, long time.

*

He stays for the rest of the day. We have dinner with Dad, and then Knightley and I go for a long walk around the orchards. We have a lot to discuss, I know, but in the end it's almost too much, and we talk about nothing—about music and books and travel, while the sun sinks below the horizon, turning the trees and vines to gold, then orange, and then deep red before they fade to black.

I don't ask him to stay the night, and he doesn't offer. He leaves around eight, but he promises to come and see me tomorrow after work.

When I go to bed that night, I lie on my side and look out at the stars. I've given up trying to analyze my feelings. I used to think life was like a library, with all your experiences, thoughts, hopes, and dreams filed neatly away on shelves in alphabetical order. But I'm beginning to realize it's more like a huge jar of jellybeans. You dip your hand in, and you might get one you don't like—spoiled milk, or dead fish. But most of the time you get strawberry or buttered popcorn or caramel or chocolate pudding. You just never know. And you can't prepare yourself for the rotten ones—they always take you by surprise, and they're always disgusting. You just have to spit them out and hope the next one is better.

I lay on my back and rest a hand on my belly. I'm afraid to hope, because I know if I do, I could end up being terribly disappointed. But it's impossible not to wish for a happy ending.

Whatever happens, though, it seems that Knightley is going to be by my side, helping me cope. I won't have to do it alone. For the first time, it feels as if maybe, whatever the result, my future might still contain a few buttered popcorn jellybeans.

*

The next day, I get up and tell Dad I'm going to do some painting. I'm not great at it—Mum was much better than me, but I like using her old paints as it makes me feel close to her. So I set up the easel on the deck, and set to painting the view.

He comes out with a coffee after an hour or two, and has a look at my progress.

"Not bad," he says.

"It's terrible," I say wryly. "But thank you for being polite."

"It's not terrible. It's… interpretative."

"That's one word for it." I look down at my phone as it vibrates. Knightley told me he'd call mid-morning, and I've been looking forward to talking to him.

Then my heart skips a beat. The screen says Dr. Susie.

I look at Dad, who's seen the name. "Answer it," he whispers.

I swipe the screen and put it to my ear. "Hello?"

"Is that Emily Woodruff?"

"Speaking."

"This is Dr. Susie Cunningham's assistant from Whangarei Hospital. We have the results of your Huntington's test, and Dr. Cunningham wonders whether you could come in today to discuss them?"

My heart is pounding so hard, I feel faint. "Um, yes, of course. When?"

"Could you make it for eleven thirty?"

I check the time—it's not quite ten. "Yes, we'll leave right away."

"Oh that's good. You know where to come?"

"To her office?"

"Yes. And will you have someone with you?"

"Yes."

"Okay, we'll see you then."

I say goodbye and end the call.

Dad pulls me to my feet and gives me a hug. "Do you want Knightley to go with you?" he murmurs. "I don't mind. We can go and pick him up. I'm sure he'd be happy to go."

I rest my forehead on his shoulder. I do want Knightley. More than anything in the world. I want to feel his arms around me. His lips on mine. I want him to kiss away all the bad things and tell me everything's going to be all right.

But this is something I need to do myself. "No," I say, moving back. "Can you come with me?"

His expression softens. "Of course." He lets me go. "Come on, then. Let's get going."

*

I don't remember the journey at all. Dad drives, and I spend it looking out of the window. My mind whirls with a complex mixture of thoughts and emotions, as if I have my hand in the jar of jellybeans and I'm swirling it around. I don't try to rein it in. I let it swirl, let the minutes tick by, and just try not to throw up.

When we finally get there, he holds my hand as we walk through the hospital. I feel lightheaded and surreal. Everything's too loud, too bright. A couple of kids are playing in the waiting room, laughing loudly. Other people are living their lives, with no idea of what's happening to me today.

We get to Susie's department and go up to her assistant.

"Hello, Emily," she says with a smile. "Take a seat. She shouldn't be long."

Dad leads me to the row of chairs and sits beside me.

The chairs are orange. The carpet is gray. The curtains are gray too, with little blue flowers. The assistant's hair is cut in a bob, one side held back by a clip with a pink flower. Her teeth have a gap in the front, a bit like Knightley's. Her lipstick is scarlet, a shade too bright for her skin tone.

I wonder whether he's rung. I've turned off my phone so I can't be sure.

I think we should fuck it up the arse and tell it that it has no power over us.

A hysterical giggle rises inside me, then vanishes as quickly as it began.

Dad puts his arm around me and squeezes. "Want a cup of water?" he asks. I shake my head.

"Emily?"

My head snaps around as Susie comes out of her office. "Come through," she says. She's sort of half smiling. Not beaming. Does that mean anything? Wouldn't she beam if it were good news?

I'm shaking like a leaf. Dad leads me into the office and sits on the chair beside me, holding my hand. An envelope rests on the table. It has my name on the front.

I want to snatch it up and open it.

But when I do, the waiting will be over, for me and the baby.

And suddenly, I understand why Bella and Gabe have never been tested. All the time they don't know, they have hope. Why didn't I understand that until now?

I don't want to know. I shouldn't have come.

Susie closes the door, comes over, and sits. She reaches for the envelope, picks it up, and turns it over. It's still intact. She doesn't know the results yet.

"Don't open it," I say immediately. "I don't want to know."

I expect her to look annoyed, but she just tips her head to the side and glances at Dad. "Are you Emily's father?"

He nods and looks at me. "Come on, sweetheart. You do want to know."

I'm shaking so much. "I don't know if I can bear it," I whisper.

"Be strong, darling. We'll cope together, whatever the result."

I look back at Susie, biting my bottom lip hard. My heart's going like a piston. He's right. I have to know.

I nod.

She holds out the envelope to me.

"Can you do it?" I squeak.

"Of course." She runs a finger beneath the seal, opens it, and takes out a sheet of paper.

Her gaze brushes down it. She reads to the bottom, then her gaze returns to the top, and she reads again, as if she's afraid of making a mistake.

I think I'm going to vomit.

Finally, she looks up at me.

I know what it says even before she speaks because her face lights up with relief.

"It's good news, Em. It's negative."

My brain grinds to a halt.

"You remember what I said about the nucleotide letters CAG being repeated?" she asks. "That a normal test is twenty-six or fewer? Your test shows fifteen repeats. You haven't inherited the defective gene. The test is negative."

Dad makes a strangled sound beside me, and then covers his mouth with a hand as tears run down his face. "Sorry," he says hoarsely, looking at me.

I burst into tears and throw my arms around him.

We sit there like that for a long time. I'm almost as thrilled for him as I am for myself. I think about Mum, and hope that, wherever she is, she's pleased, too.

I'm free. Free of the sword hanging over my head. Free to have a relationship without fear, to date normally, to grow old with someone, to have children with them.

Free to try all those things with Knightley, if he'll have me. We can have sex a billion different ways and I won't have to worry that I'm turning into a deviant. Holy shit, the guy isn't going to know what hit him.

And the baby… I don't have to get it tested. I know it's early, and a hundred other things could go wrong with the pregnancy. But if it makes it… it's also free. I have a real person inside me, and he or she doesn't have HD.

Oh God. I'm so… I don't know what the word is, but whatever it is, I feel it so strongly that I think I'm going to explode.

Next to us, Susie gets up and goes over to the fridge, gets out a water bottle, and pours it into two cups. She brings them back, then sits there patiently until we finally break apart.

"I'm sorry," I say, my voice hoarse.

"Goodness, don't be," she says with a smile. "It's wonderful news and I'm thrilled for you both. Now, take a deep breath, have a drink, and then we'll have a chat about what this means."

I tell her I'm pregnant, and I can see she's genuinely happy and relieved for me. We talk for a while about the results. I find myself more emotional than I expected as she discusses Gabe and Bella. They're going to be thrilled for me, but she tells me to prepare myself for all kinds of feelings from both sides—envy, relief, resentment, anger, joy, and guilt. "Every emotion is normal," she says. "And I'm here to talk to any of you if you need me."

It's another half an hour before Dad and I leave.

We don't say much as we walk through the hospital. It's only when we get outside, into the bright summer's day, that he turns to me, and we stand and hug.

"I'm sorry," I whisper.

He kisses my temple. "For what?"

"That Mum had it. That you've had to go through all this. It's not fair."

"No, it's not. But nobody said life was fair. It's all a lottery."

"Beans in a jar," I mumble.

He laughs. "Yeah."

We break apart but continue to hold hands as we walk down the hill back to the car. "So what now?" he asks. "You want to ring Knightley?"

I do, but I shake my head. "Gabe first, then Bella. Then I think maybe I'll surprise him at work."

"All right. Whatever you want. So are you going to call them or do you want to ask them to come up to the house?"

We arrive at the car and get in. "I would," I say, buckling myself in, "but they both know I'm waiting for the results, and it doesn't seem fair to make them wait."

"Fair enough." He starts the engine and heads out onto the main road.

"I might ask if they want to come up this evening, though. What do you think?"

"Absolutely."

"You think they'll want to come?"

He hesitates. "I like to think so."

"I wish my result meant all three of us were clear."

"Yeah, me too." He reaches out and takes my hand in his. "But you shouldn't let that tarnish today, Em. It's wonderful, amazing news, and all of us should be celebrating."

"I think I'll ring them now," I say. "Is that okay?"

"Of course."

Nervously, I switch my phone on. I've missed a couple of calls from Knightley, and a few texts asking if I'm okay. I leave them for now, bring up Gabe's number, and press call.

He answers in a couple of rings. "Hello?"

"It's Em," I say. "I'm just leaving the hospital. I got my results. They're negative."

"Ahhh…" He lets out a long breath. "Fucking hell. Oh Em, I'm so pleased for you."

Tears run down my face. "Thank you. I'm… sorry."

"Oh God, don't say that. It's fucking fantastic. Absolutely fantastic. Jesus." There's a bang of a door, and then the sound of birdsong—he's gone outside. "Wow. I feel as if you pushed me down a huge waterslide. My stomach flipped completely over."

I laugh, wiping away my tears. "I know what you mean. That's how I felt."

"Is Dad with you?"

"Yeah."

"Is he all right?"

"Shell shocked, but yeah. Gabe, I wanted to say, if you want to come up tonight and have a drink with me, I'd love to see you. But I'll understand if you'd rather not."

"Em, don't be a fucking idiot. Of course I'll come up. I'm absolutely thrilled for you. Have you rung Bella?"

"No, I'm going to call now."

"All right. What about Knightley?"

"I'd like to tell him face to face."

"Okay. He's in surgery now anyway. I'll try to keep quiet until you get here."

"Thanks. I'll see you soon."

"Love you."

"Love you, too," I squeak, and end the call.

I take a deep breath and let it out slowly. Dad gives me a smile. "Okay?"

I nod. "I'm going to be like a wrung-out rag at the end of the day." I look down at the phone in my hand.

"She'll be thrilled," Dad says.

"I know." Deep down, though, I wonder if my sister will bear a smidge of resentment because she doesn't want to know. I give a mental shrug and dial. It's all done now. It's pointless to keep debating it.

"Hello?" she says.

"It's me," I reply. "Where are you?"

"I've just got in. Called in at the supermarket on the way home." Bella teaches in the mornings at the local high school. "What's up?"

"I'm on my way back from Whangarei with Dad. I got my results, and they're negative."

She inhales sharply. Then she goes quiet.

I glance at Dad and bite my lip. "Bell?" I ask.

"Oh, Em. I'm so happy." She bursts into tears.

Relief floods me, and once again I have to wipe my face dry. "Thank you," I say with feeling.

"For what?" she asks, sniffling and snuffling.

"For being pleased for me."

"Oh, Em. Of course I'm thrilled for you. Why wouldn't I be?"

"I just thought… with the kids…"

"Love, that's my business and my problem, and nothing to do with you. I totally understand why you had the test, and it's marvelous that it's negative. I'd never resent you being free of it. I'm so glad."

We talk for a few more minutes, and then I finally end the call.

I lean my head on the rest and close my eyes. "I feel exhausted. I think I'll actually sleep well tonight."

"We all will." He signals at the roundabout and takes the turnoff toward the Bay. "So, are you excited to tell Knightley?"

I open my eyes and smile at him. "You think he'll be pleased?"

He just chuckles.

"I love him, Dad," I say.

"I know. The biggest shock is that you've only just realized."

"How long have you known?"

"Since the day after the Knight boys arrived at the house."

"Ha," I scoff.

But he just nods. "You've always adored him. You'd follow him around with these big puppy eyes, hanging on his every word. And he'd show off for you in front of his mates. Your mum always hoped the two of you would end up together. It's a shame she never got to see it."

"And that she won't get to see the baby." I rest my hand on my belly.

"Yeah." He gives a wistful smile and returns his gaze to the road.

It's strange how the day is full of such conflicting emotions. It's like the sun outside—so beautiful, but so bright it hurts my eyes.

And suddenly, all I want is Knightley, with such intensity that it hurts. I know he'll understand, and I know that when he holds me, everything is going to be all right.

Chapter Twenty-Six

Knightley

It's been a long morning in the surgery. We had a complicated case: a seal that had severe upper-eyelid trauma, and the operation to repair it has taken more than two hours. But eventually I finish the final stitch to close the wound, and together Cathy and I transfer the still sleeping seal to its crate and carry it out to the Wing, where it'll stay for a while before being put into the pool to recover.

We go back to the surgery, and I scrub my hands in the sink.

"I'm shattered," Cathy says, yawning.

"Yeah, me too."

"Great morning's work, though," she adds. "You did good there."

"Thanks." I smile and turn from the sink, wiping my hands on a cloth. "Hopefully it won't get an infection because of the…"

My voice trails off as I see Em standing in the surgery door. She's leaning against the door jamb, her hands in the pockets of her jeans. I hadn't expected to see her at work.

She's watching me, and I smile, but she doesn't return it. My heart skips a beat. I take a few steps forward, then stop. Something's happened. My heart hammers. Is it the baby? Or… has she received her HD results?

She looks into my eyes, and then her lips curve up, and it's such a beautiful smile, so filled with joy and happiness, that I know instantly what's happened.

Even so, I can't bring myself to hope. "You've heard?" I whisper.

She nods. "Just got back from Whangarei with Dad." She takes her hands out of her pockets, then walks forward to hold mine. "Only fifteen CAG repeats. It's negative, love. I don't have it."

For a moment it's as if time stops. I look into her gorgeous green eyes.

She's free.

We're free.

Free to live a normal life with all its ups and downs.

I have her forever… and the baby is free, too.

"Oh Em," I say.

A squeak makes us both turn to see Cathy covering her mouth with a hand, her eyes filled with tears. "Sorry," she says, "but I can't believe it!"

Em laughs and goes over to give her a hug, and then suddenly everyone's coming into the surgery—Lorelei and Gabe and Frankie and Naomi, and the other vets, and all the lab assistants. I'm guessing Em has already rung Gabe and Gabe has told them all, and everyone's cheering and hugging each other, because it's such amazing news.

I don't get a chance to talk to Em about it, but I don't care. We've got the rest of our lives to discuss what it all means. For now, everyone wants to celebrate with her, and I'm fine with that.

"Where's Rob?" Em asks Naomi, looking around.

"In his office," she says. "I thought you might want to tell him."

Em takes Naomi's hand. "Come on." Then she smiles at me and Gabe. "Let's go and tell him."

The four of us run across the walkway to the office block and go inside. Em walks straight through to Rob's office, opens his door, and stands in the doorway, the three of us behind her.

He's on the phone, and he looks up and throws a glare at us all. Then he sees our faces and his frowns lifts.

"Can I call you back?" he asks, not even waiting for an answer as he ends the call. He gets to his feet and limps around the desk, forgetting about his cane. "Em?" he whispers.

She nods. "I just heard. It's negative."

"Oh, Jesus." He throws his arms around her, and they exchange a huge hug. I look down at Naomi, whose eyes are bright, and I put my arm around her and give her a squeeze while she sniffles and laughs.

Rob looks over Em's shoulder at me, and I can see the emotion in his eyes. I hadn't realized until this moment how it's hung over us all for so long. Things like this touch everyone in a two-mile radius of the affected person. A positive result would have spread ripples through Em's small community, changing us all in unexpected and unforeseen ways.

Days like this are so rare. Ninety-five percent of our lives bobble along on the graph of happiness somewhere in the middle, and it's always seemed to me that the dips where something goes wrong—from daily frustrations like cars breaking down to life-changing events like illness or death—happen much more than the peaks where something wonderful happens.

But for once, this is a massive peak, a day like no other, where the future is so incredibly bright, I can't bear to look at it.

*

After a brief consultation, we agree to end the day early. We settle the animals and leave them in the capable hands of one of the assistants, and then everyone makes their way up to Hartfield House.

Em is already there with Hugh, and they've opened several bottles of champagne, and thrown together an impromptu buffet with hot sausage rolls and tiny pies and mini pizzas, as most of us haven't had lunch.

I've never seen Hugh so happy. He's carried his wife's illness and death around with him like a massive weight on his shoulders, but for once his steps are light, and he's laughing and joking with everyone as he hands out the glasses of champagne.

Then the door opens and Bella, John, and the girls come in. Bella goes straight up to Em, and the two of them standing there hugging, tears streaming down their faces.

John comes up to where I'm standing talking to Gabe and Rob, and we all exchange a bearhug. We don't say anything, but I can only imagine it's bittersweet news for John. I know he's thrilled for Em. But not knowing whether his wife and girls carry the gene must be very hard for him.

"What have you told the girls?" I ask quietly, watching them dancing around the living room with an over-excited Minnie.

"Just that Em had to be tested for a disease and it's negative. We thought it was best to tell the truth as much as we could. When they're old enough to process it, Bella said she'll get the test. If it wasn't for the girls, I don't think she'd do it, but she feels they should know it's a possibility they might have it, if that's the case."

"I'm so sorry," I murmur.

He smiles. "We've had a long time to come to terms with it all. I think both of us have accepted that she might have it, so we know where we could be headed. And we're fine. After all, life is a lottery, isn't it? Anything could happen at any time. We're not going to spend the years that we do have worrying."

"Fair enough," I say.

I stop then, as Hugh is tapping his spoon on a glass.

"Not going to say much," he says after everyone falls silent. He puts an arm around Em and pulls her against him. "Too emotional to give a long speech. I just want to say we love you, Em, and we all wish you a long and happy life." He stops, choking up.

"To Em," everyone says, toasting her with their glasses.

"To Em," I say, my voice husky.

Em just waves her hand and covers her mouth, and everyone laughs.

Rob walks off with John, leaving me with Gabe. I have a mouthful of champagne and give him a smile.

"How are you doing?" I ask.

"I'm good." He watches his sister as she picks up Lilibet and twirls her around. "I'm thrilled for her. It couldn't have happened to a nicer girl."

He looks a bit wistful, and I wonder whether he's remembering a time in their childhood when they were both young and carefree, before they found out about their mum's disease.

"Has it changed your mind as to whether to get tested?" I ask. "Has it made it easier, or harder?"

He shrugs. "Neither. I've no plans to ever get it done."

"What about if you meet someone? And she wants a family?"

"Ain't gonna happen," he says. "I'm not interested in settling down. Or in having kids. I'm thinking of traveling a bit more. Maybe going to Aus to do some more training. Or just having some time out."

I understand, and I know there's no point in arguing with him. For some reason, he's never met the right girl. He's had a couple of girlfriends that have lasted a while, but, to my knowledge, none of them has ever been 'the one'. I don't know whether his standards are too high, or whether he's purposely walked away if a relationship has become too serious. Maybe both. Is it because of the possibility of developing Huntington's? I can't help but think it is.

But there's no chance to dwell on it now, because Em's walking up to us. She gives her brother a big hug, then finally turns to me and slides her arms around my waist.

We've always been touchy-feely at home and at work, and anyway I don't think anyone's going to be surprised to see us cuddling today, but even so, warmth spreads through me as I wrap my arms around her and pull her tight against me.

We've not really had a chance to talk yet. It's all been a blur since she appeared in my doorway and gave me that beautiful smile. And there's no time, either, because not only are we surrounded by people, but I don't think I could put into words how I'm feeling. Instead, I just let it all ride over me and hold on to that feeling of happiness. I know it's like a silk ribbon that slips through your fingers, and in a week or a month's time this feeling of ecstatic bliss will slowly fade. But I think the relief and the joy will be there for a lot longer, especially now Em is pregnant, and the baby is—at least where HD is concerned—going to be okay.

Obviously Hugh knows, but I suspect Em hasn't told anyone else yet. We'll discuss it later, but I think we'll probably both agree to keep it quiet for the first three months. Oddly, I quite like the secrecy, because it's something that belongs to me and her, like a jewel we found in the ocean that the two of us can take out in private to examine and wonder at.

For now, though, it's time to celebrate. Other friends call in, and phone calls are made, and the party goes on for hours, until the sun has sunk beneath the horizon, and the stars have popped out on the black velvet sky.

*

Gradually, everyone calls it a day and departs. It's late now, close to midnight. Gabe, Rob, Naomi, and Frankie stay to the end and help us clean up, then they leave too, giving us both a long hug before they go.

"I'm off to bed," Hugh states. "I'm shattered." He smiles at me, then gives Em a long, long hug, both of them standing quietly, because there's nothing else to say. When he's finally done, he kisses the top of her head, then leaves the room, waking a tired Minnie to take her off to bed.

Em looks up at me. She also looks tired, but happy. "Will you stay?" she asks simply.

"Of course."

She takes my hand and, after turning off the lights, leads me along the corridor to her room.

Once we're inside, we brush our teeth standing next to each other in the bathroom—luckily she had a new brush still in its packet—and then we go back out, undress, and get into bed.

She curls up beside me, and we hold each other in the darkness. She feels slender and warm in my arms, her skin silky smooth.

"We're going to have a baby," she says, as if it's only just sunk in, and in fact I'm sure that's exactly what's happened.

I smile. "Yeah."

"You're okay with that?"

"Yeah, Em. I'm just fine."

She kisses my chest.

Then we both fall asleep.

*

I wake in the early hours. A pale light shows through the crack in the curtains, so it must be around five a.m.

Em lies facing away from me. Her blonde hair is spread across the pillow. She has one arm hooked over the duvet; the rest of it drapes over her body, revealing the dip of her waist, the swell of her hips.

I rest a finger on her shoulder and draw it down, scoop her hair up, and lay it on the pillow. Then I bend and press my lips to the nape of her neck. Slowly, I kiss up to her ear and touch my tongue to the lobe, then I kiss down her neck to her shoulder.

Moving a little on the bed, I begin to kiss down her back, taking my time, lost in the dark, sleepy world under the covers as I slide beneath them. Em stirs, sighs, yawns, but doesn't move, and so I continue down, pressing my lips over her hips, then down the outside of her thigh.

Gently, I push her onto her front, then I kiss over the smooth, round globes of her bottom, down to the creases beneath. I trace my tongue along them, then carefully part her cheeks and sample her there.

"Ooh," Em says, "mmm," and she parts her legs and lets me explore with my mouth, while I slide my fingers beneath her and begin to stroke her lightly. I probe with my tongue, teasing, licking, my fingers starting to move more easily as they become coated with her moisture.

Her breathing deepens, and when it turns ragged, I move back up so we're lying on our sides with her facing away from me, pull her back against my chest, guide my erection beneath her, and gently slide inside her. No need for a condom now, I think, glowing at the thought.

Making sure we're both comfortable, I slip my arms around her and begin to move.

She sighs, turning her head so she can kiss me, and we make love like that slowly, while I stroke her breasts, occasionally sliding my hand down to arouse her clit. Her hips move a little to meet my thrusts, and the two of us gradually ascend into pleasure, unhurriedly, like the sun rising over the horizon.

"Lee," she whispers, just one word, but for some reason it makes me feel emotional—it puts all the worries and fears of our youth behind us, and guides us into the present, where right now everything is warm and bright.

"Come for me," I murmur, and she gives a little nod and closes her eyes, concentrating on her own pleasure as I stroke her and move inside her.

When her orgasm finally arrives, I rest my other hand on her tummy, and keep it there as her sighs fill the air, mingling with mine as my climax washes over me. I come inside her properly for the first time, and it's as beautiful and warm and sweet as the morning sun.

We lie there like that as our breathing slows.

"I love you," I murmur, kissing her neck and giving a few leisurely, pleasurable thrusts.

"I wish you could always be inside me," she whispers, turning her face to kiss me.

"I am." I rest my hand between her breasts, above her heart. It's a cheesy line, and at any other time both of us would have laughed, but right now it seems appropriate.

*

A little later, we open the curtains and lie there in the warm rays, heads propped on a hand, studying each other.

"Should we talk about what we do now?" she asks. "Or is it too early for that?"

I trail a finger down between her breasts and to her tummy. "I'd say it's not too early."

She chuckles. "Yeah. Maybe not." She lifts my hand and kisses my knuckles. "Want to know what I think?"

"Sure."

"I think we should date for a bit. Like, a few months. Properly. Go out for dinner. Go to the movies. Get to know one another."

"Yeah, because I don't already know every single thing about you, Emily Woodruff."

She gives me a wry look. "I'm trying to slow things down. I know I'm pregnant, but it was an accident, and that doesn't necessarily mean that we're… you know… a perfect match." Her eyes are bright, hopeful.

She's trying to give me space, worried that I'll feel pushed into a relationship before I'm ready.

"We could do that," I say. "Or we could get married."

She laughs and pushes me. "We've been sleeping together for two weeks."

"Well, I've enjoyed it, I don't know about you."

"That's hardly the point."

"What is the point?"

"I don't know," she admits and giggles.

I lean forward and give her a long kiss. Then I move back again.

"We can wait, if you like," I say. "I understand what you're saying, that you'd rather do that for other people, because you think they might say we're rushing into it, although I don't think seventeen years counts as rushing in anyone's book." I cup her face and brush her cheek with my thumb. "We fell in love years ago, Em. But we had to wait until the timing was right. And now it is… do you really think any of our friends or family will think we're rushing it?"

"No, I suppose not," she says, a little shyly.

"We'll wait a bit, if you want," I say. "But I'd like to marry you before the baby comes."

She meets my gaze and smiles. "Okay." She bites her lips then. "I didn't think I could feel this happy."

"I'm sure we're all feeling like that today."

"I hope so. I worry about Gabe and Bella. They've been great, but it must give them mixed feelings."

"Yeah. Dad's happy though."

Her eyebrows rise. "That's the first time I've ever heard you call him Dad."

I hadn't even realized I'd said it. "Oh. Um, yeah."

She intertwines her fingers with mine. "Are you going to see Steven again?"

"Maybe."

"I think you should. If he doesn't have long."

"Yeah. I'll think about it."

She sighs. "Dad will be over the moon if we get married. But sad when we move out. I hate the thought of leaving him alone, rattling around in this big house."

"I was thinking about that," I say. "Obviously it's up to you and I don't know what he'd think, but I wondered whether I should move in here, with you."

Her face lights up like the sun coming out from behind a cloud. "Really? You wouldn't mind?"

"Oh, it's more than that. It's my childhood home too. I love it here. On a practical level, it would mean we wouldn't have to save up for a house or rent somewhere small. We'd be close to HWH, and we'd also be around to help Dad on the estate at times. And we'd have a babysitter on call." I chuckle.

"I think it's a wonderful idea." She looks genuinely thrilled. "We could move into one of the bigger bedrooms, near where Bella and John stay when they come up. The east wing is practically self-contained anyway."

"Yeah. You sure you wouldn't prefer your own place?"

She shakes her head. "You know I love Hartfield. I've been here all my life. It's a part of me. And I'm a homing bird. I'll always return here at the end of the day." She traces a finger down my chest. "Do you mind that I'm not very adventurous? That I'd rather be here than traveling around the world?"

"I've done my share of traveling, and I enjoyed it, but I'm ready to settle down. And I'm more than happy to do that with you."

We study each other, smiling, as it gradually sinks in that this is our future—safe at Hartfield, surrounded by our family and friends.

"I've got one more thing to tell you," I say. "About HWH."

"Oh?"

"Yeah. Rob wants to make you Property Manager."

Her eyes widen. "What?"

"You practically do the job anyway. You know more about the running of the site than all of us put together. You're the oil that keeps the place working smoothly. He's going to call you in to promote you officially, but I thought he wouldn't mind if I told you. What do you think? Would you like to do it?"

She gives me a beautiful smile, eyes shining. "I'd love to. I couldn't be happier right now."

"Aw."

"Life's pretty good sometimes, isn't it?"

"Right now, it's amazing," I reply, and I pull her back into my arms for another kiss.

Newsletter

If you'd like to be informed when my next book is available, you can sign up for my mailing list on my website, http://www.serenitywoodsromance.com

About the Author

USA Today bestselling author Serenity Woods writes sexy contemporary romances, most of which are set in the sub-tropical Northland of New Zealand, where she lives with her wonderful husband.

Website: http://www.serenitywoodsromance.com
Facebook: http://www.facebook.com/serenitywoodsromance

Printed in Great Britain
by Amazon

61337808R00151